DARREN RUMBOLD

Trek Through a Ravaged Land

Prequel to Book One of the Phoenix Treks

First published by RHR Publications 2026

The Library of Congress Control Number (LCCN): 2025927108

This novel's story and characters are a work of fiction. Any references to institutions, agencies, public offices, real people, or the conditions of real places are used fictitiously.

First edition

ISBN: 979-8-218-89483-2

Cover art by Maxim Mitenkov

This book was professionally typeset on Reedsy. Find out more at reedsy.com

This book is dedicated to my wife and life partner, Susan Ruth Healy, without whom I would surely be lost. Together we have lived and continue to live an incredible life. She has been my strongest supporter throughout and recently in becoming a novelist, encouraging me to commit to writing full-time and enduring hours of endless talk about my books. She was also my first and best beta reader and contributed many great ideas.

Contents

Acknowledgments

My thanks go to my Reedsy's copy editor, Adrienne Kisner for her help in improving the manuscript. I'm also thankful to my other beta readers: Patrick Freal, Mandy Krupa, Sammi LeClair, Katie McFarland and my son, William Rumbold as well as others whose encouragement and feedback were invaluable. I also want to acknowledge the exceptional cover design by Maxim Mitenkov. Finally, for those who read this book, thanks for taking this journey with me. Let's hope the events in the book never come to pass.

Chapter 1. The Ghost Town That Wasn't

It was the horrible smell that told me I'd made a mistake that could get us both killed. The ominous orange smoke that had hung in the air all summer had concealed the fact that the town we were entering wasn't as dead as I thought.

From returning trekkers, we knew the wildfires that had plagued the southwest now engulfed the midwestern states of Ohio, Michigan, and Indiana. The smoke was as thick as I'd ever seen it; if you waved your hand, I'd swear you could see swirls in the smoke. It was like living in the billowing smoke from a campfire. You know how, when you're sitting around a campfire, and no matter where you move, the smoke follows you and blows in your face, burning your eyes. It was like that, but there was no breeze, so the burning eyes and throat were constant.

It wasn't just the disgusting urine and feces smell that bothered me, it was also the sharp chemical odor of burning rubber or plastic that told me this wasn't a ghost town. I hadn't expected squatters to be living this close to our village, or I'd have been more cautious walking into town. I thought it was just another empty town. The acrid smell that you could taste originated from something they were burning in 55-gallon drums along the street, probably for the light. I got it; we hadn't seen the sun through the orange haze in months. At first, it'd been eerily quiet as we entered the town, but now, I began to make out new sounds, murmurs of, "*Who are these two strangers?*" I also began seeing shadows move in the doorways of the abandoned buildings. I just wish I hadn't brought Ruth into this cesspool of human tragedy.

As calmly as I could, I whispered, "Stay calm. Don't stop; we'll just walk on through."

"I'm not scared," Ruth said.

I thought I heard her voice quiver but I might have imagined it.

We were just passing a deserted auto supply store when a group of teenagers suddenly appeared in front of us, blocking our way. They brought a new smell with them; clearly, they hadn't taken a bath in a long time, if ever. I couldn't make out many details because of the orange haze, but I could see they were carrying various weapons: knives, hammers, a 2x4 studded with nails, and a baseball bat. The tallest kid, who was short by any standard, only a hundred and fifty centimeters, was swinging a crowbar menacingly. He appeared to be about nineteen and had a scraggly beard that covered up some of the pox marks on his face. The patchy beard matched his long, stringy, greasy hair. He was wearing baggy, ripped blue jeans and a torn black T-shirt that he'd scavenged long ago. You could no longer read what had been printed on the front.

2

Sizing us up, he said, "Hey, Grandpa, this your daughter? She's fresh." He moved a step closer. "Where you goin' so fast? And whatcha got in those fancy backpacks?"

He turned so his gang, if you could call them that, could hear him and said, "I wish I could find the store you hit—I carry my shit in a garbage bag. Why don't you give us those fancy backpacks, and maybe we won't kick your ass."

When he spoke, I could see he was missing several teeth. Ruth swung her backpack around as if she were going to hand it over to him. I pulled out my long knife to let her know we weren't giving anything up. I figured I could take the kid because I'd have greater maneuverability and speed with the knife over the crowbar. And if I injured him, the other kids would run away.

"Let us pass," I said.

"You ain't goin' nowhere," he said.

A girl with a very pale face, sunken eyes, and her own set of pox marks moved up next to him and said, "Crowbar, lookit her boots. Get 'em for me." The girl then coughed. I couldn't be sure, because of the haze, but I thought I saw a dark liquid—blood maybe—on her hand as she wiped the spittle away.

"Okay, Princess. You heard her, Grandpa. Give us your packs and boots, and maybe we'll let you live."

We go to great lengths to blend in with the people living outside our village who rely on scavenging to meet their needs, including clothing. Our backpacks, although crafted for us, were washed repeatedly with stones, intentionally ripped and mended, and stained to appear old. The same with our boots and clothes.

"We're not giving you our shoes or our backpacks. What if we give you some food?"

3

Ruth made a show of rummaging around in her backpack.

"Quit fuckin' around and hand over the backpacks."

Just then, the smallest, scrawniest kid whispered, "Crowbar, old man Vincent's coming."

The kids all turned and looked at the large shadow coming up from behind them and scattered—all but Crowbar, who just stood there, defiantly.

A grim-looking man, a few years older than me, wearing what looked to be a faded uniform with epaulets and pintucks running down the front of the shirt walked up and with one blurred smooth motion grasped the kid's hand holding the crowbar in such a way as to prevent him from dropping it and swung them both up and hit the kid on the head. Blood and bits of something flew; some landed on Ruth. She retched. The kid folded up and dropped like a stone. If he wasn't dead already, he soon would be with no medical attention available.

The man didn't give the kid a second look and instead swung the crowbar again and smashed my hand holding the knife. I dropped it, of course; the pain was excruciating.

Then, he began smacking the crowbar against his other hand, splattering more of the kid's blood. The man they called Vincent had a full beard that actually appeared trimmed. His hair was greasy but also trimmed, cut close to his head, similar to a military crew cut. He was of normal stature and had no pox marks because he was born well before the collapse and had been vaccinated against chickenpox. His teeth were jagged and black to the gum, and he smelled horrible.

"That kid's been givin' me shit for a long time! I warned him not to mess in my business."

I moved to put myself between Ruth and the man. *I wasn't there to protect April and the girls, but I'll die before I allow*

4

anyone to hurt Ruth. While I was sure I could take the kid I wasn't too sure about this guy but as my dad had taught me—don't ever let them see you're scared.

"Just let us go; we don't want any trouble," I said.

"Did he tell you his nickname was from his 'weapon of choice'? He's always telling people that. I gave him that nickname when he was a baby. When his mother showed him to me, I noticed his penis was misshaped. It looked like a goddamn crowbar. I guess his little princess likes it. Or,"—he looked down at the kid dying on the ground—"liked it."

He turned to me and said, "Okay, buddy, let's start these negotiations over. You give me everything you got, including your woman here, and I may let you live." Smiling at Ruth, he said, "We don't see the likes of you round here with that hair. The kid was right; you do look fresh. Buddy, whatcha trade for this bitch?"

Ruth and I were married almost eight years ago after my first wife was killed by raiders. She was twenty-seven and beautiful, with lovely long reddish-brown hair that she refused to cut for this trek. I had no idea why she married a slightly overweight, grizzled older man who was an emotional wreck at the time. Nor did I understand how she convinced me to bring her along on this dangerous trip.

I heard Ruth behind me rummaging in her backpack, but couldn't see what she was doing, and then the man smiled and said, "Come on, pretty lady, that might have scared the kids away, but I know you don't have any ammunition for that thing."

I turned my head slightly and saw that Ruth had pulled her gun from her backpack. She carried a .22LR pistol while I carried a 9mm. Even with the greater accuracy of the 22, at

5

this angle, she was just as likely to shoot me in the shoulder or blow my head off as to hit him. Suddenly, the side of my head exploded with agony from the concussion and the gunshot's earsplitting report. I jerked sideways reflexively and fell to my knees. I looked up at her and yelled, "Jesus fucking Christ!"

Her shot had missed Vincent, but he'd dropped the crowbar as he ran away. I tried to regain my composure even though I was holding the side of my head with my throbbing hand, which was already swollen, having been hit with the crowbar. All I could hear was a loud ringing, like a fire alarm going off. With my left hand, I picked up my knife.

From behind the corner of a building, Vincent yelled something about wanting the gun and ammunition, hunting us down and doing unspeakable things to us, but I couldn't hear him very well due to the fire alarm.

"Put that away and let's go," I said.

* * *

We walked out of town without further interference. As we passed the last building on Main Street, we heard a girl scream, "You kilt him." Thankfully, the horrible smell faded, but I'd have to wash the awful taste out of my mouth later.

"Ruth, can you please walk up here with me? No, my other side. I can no longer hear out of that ear. And can you please pick up the pace a little?"

She'd had blisters the first few days of the trek but they were healed now, so I'd been after her to walk faster. I'm taller, so my stride is longer, but she seemed to have only a single speed.

"Babe, when we're confronting someone like that, it's best if you're behind me, but when we're walking, it'd be nice to have you up here, okay?"

"Okay, George."

She came up beside me.

"You could have killed me!"

"I'm sorry George, but you were in my way, and I didn't want him to kill you. Besides, I wouldn't have hit you. I'm a better shot than that, remember."

"But I told you that bringing the gun out and shooting were the last resort. I asked you to keep it hidden. We don't want, or didn't want, people to know we had guns with ammunition. Besides, having guns makes it too easy to shoot people. Would you've shot him?"

"To save you, yes," Ruth said.

"You realize that these days, with no medical attention available, almost any gunshot is likely fatal?"

"Yes, I do."

"I don't think you appreciate what killing a person does to you."

I knew from personal experience that killing changes you for life. We walked on in silence for several hours.

"Babe, I'm sorry I put you in that position. I should've been more careful entering the town. It must have been very frightening for you."

"It was, but I had faith you'd get me out of there, George."

"Then why didn't you let me handle Vincent?"

"I knew you'd protect me but wasn't sure you'd protect yourself."

I let it drop because I had no idea what she meant by that.

* * *

As darkness fell, we found an abandoned farmhouse over-grown with vegetation. The roof had partially collapsed, probably under the weight of too much snow since there was no one to rake it, but it was still attached. A few windows remained, but most were cracked or missing. The field behind the house was returning to forested land. We'd split up to search the house for squatters, wildlife, or corpses when I heard Ruth gasp. I ran into what must've been the master bedroom. She'd found the long-decayed corpses of a family lying in the bed together and a large dark spot on what had been the headboard.

I went over and put my left arm around her.

"Dad and I found many of these on our trek. People took control of how they went out during the Time of the Great Dying."

I suddenly realized I'd heard her gasp and heard myself talk with my right ear. *So I wouldn't be deaf in that ear for the rest of my life.*

In case Vincent or someone else were following us, I decided we shouldn't have a fire that night or even use the small solar lamps we were issued before leaving on the trek. We simply sat in the moonlight at what remained of the dining-room table and quietly ate salt-cured ham we'd brought with us from home, along with some berries that Ruth had foraged the day before. I wouldn't have been able to hunt anyway, being incapable of drawing and steadying an arrow with my swollen hand.

Ruth broke the silence when she said, "I can't believe he killed his own son without any remorse."

"Babe, you've got to understand that life has little meaning to some people out here."

"Well, I guess a fast death was better than what he had to look forward to with TB."

"TB?"

"Yeah, Crowbar's girlfriend had clear signs of an active tuberculosis infection. We've had two active cases in trekkers coming back from out west in the past couple of years. Fortunately, we caught them while they were still in quarantine. And did you notice all the pox marks? From chickenpox, I bet. Thank God Dan didn't have to grow up like that."

"I thought we agreed not to talk about Dan—it just reminds us how much we both miss him."

"I know, I'm sorry, hon."

"I wonder how he's doing. Do you think he ever stopped crying?"

"Of course he did, hon. He's probably got his nose stuck in a book with Otis lying beside him on the bed."

After a few minutes, I said, "Well, I guess putting your hair up into a hat didn't work, maybe you could cut it off? And I wish you'd let yourself get dirty. My skin is hidden by my gray beard, but your complexion is nearly flawless."

9

"Thank you."

"Okay, I'll leave that as a compliment, but please consider cutting your hair. It's not even greasy."

"That's because I brush dry shampoo through it every night."

"Is that what you're doing with the fancy silver hairbrush you brought along, despite my objections?"

She didn't answer me, but got up in a huff, unrolled and laid out her sleeping bag, and climbed inside. We'd brought sleeping bags that could be zipped together, but hadn't even tried since leaving on the trek. At least she'd get some sleep; I was planning to stand watch all night.

* * *

As I lay there, I couldn't help but think, *I should never have brought her along. She's been sheltered all her life. She has no idea how much worse it's going to get.*

I hate arguing with Ruth because I'm not very good at it. Invariably, I lose my temper, say something stupid that hurts her feelings, and so end up apologizing and losing the initial argument. I clearly lost the argument about her coming on this trek. Was it only a few months ago? I replayed the scene in my head, trying to figure out how she outmaneuvered me.

I'd come home from work and told her I was going on the trek to Florida again. I told her I'd talked John into coming with me.

From her facial expression, I thought she was going to laugh at me, but instead she calmly said, "You'll never get approval to go, even if I've got to go to Ralph and tell him you're still having the nightmare. You're just not ready." Then she turned and walked into the kitchen.

"You can't do that," I yelled after her as I followed her into the kitchen. "You've got to support me on this. It's important. How are we to know when it's the right time to restart society? And who is going to collect all the environmental data we need?"

"I know these treks are vital to the Center's mission, but why does it have to be you that goes down to Florida?"

I sighed. "We've been over this all before. Continuity of who takes a trek is crucial. I've done this trek before, so I'm the most familiar with the route, the people, and the environmental conditions. No one's better suited to gauge the extent of any changes that have occurred over the past ten years since the last trek. And as you already know, I hope Dan will take over this trek when I'm too old, so he can find his legacy within the Center. If I give it up now, his chances of taking it over are limited."

"Has John told Libby he's going? He treks up to Newfoundland already, and now he's going down to Florida. That's ridiculous. She's never going to let him take this on."

"No, that's the beauty of it. John won't do this trek next time. Dan and I'll go."

"So you're already planning the next one. If anybody goes with you, it'll be me."

"Now who's being ridiculous? Women aren't allowed to go on long-haul treks—it's too dangerous."

"If it's too dangerous for me, it's too dangerous for you. Besides, I heard Jessica is going with her husband on his trek to Vancouver."

11

"Come on, that's Canada and the northern U.S., not down the eastern seaboard with all its population centers. And don't play dumb—you know that the dangers for women are different than for men. That's why women weren't allowed to go on the first treks fifteen years ago."

"Don't you be naive; you know men can be raped too. Besides, conditions must have improved out there since the Blackout War twenty-five years ago."

"We don't know that."

"The only way I'm going to support this is if I'm going with you. I can help. I'm a nurse, so if you get hurt, I can take care of you. And if you take me, there's no chance someone else would take over this trek in the future."

"But I couldn't go on if something happened to you. I can't go through that again."

"Nothing will happen to me. You'll be there to protect me."

"How are we going to tell Dan? And who is he going to stay with while we're away?"

"Well, he can't stay with Sandra. She still blames you for the death of April and the girls. She spends all her time telling him stories about them to turn him against you."

"I'm not going to be there when you tell your parents. They already hate me for marrying you."

"They don't hate you, and they love Dan and won't turn him against you."

She kissed my cheek and smiled in a way that told me she had won the fight.

I was snapped back to reality by a noise outside. I got up quietly not to wake Ruth and checked the backyard where the noise originated, but it was only a raccoon. Nonetheless, I scanned the backyard expecting to see Vincent.

Chapter 2. Learning a Hard Lesson

The dawn came with another smoky haze. We had a cold breakfast of water and pemmican brought from home. As we sat there eating our breakfast, a cat walked into the room and sat down in front of Ruth.

"George, it's a cat. I thought you said all the pets were eaten just after the blackout?"

"They were. I don't consider cats to be pets. And they certainly aren't pets now. Don't get too close to that cat—it'll scratch you, and it'll get infected and you'll die."

"Don't be so melodramatic." She reached out, and the cat sniffed her hand. "Hi, little guy, where'd you come from? Do you want some of my pemmican?"

"Don't. He's feral. Besides, they have plenty of food—rats, birds, and, above all else, human corpses. That's why they're still around, and man's best friends aren't."

"I can love cats as well as dogs. Our Otis is precious, and without a doubt, the smartest and best dog in the world. But this guy is so sweet, and he looks like the cat I had as a kid. I'm going to call him Charley."

"Well, we can't take him with us, Ruth."

"I know, but I'm giving him some food anyway," she said as she began petting him.

I just shook my head, but I thought I heard it purring.

I wanted to put an end to that, and so told Ruth it was time to pack up. As usual, I was ready to leave well before Ruth and had to wait for her. The cat followed us to the threshold of the front door, where he sat down. I guess the house was his.

Fortunately, the Blackout war and the EM pulses occurred at about one o'clock in the morning, so few cars were on the road for us to have to avoid now. There were, however, lots of blowdowns that we had to climb over or walk around, sometimes into the woods. Ruth and I had our usual squabble about pee breaks. She preferred fewer, longer rest stops, and I didn't. But that was all part of getting used to hiking together and finding our rhythm.

After a couple of hours of walking, we came upon a family composed of a man, a woman, and two boys in their early teens walking south as we were. We were walking at a faster pace, or at least I was, and, for a change, Ruth deemed to walk beside me. I made some noise as we approached so as not to startle them. One of the benefits of traveling with a woman was that as a pair, we appeared less threatening than when I had walked with another man, my dad. Within a meter of catching up to them, I smelled them; I wondered when I'd get used to smelling the body odor of people who no longer took showers or baths. But then again, Ruth was constantly complaining about my BO. The family was all dressed in ill-fitting rags. Ruth said hello as we passed, but none of them responded. The two boys looked up at the man, who just shook his head. The woman made eye contact with Ruth and smiled.

When we were well out of earshot, I said, "Ruth, you can't engage with people on the road. It's just inviting trouble. You're putting yourself and me at risk."

"You're a shit," she said as she stormed off.

Later, we passed a man and a woman alone. They were dressed in better-looking rags, and the man had a small backpack, something a child might use to tote books to school, slung over his shoulder. Ruth again said hello.

This woman made eye contact with Ruth and asked, "Do you have any food you can spare? My husband and I are starving."

Before I could do anything to stop her, Ruth pulled her backpack around and found a plastic bag full of goat jerky. Plastic bags are forever, and you can scavenge them in almost any store; they're very useful. She handed the bag to the woman and said, "Here you go."

I grabbed Ruth's upper arm, but before I could get her moving again, the woman asked, "Do you have any clean water?"

Ruth pulled her arm free and handed the woman her water bottle. The woman turned and handed it to the man.

Replacing my grip on her upper arm, I pushed Ruth forward but shouted to the man, "Keep the bottle!"

The man and woman stood there devouring the jerky and gulping down the water. I continued to push Ruth forward using the grip I had on her upper arm. Fortunately, the couple didn't follow us immediately; they were too busy scarfing down the jerky and water. But after only a few minutes, we heard yelling and the sound of people running coming from behind us. I got us off the road and into the woods as fast as I could. We then saw the man and woman run past on the road, being chased by a group of ten people screaming for them to stop.

Ruth whispered, "George, we've got to do something."

"We can't."

"But we have guns."

"We can't!"

We then heard the woman screaming, "You're killing him." They must've caught up to them.

"Come on, Ruth, we've got to get away from here." I grabbed her arm and started pulling her farther into the woods; she was going to have a bruise that I'd have to answer for later.

"Ruth, please, we've got to get out of here before she puts them on to us."

We moved farther back into the woods.

* * *

We slowly found our way through the fir trees, which is no easy feat because they grow so densely, and the dead lower branches seem to aim for your eyes. Having to navigate around all the deadfalls and blowdowns makes it difficult to maintain a constant direction. Fortunately, I had a compass. Eventually, we found a game trail and followed it to a clearing and sat down. Ruth was crying; I thought she was going to be sick.

"Ruth, you need to learn the hardest lesson a trekker must learn—you can't help everybody. We're going to see some horrible things over the next year and encounter some very desperate people. We can't help them all."

"It was my fault they were attacked. I shouldn't have given them the jerky or the water."

"No, you shouldn't have. Even acts of kindness can have undesirable consequences in this environment, but they should've known never to let anyone see you eat or drink unless they themselves are eating and drinking. But that might not have been the reason they were attacked. Did you notice how much they resembled us?"

"Are you saying they were attacked because they looked like us?" she asked. "Why would...You think those people were after the guns?"

"I think it's likely there are people out here looking for a man and woman with long hair wearing unusually nice clothes carrying fancy backpacks," I said.

"Either way, it was my fault then, and we allowed those two people to be killed or worse."

"Should we have fired a warning shot?" I asked. "That would've just confirmed we had ammunition. Should we've tried to shoot all the attackers? There were two of us and ten of them—sure, if we'd had greater numbers, they might've run off, but not from just the two of us. And they would've wanted our guns and ammunition more than even food or water. Our mission will improve the lives of hundreds of thousands of people, if not more. Do we put that and our lives in jeopardy for just two people?"

"You're right," she said. "But it's just so hard not to do

something."

"It's a hard lesson to learn," I said. "Having worked as a nurse helping trekkers through their post-trek depressions, including me, you should know the guilt we return with better than most."

She reached up and caressed my face and said, "Well, you were a special case."

"Yes, I was," but I didn't smile, *thinking of the guilt I still carried around.*

"Yeah, I heard the stories," she said. "The ones they'd share"—she looked pointedly at me—"but I didn't think it would still be this bad out here after all this time."

To break the ensuing silence, I said, "The social scientists at the Center are also surprised by how bad things still are. They expected the extreme violence to have ended by now and that there'd be more cooperation among people working for the common good."

"But why hasn't that happened yet?" Ruth asked.

"Well, some at the Center worry that natural selection during the Time of the Great Dying burned out cooperative behavior in favor of individualism. I mean, the only reason someone like Vincent survived this long to grow 'old,' and he is old by today's standards, was if he was already a monster, even lacking the drive for kin selection."

She shook her head. "Then why don't we just give up, lock ourselves away in Phoenix, and enjoy all that we have for as long as we can?"

The village of Phoenix was built decades before the collapse ostensibly to support a small liberal arts college, but its real purpose was the creation of the Center for Climate Mitigation. The name of the village was to confuse anyone who someday might go looking for it. Surprisingly, the name was unremarkable considering the names of surrounding towns like Berlin, Belfast, Mexico, and China.

"We can't give up!" I said. There are good people out here who want to work together for a better future. We've just got to trust that we'll find lots of examples of that on this trek, so we can convince the Center it's safe to move into Phase 3 of our mission."

"I hope so. I can remember as a girl, my father would talk about all the things that needed to happen before the Center would move into Phase 3. He was very proud of the work he was doing to genetically engineer food crops to make them more drought and heat-resistant."

"You know, I was surprised you didn't end up working in the lab with your father."

"I enjoy working with people too much to be stuck in a lab. George, I know you feel my father doesn't like you, but he's impressed with the work you're doing on the model and recognizes its importance to the Center's mission."

"That's nice to hear, but I've got to get the damn thing to work first. But to solve the more immediate problem, I think we should get off the main roads, at least for a while, in case there are people like Vincent looking for us."

* * *

I spent the next half hour reviewing my maps. Trekkers are issued sets of different printed maps before leaving Phoenix. My dad used to call one particular set of maps a Triptik because it looked similar to something his dad used when driving down to Florida before the collapse. Unfortunately, the Triptik wasn't very helpful if you had to deviate from the planned route, so we had other maps and old satellite images. If needed, we could also scavenge additional road maps at welcome centers or truck stops along the way. After examining the maps, I had our route plotted all the way to New Jersey.

We followed the game trail for several more kilometers until we came upon a county road.

"Okay, this road shouldn't be as heavily traveled as the others we've been using."

"Where exactly are we going, George?"

"We're headed to a trailhead for the Appalachian Trail. We're going to take it south for a few hundred kilometers before getting back on the roads."

"I know you told me about this when you planned our trip, but I wasn't really paying attention. Why are we taking it? And weren't we supposed to take it back to Phoenix, not going south?"

"I'm still planning on taking it home, but we need to get off the main roads; the number of people moving around on the roads surprised me. But there should be a lot fewer using the trail."

"But are you sure there's still going to be a trail to take? Shouldn't it be overgrown if no one's using it?"

"Yeah, it'll be overgrown in some areas, but Dad and I used it coming back on our trek, and it was in surprisingly good shape. They used long-lasting oil-based paint for the blazes to mark the trail; depending on the tree species, it can last for decades."

"Why did your dad think of taking it in the first place?"

"My granddad used to talk about the 'AT' all the time. He hiked it as a teenager right out of high school. It was like a rite of passage. Dad thought taking it would be a way to avoid people as we traveled north, and he was almost right. We found a few people still using it back then. They told us they'd hiked it before the collapse and blackout and had come back to hide from the crazies escaping the cities and then continued using it to travel from area to area. There were some preppers using it too. We even found people living in the shelters. So, to answer your question, I do expect to find the trail still there. Those people maintained the trail by using it, and so did wildlife. We saw lots of wildlife using the trail."

"Should we get a bear bell?"

"I don't think those things work. It's better if you just talk loudly or clap your hands while on the trail; that way, animals, including bears, will move off."

"Are you sure? I think we should get a bear bell."

"If it'll make you happy, we can try to scavenge up a bell."

"You know, George, if we can hike it, I guess you'll be making it a family tradition."

* * *

21

Even on the back roads, we continued to see people, mostly walking south. I guessed that almost everyone was a climate migrant these days. Although Ruth continued to acknowledge them as we passed, most just stared back in disbelief that she would attempt to interact. We scavenged a replacement water bottle for Ruth at a service station we passed; I grabbed more plastic bags too. The good news was that the smoke had lessened; it wasn't gone, but it wasn't as bad.

One afternoon, we passed a few houses built close together, signaling a town up ahead. I pulled out my monocular telescope.

"What's that?" Ruth asked.

"It's a compact telescope to surveil the town before entering."

"Oh, that's a good idea. It would've been handy for that last town."

"Give me a break. The poor visibility from the smoke that day would've made any attempt pointless."

"How's this town look?"

"It looks burned down."

As we walked down the main street, we found hulks of burned, rusted-out cars sitting on rims. We also saw carbonized bones that could only remotely be recognized as human remains in the doorways of some buildings.

"What a horrible way to die," Ruth said.

"They were probably dead before the fire."

"Oh, that makes me feel better," she said. What do you think caused the fire?"

"Impossible to say, but considering the degree to which the skeletons have deteriorated, and the vegetation has grown, it's likely that it burned a long time ago but well after the

22

blackout," I said.

"How do you know that?" she asked.

"If it had burned just after the blackout, those bones would've decomposed completely by now out in the open."

"Then maybe it was much more recent?" she asked.

"Maybe, but you've also got to look at the size of trees growing out of the asphalt and from cracks in the cement. And it also doesn't have a strong smoky smell. The little smoke I can detect is coming off us from the past few weeks."

"I'm surprised you can smell anything above your own BO," she said.

"Thanks."

"Go on, George. Sorry I interrupted."

"Let's get through the town and make camp early tonight. I want to try to hunt us some dinner."

Ruth looked skeptical but said nothing. I'd had little luck the past few days even though game was plentiful. I am not the 'big-game hunter,' and my hand was still sore.

* * *

I let Ruth set up the tent while I built a fire. I prefer constructing an upside-down fire because it gives off far less smoke and requires less tending. It's kind of a thing with me. The first time I let Ruth build a fire, she did it all wrong. She stormed off in a huff when I rebuilt it in front of her. In the past couple of weeks, we've had several arguments about my micromanaging everything she did.

After I got the fire started, I assembled my takedown recurve bow and went in search of dinner. I'd also keep an eye out for a source of clean water to replenish our supplies. I got lucky and shot a turkey. I hate plucking birds because I invariably end up covered in mites. I especially hate it when they crawl into my ears, but I plucked it and dressed it in the field. When I walked back into camp with the turkey, I was all puffed up with pride.

Upon seeing me, Ruth said, "That's great hon, I'll brine it overnight, and we'll eat it in the morning. Put it in the largest stackable pot over there."

I'd hoped for a more enthusiastic response to my hunting prowess and was very disappointed we wouldn't be having roasted turkey for dinner. But she was right; it would taste better brined overnight, and we could have the leftovers for lunch. I'd just have to be satisfied with the salt-cured ham and beans we'd brought with us, and the leeks Ruth had foraged that we would grill. She'd also found some 'Chicken of the Woods' but said we'd save the mushrooms till breakfast because she wanted to cook them with drippings from the turkey. The thought made my stomach growl. At least I should have better dreams tonight.

After the disappointing dinner, I rummaged in my backpack and found my field book and sat down with a cup of birchbark tea to begin my journal while there was still daylight.

"What're you doing?" Ruth asked.

"I'm writing my congressman to tell him he is doing a shitty job."

"Why do you have to be a smartass? Can't you just tell me

what you're doing?"

"Sorry, that was the silly retort my dad would use anytime Mom asked him what he was doing when he thought it was obvious what he was doing."

She didn't smile.

"I am writing in my journal."

"You keep a journal? Why haven't I ever seen it?"

"Only while I'm on a trek and it's not a diary. We're asked to record all our observations in field books. When we get back, they're scanned and distributed to everyone at the Center so the data and information can be used by anyone who needs it."

"Shouldn't I keep one too, then?"

"Yes, you should." I got up and rummaged through my backpack and found a blank field book and pencil which I handed to her.

"What do I write about?"

"Well, first, keep in mind you're writing it for them. It's not a personal diary. You record any specifics you learn about the groups of people we meet, in particular, your impressions and specifics about their social organization like are they a clan composed of few family members or a large band of unrelated people cooperating in survival; do they have a single leader or do they have a council; is the leader male or female, and how do they get people to do what they want; do they have a standing army, that sort of thing."

"Okay, I get it."

"They also want to know if they are religious, if it's something you recognize or a new wave religion; if their kids are allowed to be kids or given adult tasks; are they being taught to read and write? Another important thing to determine is

25

whether they're nomadic or settled in one location and, if settled, whether they're farming."

"So this goes back to the conversation we had earlier about people working together?"

"Exactly. The social scientists back at the Center will use your observations to score the community's readiness for recovery. Additionally—and this is important to my group at the Center—you should record anything you can learn about the weather they've been experiencing over the past five years or so; not just extreme events, which they'll want to talk about, but general conditions too. We should also record the environmental conditions we observe during the trek: the weather, forest types, and any animals we see on the trek. We pay particular attention to the forest types because we can infer a lot about the suitability for nesting, roosting, or foraging for different wildlife species from the snapshots the forest type provides during our short visits. Once we travel farther south, I'll start collecting meteorological and water quality data using instruments I have in my pack; I'll show you how to use them later. We don't need to take any measurements this far north since we're so close to Phoenix and share the same weather. I have only one more book that you can use if you fill that one. So write small and use every millimeter of writing space. You'll be surprised how fast they fill up, so be succinct."

"What happens if I lose it?"

"Don't. Once filled, those field books become the most precious things we have, other than our lives. The observations and measurements must get back to the Center, or this whole trek will be for nothing. The paper in the book is coated, so it won't deteriorate when it gets wet. I have a couple of extra pencils, but if you lose them, we'll have to scavenge some more. Any more questions?"

"Can I look at yours later to get an idea of the format?"

"Yeah, but after that we should try to keep our impressions to ourselves so as not to bias the other person, particularly about their read on a group's social organization."

"Sounds reasonable. Okay, then I'm going to clean up while you work."

"Alright, once I'm done with this, I'll let you look at it. Then I'm hitting the sack so I can get up early for that breakfast you promised."

* * *

Journal entry: 3 October 2081, Near Norwich, NH

First journal entry by George Reynolds in Field Book One on trek to Florida. This marks my second trek to Florida; previous field books authored by my dad, William Reynolds, and me should be on file. I am accompanied on this trek by my wife, Ruth Reynolds; she will keep her own journal with her own perspectives and will turn it in on our return.

Reduced atmospheric mixing assoc. with a thermal inversion continues to weaken winds and trap smoke from wildfires near the ground. Breathing all the smoke makes walking all day difficult.

Plants are now showing signs of stress, e.g., faded leaf color, dropping of leaves, etc., from sunlight dimming and from being coated with ash. Although the inversion has moderated daytime temperatures, the haze is preventing radiative cooling at night.

A week ago, we entered what I thought was a ghost town; however, it was occupied by squatters: a mix of adults and teens. As obs. on previous trek and continued to be reported by other trekkers, most teens had pox marks from the chickenpox epidemic following the collapse and blackout, as well as stunted growth due to poor prenatal nutrition. More worrisome, we obs. at least one individual with active tuberculosis.

While in the town, we were accosted by squatters—a group of teens and then by an adult male, who may have been a former police officer or security guard based on clothing. We escaped with no injuries or loss of equipment; however, one of our guns was discharged in making our escape, so the townspeople know we have ammunition. To escape possible pursuit, we have been moving as fast as possible for the past few days, but cannot keep up this pace much longer.

I am concerned that such dangerous people are squatting so close to Phoenix. I strongly recommend we take some kind of action to reduce this threat. This could range from giving squatters time to relocate and then burning the town to the ground, or better yet, recruiting individuals from Phoenix to move into the town and work with townspeople to improve living conditions while forcing dangerous individuals out. Taken to its logical conclusion, the Center could support the town with food and other resources and have it serve as a satellite village and first line of defense for Phoenix.

Obs. surprising number of migrants traveling south on the roads (> number than obs. on previous trek), probably escaping *the smoke or migrating ahead of the coming winter. Some of these individuals are desperate and therefore dangerous; we've obs. acts of violence on the road. I feel we would be safer if we got off the road, particularly if people are searching for us and our ammunition. I'm therefore headed toward a trailhead for the Appalachian Trail. I plan to take it south, exiting in NJ to visit Asbury Park to begin collecting sea level data.*

General environmental conditions obs. on the trek south: the mild drought that followed the early snowmelt last winter continues; there was no measurable precipitation during this period. I cannot be certain without long-term monitoring and more detailed study, e.g., growth rings, etc., but increased CO_2 has likely accelerated the growth of the forest as it has around Phoenix. There is an incredible amount of woody biomass that has accumulated. However, obs. heavy infestations of balsam woolly adelgid and white pine needle disease. Dieback of spruce and fir trees and replacement with hardwoods well underway. Consequently, all the essential ingredients are present for a catastrophic wildfire here: high fuel load from accelerated growth, prolonged spells of hot, dry weather this past summer, and high evaporation rates causing plants and soils to dry out, forest dieback due to disease and heat stress, and particularly the lack of forestry management, e.g., prescribed burns, firebreaks, etc. One lightning strike could ignite a blaze, which could put Phoenix at risk. Recommend widening the firebreak around Phoenix.

Glossy buckthorn continues to take over the understory in New England forests. We obs. numerous, red-bellied woodpeckers and heard lots of songbirds but boreal chickadees noticeably absent; there will always be winners and losers in distribution shifts. Frog calls down, especially the easily recognizable call of Spring Peepers. Reduced populations of frogs are likely because of

29

shifting seasons and drying of vernal pools in this drought; turtles are also likely to be negatively affected by drying pools.

Chapter 3. Falling into a Trap

We'd been hiking the Appalachian Trail for a couple of days, with me in front and Ruth following behind. Having joined the trail south of the White Mountains and Killington, the terrain here wasn't too bad. We were also well south of the stretch of the AT that I never wanted to see again, but that's another story. Of course, there'd be lots of extra steps up and down, over the horizontal ground distance, so our progress had been slower, but we also hadn't seen another person, so the trade-off was worth it. Sections of the trail were overgrown, but we found our way; the blazes were faded but still visible. Fortunately, the wind continued to keep the smoke away, so we were favored with amazing vistas and, although it was late in the season, we saw the fall colors that'd been less impressive farther north. Most stunning were the reds of the maples, the oranges of the flagging cedar leaves, and the yellows of the black birches. Of course, while the panoramic vistas of autumn foliage were impressive, to really appreciate it, you had to examine it up close and notice that often the change began only with a single branch at first, and if you looked carefully, you could see patterns of green, yellow, and red on a single leaf. But if you spent too much time looking up at the leaves, you could trip and fall; I knew that from personal experience.

Water was more plentiful at this elevation, but I was having difficulty shooting anything but squirrels; my hand still bothered me where Vincent had smacked it with the crowbar. All the supplies we brought from home had been eaten. We weren't starving—we reserved that term for people who were truly at risk—but we were hungry all the time. We'd need at least 3000 calories a day under this kind of exercise load, or our bodies wouldn't be able to repair the muscle damage from all the hiking.

When I woke up on the third day, I found Ruth had already revived the prior night's campfire from the ashes and was steeping twigs of black and yellow birches in boiling water for tea.

"Morning, hon."

"Morning, babe. After I've had a cup of your tea and wake up, I'll try to shoot something more substantial than squirrel for breakfast. Even a couple of rabbits would have more meat."

"Squirrel would be fine with me. I'll go foraging. There's bound to be some mushrooms or berries."

"That'd be great, but we need protein too."

After my tea, I grabbed my bow and headed off following the white blazes. It'd be easy to get lost up here. After a few minutes hiking, I spotted a deer. Not wanting to be wasteful, I usually tried to take only small deer but this was a big basket

8-point buck. Although it represented much more meat than we could use, even drying meat for jerky, I hadn't been able to hit a deer since leaving Phoenix. I shot and hit it, but it didn't go down. Noting the last spot the animal had been, I listened for breaking branches.

Rushing forward and navigating all the deadfalls, I found blood. It was dark, suggesting I hit the liver. I followed his blood trail. After a kilometer, the deer got onto a game trail; he was probably headed toward his primary bedding area. I desperately wanted to find that deer not only for the meat and to prove to Ruth that I could hunt, but also to end its suffering. I was rushing too fast along the trail when I spotted the trap. To avoid it, I stepped on a log to the side of the covered pit, but the log was rotten. My foot went through and I lost my balance and fell, and then slid into the pit.

Sliding down the side of the pit was bad luck but it was better than falling headlong into it; I was only impaled by one of the sharpened stakes at the bottom. It pierced my upper arm, punching a hole in the deerskin coat my mom had made for me. The pain was excruciating. Beads of sweat broke and ran down my face. I wished I'd had something other than tea to puke up, but it felt as if it were burning a hole in my stomach anyway, so no great loss. I sat there for a few minutes clenching my teeth until the pain ebbed. Then I slowly pulled my arm free, screaming all the while. Ruth says I am a big baby when it comes to pain; she didn't use to when she was my nurse but now I think its just banter. I felt weak and thought I was going to be sick again, but I had nothing else to puke up. Fortunately, I had a bandana scarf around my neck; I wouldn't have been able to rip my shirt with only one hand. After wrapping the bandana around my arm and tightening it as best I could using only my teeth and my other hand, I sat there for a few minutes taking deep breaths to calm myself. I then started shouting.

"Ruth! Ruth! Help! I'm trapped in a pit!" After about twenty minutes of shouting, I heard someone approaching in the woods.

"Where are you?" Ruth shouted.

"Down here." I waved my good arm—my hand extended just above ground level.

When she peered over the pit, she said, "Shit, how badly are you hurt?"

"I was lucky; only one stake pierced my arm, but it hurts like the devil. And I think I have splinters."

"What happened?"

"I saw the trap at the last minute while running on the trail and stepped on a log to avoid it."

"You know that's basic hiking-in-the-woods 101—you don't step on a log because it may be rotten."

"I know, but I was attempting to avoid falling into the pit."

"Well, congratulations, you managed to do both. Can you get out?"

"No, the pit's too deep and the sides are too straight. The dirt just falls apart when I try to climb up. Can you give me a hand?"

She lay down on the ground and reached in and grasped my good arm, but it was soon apparent that I'd pull her into the pit if I tried to use her as an anchor point to pull myself up.

"I don't think I can pull you out. I'll have to go back to camp and get some paracord."

"That won't work either. I wouldn't be able to pull myself up with my bad arm, and I don't think you can pull me out.

Maybe if you found a few logs and rolled them in, I could have something to step on."

After looking around, she said, "I see nothing up here we could use. They're all rotten. How long ago do you think this pit was dug?"

"I don't know, but the vegetation that covered it wasn't long dead, so relatively recently."

"Then I'm going to go look for help."

"You can't. They might be crazy mountain people."

"Don't worry, I've got my gun."

I was growing worried she was becoming too reliant on that gun to get us out of trouble. I had my bow, but had lost my quiver in the fall, so I pulled up a stake to use as a weapon. I stood there for an interminably long time and was going to try to sit down when I heard something big approaching.

"George, I found help. He was on the game trail butchering a deer."

A burly young man, who looked like he was dressed up to look like a stereotypical mountain man, glared down at me over the rim of the pit. He was big-boned, fleshy, with long, straggly light brown hair and peach fuzz on his face. Dressed in furs and jean cutoffs that were no longer blue, he held a long-handled spear in one hand and an arrow in the other—my arrow.

Pointing at me and then at the arrow, he grunted, "You?"

"Yes, mine. I shot the deer and was tracking it to kill it when I fell into this pit."

He seemed satisfied with my answer because his frown softened. He then stuck the spear into the ground, knelt, reached down for my arm, and in one swift motion pulled me up.

35

He then pointed down at the pit and said, "Me."

As I rubbed my arm, I said, "Thanks a lot." I think the sarcasm was lost on him. I looked around the brush on the other side of the rotten log and found my quiver. The mountain man kid was eyeing it. I gestured at the arrow he was holding, and he handed it to me.

"What's your name?"

"Russ."

"I'm George, and she's Ruth. Did you already introduce yourself, Ruth?"

"No. I didn't. What are we going to do now, George?"

"Come," Russ said.

We walked along the game trail back to the deer. It was obvious he had been in the middle of removing the organs when Ruth had found him. Russ pointed at the deer and then at me and then at himself. I guessed we were going to share it. I nodded and said, "Okay."

He knelt and finished what he'd started. I pulled my knife with my left hand to help, but when he saw it, he shook his head and waved his hand. I guess he wanted to do it himself. It didn't take him long before he stood up, picked up the carcass, and threw it over his shoulder. He then gestured to me that I should lead. We walked back to our camp.

When we got to the camp, Russ dropped the deer and then made a sweeping gesture and said, "Come, cabin," and pointed to himself and then into the woods.

Ruth and I looked at each other, and both shrugged, and I said, "Okay."

* * *

We packed up our camp and followed Russ back to his cabin in the woods. He packed out the deer. It was a small cabin with a turf roof and a covered, narrow front porch made up of rotted planks on the ground extending the width of the cabin. Smoke was coming out of the chimney. As we approached, a girl a couple of years younger than Russ opened the door. Her straw-colored hair was chopped off irregularly as if someone had cut it with a knife. She was dressed in tattered rags that looked as if they had once been a woman's dress. What remained of the dress appeared clean but was threadbare due to age and frequent washing. She was holding a crying baby wrapped in what appeared to be the same material as the dress. When she saw us, her round face lit up with a smile. Russ dropped the deer and went over to the girl and pointed at her and said, "Jess."

Ruth walked over and placed her hand on Jess's arm, smiled, and then pointed to herself and said, "Ruth." She then pointed at me and said, "George." Ruth then smiled down at the baby and pointed and asked, "Name?"

Jess answered, "Baby."

I thought, that's as good a name as any. Jess stepped back into the cabin, inviting us in. It was a small cabin with a bed next to one wall, a wooden plank along the other wall serving as a counter, a small table with three chairs—one was sized for a child but not a baby. The fireplace was lit. Something was boiling in a pot suspended on a fireplace crane over the fire. The cabin had no windows and was illuminated only by the fire, and so was dark. We took our packs off and laid them on the floor. I was careful not to jostle my injured arm too much. I placed my quiver and bow on top of my backpack. Ruth immediately began rummaging through her backpack and pulled out the first-aid kit. She then grabbed her water bottle.

Turning to me, she said, "It's time I tended your wound." She smiled at Jess and pointed at my arm. "We're going to go back outside where there's more light."

I noticed then that Russ hadn't come into the cabin behind us. We went back outside, and I sat on a log in the dooryard that was obviously used as a seat. The top was worn down and wasn't covered with moss like every other surface. Ruth unwrapped the wound, cleaned it using her drinking water, and then poured some of the powdered disinfectant we'd brought with us on it and bandaged it. All the while, Jess watched with great interest.

Ruth patted my head and said, "All done, and you didn't cry like a little girl. I'm proud of you."

I smirked at her. "Can I have a sip of your water, please?"

Jess laughed at our exchange. Then Ruth, Jess, and Baby went back into the cabin leaving me alone. I looked for Russ. I wanted to give him a hand with the deer. I found him not too far away in an earthen larder, hanging the deer. He had an impressive larder with a couple of ducks and another small deer already aging. He smiled when I came in. I smiled at him, shaking my head in a gesture of approval. He'd already removed the tenderloins.

I followed him back outside. He turned, pointed at me, and asked, "Where from?

I gestured with my good arm, pointing to what I thought was north, and said, "A ways from up north."

Nodding his head as if he understood, he said, "You, Ruth, stay here this night, share food?"

As he spoke, I'd noticed his gums were bleeding, but I simply said, "Yes," nodding my head.

He then noticed my hand, which was still bruised but no longer swollen from the smack of the crowbar. He pointed at it and then pointed to several bruises on his arms and legs that I hadn't noticed before.

I wasn't sure what he wanted, so I just nodded my head again and said, "Bruises."

We went back into the cabin, where I found Ruth examining the baby. When she saw me, she handed it back to Jess and came over and said, "George, let's step outside for a minute."

We smiled at both Russ and Jess and stepped out the door onto the porch out of earshot.

"George, that baby is only a week or two old. I don't think Jess knows how to raise a baby. The baby is extremely malnourished, but so is Jess. And she's not eating the right foods to help breast milk production. Hell, I'm surprised she even knows how to breastfeed. They're one step above being Ferals."

"They probably saw animals suckle, so had a general idea, and it's kind of instinctive for the baby, isn't it?" I said.

"George, I also think Jess is suffering from a mild case of scurvy."

"Scurvy? Is that why Russ is bruised all over, and his gums are bleeding?"

"Yes. I think her case isn't as bad, which is fortunate, or she might've died during childbirth. That birth must've been

39

an interesting few hours."

"I've heard other trekkers report seeing people with scurvy, but I don't think Dad and I ever saw it on our trek."

"The first thing we've got to do is to increase their vocabulary so we can communicate better. I also need to teach her, and I guess Russ, how to hold that baby correctly. Then I'm going to show her what plants to forage for vitamin C and to fortify her breastmilk and, I guess, what to feed a baby later."

"That all sounds well and good, Ruth, but they've got to be crash courses; we need to keep moving."

"I understand and haven't forgotten what you said the other day, but we can help these people. Before we leave, I'm also going to give her some of my clothes. I can always scavenge some clothes once we're back on the road. Jess has no diapers for the baby, and so is wrapping it in material ripped from what I believe were her mother's old clothes that she's been wearing. Soon she won't have anything to wear and will be out of diaper material."

"What can I do to help speed things up?"

"You've got to convince Russ to leave the mountain and take him down into a nearby town to scavenge things for the baby and maybe even locate people he and Jess can safely interact with, or these three will never survive. And we don't want the townsfolk mistaking them for Ferals."

"Okay, but can we go in and communicate that I need something to eat? All I've had this morning was tea, and I puked that up when I was impaled, falling into the pit of death."

"Come on, you big baby, let's go back inside."

After our eyes readjusted to the low light of the cabin, I noticed Russ examining my bow.

"That's a bow," I said, as I went over and carefully took it from him. Then, with some difficulty because of my bad arm and still sore hand, I notched an arrow. I pointed outside and said, "I'll show you how it works later."

"Good." He then pointed at me and said, "Maybe help?" He went over to the fireplace and pulled down a rifle that I hadn't noticed hanging above the mantel. "You have bullets for 'Shoot Bang'?"

I took the rifle and examined it. I doubted it would still fire, but it wasn't loaded. "This is called a rifle, and no, I don't have any bullets or 'cartridges'." I guessed he was old enough to have gone shooting with his father before he lost his parents. While this was going on, Ruth was busy attempting to communicate with Jess and showing her how to hold the baby correctly.

Jess then looked at Ruth, turned to us, and hesitantly announced, "Lunch?"

Russ turned and smiled at her, no doubt, with pride in her for learning a new word.

They only had three bowls, so Jess didn't eat with us and instead just stood and held the baby, which I noticed she did a bit differently than before, supporting the head more. Ruth and I were seated at the table while Russ sat on the bed. There was no way the small child's chair would've supported him. It was interesting but not surprising that neither he nor Jess had any pox marks, and, except for the symptoms of scurvy, bruising, and bleeding gums, and malnourishment, they both looked relatively healthy.

Lunch was a venison stew that tasted good, especially having only eaten squirrel and cold food brought from home for the past several days, but it wasn't as good as Ruth's. It

41

didn't have potatoes or the right vegetables and spices. There were just some strange greens in it. Ruth was right. Jess needed some lessons in foraging for plants. While eating, we tried to get to know our hosts better and teach them some vocab.

Ruth began. "How long have you lived here in this cabin?"

"Born here."

"What about Jess?" Ruth asked.

"Born here," Russ said, without looking up from his stew. It was clear that Russ was the talker.

Ruth then asked, "Her parents and your parents lived here together?"

Russ looked up with a quizzical expression. "Parents?"

"Mother, father," Ruth responded.

"Oh." And using his spoon, he pointed at Jess and then back at himself and said, "Same." And went back to eating.

Ruth and I exchanged glances, and after a moment, both shrugged.

"Where are your parents?" Ruth asked.

Using his spoon again, Russ pointed outside. "Long dead."

"Oh, they died a long time ago, and you had to bury them. That's very sad." She was trying to teach them some new vocab.

I wondered if their parents had fled to the AT and built this cabin to avoid the crazies after the blackout.

Remembering the task Ruth had assigned me, I then asked, "Have you gone into town where other people live?"

"No. Father say to stay here and never go where people are."

We finished our meals, and Ruth went over and cleaned her bowl in a bucket of water I hadn't noticed before, and then served Jess some stew and gestured for her to sit. Ruth took the baby, and Jess smiled and sat down to eat.

I watched as Ruth played with the baby. It looked a little odd, and I wondered if she was giving it an Apgar test or something similar. Then she looked up and smiled and nodded at me; I guess it was healthy.

To Russ and me, Ruth said, "Just bring your bowls over here; I'll clean them later. You two go out and do man things."

"Works for me," I said, and grabbed my bow and quiver.

Russ grinned and eagerly followed me outside like a puppy—a giant muscle-bound puppy. I spent the next couple of hours teaching him how to shoot. This was made more difficult by not being able to shoot an arrow myself because of my injured arm. In the end, he could shoot fairly accurately; he was a natural, and was very excited by the possibility of a new 'hunting tool' as he called it. It took several attempts, but he communicated that, no longer having the 'shoot bang,' he had to rely on the pits for catching anything larger than small game he could snare. We then spent what remained of the afternoon making a crude bow and some arrows. We used maple for the bow stave, some well-worked deerskin for the string, and cedar for arrows. Our biggest challenge was making the arrowheads. But when I pointed to the heads on my arrows, Russ nodded and ran into the cabin.

I heard Ruth yell, "What are you going to do with those?"

Russ returned with two spoons. I shrugged and nodded when I saw them. He then ran over and went into the larder and came back out with a very rusty metal file. We got to work. While we fastened the archery set together, I convinced Russ that we needed to go to town. After trying to explain that the baby needed things like diapers, I took the expedient route

43

and lied to him to get him to agree to go. I told him we would find cartridges, bullets, for his 'shoot bang'.

Later, I set up the tent outside the cabin. It would've been too crowded inside for all of us, even with us sleeping on the floor. Ruth and Jess had been busy while we menfolk were doing man things. They'd roasted the tenderloins from the deer I'd shot. The venison tasted delicious; Ruth had shown Jess some plants to forage to use as spices for the roasting meat. Russ noticed the difference in flavor immediately and went over and kissed Jess on the forehead. Jess beamed with pride. I thought he was going to kiss Ruth too, but he looked at me first and, smartly, decided against it. Ruth and Jess had found some split wood we could improvise as plates, so we were all able to eat at the same time. Dinner also included mushrooms and a few acorns. I guess oaks were expanding to higher elevations due to climate change. I also recognized stinging nettles, which I've been told are an excellent source of iron and calcium. We also had tea that tasted like the smell of balsam fir trees. Russ didn't like it and put it down, but Jess, after looking at Ruth, got up and picked up the cup and handed it back to him. He looked surprised she'd do such a thing, but drank it. I smiled and felt sorry for him. His life would be different now that Jess had spent time with Ruth. I'd stopped arguing with Ruth about any food she served to me a long time ago.

After dinner, we all went outside and watched the fireflies. It was some consolation not to have to worry about fireflies all dying out from light pollution.

* * *

The next day, Russ and I walked out of the forest into town. We took our bows and my quiver of arrows; I wanted to avoid having to carry my backpack so I didn't have my gun. After a few kilometers on the trail, we found an overgrown logging road that led to a country road and to town. After a few hours, we started passing houses that looked to be in amazing shape. We then came upon a small post office, a church, and one of those 'Dollar' stores. I wasn't sure which Dollar store it was because part of the sign was missing, but, regardless, what luck to find a store selling general consumables. The door wasn't locked, so we didn't have to break the glass to get in.

When we entered, I turned and found Russ open-mouthed with awe, gazing at all the merchandise. The store was surprisingly clean—it didn't look ransacked at all. Not surprisingly, there were no food items. No cans of green beans, or soups, or boxes of crackers or candies. The shelves were just empty. There were also no diapers, neither disposable nor cloth, but we did find stacks of dish towels that could easily serve as diapers. I dumped them all into a cart that fortunately no one appeared to be using at the moment. We found blankets that could be used for warmth or could be cut up to serve as more diapers. We also found three bags of safety pins; what a godsend. I grabbed several pairs of scissors. The biggest surprise was that we found denim jeans. I grabbed a pair and threw them at Russ and mimicked trying them on. He tried them on and then several others. He found one that fit

45

him. Because he couldn't read the size label, I went over and read it—he wasn't sure what I was attempting to do when I grabbed a belt loop, but let me peer down to read it. I searched and found several more his size. He then tried on shirts too. He decided to wear his new clothes out of the store, discarding his furs and jean cutoffs in a waste bin.

What we didn't find were many women's clothes; only a few dresses and blouses were hanging on the rack, and none would come close to fitting Ruth. Someone had looted the store, but without leaving a mess, or someone had straightened up afterwards. We would need to hit a couple of houses on the way back to the cabin to look for women's clothes. But we grabbed some smaller-sized denims and some small-sized men's shirts that I thought would fit Jess, just in case. We also found boots for both of them: work boots and cheap hiking boots. We moved over to housewares and picked up bowls, plates, and several spoons to replace the ones we used for arrowheads. I was pleased to find a handsaw. They were going to need to learn to make baby furniture, including a crib, or spend the next few years with a baby sleeping with them. I wasn't surprised when we found no rifle cartridges. This type of store wouldn't have carried them. But I didn't think Russ was thinking of bullets with everything else we were finding. When he walked past a display of stuffed animals, he stopped, turned, and looked at me with a huge smile. I nodded, and he started picking toys to bring home for the baby. Because the cart wouldn't travel well on the trail back to the cabin, we dumped all our selections into two heavy-duty trash bags. The handsaw wouldn't go into a bag without slicing it, so I fastened it to my belt.

On our way back to the cabin, we passed two houses, one

on each side of the road. I motioned to Russ that we would leave the bags at the bottom of the drive and go inside the house. He shook his head no. It took some convincing, but he reluctantly agreed, and we went up the drive to the house. This time, the door was locked, so I had to break a window to get in. We searched the house and found no one. Like the store, the house was in surprisingly good shape. It didn't look ransacked at all. I didn't voice it to Russ, but I looked for cartridges for any type of gun, but didn't find any. But we found dresses, women's slacks, and blouses. Their style was for an older woman, but they were small enough that Jess could wear them if she preferred them over the jeans we had already picked up for her. After all, she'd been satisfied with her mom's old clothes. We also discovered a sewing kit. Maybe Ruth would find time to teach Jess how to sew too. Before leaving, we straightened up any mess we'd made, and Russ found a cookie sheet to wedge over the glass that I'd broken to get in.

We walked down the drive carrying our bows, a bunch of women's clothes, and a sewing kit, only to find an old man, at least seventy years old, standing over our garbage bags full of loot, holding a shotgun. He was by far the oldest man I'd ever seen outside of Phoenix. All I could think was, how the hell did this old man survive this long and the Time of the Great Dying? He was nearly bald but had little tufts of white hair on either side of the receding hairline and wore an old man's threadbare plaid flannel shirt and tan cotton work pants held up with red, now pink, suspenders.

"What are you two fellers doing? You planning on stealing all those dresses?" He asked the last part with a quizzical expression on his face.

"I can explain, Sir. We're not looters—well, we are kind of, but it's an emergency. Russ here just had a baby, and we needed a few things."

"He had a baby?"

"Well, his...his wife did. My wife is with her back in their cabin in the woods. They have nothing for the baby."

"And you took the dresses for the baby? And he looks like he is wearing new clothes straight off the rack."

I dropped the dresses into the garbage bag we'd filled at the Dollar store, put my bow and quiver down, and raised my hands. When I thought he was satisfied, I wouldn't do anything rash, I knelt over the garbage bag and opened it.

"No, sir. We were at the Dollar store picking up a few things for the baby..." I rummaged through the bag and, fortunately, I'd picked the right one and pulled out a couple of stuffed toys, and showed them to him. "While we were there, we thought to pick up some new clothes and things for the parents, who've been living alone in the woods all their lives. But there weren't any women's clothes left in the store, so we stopped here to have a look."

"And I bet my house woulda have been next."

"No, sir, we found everything we needed and probably couldn't have carried any more, anyway." I realized immediately that I shouldn't have added the second part.

"So, you also ransacked my Dollar General?"

"No, sir, we didn't ransack. We appreciated the condition the store and house were in and were careful to leave both the way we'd found them. If you don't believe me, let's go up and look in the house. We even improvised a repair to the window I broke to get in."

"Fine, tell him to drop that stuff and let's go see. There's

48

no more of you, is there?"

"No, sir."

He was impressed with the job that Russ had done to cover the window I'd broken. Fortunately, we'd left the door unlocked, so we didn't need to smash another to get inside. He saw we hadn't ransacked the place in our search and was satisfied. He lowered his shotgun and said, "All right, while I can't condone breaking and entering and thievery, I understand you were in a bad spot with the new baby, so I'll let it go this time."

I rubbed my chin and said, "Um, sir, ah, Russ here, he doesn't talk much. He may need to come back to town in the future for some other things they don't have. For the child as it grows up."

"Yeah, so what?"

"Well, I was hoping you wouldn't shoot him if you saw him around here again. He's a good guy. Maybe he could stop in and check on you on his way into town. Maybe even bring you some meat. He's an excellent hunter."

I could see on the old man's face that the possibility of Russ bringing meat interested him.

"That might work," he said. "To be honest, I don't have any shells for this shotgun and can't hunt worth a damn without it. My wife and I have been worrying about how we'd make it through another winter without enough food and firewood."

"I bet Russ could help with that too," I said.

Russ nodded and said, "I help," and he pantomimed chopping wood.

"Sir, you mentioned you had a wife. What's her name?"

"Alice."

"And yours?"

49

"My name's Robert."

"Nice to meet you, Robert." I reached out and shook his hand. "My name is George. I'm just passing through. If it would be okay with your wife, maybe Russ here and his wife, whose name is Jess by the way, could come visit you. Jess is new to motherhood and might need advice."

"I'm sure Alice would love that, but let's go ask her, and I'll introduce you."

Alice was a sweet old lady with severely cut white hair and a big smile. The blouse she had on did not cover all the loose skin and protruding bones in her neck and shoulders. When she saw Robert hadn't been killed by the two fellas he'd confronted on the street, she was overjoyed and ran— actually, it was a waddling gait—and hugged him. She'd probably have agreed to anything at that point, but seemed overjoyed at the prospect of receiving visitors, especially if they brought food and a baby to play with. She wanted to feed us, but it was obvious they didn't have enough food for themselves, so we said our goodbyes with Russ promising to return soon with Jess and the baby. We headed back to the cabin. I was very pleased with myself for accomplishing my assigned tasks. Ruth would surely be pleased with me.

Ruth was pleased. We stayed for another three days. Long enough to make two batches of jerky out of the deer that I'd shot. Ruth also showed Jess how to make pemmican. I almost died getting the fat for the pemmican, however. Russ was so excited about the new bow that he wanted us to go hunting constantly . He was also following me wherever I went. He must've really missed his dad. One day, he came up with the idea that we should hunt a nuisance bear he'd been dealing with that wouldn't fall into one of his traps. I could barely draw my bow with my arm the way it was, but I think he really wanted to borrow my arrows, but didn't know how to ask. I had more of them than he did, and the tips were better. We would need all of them to bring a bear down. It didn't take us long to find his bear. It was nice and fat, preparing to hibernate. I ended up serving as the bait for the bear while he repeatedly shot it with my arrows, but he brought it down, and I wasn't killed.

When we said our goodbyes, both Jess and Ruth were crying. I wasn't sure how Ruth had done it, but Jess was talking up a storm. Even after only four days, both Russ and Jess and the baby were looking much better. I'm not much of a hugger, but I let Russ hug me without pulling away. He walked us back up to the main trail so we wouldn't get lost, and soon we were looking at white blazes. Ruth was silent for the next several hours on the trail.

* * *

We fell into a routine as we hiked south for the next two weeks. Despite my sore arm, I even managed to shoot some game to augment the provisions we'd resupplied from Russ and Jess. Although it was a challenging hike with the trail overgrown in many places, it was fine. Importantly, we didn't see another living soul on the trail but did occasionally see smoke, showing people were close. When we missed the double white blazes indicating a turn, we simply backtracked until we found them. Ruth was especially good at spotting them. The stone-walled shelters were still in great shape, so we didn't have to set up the tent each night; although the rocky floors were hard on my hips—my sleeping pad was just too thin. When I complained about it, Ruth called me a big baby.

During those two weeks, the most notable incident was one night we were awakened by growling just outside the camp.

"Hon, what's that noise?" Ruth asked.

"It's wolves. I let the fire die out, damn it."

"What are we going to do?"

"Get your gun out, but don't use it unless they attack and start dragging me off. I'll throw another log onto the fire. And then I'm going to make as much noise as possible."

Although the wolves stood their ground for a time, jaws snapping at the air, the fire restarted, and the plan eventually worked; they ran off. But they came back the next day and shadowed us for several more. During daylight, they kept their distance, especially after I shot one in the shoulder. But they kept us awake each night by howling and coming into the campsite and growling; their damn eyes shining in the firelight. I think they were just trying to prove they were no longer intimidated by humans. There was so much game around to feed on, they weren't interested in eating us. It was fortunate they were red wolves and not the larger, more aggressive gray wolves found farther north. If they were, they would have likely killed us just for being in their territory. Eventually, we walked out of their territory, and they didn't follow.

The other bit of excitement was that I violated another

hiking 101 rule and didn't take care of my feet properly, so I came down with swamp foot. You can imagine Ruth's response as I screamed each time I yanked a toenail off. We left the trail just inside New Jersey and set off on our way to Asbury Park to see the ocean and measure the sea level.

* * *

As we walked off the trail we could see glimpses of a large, beautiful lake off to the east. When we reached the empty parking lot, which had likely served day hikers in the past, we could see that there was a marina on the lake. Fortunately, we saw no activity, but I could smell smoke. It was a chilly late-October day, so I figured the smoke was coming from a fireplace in one of the luxury homes that rimmed the lake's shore. There had been plenty of ponds and streams on the trail to wash up, so we weren't in dire need of a bath, and I don't swim, so I convinced Ruth to bypass this lake and not go swimming. I wasn't keen on talking to anyone, so we set a brisk pace.

After leaving Lake Shore Drive with all the big houses and docks, we turned and headed east on a road that looked as if it were a county road but claimed to be a turnpike. I think we both were enjoying a flat, unobstructed road to walk on for a change. We'd been walking in silence for a few hours when I asked Ruth, "Are you looking forward to seeing the ocean for the first time?"

"I can't wait," she said. "I bet it's amazing—all that blue as far as the eye can see. I hope it's warm enough to swim."

"Well, I don't want to burst your bubble babe, but it may be more green than blue because of all the phytoplankton, and if the weather there is anything like it is today, I don't think we'll be swimming."

"Come on George, didn't they used to have events where people would jump into freezing cold water during the winter?"

"Yes, they were called 'polar bear plunges', but I'm not a polar bear, and besides, I think we'd have to change the name; polar bears all went extinct."

"George, you can be such a downer sometimes."

"Well, life can be a downer sometimes. Right now do you want to play 'Would You Rather' again? I might be wrong but I thought you enjoyed playing it when we first started the trek."

"Okay George, but just for a short while. You ask insipid questions sometimes."

"Insipid, thanks. Right, I'll start. Would you rather sleep in a tent or an abandoned building?"

"It depends," she said. "Is it going to rain, or will there be wolves at my tent flap?"

"Alright, next question: would you rather hike in very hot weather or freezing cold?"

"Since I'm cold now, my answer is very hot, but I reserve the right to change that answer later."

"Would you rather camp in the mountains or by a lake?" I asked.

"Well, we just camped in the mountains for two weeks, so

I'm bored with that, but we also just walked past a beautiful lake surrounded by huge vacation homes. So, I'd rather camp by the ocean."

"Babe, it'll take us a few more days to reach Asbury Park and the ocean. Your turn."

"Okay. George, would you rather do it missionary style or doggy style?"

"Ha ha. We're not going there."

"Why not, hon?"

"Because it's the middle of the afternoon and there are many more kilometers to walk before setting up the tent. And besides, you said my questions were insipid."

Just then, we spotted a man standing on a small bridge a hundred meters in front of us, waving his arms.

"I think he's trying to warn us to get off the road," Ruth said.

I looked around for a place to hide. We'd just walked past a small single-story building advertised as a 'Deli and Pub' and were now in front of what looked like a two-story garage or auto machine shop with three bay doors that were all closed. There were lots of rusted-out cars sitting in the gravel parking lot too.

"Come on, let's hide in there and get up to the second floor to watch the road."

We found the side door unlocked and went in, locking it behind us. It opened into what once had been an office. There was a desk, filing cabinets, and papers strewn all over the floor. We hurried to the inside door that led to the stairs up to the second floor. We were in a hurry and, foolishly, hadn't considered the place might be occupied. When I stepped into what I assumed would be the front room, someone grabbed me by the arm and put a knife to my throat.

"Make a sound, and you die."

The threat had been whispered into my ear by a woman. The room was filled with boxes and filing cabinets, and the floor was littered with broken glass from the windows that had either blown in or been smashed by someone throwing rocks.

Just off to my right, I heard, "Please don't hurt him." It was Ruth who had just come through the door. I could feel the knife bite and blood dripping down my neck.

"Be quiet, or I'll kill him."

We stood there for a minute or two staring at each other before I whispered, "What are we hiding from?"

"Shut up."

"We don't mean you any harm and promise to be quiet," Ruth pleaded in a whispered voice.

I heard a commotion coming from where Ruth must've been standing. I couldn't see because I couldn't turn my head without my throat being sliced open, but I heard another woman's voice whisper, "Debby, let him go. They aren't Rangers."

"How can you be sure?"

"Because they aren't sunburned or filthy."

The knife was removed from my throat, and I was released.

The second woman, who was obviously in charge, was in her 30s, had short dark hair, a pretty face, and was dressed in a green jacket and pants that looked as if they'd been tailored; they were worn and dirty now. She carried what looked like an expensive crossbow.

She whispered, "Now, all of you get down and be quiet." Crouching low, she moved silently over to one of the two windows and peered out. "They're coming."

Just then, we heard grunts and the sound of stomping boots from the road below. I tried to inch over to the other window from my squatted position, but Debbie glowered at me. The other woman then nodded, so I continued. When I looked out, I saw six men in baggy camouflage jackets coming from the direction that we had been headed. A few had spears, while the others carried fierce-looking crossbows. The sound of running became louder as they passed in front of the garage. Everyone held their breath. Then I watched as the band of men moved off and the sound of pounding boots receded. In unison, we all exhaled and started breathing again.

After a couple of minutes, the woman in charge stood up, and then so did Debbie. Ruth and I followed suit.

"Who are you people, and why aren't you sunburned from working in the fields?" the woman in charge asked.

Before I could answer, Ruth said, "My name is Ruth, and this is my husband, George. We're just passing through on our way to the coast."

"Well, you're lucky you weren't caught by the Rangers."

Before Ruth could, I asked, "Who are they and why do we have to hide from them?"

"They control the area south of here and patrol all the way to the lake's south rim. They don't like strangers."

"So where are they from?" I asked.

"West Milford."

"How many people live there?" I asked.

"I don't know."

"But they must be organized," I said. "Is there a warlord or what?"

"I don't know."

"But they've got a standing military force?" I asked.

"Yeah, I guess you can call the Rangers a standing military force."

"And you? Where are you two from?" I asked.

"My name's Joan, and this is Debbie. We live a few miles from here on the west side of the lake. We're here just scavenging some parts for a pump."

"Well, thank you for not letting Debbie here slit my throat."

"You're welcome, but I only stopped her because I was worried your woman would scream."

"Well, thanks anyway."

Ruth then asked, "How long do we wait until we know it's safe to leave?"

"A while. I'll let you know."

So we stood there staring uneasily at each other. Debbie, who was in her early 30s, had close-cropped blonde hair and a very narrow face with a sharp nose, was becoming fidgety, pacing and looking out the window. Her body odor also had an "acrid" quality. She was making me nervous. Ruth and I exchanged glances, and I could see she was also becoming worried.

To break the silence, I asked, "Do you two live alone by the lake?"

Joan frowned at me and said, "You ask lots of questions."

"People have told me that before," I said.

"Although it's none of your business, we don't live alone. Our men are likely hiding someplace out there waiting until they're sure the Rangers have gone." Looking at Debbie, she added, "But I'm sure they're safe or we woulda heard a commotion when they were captured and seen 'em get dragged off." Glancing back at me, she said, "So don't you

58

try anything, or when our men come for us, they'll find you."

"Are you part of a community where you live?"

"Shut up!" Debbie whispered.

Just then, we heard someone breaking in downstairs.

Chapter 4. Let's Try That Again

We'd been holding our breath for what seemed like eternity when a man called out. Both women exhaled, glanced at each other and smiled. It turned out their men felt it was now safe to leave, but were forced to break into the garage because Ruth and I'd locked the door. They were disappointed that Joan and Debbie hadn't found the parts they needed and were even less happy to see Ruth and me. They wanted nothing to do with us, especially after I tried to pump them for more information on the Rangers. So we left them with a 'Good luck', and Ruth and I continued on our way.

We walked the rest of the day, hoping to put as many kilometers as possible between us and the Rangers' territory, even though we weren't sure how much of a threat they were. We stopped for the night near another lake. I built the fire while Ruth put up the tent. After I got it going, I found some grubs to use as bait and caught a few fish for dinner. Ruth foraged and contributed stinging nettles and cattail heads, which we boiled and then grilled. We sat around the fire looking up at the stars. Since the smoke still hadn't returned, the sky was clear, and the stars actually twinkled. I found myself dozing off as Ruth chattered on excitedly about what we had experienced on our journey so far. It was all just a big adventure to her.

The next day, I caught some more fish for breakfast, and we got underway. After a few hours, we began passing deserted houses built close to one another, indicating a town was up ahead. I got out my monocular telescope and surveyed the town.

"What do you see?"

"It's difficult to see very far with all the trees but it's not a big town. Although I can see a few commercial buildings, there aren't any that are multi-story. About a kilometer down the road, there's a roadblock of rusted cars, refrigerators, and other debris blocking the way into town." Lowering the scope and turning to Ruth, I said, "I wonder if someone like the Rangers have cars or trucks that still run; maybe the roadblock is to prevent a motorized attack?"

"I didn't know any cars survived the Blackout War?"

"Oh yeah, Dad and I saw some on our trek. A few of the older models survived, but fuel goes bad after a while, so you need to convert to biodiesel or wood gasification. And things break down. Local auto supply shops have only a limited inventory, and cannibalizing other cars for parts only takes you so far. I'll be surprised if we see any cars running now, twenty-five years after the blackout."

I turned my attention back to the roadblock. "There's three men standing at the roadblock. One of them looks to be about my age; the other two are younger but not kids. Only one appears to be armed. They don't look very intimidating."

I closed the telescope. "Okay, before we enter the town, I want to go over a few things. I'll go in first while you hang back watching from here for trouble. I'll leave you the scope." I handed it to her. "Don't come in unless I signal you. If you can see I'm in trouble, you can approach and shoot a few arrows to cause confusion to give me a chance to escape, but don't put yourself at risk. And don't use the gun. If I don't signal or you don't see me, give me a day or two, and if I haven't come out by then, abort the trek and return to Phoenix. Do you got that?"

"Yeah, I got it. I abandon you if you get into trouble."

"Yep. Do you think you could find your way back to Phoenix if I leave you my backpack with the maps?"

"Yeah, but I am not leaving without you."

"What if you see them kill me? You'd return home then, wouldn't you?"

"Yes, of course."

"And if I signal it's safe, when you come in, be very careful about what you say, even if they seem like nice people. Obviously, you never tell anyone where we're really from, ever! If asked, just say something like, 'We're from a ways up north.' And of course, never discuss conditions back in Phoenix with anyone. We don't want to give them any reason to go looking for it. When they ask what we're doing, simply say something like, 'We're just looking for a better place for our people to move that's not already overcrowded. We want to avoid any trouble.' This story allows us to ask questions about the local conditions, like weather and warring neighbors, and doesn't create too much suspicion. And don't drink or eat anything unless it's just come out of the fire or you know it's been boiled; it could be host to bacteria and other germs that could make you sick."

"You remember I'm a trained nurse, right?"

I ignored her and continued, "Tell them you already have water and food and don't want to deplete their supplies. Any questions? Right, now let's change into our dirtiest and smelliest clothes so we'll blend in."

After I changed into my filthiest clothes, some spotted with dried blood and gore from cleaning squirrels, fish, and other goodies for dinner, I looked at Ruth. "Is that all you got? You cleaned the fish for breakfast this morning; how do you stay so clean? I swear I am going to throw mud on you."

"Is it my fault I'm tidy?"

Ruth always looked as if she had stepped out of one of the magazines the Center had archived. In Phoenix, we all had access to clean, well-made clothes, but they looked different on Ruth. They actually fit her, and she took the time to put together outfits. She stood out in a good way in Phoenix. Out here, her looks put her in danger.

I left my backpack with the maps, and my bow and quiver with Ruth, and walked slowly toward the roadblock. On the way, I walked past several houses that appeared to have been dismantled, possibly cannibalized to repair other houses or for firewood.

As I approached the three men, I noticed all three had beards of varying length and fullness. One man, the guy with the fullest beard, was balding, while the other two had trimmed hair; one of whom had some gray at the temples. They wore clothes that had been clearly mended, but that were only moderately dirty. They all looked thin and haggard and seemed more nervous than I was. Only one of them appeared

63

armed with an old rusty sword.

As I approached, the tallest man, who was wearing a New York Mets baseball cap, said, "We don't want any trouble."

I gave him a wide smile and said, "Good, neither do I."

"What do you want?" the balding man asked.

"I'm just passing through, looking for some information."

"What kind of information?" the balding man asked.

"I'm from a ways up north, looking for a place with better weather for folks in my town to move to...but not to an area that is already densely populated. We don't want to fight anyone."

"Well, as you can see, there are people living here already," the balding man said.

"Besides, the weather here sucks too," the guy with the baseball cap added. "One day it's snowing, the next rain, followed by tornadoes, and then no rain for months. It kills the crops."

"So, you plant crops?" I asked.

The balding man gave me a stern look and said, "That's none of your business."

"Listen, my name's George Reynolds, but most people just call me Reynolds. I'm also looking for possible future trading partners. Do you have anything worth trading?"

"Again, that's none of your business," said the balding man, who was becoming irritated with me. "You could be attempting to find out if we have anything worth raiding the town for."

"Well, is there someone else I could talk to about this?" I asked.

The three men exchanged glances, and then the tallest guy said to the balding guy, "We could take him to see Martha."

The youngest man holding the sword, who hadn't spoken yet, said, "No, let's send him on his way. He's probably lying and is just another refugee from New York. How do we know there's not a hundred more just like him up the road waiting to come in and steal all our food like last time?"

"I can promise you I'm not a refugee from New York or anyplace else. And I'm not here to steal your food."

Just then, three women walked down the road from the town.

"Bob, what's going on?" one of the women asked. "Who is this guy?"

The balding man, whose name was apparently Bob, said, "He says he's just passing through, looking for a place for his people to move, but doesn't want any trouble. He also says he may be looking for future trading partners."

"Do you believe him?" she asked.

"No!" the man with the sword said loudly.

"Then send him on his way or stick him with your sword," the woman said. "We don't need any strangers surveying the town."

I noticed they were all now looking behind me up the road. I turned to see Ruth walking toward us with both our packs. *For fuck's sake*, I thought.

When she came up, she said, "Hello, everyone, my name's Ruth. I'm George's wife."

They all exchanged glances.

"Hello Ruth, my name's Martha Remis. I must say, you certainly are a pretty girl."

I noticed the emphasis on the last word. Ruth is fourteen years younger than I am.

"Ruth, this is my husband, Bob," Martha continued.

"That's Charles in the baseball cap, Chester with the sword, and Jean and Daisy. We're the town council running things here."

"It's wonderful to meet you all," Ruth said. "Would it be okay if we visited for a while and asked you some questions? George and I are from a ways up north and are looking for a place to move our town that wouldn't upset anyone. We don't want any trouble."

I wanted to yell at Ruth for not following directions, but I bit my tongue; I couldn't yell at her in front of these women. If the men noticed similarities in Ruth's and my scripts, they didn't mention it. They were too busy ogling Ruth.

"I guess that'd be okay," Martha said, looking intently at Ruth.

It was clear that Martha ran things in this town. She was of average height, had short blonde hair beginning to go gray, a round face, and ruddy cheeks. She was wearing linen pants and a polyester jacket. The other two women were wearing faded blue jeans, Daisy with a windbreaker, Jean a sweater. Jean had a pointed face and light brown hair in a ponytail, while Daisy had her blond hair down around an unusually large face. All three looked very thin in their clothes that no longer fit. It wasn't clear whether Jean and Daisy were married to Charles and Chester.

Ruth and I walked through the opening in the roadblock.

Martha turned to Bob and said, "Why don't you carry their backpacks for them?"

"No, that won't be necessary," I said. "We can carry them."

I couldn't let him search the backpacks; I wouldn't be able to explain all the tech or the guns with ammunition.

"No, I think it'd be better if Bob carried them for now,"

Martha said.

"Okay," but I wasn't planning on letting Bob or our backpacks out of my sight.

"Chester and Charles, why don't you stay here on sentry while we all go talk?"

In a surly tone, Charles answered, "Yes, Martha."

We followed Martha, the two other women, and Bob up the street past an abandoned daycare, a bar and grill that didn't look as if it had poured any beers lately, a U-Haul rental place, and several houses, a few with smoke coming out their chimneys. Although the surrounding forest was encroaching on the town, there were obvious signs the townsfolk had been attempting to keep the vegetation takeover at bay for at least a little while longer.

We stopped and went inside a building that had once been a cafe. The place was clean and well-lit from natural light coming through a wall of oversized windows with views of the street outside. There were several tables with chairs, a counter with several stools with red vinyl padded cushions, which were now cracked, and a chalkboard that had presumably advertised daily specials in the past. It now appeared to list job assignments.

As we entered, Martha said, "Daisy, could you find us some coffee?"

Daisy walked into the back of the cafe, followed by Jean. After Bob unceremoniously dropped our backpacks on the floor, he followed them. I guessed they'd seen these interviews before and were no longer interested in hearing from new strangers.

As Martha sat down, she said, "Take a seat. So who are you and what do you really want?"

67

"We've already told you who we are," I said. "We're searching for a place to move our small community that has better weather for growing crops. We want to avoid any trouble, so we're looking for a deserted town. We're also hoping to find one that might have neighboring towns we could trade with once we got settled."

"Well, you can understand our concerns about being over-run with refugees. It's been years since the last flood of refugees came in from New York, but they come in waves following some disaster, so we've got to keep our guard up. We no longer have the resources to accept any new people. We can't feed them or keep them warm in the winter."

Before I could ask about the barricade on the road, Ruth asked, "Martha, you said before, that you no longer have the resources. Has something changed to reduce your re-sources?"

"How do I know you aren't here to learn everything you can about us so you can come back later with a raiding party? Why don't you tell me a little more about yourselves first? Where do you come from?"

I answered before Ruth could, "We're from a ways up north in New England. Although the average temperatures aren't too bad, the amount of winter snow has increased dramatically, and what's worse, the timing of the seasons is so erratic that we haven't had a successful crop in several years. We're slowly starving and need to move south."

The story I told wasn't entirely true. The weather back in Phoenix was as undependable as anywhere, but we en-joyed food supplied by a vertical farm or, more precisely, an advanced and intensive form of hydroponically based agriculture known as 'Controlled Environment Agriculture.'

It allowed us to raise crops despite the erratic weather outside. But the vertical farm was made possible only because of the electricity generated by our microreactor to power the irrigation pumps, lights, and geothermal pumps to control the temperature.

"Tell me about it," Martha replied. "Charles, you met him earlier. He's our farm manager. He tells me our crops are either rotting in the ground before they sprout because the soil is waterlogged from heavy rains or the soil is too dry from flash droughts. There's no winning."

"Apparently not," I said. "At least not until we can predict the variable weather better without all the technology we relied on before."

At that point, Daisy came in with coffee, or what they considered coffee. I could tell it was birch bark tea, but didn't comment.

"So how long have you two been together?" Martha asked.

I almost choked on my tea.

"We've been married for over seven years," Ruth replied.

"You must've been very young then, darling," Martha said, giving me a dirty look.

"Yes, but I knew what I wanted, didn't I, George?"

I just smiled.

Wanting to change the subject, I asked, "The roadblock you have; was it constructed to prevent a mechanized attack?"

"Alright, I guess I can trust you enough to reveal a few things. Yes, early on, we were attacked by marauders with modified cars, but we haven't seen any in years and have only needed to fight off the occasional raiding party. But don't get the wrong impression; we're very well armed."

I could tell by her expression that the last part was to

disabuse us of any notion of attacking, if we weren't who we said we were.

"Martha, can we go back and discuss what changes have occurred recently that've reduced your resources?" Ruth asked. "Was it just because of the problems with farming you mentioned earlier?"

"Yes, I guess so. Early on, we were fortunate to have several consumptive-use natural gas wells from all the fracking that had taken place before the collapse. After the blackout, we rigged a way to distribute the gas for heating and cooking and to run a few old-model trucks that survived the EMPs. So we had a car and a couple of trucks that ran too. That improved our farming capabilities. But the flow of gas slowed over the years, and we suffered a major explosion a few years ago when someone tried to steal gas using propane tanks that aren't meant for natural gas. We modified the trucks to burn biodiesel, but over time, they broke down. So we now must rely on manpower and, of course, womenpower to farm and burn wood to stay warm during the winters."

Getting up from the table, she said, "Why don't we take a break from this for some lunch? Would you like to stay for lunch and maybe even stay the night? Later, we can talk about some of our neighboring towns that might be suitable for you, but, as I've said, we've got erratic weather here too."

Ruth and I started getting up.

"We'd like that very much," I said. "I'd be very interested to hear more about the local conditions."

"Don't get up," she said. "I'll see about lunch. I'll send Bob back in; he can show you where you can freshen up before lunch and stay over tonight."

As soon as she left, I got up and retrieved our backpacks.

After a few minutes, we heard some arguing in the back of the cafe, but couldn't make out what was being said. Then Bob came out and walked outside, and started walking down the road. We followed.

When we caught up to him, he said, "George, I should explain about Chester. He's got issues. His parents were killed early on by raiders. We wouldn't have let him stick you with his sword; not unless you did something to deserve it."

"I understand completely," I said.

"Good. So I hear you're staying with us for a while." Pointing to a yellow house down the road, he said, "You can sleep in that house over there. It's temporarily empty. There's a cistern in the back with clean water that you can drink and use to wash up. There's also a privy. When you're ready, come back to the cafe, and we'll have something to eat."

"This is very generous of you all to allow us to stay and feed us," Ruth said.

"Yes, it is." He stopped walking and turned to us, "Please don't take advantage of Martha's feelings."

"What do you mean?" I asked.

"The only reason she allowed you in and is allowing you to stay is that Ruth reminds her of our daughter." Looking at Ruth, he said, "I can see the resemblance, although our Debby was younger when she died, but it's there, and in how you present yourself. It's uncanny."

"I'm sorry for your loss. How long ago did she die?" Ruth asked.

"It was almost ten years ago. She was only fifteen when she died of some damned flu."

"I'm so sorry," I said. "I know what it's like to lose a child."

He nodded, then turned and left us standing there. We

71

walked over to the empty house. It needed some repairs, but had a roof and windows, and would keep the weather out for a little while longer. It was dusty but clean otherwise inside. We found a queen bed in one of the bedrooms, while the others had twins or a full-sized bed. We chose the queen. It didn't have linens, but our sleeping bags would suffice. Ruth sat on the edge of the bed and bounced a few times to see how firm it was. She had a smile on her face when I tore into her.

"What were you thinking, not waiting for my signal that it was safe to come into town? I could've been caught in a lie that might have gotten me or both of us killed."

"Well, it turned out it was a good thing I showed up, wasn't it? You would've been sent away or possibly killed if I hadn't come in. Besides, I figured if they were going to kill you, they would've done it already."

"That's beside the point. You've got to follow my directions if we're to survive this trek."

I sat down in a huff.

"Now that you've got that out of your system, what do you think?" Ruth asked.

"I think this bed is going to do wonders for my sore hip."

"No, about everything they told us?"

"It's all very sad."

"What do you mean?"

"Everything. Martha and Bob losing a child, their seeing a resemblance in you, and the town losing what little advantage it had after the blackout and now sliding backwards. Sounds like they're barely holding on."

"Is there anything we can do to help?" she asked.

"Not in a meaningful way. If they were located closer to Phoenix, we might fabricate and supply replacement parts for their vehicles and possibly get their gas wells flowing again. Maybe even give them some of the genetically modified seeds your father's working on, but the Center isn't prepared to move onto Phase 3 yet."

"But how long before that happens?" she asked.

"We talked about this. It depends on a lot of things, including how long it takes me to get my model working and how long before people pull down the barricades and stop sending out armed Rangers."

"Well, that sucks," she said.

"Yes, it does."

"Okay, I guess the only thing to do is to take advantage of their hospitality. I never thought I'd look forward to using a privy, but it's better than squatting in the woods." Ruth got up, pulled off her jacket, and laid it on the bed. "We can then clean up and go to lunch. I'm sure we can find ways to help them, even if they're only in small ways."

* * *

We had a satisfying meal of chicken stew with potatoes and carrots for lunch. It tasted as good as it smelled. I got a stern look from Ruth when I asked for seconds, though. After lunch, Martha showed us around town, pointing out some of their workarounds after losing power from the natural gas. They were fortunate to be located so close to a reservoir, so had no problems getting water to drink, but it took a lot of manpower to collect and distribute water for irrigation. Someone knew enough to fashion something similar to a dhone, used in rural parts of India, consisting of a wooden trough that a person would stand on, and by shifting their weight would seesaw across a log to raise water from the reservoir and deliver it to the irrigation ditch. It wouldn't move much water, but enough to flood the field if they supplied the manpower. It sounded as if they were doing an okay job of disposing of their waste, but I suggested they start collecting their urine to use as fertilizer. After the heavy noontime meal, we had only a light dinner before going to bed. And it was a wonderful bed.

Despite their friendly attitude and obvious fondness for Ruth, I couldn't sleep much that night. Instead, I lay there listening for sounds of people sneaking in to kill us. Eventually, I fell asleep. I couldn't help it; the bed was so comfortable after sleeping on the ground for weeks.

* * *

We stayed for three nights. Ruth and I found different ways to help. Using her nursing skills, she treated several people for cuts and broken arms. Fortunately, no one was suffering from any raging infections; I was in no mood to argue with her about using the antibiotics we'd been supplied for our trek. For my part, I educated Charles about the advantages of agroforestry without letting on that back in Phoenix, we had ample food from the vertical farm and only used the agroforest to test out our new genetically modified, climate-resistant crops and to raise goats and rabbits. I emphasized that growing crops within an established forest and incorporating understory and ground cover would provide better shade and, thereby, reduce evapotranspiration and irrigation needs. And that it would also serve as a windbreak.

Before we left the village, I wrote up my notes from the past couple of weeks.

* * *

Journal entry: 28 October, Small Community on Wanaque Reservoir just South of Erskine, NJ

Accessed the Appalachian Trail from a trailhead near the Connecticut River and Dartmouth College. The AT remains a viable route; we encountered only one family while traveling 300 km (noteworthy, they were suffering from scurvy), but saw evidence of other people living just of the trail. Exited AT near Greenwood Lake at the NY – NJ border. Encountered a small group of people who alerted us that an armed group (known as Rangers by locals) was patrolling the area; the armed group was reportedly from West Milford. We were told this militaristic group enslaves captives, but this was not confirmed.

75

Having avoided the Rangers, we arrived here three days ago to find a community of approximately 25 families organized beyond chiefdom; it has a town council of three women and three men, but is run principally by a woman named Martha Remis. While townspeople are armed with bows, etc., and stand sentry, they do not have a standing military force. They send out small patrols, but they are told not to engage unless necessary for defense. They have occupied this town since before the collapse and blackout. The town is in moderate to good condition—clean potable water and sanitary disposal of wastewater—but appears to be backsliding. Crops are less productive due to weather-related issues and reliance on human labor. Observed only a few kids who were required to take on adult tasks. They also have individual gardens and very limited livestock: chickens, turkeys, and three goats. They had natural gas wells from before the blackout to run pumps to pull potable water from the reservoir; heating and run a few vehicles, but no longer have access to the natural gas. Now rely on cisterns and manual labor to distribute water. It is very troubling that this settlement is no longer sustainable. They tell us that besides the Rangers to the west, there are two towns with squatters that we should try to avoid to the east.

Meteorological data collected at this location are tabulated on the previous page. I interviewed several people about the weather they've been experiencing over the past few years. Most reports centered on recent extreme storms: torrential downpours, hail, and heavy snow. They report being most surprised by the heavier snows under global warming. I explained that climate change can paradoxically cause more snowfall in some regions because warmer temperatures increase the amount of moisture the atmosphere can hold—if temperatures dip below freezing, this extra moisture can result in heavier snowstorms.

They felt the average temperature had remained unchanged, but that the frequency of prolonged heat waves of a duration of a week or more had increased. Last winter, they had extensive runoff, flooding, and damage following the sudden melting of snow that had accumulated over much of the winter following a sudden heat wave and a significant rain event. But all agreed that the erratic weather during the shoulder seasons was the biggest problem.

* * *

The day we left, Martha and Bob both hugged Ruth; I thought all three might cry. Martha had become very fond of Ruth; the feeling was mutual—I think Ruth missed her parents. They allowed us to resupply, providing us with a couple of jars of preserves, a jar of honey, a few vegetables, and venison jerky for our travels.

We took I-287 south to avoid New York City as we traveled toward Asbury Park on the coast.

While walking past a few burned-out suburbs, Ruth asked, "George, do you think someone intentionally started those fires?"

"Maybe, but it could've happened after the blackout or, more recently, from lightning strikes. During the trek with my dad, he told me he thought there must've been scores of fires in urban areas throughout the country after the blackout because of natural gas leaks. The lack of resources prevented people from extinguishing the fires, so the fires just burned until they encountered some form of firebreak or it rained. But now, most fires are started by lightning strikes. Unfortunately, the type of cloud-to-ground lightning that starts fires has increased in frequency."

A few days later, Ruth asked about something I'd hoped she wouldn't notice.

"Hon, why are the roads here littered with so much trash, and especially all the shoes?"

"We're moving into more urban areas, and so greater numbers of people traveled on these roads after the blackout. As they walked, they discarded items they no longer wanted or could carry."

"And all the shoes?"

"Some of them are simply shoes that fell apart while those thousands of people walked along the road."

"You said some; what about the other shoes?"

"Well, remember I told you that even bones will decompose after years of exposure to the elements. The rubber or plastic soles of shoes, particularly athletic shoes, take longer to decompose."

"What are you trying not to say?"

"Some of these shoes are from people that died or were killed on the road. The people decomposed, including their bones and clothing, some of it having been scattered by the wind, but their shoes remain."

"Oh, Christ, George. Why'd you tell me that? I'm going to cry."

We walked on in silence for a long while.

* * *

Because we were in a hurry to reach the coast, we walked later than usual one day and realized dusk was approaching. We then smelled smoke. After scanning the sky above the suburb, we spotted a plume of smoke coming from behind a house a few blocks away. Then we smelled roasted venison; I have a knack for identifying roasting meats by their aroma. We'd been subsisting on the jerky and other foods from Martha and Bob and hadn't had hot food in days, so our mouths began watering. Because it was later than usual, too late to hunt even for rabbits in the suburbs, we foolishly thought it was worth the risk. So we got off the highway and walked toward the house. But I wasn't foolish enough to approach it directly, we scouted it out first. It was fortunate that I had, because no sooner had we found a vantage point to spy on the house, when we saw three people walk up, call into the camp, and walk to the rear of the house. Ten minutes later, we heard screams. We couldn't be sure who killed whom, but no one came out from behind the house, and we didn't care enough to learn who won. So we got out of there fast, walking a few more kilometers before settling for a dry, cold camp inside an abandoned house.

"I think it was a trap to lure people in," I said while chewing

79

on my jerky. "They could then kill any takers for their belongings."

"Well, I think the three newcomers that showed up for the roasted venison wanted more than just to share dinner."

"We'll never know, but it should reinforce the notion that we must always be on guard," I said, staring pointedly at Ruth.

The next day, we walked as fast as we could with only brief breaks, but we stopped early enough to allow me time to hunt. We camped in a large, wooded area surrounding a Walmart Supercenter off Route 18. We avoided the store because it had clearly already been looted by people who didn't clean up after themselves. All sorts of refuse and debris were strewn over the parking lot. We doubted there'd be anything of value left inside. Because we didn't want to attract attention in the urban environment, we made camp back in the woods where I dug a deep pit in which to build the upside-down fire. This would minimize the leakage of light from the fire. I was able to shoot three eastern gray squirrels, so we had our first hot meal in many days. Ruth had foraged and found some oyster mushrooms and Japanese barberries. She had also collected some twigs from spicebush for tea in the morning. Because we wanted to get an early start the next day, we climbed into our sleeping bags as soon as we finished eating. Both of us were eager to get to the coast; Ruth wanted to see the ocean for the first time, and I was anxious to see how much sea level had risen since the last time I was there.

Chapter 5. Romantic Getaway at the Seashore

The next day, we hurried along, eating while we walked, and reached Asbury Avenue by mid afternoon. When we reached the end of the street, Ruth got her first glimpse of the ocean.

"It's breathtaking. It's so vast, so endless! But you were right; it's more greenish-blue than the blue I'd expected. I wish the sun were out. And the smell." She inhaled several times through her nose. "It's... different. It's not perfumy like the forest can be. It's fresh."

Ruth tried to take her boots off standing up with her backpack still on, but quickly realized she was going to fall; it was comical. So she handed me her backpack, sat down, and removed her boots and socks. She rolled up her pant legs and then ran to the water's edge to get her feet wet. Small waves were rolling in. I stood there holding both backpacks and surveyed the area for any threats. I didn't see any people. We'd seen no one for days after heading more easterly than southerly. The location of the water's edge and the width of the beach didn't look much different to me than on my previous visit, but I couldn't be sure. I also didn't know what stage of the tide I was looking at. From this vantage point, I could see the coastline had more of a scalloped appearance than my memory of it; likely from sand being distributed around the rocky groins. While Ocean Avenue wasn't flooded, it was now covered by a thick layer of sand. There was also much more damage to the boardwalk and adjacent buildings than I remembered.

I was roused from my damage assessment when Ruth shouted, "The water's warm! Come on, let's go swimming!"

"But I bet it'd be freezing when you got out!" I shouted back.

It was about 10°C, but the sea breeze made it feel much colder.

"Perhaps tomorrow, with the warmth of the midday sun, we can take a swim!"

"No, I want to take a swim before dinner! I need a bath anyway!"

"Well then, maybe I can get a fire going so we can warm ourselves after getting out and dry quickly!"

"Okay, but let's hurry!"

Ruth ran up, grabbed her boots and socks, and then raced back down the beach face. I followed and handed her backpack to her. We walked along the beach north towards the Convention Hall, where I planned to spend the night. We couldn't walk on the boardwalk; there were too many sections missing, likely blasted up by storm surge. All that remained was a lot of deck boards lying jumbled on top of one another, making it impassable.

As we walked, Ruth asked, "What are those birds?"

"Which birds?"

"The ones making all the noise."

"Seagulls."

"And the large ones diving into the water?"

"They're called pelicans."

"Why do they do that?"

"To catch fish."

"Well, it's amazing. How do they do it without hurting themselves?"

As we approached the Convention Center, I could see that the section of the building nearest the ocean had sunk into the sand, and so the building looked as if it were broken in half. The massive stones that I remembered lining the beach in front of the Convention Center to armor it from erosion were now located a hundred meters offshore, serving as a true breakwater. With this perspective, I could see the beach was much narrower than during my previous visit. We walked up the beach to the boardwalk just beyond a building with unusual architectural features and a strangely peaked roof that was immediately south of the Convention Center. All the pentagon-shaped windows of the building were blown out. The ramp encircling the building was also covered in a thick layer of sand. I had no way to determine if the sand had been blown there or carried by a storm surge.

Besides breaking in two when part of the Convention Center had settled into the sand, many of the sculptures on its facade were crumbling or missing entirely. Murals that I remembered being amazing years ago were now faded and unrecognizable. I also noted that the park that had been on the west side of Ocean Avenue was now flooded and looked more like a wetland than a greenspace. That was different. When we entered the Grand Arcade, it was how I remembered it, except we now had to step over a wide crack in the floor. We found that the windows and doors facing the ocean were missing, as were most of the glass panels in the ceiling. There were piles of sand in various locations inside the arcade. Clearly, storm surges had blown through the building on at least one occasion. Few of the interior glass panes remained.

"Let's dump our gear over there by the openings, so we can look out on the ocean tonight," I said.

"That'd be nice and kind of romantic," Ruth said with a smile.

"Alright, you unpack while I look around to make sure we're alone."

The interior of the building didn't look much different from the last time I'd been here. It appeared as if it'd been gutted well before the blackout. No furniture or displays, not even much debris on the floors. The shops were empty, and the bleachers and stadium seats in the Paramount Theatre were just a jumbled mess of rusting metal and plastic. But the walls and ceilings were in worse shape than before, with entire sections crumbling and falling to the floor.

When I returned to Ruth, I found her zipping the sleeping bags together.

"There's no one about," I said.

"Good. The building's in awful shape, isn't it?"

"Yeah, but I'm surprised it doesn't smell musty. I guess it's the salt air that prevents mold from taking over. Anyway, the priority now is to get a fire going."

"You can't start one in here, can you?"

"No, I looked for something to repurpose as a fire pit, but

found nothing we could use. We could have it on the covered walkway outside, but I think it'd be better to have it down on the beach."

"I like that idea," she said, again with a smile.

"First, I need to figure out where to place it so that it's not flooded and extinguished if the tide comes up too far. Then I'm going to dig a pit again so we don't generate light that might attract unwanted visitors."

"Okay, what can I do to help?"

"You can collect wood to burn. There should be plenty from the boardwalk."

Because the concrete steps closest to the ocean had been ripped off the building, we had to use the second set of steps. It wasn't too difficult to determine how high the tide would come up the beach based on the location of the wrack line of algae, shells, and debris, and the watermarks on the side of the building. I'd have to take some measurements tomorrow when I'd have more time, but figured a narrow strip of beach would still be exposed at high tide. So, I dug the pit on the south side of the building. By the time I dug the pit and got the fire going, it was early evening.

"Okay, I'll try to catch some fish for dinner."

"What about our swim?"

"It's getting late, babe, and I need to catch some fish before dark if we want a hot meal."

"I'm fine with jerky again."

"I don't think we have enough jerky left for dinner. Besides, it's cold with this wind. Maybe tomorrow at midday it'll be warmer."

"You can go fish if you want, but I'm going swimming."

"Okay, but don't swim out too far. I'll keep an eye on you

while I'm fishing." *I didn't know what I'd do if she got into trouble—I don't know how to swim.*

She ran down the beach, stripping off clothes. I went up and got my fishing line out of my backpack while looking for something to use as a pole. After failing to find any insects to use as bait, I ended up relying on an artificial mirrored lure I'd fashioned out of a spoon some time ago. With luck, there'd be sufficient light remaining for it to reflect. It worked, and I'd caught several fish by the time Ruth was running up the beach to the fire to get warm.

"You look as if you're freezing."

"Nooo, it's fine."

I could see she was shivering and turning blue.

"Well, I brought down some dry clothes for you to put on, but if you're not in any hurry?"

"Give me the damn clothes. Jerk."

After a few minutes, she said, "Thanks for bringing down the clothes, but I wish you'd come out swimming with me."

"Maybe tomorrow. But I'll clean these fish and have dinner ready in a few minutes."

We still had some vegetables left from what Martha had given us to have with the fish.

"You know, I think I prefer saltwater fish over freshwater fish," I said, as I was eating. "It doesn't have that fishy taste."

"Thank you for catching our dinner, George. The fish is delicious and is better than having the cold jerky."

* * *

After dinner, we bundled up and sat in front of the fire and stared out over the ocean.

"It's so beautiful, and I love the sound of the crashing waves," Ruth said. It's so calming. I could stay here for days. Maybe we could work on our tans."

"It is beautiful," I said, "but we can't stay long. We've got to get farther south before the snows set in, and we don't want to be caught in Florida at the height of the summer."

"That makes sense," she said. "Are you getting cold? Why don't we head upstairs and get out of this wind?"

"That sounds like a wise idea; I'm kind of tired."

When we got upstairs, Ruth kept looking at me as if she was waiting for me to do something.

"Babe, I think we should move the sleeping bag over into the alcove to get out of this wind, or we'll freeze without a fire," I said.

"Fine."

I could tell something was suddenly wrong.

We moved our gear over to the alcove, dressed in our sleeping clothes, and got into the zippered sleeping bag. I was exhausted from the long day and thought I'd be asleep in no time, even with my insomnia.

Just as I was falling asleep, I heard, "George, are you asleep?"

"No, why?"

"Is everything okay between us?"

Being careful not to let my tone reveal the irritation I was now feeling, I said, "Of course, why?"

"You've been snappy with me lately, and tonight you missed all my cues that I wanted to have sex. We haven't had sex since we left Phoenix."

87

I exhaled quietly, trying not to let my frustration show. "I've been a bit anxious with all the people wanting to rob and kill us and rape you."

She was quiet for a while, and I thought she'd accepted that, but then she said, "But there wasn't any danger here today. It was perfect—like a romantic weekend getaway at the seashore."

"I don't know what to tell you, Ruth—it's just that I've got a lot of things on my mind."

"Are you sure that's all it is? I felt we were drifting apart even before we left Phoenix. I know you don't love me like you loved her, but I thought we had something worth fighting for and thought this trip might bring us closer together. But I guess I was wrong."

Shocked by what she'd said, I didn't know what to say. She was crying. I rolled over to face her and started rubbing her arm.

"Babe, I don't think we're drifting apart. How could you think that? I don't know what I would've done without you."

"So that's why you married me? You were grateful to me for taking care of you? I don't need your gratitude. I need your love!"

She rolled over, away from me.

"How can you even think that I don't love you?"

Without turning to look at me, she said, "But you were ready to leave me behind and go on this trek without me. If you loved me like I love you, you couldn't imagine being apart."

"That's different. It wouldn't have been forever. And remember... I'd left April and the girls behind to go on my first trek." Now, I was crying.

Ruth looked stricken when she rolled back over to face me.

She hugged me and whispered, "Oh, hon, I'm sorry I brought it up. I'm okay. Go back to sleep."

We held onto each other until her grip on me released, and I could feel her breathing steadily. She was asleep, but I wasn't going to fall asleep anytime soon. If I did, I was sure I'd have the nightmare. I'm plagued by a recurring nightmare of finding April and the girls brutally murdered. So I lay there listening to the crashing waves and tried not to fall asleep. I reviewed what I had to do the next day. Then, I went over the route we'd be taking after we left Asbury Park in my head. Eventually, I could no longer resist the magic of the sound of the crashing waves and I fell asleep.

* * *

I awoke with a start. I'd been in the middle of the nightmare, but something woke me up. I didn't move but strained to hear if there was any new noise. All I could hear were the crashing waves. Slowly, I lifted my head and looked around to see if there was something or someone nearby. I couldn't see any movement but kept listening. After a few minutes, I rolled over in the sleeping bag and tried to get back to sleep. I've always had trouble getting back to sleep after waking, and tonight I kept thinking about what Ruth had said—that I didn't love her as much as April. Then I thought about the time I'd first realized I'd fallen in love with her.

It was when she'd been my nurse ten years earlier. I'd been living in a long-term care facility for almost a year...it was actually a dorm for the college. They'd had to reopen the dorm as a care facility after so many of the scientists working at the Center had attempted suicide after returning from the first series of treks following the 'Time of the Great Dying.' I'd tried twice after coming out of a catatonic state. Although all of us had witnessed horrors on our treks, my problem stemmed from guilt. At least that was what I was told by my counselor, Dr. Ralph Jameson.

But that day had been different. I was actually looking forward to what the day would bring. Ruth was scheduled to work. I was busy straightening up my room when Ruth came in. She was as beautiful as ever. Her long reddish-brown hair flowed down below her waist. Today, it was swept back and tied in a ponytail. She had lots of freckles to go with her reddish hair. She was wearing the tight jeans that I liked. She was one of the few nurses who didn't wear a uniform. Was she dressing up for me? No, I was imagining things. She was never anything but professional with me.

"How are you doing today, George? Please take a seat so I can take your blood pressure and temperature." She wrapped a sphygmomanometer cuff around my arm and stuck a thermometer in my mouth. "How was your night? Are you sleeping?"

I mumbled around the thermometer, "I don't really have a choice with the pills they force me to take."

As she pulled the thermometer out of my mouth, she said, "Hopefully, you aren't having any more nightmares."

"No nightmares."

I'd stopped telling them about my nightmare.

"I'm ready to get out of here and go back to work."

I knew it was naïve to think there was anything more than just a nurse-patient relationship between us. After all, she was much younger than I was. But she had seen me at my worst and hadn't turned away. Even so, I bet that was how she was with all her patients. She was just doing her job.

"George, we have a very special surprise for you today. Dr. Jameson convinced Gerald and Sandra that Dan needed to see his father. In a few minutes, he'll bring Dan in. George, I'm so sorry you've been subjected to their misplaced resentment. You weren't to blame."

I'd been told that many times before by others, but coming from her, I could almost believe it. At that moment, Ralph came in carrying my infant son. He walked over and placed Dan in my arms. I looked down and cried, and for the first time in a very long time, they were tears of joy. I looked up at Ralph, who was smiling down at me, and then at Ruth. She was crying too. It was then that I realized I loved her.

At that moment, Ruth let out a snore. She rarely snored; maybe it was the sea air or all the emotions from last night. That had likely been the sound that had woken me up from my nightmare. I rolled onto my back. *But did I love her like I had loved April? I couldn't. April had been my childhood sweetheart. We grew up together. She was the mother of my two beautiful daughters and my son. I had no right to feel the same way about Ruth. That would be a betrayal.*

* * *

91

The next morning, I awoke to find Ruth gone. Her backpack and gear were still here, but she was nowhere to be found. I started to panic, thinking she might have gone swimming again. I ran out to the covered walkway and scanned the ocean, but no Ruth. It was a cold and gloomy morning that matched my mood. I then spotted her a ways down the beach, walking back toward the Convention Center.

Furious, I bounded down the stairs to the beach. When she came up, I practically yelled at her.

"What were you thinking, going off by yourself? You scared me half to death."

"I'm sorry. I didn't think you'd wake up before I got back." Pulling her gun out of her jacket pocket, she said, "I took my gun with me."

I shook my head and sighed. "You've got to be more careful."

We walked back up to our gear, and I changed out of my bedclothes. "Why don't you restart the fire, and I'll go catch us some fish for breakfast?"

As Ruth replaced her gun in her backpack, she said, "Fine, and I'll also start boiling some water for tea."

Her coldly efficient response told me she was mad at me for being so gruff before. She always got angry with me when I was mad at her.

* * *

After breakfast, I grabbed my backpack and pulled out the portable weather station and the instrument to measure water quality that I'd been supplied before leaving Phoenix. I'd show Ruth that I could be as cold and businesslike as she was.

"I've already shown you how to use the portable weather station. Today, we're going to use this instrument to measure various water quality parameters of the ocean. It has probes to measure pH, water temperature, and conductivity; from that, it automatically calculates salinity for us. After we're finished, I'm going to take this opportunity to charge the batteries using this solar panel since no one is around; it'll charge even though it's cloudy. Besides recording all the collected data in our field books, we're also supposed to record our observations of general conditions, like storm damage and particularly the current location of the edge-of-water. Dad and I placed small metal disks as survey monuments on the base of this and a couple of other buildings. From the information in Dad's and my journals along with old satellite images, the GIS folks back at the Center determined ground elevation. So all we need to do on this trip is to measure the distance from the monuments to the water's edge. Now, we saw how high the tide came in last night, and so we know it's low tide right now. We'll record that, but when we get back, the folks at the Center will look up the tidal stage for this area based on the date and time and then, based on what they know about the elevation here, calculate local sea level. Besides all that, we're supposed to make notes on the location of any sediment overwash deposits that might have been carried landward by storm surges. I also want to note the flooding we can see on the other side of Ocean Avenue and take some readings to determine if it's inland freshwater flooding or just storm surge that's been trapped because from here it doesn't look tidal."

My monologue had done nothing to improve Ruth's mood.

"Got it," she said.

It took us the rest of the morning and a good deal of the afternoon to take all the measurements, but it was nice working together as a team. Ruth's mood softened, signaling that we weren't fighting anymore.

When we were done taking measurements, Ruth asked, "Since we measured sea level here, why do we have to walk all the way to Miami and take measurements there too?"

"Because local sea level varies due to many factors like ocean currents and winds and, to a lesser degree, ocean temperature and density, this is termed 'sterodynamic sea level change.' It also depends on local factors like subsidence or post-glacial rebound."

"Do you talk to your interns that way?"

"Why?"

"Just asking"

"Anyway, that's why we take measurements at several locations. Besides measuring it here and in Miami, I also plan to stop in Wilmington, North Carolina to take measurements there, just as Dad and I did ten years ago."

"Okay, but what does that have to do with your Bayesian model that you go on and on about ad nauseam at get-togethers back home?"

I nodded and smerked. "The data we collected today, and collected by other long-haul trekkers, are used in a lot of different models by folks at the Center, many of which try to predict weather systems driven by gradients in temperature across the globe. My model takes output from their models, integrates it with information on the sensitivities of different crop species, including the genetically modified crops your father's working on, to predict which will be successful across broad geographic regions."

"It sounds complex."

"It is, and unfortunately, it requires lots of data. In the past, scientists relied on the massive amounts of data generated by satellites to develop and test their models. But we lost all the satellites in the Blackout War."

"I know," she said. "And that's why we have to go on these treks. See, I do pay attention sometimes."

"Okay, smart ass."

"What's next on today's agenda?" she asked.

"If you'd like, you can copy the data from my field book into yours, so we'll have two copies. You can also record your own observations of local conditions, but remember it's meant for people at the Center and isn't a diary."

I thought I saw her flush. *Oh God, what had she written in the journal that I'm going to be embarrassed by when my colleagues read it?*

I restarted the campfire to make tea and finished writing up my notes before handing the field book to Ruth for her to copy.

* * *

Journal entry: 29 October, Asbury Park, NJ.

Encountered less traffic on the roads since turning east; suggests most are migrating due south. Yet, we continued to see conflicts on the road. Also noteworthy: as reported by other trekkers, fewer skeletal remains were observed on the roads, likely as a result of the decomposition of bones over time.

We arrived here yesterday and found it deserted. Meteorological, water quality data, and distance to water's edge collected at 1430 hrs this date and tabulated on the previous page; we were able to locate and use survey monuments placed at the base of Asbury Park Convention Hall and other buildings (see journal entries from the previous trek). Should've been low tide or nearly low tide when we collected data based on tidal cycle obs. yesterday, but someone will need to check tidal stage records. At typical high tide, only a narrow strip of beach remains. Some inland flooding is occurring west of Ocean Ave., which is also covered by extensive overwash sand deposits. Most of the buildings on the boardwalk remain standing but have extensive damage, likely due to wind and storm surges; there is evidence the Convention Hall has flooded in the past.

* * *

We had a quick bite for lunch, finishing the jerky. By the time we were done, the sun had come out and had burned off the sea fog. So I suggested we go for that swim. Well, Ruth swam; I waded out until the water came up to my chin and stood there sculling the water around. I really needed to learn how to swim. Ruth hadn't lied—the water was warm. After a few minutes of playing around and teasing each other, we ran back up to the blanket we'd spread out near the fire and made love.

It was chilly. But I thought *it could've been colder. Thank God for climate change!* The sex was very satisfying, but I think we both realized that it wasn't spontaneous. And sand got into all the wrong places.

Afterwards, we dressed, and I let her talk me into taking a walk on the beach. *I thought taking a walk was a bit foolish since we'd been walking for weeks now and had many more months of walking ahead of us. I thought we should've sat and relaxed while staring out at the ocean.* Nonetheless, we held hands and playfully kept bumping into each other.

On the walk back, I asked, "So you begged me to bring you along on this arduous and very dangerous journey to strengthen our marriage?"

She looked up at me and said, "I wasn't sure if our marriage would've survived you being away for more than a year."

Again, I was completely taken aback by her statement and didn't know how to respond. Before my silence became awkward, she said, "I was also worried about you. I know how your nightmares affect you. I thought you were too fragile to make the trek and so wanted to be here for you."

She was back in her nurse-mode, and I was now the patient again.

To hide the fact that I didn't know what to say, I stopped and pulled her tight and hugged her, but I thought *that explained a lot; she feels she needs to protect me.* She relaxed a bit, but it would take more than a hug to make things right.

After our walk on the beach, we went over to the other side of Ocean Avenue and washed the salt and beach sand out of our hair and off our bodies with the water from the new marsh that we'd found earlier to be only slightly brackish. Later, we returned to the beach where I caught some crabs that were hiding among the rocky groins. We cooked them with the remaining supplies from Martha. We saved a bit of honey for our morning tea. We were both very relaxed sitting around the campfire that night, possibly more relaxed than we'd been since starting the trek. *I guess there's a lot to be said for 'maintenance sex.'* I slept without having any nightmares.

We left the next morning after breakfast. I planned to take I-195 to I-276 to skirt west of Philadelphia. I hate cities; there are too many crazy people and skyscrapers that could collapse on you at any minute.

* * *

On the second night after leaving Asbury Park, I was hunting in the woods of Bear Swamp off I-195 when I heard branches breaking and something rushing towards me. Whatever it was, it sounded large, maybe a hog or possibly a bear.

I hadn't been able to shoot anything the night before, so all we'd had to eat was greens and mushrooms that Ruth had foraged. I had an arrow nocked and readied myself for something big when a piglet the size of about three footballs came running out of the brush. I had only a minute to aim. Fortunately, the piglet was as surprised as I was and turned to avoid me. My arrow struck him just behind his left shoulder, and he went down. I stood there for a second, surprised I'd made the shot, before I dropped my bow, pulled out my long knife, and dispatched him before he got back up. I needed to work quickly before rigor mortis set in, since I wouldn't be able to cool the carcass down or age it properly. So I dressed it using the gutless method that allowed me to forgo having to open up and clean out the body cavity. I skinned and quartered it. Then, I carefully separated the backstrap from the rib cage and removed it, making sure to include as much of the fatback as possible.

When eating so much protein as we were, it was crucial to eat fat when available, or you could suffer from protein starvation. In the early days of America's expansion west, this was called rabbit poisoning because they ate a lot of rabbits but it was just as appropriate now because were relying them too.

I then located and removed the tenderloin. I flipped the piglet over and repeated the process. It took me only twenty minutes. I picked up the four slabs of meat, juggling them, and hauled them a couple of hundred meters back to wash in a small stream next to the trail. I left the meat submerged in the stream to cool and walked back to the camp to get the tarp I sometimes used as a tent cover to carry the meat.

Fortunately, Ruth had been foraging and hadn't yet un-packed or set the tent up. I told her I'd shot a pig. She seemed surprised, but I let that pass. I explained why we should put distance between us and the carcass that would draw predators. We gathered up our gear and went to collect the meat from the stream. We then got back on the road and walked for an hour before deciding it was far enough. Rather than setting up camp in the woods off the highway, we thought it'd be faster and more efficient if we found an abandoned house to work out of. We found one that wasn't in too bad a shape and that had no corpses, wildlife, or squatters. Ruth and I made two separate fires using wood from several chairs and a table I'd broken up: hers to roast one of the tenderloins, mine to dry the meat from the backstraps for jerky. I started the second fire and then went back inside and cleaned off a counter in the deserted kitchen and began slicing the meat into strips, cutting out as much of the fat as possible. It took me over an hour to get an improvised drying rack set up, hang the meat strips, and cover it so it would dry slowly overnight.

I'd timed it well because Ruth announced the tenderloin was done. That night we had a wonderful meal, and we could look forward to having jerky for days. When we were done with dinner, I banked the fire, drying the meat. I then went back inside to find Ruth had cleared an area on the floor of the front room and spread the sleeping bags out. We were both exhausted and fell asleep in no time.

* * *

The next morning, I woke up before Ruth for a change

and went outside to restart the fire she'd used to cook the tenderloin. I then went over to the drying fire and pulled a piece of jerky off a hanger to see how it'd come out. I'd left too much fat on some of the jerky. It'd be very chewy, and we'd have to eat it fast, or the fat would turn rancid. Eating it fast wouldn't be a problem.

I cooked the remaining tenderloin that we hadn't dried. We had wrapped it in the tarp and left it submerged overnight in the community's stormwater pond behind the house, so that it would be more tender. As the tenderloin cooked, I boiled some birch twigs that Ruth had collected the night before for tea.

As I was busy with that, I heard a voice behind me say, "Good morning, hon. How did the jerky come out?"

"It's going to be chewy but edible. Here's some tea. The tenderloin will be ready in twenty or thirty minutes."

"What a treat."

At least I didn't burn the tenderloin. As we were eating, Ruth brought up a painful subject.

"George, I know we agreed not to talk about Dan as much, but I think we made a mistake."

"A mistake in not talking about him? He's all we talked about the first week on the road."

"No, I mean, we made a mistake by leaving him. I want to go back."

"Go back? Go back now? I miss him as much as you do, but we haven't completed the trek. Who'd finish it? It's too late in the season for someone else to start; they'd have to wait until next year. And it would ruin all my plans. Steven would win, and Dan wouldn't take over this trek and possibly wouldn't even get a spot at the Center."

For a second, I thought, *and what would forcing me to turn back now do to our marriage?* But of course, I didn't say that.

"I know all that," she said. But last night I had a dream. It was of him sobbing at my parents house. I could see his pathetic, little, sad face. It ripped my heart out and left me with an ache in the pit of my stomach; I miss him so much."

"I know. I miss him too; sometimes he's all I can think about, but we couldn't very well have brought a nine-year-old along with us. It's far too dangerous."

"Of course not, but his well-being is more important than collecting data for a bunch of mathematical models."

"It's more than that, and you know it. Those models could improve the lives of many people. And what would we tell everybody? What would we tell your mother? She was so proud of you, telling everyone on the village council and at the church your family attends you'd be one of the first female long-haul trekkers. And what about your father? You know, they both surprised me when you told them. I thought they'd be against the idea and hate me even more for taking you. But they recognized the importance of the larger mission, not to mention what going on a long-haul trek would do for your standing within the community."

"I know, but I can't bear the guilt of him being there all alone."

"He's not alone. He's with your parents, and he has Otis."

"I don't care, I have to go back."

Once again, I didn't know what to say, so I punted. "Let's think about it over the next couple of days. We're heading west right now. It's the same direction we'd travel if we were going back. Maybe you'll feel differently once you've had more time to think about it."

"I doubt it," she said.

We packed up and got back on the road, but our pace was sluggish.

* * *

As we walked, I unintentionally let my mind wander back to the day we'd dropped Dan off at Ruth's parents. *He'd cried and screamed. By then, he'd given up the idea of coming along with us. So he now screamed that he wanted to live with his 'real grandparents.' I'd had to peel him off Ruth when he wouldn't let go of her. He screamed that he hated me. He even refused to let me hug him when I handed him Otis, our dog, and told him it was his responsibility to take care of him now.* I was roused from this painful memory when I tripped over a rusty muffler lying in the middle of the road. There weren't many rusted-out cars on the road that we had to walk around, but I still needed to pay attention to where I was going.

We didn't talk about it again until the fifth day after leaving Asbury Park. It was at breakfast, and we were still eating bacon jerky. I'd shot a couple of rabbits the night before for dinner, but hadn't been able to find any game this morning.

"George, I know we've turned south. You promised we could consider returning home."

"When you didn't bring it up again, I thought you'd resigned yourself to continuing on."

"No, I still want to turn back."

"Babe, isn't there anything I can say to change your mind?"

"George, why don't you continue on with the trek, and I'll find my way back to Phoenix?"

I sighed and said, "Babe, you know I couldn't let you try to go back on your own. Alright, if your mind's made up, let's walk to the next town first. Maybe we can trade for some supplies for the trip back. I can't eat any more of my lousy jerky."

"It is pretty horrible, isn't it?"

She smiled for the first time in days.

We packed up and got underway; both of us moving faster, knowing the decision had been made. Walking until early afternoon, we took an exit off I-295 to look for a small town with people. We walked past a quarry filled with water, a railroad crossing, and then a large mall with lots of carts and debris strewn across the empty parking lot. Up ahead, we saw a street with houses on either side. I smelled smoke.

"Okay, you know the drill. You stay back here with our packs, and I'll see what kind of reception we'll receive."

Chapter 6. Supercell Tornado

As I walked down the street, I saw a golf course between the houses. Someone had been farming the fairway. Yet, there wasn't any evidence that the encroaching vegetation had been cut back recently. Discarded furniture and rolled-up carpets lined the street. The houses were in terrible shape with broken and boarded-up windows, decorative shutters missing or hanging by a single nail, and peeling paint. Muddy water stains on the walls of the houses showed they'd been recently flooded.

As I continued to walk, I startled a woman coming out of one of the houses. She turned around and went back inside. The house she'd come out of was larger and in better condition than the nearby houses, except its garage door was missing. A moment later, a man came out. He was carrying a long knife. The woman followed. They walked down the drive containing a rusted-out Tesla pickup with flat tires. The man was in his 30s, with a classic little boy's haircut neatly parted on the side and a trimmed beard. His clothes appeared clean but mended. Despite his otherwise youthful appearance, his face betrayed worry lines. The woman, who was his age or older, had shoulder-length brown hair, with a narrow face and a pointy nose. She was wearing a black turtleneck sweater and jeans that were in good shape but cinched too tightly.

"What do you want?" the man asked.

The knife wasn't pointed at me, but it was angled upward.

"Hi, my name's George Reynolds," I said, while extending my hand.

He didn't take it.

"What do you want?"

"Don't worry, I'm just looking for some information."

"What kind of information?" he asked. "Are you from Philly?"

"Chad, why don't you at least offer George some water?" the woman said. Turning towards me, she said, "George, we have a source of clean water, if you care to have some."

"He doesn't need any water, Gloria. So what information do you need, George?"

"I'm from a ways up north and am looking for a place to move my family and a few friends that has better weather than we're having to deal with now. We're looking to establish a settlement—we're not squatters. And we don't want any trouble, so we're looking for someplace that has space and resources. Do you know any places nearby that might work for us?"

Chad shook his head and said, "No, I don't."

Gloria then added, "C'mon, Chad, if he waits long enough, this town will be empty."

Chad glared at her, but turning back towards me, she went

on. "But the weather here is horrible, too. The entire town flooded just a few weeks ago."

"Oh, I'm sorry to hear that. What happened?" I asked.

"A storm came in off the ocean and sat on top of us for three days, dumping a lot of rain," Chad said. "It was the third time we've flooded in two years."

"Many of our neighbors have already moved out," Gloria added.

"But that doesn't mean there aren't plenty of people here prepared to protect what we have," Chad said, looking at me.

"Do you know where your neighbors went?" I asked. "Perhaps we could check that area out too."

"Why don't we continue this conversation in the shade?" Gloria suggested. "George, come up to the house. We've got some chairs in our garage. It's sort of a meeting place for the entire neighborhood. I'd invite you into the house, but it's a mess and always smells musty."

"Thank you, Gloria. May I invite my wife to join us? She's just down the road a ways? I'm always cautious when entering a new town."

"Sure, the more the merrier," Gloria said. "I'll go fetch a pitcher of water."

"Are there any more of you down the road?" Chad asked with a stern expression on his face.

"No, it's just her and me. I promise." I turned and waved my arm to signal Ruth, and within a few minutes, she came walking up carrying our backpacks and my bow and quiver.

"Chad, this is my wife, Ruth. Ruth, this is Chad. He and his wife, Gloria, have agreed to talk to us and offered us some clean water to drink."

"Oh, how nice," Ruth said as she handed me my backpack

and bow and put her hand out. "Lovely to meet you, Chad."

He switched the knife to his other hand and then reached out and shook Ruth's hand. "Nice to meet you, too." The knife was now pointed down.

We went up to the house and joined Gloria in the garage, which contained several plastic chairs arranged in a circle. We politely refused the offered water, saying we wanted to err on the side of caution when it came to introducing new bacteria to our stomachs. Then Chad surprised me by offering us hard apple cider. He suddenly seemed much friendlier. He explained how he boiled down some of the maple syrup they collected for sugar and added it to the processed apples they got from a nearby orchard that was still producing. It was one of his major contributions to the community. He also bragged about making biodiesel for heating.

"Come on, George, have some," he said. "The alcohol will kill any bacteria."

"Thanks, but no thanks," I replied, knowing the alcohol content wouldn't be high enough to disinfect the unpasteurized cider.

But Ruth said, "I'll take some."

"That's the spirit, Ruth," Chad said with a smile. "I knew there was a reason I liked you."

I just shook my head and gave her a look, but she ignored it.

We talked for an hour before neighbors began dropping by. Some neighbors, hearing that Chad and Ruth were drinking cider, went back to their houses and returned with their own hard apple cider. Apparently, it was a thing here. I learned Chad's parents had owned a craft brewery before the collapse, which explained his interest in making hard cider. I also learned that this neighborhood had fifty or so families still living in it and was on the outskirts of a town that'd barricaded itself. The few families on the other side of the barricade didn't associate with these folks. They were even more distrustful of strangers because they'd been overrun by refugees escaping Philadelphia.

Like most people I met, nobody wanted to talk about what had happened during the Time of the Great Dying. But I learned that besides ruining several houses, the recent flood had killed the potato crop they were growing on the golf course

Ruth and Gloria hit it off. Ruth also spent a lot of time talking to a young woman by the name of June. June was in her late twenties and had coal black hair swept back into a ponytail. I couldn't overhear what they were discussing, but June spoke with her hands and seemed very earnest. I also met June's boyfriend, Bill, and Carol and her daughter Margaret; Carol's husband was out hunting with a couple of other men. From the deference that everyone showed, I knew Chad was the leader of the neighborhood.

As the party wound down with a couple of people leaving, Chad surprised me again when he invited Ruth and I to stay the night. We accepted.

Chad and I then walked over to a neighbor's house to invite him to dinner, but our real intention was to ask if he would contribute venison steaks for dinner. Apparently, this fellow, Joe, was an excellent hunter and shared his bounty with his neighbors. We found Joe inside his garage with Chad's brother, Chris, and Phil, who was Carol's husband. They had all just returned from a successful hunting trip and were hanging a deer. Chris and Phil both said they needed to get home to their wives and couldn't come to dinner. Joe accepted with a grin and offered to bring some bear meat he'd been aging.

The black bear steaks were delicious, even better than the bear steaks we'd had with Russ and Jess. Joe had seasoned the steaks before grilling them with spices he'd developed over the years. We sat around in the light from beeswax candles and talked about the weather and how bad the refugees from Philadelphia were. Gloria had been right earlier; their house had a strong musty odor from being flooded. The walls were probably full of black mold. But why bother ripping the drywall down—there was nothing to replace it with. Gloria told Ruth they'd cleaned everything with bleach they'd scavenged from the mall.

Towards the end of the evening, Ruth revealed we were heading home the next day and, without providing details, explained about Dan. Everyone was understanding. Gloria then shared their personal tragedy of losing their two sons to a chicken pox epidemic that had swept through the town years earlier. Many families in the neighborhood had lost children. After Joe went home, we took turns using the outhouse and prepared for bed.

Gloria gave us some linen and showed us to a bedroom we could use. It'd obviously belonged to one of their sons.

Once we were alone, Ruth said, "That was very nice, wasn't it?"

"Yeah, the steaks were delicious."

"What do you think of the people?" she asked.

"They were all very nice. Chad was a bit controlling, though."

She pressed her lips together. "I didn't think so."

"Well, he certainly liked you."

She shook her head and said, "Come on, don't be silly."

"One minute, he doesn't want to offer me a drink of water, and the next, he is pouring you hard apple cider and inviting us to stay the night. Why did you drink that cider? I hope it doesn't make you sick later."

Ignoring my reprimand, Ruth said, "Gloria and June were very nice."

"Yes, they were."

"Do you think they'll trade food for our trip back?" she asked.

"I'm sure they will, but we're going to need to come up with something to trade. But let's think about it in the morning. I'm enjoying this comfortable bed with real sheets. Do you know how long it's been since we've had real sheets?"

"Yeah, hon. I was right there with you."

* * *

Both Ruth and I slept soundly in the glorious bed. She woke up when I started moving around, getting dressed.

"Good morning, hon. What time is it?"

I checked my pocket watch. It was self-winding and, besides the time, it showed the date and day of the week. On a trek, it's easy to lose track of what day of the week it is, let alone the date. "It's 7:30."

"Wow, I haven't slept this late in a long time."

"Maybe it was all the cider last night?"

"Ha, ha. I only had one glass."

I left her to get dressed and went out to the privy.

When I was done, I found Chad in the garage with several people. "Good morning, George." Let me introduce you to Donna, Clark, and David. You already know June, Bill, and my brother, Chris. We've got a storm coming in, and some of us are jumpy after the last storm and flood."

I turned and looked at the sky and saw that, indeed, very ominous clouds were on the eastern horizon.

"Who is this guy, Chad?" the man introduced as David asked.

David was in his late 30s, older than anyone else I'd met so far in this neighborhood, and could only be described as portly. But what really surprised me was his goatee. I hadn't seen anyone with a goatee since I was a kid. He was dressed in what I took to be his father's golfing outfit, or perhaps he had scavenged the pants and pink polo shirt from the mall down the road.

"George is just passing through with his wife," Chad replied. "I can assure you they aren't refugees from Philly."

"Okay, whatever. What are we going to do about the storm?" David asked.

"There is not much we can do except prepare," Chad replied.

"As a precaution, we need to fill up as many containers as possible with clean water," June suggested. Looking to her husband, Bill, for support, she added, "And secure any food above the previous high-water mark in case we flood."

"I was just going to suggest that," Chad said. "I guess we should also begin securing anything outside that might fly around in the wind and try to board up any broken windows."

"I'll assemble all the remaining first-aid supplies and medications," Donna said.

"Shouldn't we also fill all the privy holes to prevent waste from being washed out and spread through the neighborhood?" June asked.

Her husband put his arm around her and said, "That's an excellent idea. I remember how bad it was after the last flood."

"Yeah, it stank for days afterward," Clark added.

"Okay, I think we all know what needs to be done," Chad said. "On your way back to your houses, stop at your neighbors and tell them what's going on, and ask if they need any help. George, I know you and Ruth were planning on leaving today, but maybe you could stick around and help. You'd be safer here than on the road, anyway."

"Yeah, we'll be glad to help in any way we can, and thanks for offering us a safe harbor," I replied.

"Chad, can you assign someone to come to my house to secure everything and fill my privy hole?" David asked.

"David, you've got plenty of time—you can do it yourself," Chad snapped. "I've got other people who really need our help."

I went in to tell Ruth why we wouldn't be leaving today and found her already helping Gloria find containers to fill at the hand pump. I went back out to the garage to ask Chad what needed to be done, and he handed me a shovel and a hammer.

"Let's go. I know several widows with children who might need our help."

"Right behind you."

We worked most of the day, taking a break only for lunch. All the while, the cloud bank in the east was getting closer and darker. We returned to his house just before it began to rain.

It wasn't heavy at first, and I could see Chad begin to relax. But then we spotted an approaching cloud wall indicative of supercell formation. I was worried about the flanking wall I could see off to the south. The updraft could spin off a tornado. The sky was glowing an eerie green and blue—straight out of a nightmare. It became deathly quiet. Then it began to hail. The noise of the hail hitting abandoned cars and the road pavement was deafening.

"Chad, I think the storm is going to spawn a tornado. Do you have a basement?"

"No, but the high school does. Let's get the girls and start knocking on doors."

We ran toward the high school, yelling, "Tornado's coming; get to the high school."

The hail was getting larger. It hurt when it struck. Once we arrived at the school, we found Joe and June already there, getting people inside the building. The wind was picking up.

June was shouting at people. "C'mon, hurry! It's coming! No, leave that stuff. You can't bring it with you into the basement."

People were slipping on the layer of hail on the ground. Joe and June would run out and grab them and pull them inside.

Ruth and Gloria were inside helping people down the stairs into the basement, which was quickly filling. Someone had the presence of mind to bring candles.

Chad, Joe, and I were together in the entrance hall watching for any stragglers out the open doors when Chad asked, "Joe, have you seen Rebecca and her kids?"

"I don't think so."

"Damn, she said she'd be right behind me. I've got to go find them."

"I'll go with you. No, you and George get the rest of these people down into the basement or into an interior room. I'll be back." And he ran out the door.

Joe and I made sure everyone had a place to hide and then went back to the entrance hall to watch for Chad's return.

"Holy crap, look at that funnel," Joe said. "It must be a mile wide."

"Look at the cloud of debris being tossed up in the air," I replied.

Joe just shook his head and said, "We're fucked."

"Chad better get back here soon," I replied.

"Can you hear that low rumble and that high-pitched whining?" Joe asked. "Jeez, it sounds like Satan's army coming to drag us all straight to hell."

Joe's description struck home with me but even now, I was intent on not allowing anyone see how scared I was. We exchanged a look and knew the moment had come to take shelter. We'd prearranged where we'd each go. I ran to the basement to be with Ruth, while Joe ran to the office, where we'd put two late-arriving families. I'd have the unenviable task of telling Gloria that her husband hadn't returned and was hopefully hunkered down to ride out the tornado somewhere else.

Chapter 7. The Aftermath

The building shook for what felt like an eternity. All the while, we had to suffer the roaring noise from the tornado outside, but it couldn't drown out the sound of people sobbing or praying out loud. People were also coughing from the dust from the shaking building. We were all certain the building would be ripped off its foundation any second. I kept picturing the whirling house swept up by the twister in the *Wizard of Oz* movie I'd watched as a kid before the blackout. Gloria was beside herself with worry about Chad, but she was clutching a little girl who had her hands clasped over her ears. Ruth and I just held each other. I was worried about Joe and the two families above.

Once the shaking and noise stopped, and we felt the tornado had passed it took two men to force the door open. It was eerily quiet after the horrible sound of the tornado. As we exited the basement, we were shocked to see light coming from where the south wall of the high school had been. Rain was pouring in through a missing section of the roof. We were relieved to find Joe and the two families, which included three kids. All were safe but shaken.

We all walked through the opening where the school's front doors had been just a few minutes earlier to find complete devastation. All the homes surrounding the school were damaged, with missing roofs, collapsed walls, or both. Two appeared to have been lifted into the air and then smashed down, their contents now piles of rubble. One house was almost cut in half by a fallen tree. Where a house stood a few minutes ago, there was now an empty lot. Trees, some possibly over a hundred years old, snapped. Power and telephone poles were down with wires in the water—it was fortunate the electric grid was dead. Ironically, this time the blackout had probably saved lives. Cars that hadn't moved in twenty-five years had been picked up and tossed into houses. Debris, including the trash left out after the last flood, had been swept up and now littered the street and yards. There wasn't a square meter of ground that was free of debris. The rusty chain-link fence that surrounded the football field and track was plastered with debris. We just stood there in shock.

Someone screamed, "It's not fair! It's just not fair! First the floods and now this. Damn it to hell."

June was the first to pull herself together. She turned and addressed the group. "The first priority is to do a headcount. Then we'll search for anyone not accounted for. Bill, can you find some paper and start taking names? Everyone, make sure you check in with Bill before you leave. Then we'll start going door to door. Now, does anyone already know someone who's missing?"

Gloria raised her hand and said, "Chad went off to find

Rebecca May and her kids and didn't get back in time."

"Okay. Joe, and I'm sorry, I've forgotten your name. Can you two go to Rebecca's house and see if she and her kids are alright and whether Chad's there?"

"Will do," Joe replied.

I squeezed Ruth's hand and walked over to Joe and patted him on the back. "Man, I'm glad to see you."

"I'm glad to be seen."

Joe went over to Gloria and said, "We'll find him."

As we were walking away, we heard June ask, "Is Donna here?"

"Yes, I'm over here."

"Thank God. Can you get your medical supplies and find someplace to set up a makeshift hospital in the high school? I'm sure there's going to be injured."

"I'm on it. Clark, can you give me a hand setting something up?" Donna asked.

As Joe and I were leaving, I heard Ruth's voice, and so I turned and saw that she had her hand up. "June, I'm a trained nurse. I'll give Donna a hand."

Joe and I ran to Rebecca's house. When we got there, we found, by some miracle, hers was the only house still standing on the street. We heard screaming from inside and found Rebecca and her girls hiding in a bathtub covered by a mattress. A chest of drawers, painted pink with flower stickers, had landed on top of it, and they couldn't push it off.

After we freed them, Rebecca told us that, as far as she knew, Chad had never made it back to them. We told them to go to the high school and check in. Joe and I split up, working both sides of the street, picking through the wreckage looking for Chad, telling anyone we found to go to the high school. I had to administer first aid to a couple of people with minor injuries. Joe yelled that he was having difficulty navigating—that all the landmarks were gone. I shouted back that we should check Chad's house in case he'd gone home. I also wanted to know if my backpack with all my instruments had survived the storm. On the way, we had to rescue a family that couldn't escape from their house because trees had fallen and blocked both the front and back doors. It took almost an hour of rummaging through the nearby houses and garages to locate handsaws.

We managed to find Chad's block, and, by some strange twist of fate, his side of the street was untouched while the houses on the other side were demolished. He wasn't there, but at least Ruth and my backpacks weren't lost. It began to get dark, so Joe and I returned to the high school to organize people with torches to continue the search for survivors. I checked in with Ruth, who was busy helping Donna care for the injured. When she was done stitching up a nasty cut on a woman's arm, I pulled her aside and hugged her.

"How are you doing?"

"George, it's terrible. These people have been through so much already. Many of them have PTSD from the horrors they had to endure after the blackout. I don't think they can cope with this. Most of them just want to lie down and go to sleep and never wake up."

"I know, babe."

"I don't think you do. You and I can leave and return to our normal lives in Phoenix. These people have nothing and nowhere to go. They feel utterly defeated. And no one's coming to help them."

Once again, I didn't have an answer, and so I just continued to hug her. I recognized she knew what she was talking about since she used to nurse suicidal long-haul trekkers, including me, after I lost April and the girls.

"George, you and I have emotional reserves. Their supply's been exhausted—we've got to help them."

Just then, Joe came up and said he'd rounded up a couple of volunteers and had made some torches using tallow-soaked rags and was ready to go back out. I kissed Ruth on the forehead and left with Joe. We searched all night and into the morning. That's when things went from bad to worse.

We were in the high school gymnasium. There were fifty or sixty people spread out on the floor, sleeping. Several of us were huddled around a table in a corner, shoving food into our mouths and gulping down hot tea when Clark came running in. He stopped, surveyed the room, then quietly walked over to us. We could tell from his expression that something was very wrong.

When he came up, he quietly said, "The water level in the river has risen three feet and is still rising."

"Oh shit, that's what happened last time," Bill whispered. "Runoff in the upper watershed is flushing downstream to us."

"Goddamn it! I can't take any more of this," Carol exclaimed suddenly.

"Carol, it's going to be okay," Gloria said, putting her arm around Carol and hugging her. "We're going to make it through this. Think of Margaret."

Both women began sobbing quietly.

"One thing we don't want to do is cause a panic," June said. "And we don't know if it's going to be as bad as last time."

I raised my hand slightly to signal I wanted to ask a question.

"Can I ask how long it took for the river to crest last time?"

"It took two days," Clark answered. "I live on the river, and so monitor water level."

"So, we have some time," I said.

"What can we do?" Clark asked, looking around the assembled group.

"We should leave," Joe said, surprising everyone.

"Do you mean leave altogether as a group and abandon everything?" June asked.

"Yes. We can't repair all the damage. There's no reason to stay here any longer. We should get out before the water rises and makes leaving impossible."

Suddenly, the guy with the goatee came up and rudely interrupted. "Hey, what are you people talking about, leaving? Where's Chad?"

"David, please keep your voice down," June said. "Chad is missing."

"We're considering recommending people leave because the river is rising," Joe said.

"Well, I'm not leaving," David replied.

I could see Clark was becoming visibly upset.

"That's fine for you, David. Your house sits on the hill, didn't flood, and was spared by the tornado. Mine's now missing a roof, which is good because it still hasn't dried out from the last flood."

David turned to Clark and said, "You shouldn't have built on the river."

"You're an ass," Clark hissed.

"This is getting us nowhere," June said. "David, you're free to stay."

David stormed off, shaking his head and muttering.

"He'd better not start anything," Joe said.

"Okay, what would we need to do if we were going to move all these people to a new town?" June asked.

"Why don't we ask George and Ruth?" Gloria said. "They're thinking of moving their town. They must have given it a lot of thought."

The question caught me by surprise. First, because it came from Gloria. Apart from consoling Carol, she'd been withdrawn and very quiet since I told her that Chad was missing. And second, because while I'd used that line about finding a place to move my people many times to set the stage for asking a lot of questions, I'd never given much thought to actually doing it; few places, if any, in North America could be better than what we had back in Phoenix. Ruth saved the day before my silence became awkward.

"Well, first you need to know where you're going. That's what George and I are doing on our trek—looking for a suitable location to resettle."

"We don't have time to go searching for the perfect location," Joe said.

"Maybe we could resettle near where my cousin lives," Chris said. "He lives next to an Amish community. They've got farms and were living off the grid long before the collapse and blackout."

Joe nodded and said, "Yeah, I like that idea."

"Yes, that's an excellent suggestion," June said. "Do you know how to get there, Chris?"

"I know the name of the town; it's just outside of Lancaster, but I've never been there and wouldn't know the best way to go."

"George can help with that," Ruth said. "He's got all sorts

of maps."

I couldn't believe she'd just revealed that information and, in doing so, had volunteered our help.

"I do have some maps that might be of use," I said.

"How long would it take for us to walk there?" June asked.

"I don't know. I'd have to consult the map. It would depend on how fast we could walk."

"Understood, would you check and let us know?" Looking pointedly at Ruth, she asked, "What else?"

"Well, you'd obviously need to bring as much food and water you could carry along for the trip and, if you have any, seed to plant crops once you've settled."

"You'll also need to tell people to dress appropriately for walking long distances, especially their shoes," I interjected. "And to bring tents and sleeping bags, if they have them."

"We'll need to designate people to hunt for us while we travel and to defend the group," Joe said. "George and Ruth would know better, but I've got to believe it's very dangerous on the roads."

I was now resigned to the idea and said, "Yeah, that's a good point."

"We'll need to find wagons or buggies to take any belongings we want to bring with us," June said.

"There are a lot of pushcarts in the mall's parking lot," Chris interjected. "Some of them must still work. We could also use the wheelbarrows we've been using to transport bodies."

We'd been transporting the dead to a makeshift morgue in the fire station, making certain their loved ones didn't see us unceremoniously load them into wheelbarrows.

Looking around, Bill quietly asked, "What shall we do with

123

all the dead? We haven't even begun to bury them all."

"We should split up into teams," June said. "One to bury the dead, another team to find any type of wheeled conveyances, and a third team to get people started packing. Ruth, could you find Donna and tell her what's going on and help her get the injured ready to go?"

"Okay, but we also need to designate someone to take responsibility for the kids who just lost their parents."

"Ruth, would you mind finding someone to do that?"

"I'm sure Donna and I can find someone, or I'll do it myself," Ruth replied.

I suspected she'd already planned to take on that responsibility.

"Okay. Joe and George, I hate to ask, but can you take the burial detail?"

We both nodded.

"And Chris, can you find some volunteers to gather buggies or pushcarts, as you call them, or anything else we could use to move everything?"

"Will do."

I'd noticed she hadn't yet assigned anything to Gloria.

"Okay, and maybe Gloria and I can go around and convince people we need to leave, and that we need to do it as soon as possible."

That role made sense for Gloria since her husband had been the informal leader of the neighborhood. It'd also give her something to do rather than grieve. We broke from our huddle and got to work.

Before I left with Joe to find some shovels, I went over to Ruth, who was with Gloria, continuing to console Carol. I'd just learned why Carol was so upset; Joe told me they'd found

Phil's body a few hours earlier. I motioned to Ruth that I wanted a word.

"I know you wanted to help these people, but are you sure you want to help lead them to a new town? Don't you want to go home?"

"George, they need us. The immediate danger of the potential flood may snap them out of the shock from the tornado, but they still need all the support we can give."

As she said that, *I wondered to myself whether I'd have volunteered to help move them if she weren't with me. She makes me a better man, but at what cost?*

It took most of the day for Joe, me, and six other men to bury the recovered bodies. We buried them on the golf course, where the neighborhood had been farming. Afterward, people gathered for a brief ceremony. A few people spoke, but it was mostly everyone hugging and crying, especially the kids who had just lost one or both parents. David upset a few people when he asked to speak. They told him to be quiet or go back to his safe home on the hill. At the end of the ceremony, June suggested everyone take a break from their jobs and find a place for a good night's sleep—the work would have to wait till tomorrow. I think everyone welcomed that suggestion because some of us hadn't slept for 48 hours.

Ruth and I returned to Chad and Gloria's. Because they didn't have any place else to go, Carol and her daughter, Margaret, along with a woman named Emma, came too. Ruth had warned me to give Emma lots of space because she'd panic if any man got too close. She'd wandered into town a few years earlier, practically naked, after suffering some traumatic experience. Despite her grief, Gloria tried to be a good hostess. Ruth helped her get everyone settled. I made a fire out back and cooked more of the bear meat gifted by Joe. His house was spared as well, and he was hosting the two families he rode out the tornado with. Although, like everyone else, I was mentally and physically exhausted, I couldn't get to sleep, so out of habit I used one of Gloria's candles and wrote up my notes in my journal.

* * *

Journal entry: 3 November, Outside of Norristown, PA, near Schuylkill River

Arrived three days ago to find a community of approximately 150 people in this neighborhood organized at/approaching chiefdom stage; a man named Chad was the informal leader (he is now likely deceased; killed in tornado described below). People are armed with bows, etc., but do not have a standing military, stand armed sentries, or organized law enforcement; however, they appear to be living under a sense of order, possibly because of informal social control. They also report a continuous stream of refugees traveling west from Philadelphia, which they perceive as the greatest threat. As a result, the adjacent town center for this suburb has barricaded entry points, which also excluded this community. This act of isolation put these people at greater risk. Yet, no reports of raiding parties; only small groups of refugees seeking help where none can be offered because of a lack of resources. Some townsfolk have lived here prior to collapse and blackout. They are moderately religious, being mostly Christian. Kids take on some adult tasks, no formal schooling. Neighborhood was maintained in good condition: clean potable water and sanitary use of wastewater. Their main challenge is the intensification of the hydrologic cycle; they have flooded several times in the past 5 years with no possibility of making significant repairs. Most households report mold inside their homes. Only moderate success farming; hampered by flooding and by hail shredding crops. Increased flooding is likely a direct result of poleward shift in atmospheric rivers because of changes in the jet stream and ocean temperature gradients.

Less than 48 hrs ago, this area was hit by a supercell tornado— gauged to be an E4; however, there was no time to collect meteorological data. Almost complete devastation and 45 people missing or dead. As other trekkers have reported, supercell activity appears to have increased, resulting in more frequent tornadoes. Outbreaks of these deep convective storms have shifted to the east and are now moving north to include New England states as well as the mid-Atlantic; tornado season is also longer—now extending into November. This is a result of increased moisture and energy in the atmosphere of these regions from the warming of both the Gulf of Mexico and the Atlantic.

Worse, due to runoff in the upper watershed, the Schuylkill River is now threatening to flood and should crest in another day or two. These people have suffered greatly and have decided to leave en masse before it floods. They hope to relocate 100 km SW to Lancaster County and seek aid/guidance from the Amish community in that area. Ruth and I have agreed to assist them with that relocation.

* * *

When I finished my notes and got into bed, I found Ruth still awake.

"You don't usually have a problem getting to sleep, even when our lives are in peril. What's keeping you up tonight?" I asked.

"George, how are we going to move all these people over a hundred kilometers?"

I put my arms around her. "I wish I knew."

Chapter 8. You Can't Get There from Here

Completing all the preparations for the migrant caravan took longer than anyone had expected. It was a sad wagon train of pushcarts, wheelbarrows, garden carts, baby strollers, and little red wagons hitched to a few bicycles. They were piled high with people's most cherished belongings: boxes of photos, clothes, tools, and family heirlooms salvaged after the tornado. Some carts were full of water jugs and plastic containers of food. Some had tarps or blankets to keep the prized possessions from falling out of the overstuffed wagons.

One of the most prized cargoes was a beehive. A husband-and-wife team had elicited three volunteers to help them transport the queen within nucleus hive or what they called a nuc, along with enough honey to feed the bees over winter. They weren't likely to succeed, but they wanted to try anyway. It was interesting to watch them use smoke to calm the bees when the wagon was jostled going around an obstruction in the road.

The headcount was eighty souls, including six newly or-
phaned children, one of whom was a baby that Gloria took
charge of, carrying it in a sling she belted across her chest; I
think Ruth was jealous. Everyone was surprised and generally
displeased when David, the troublemaker with the goatee,
announced he was leaving his house on the hill and coming
with us.

It had stopped raining by the time we got the ragtag group
rolling, but the river had crested. The plan had been to take
U.S. 202 to U.S. 30, but we immediately encountered flooded
roads, so we had to detour. Where it was only ankle deep, we
waded through the rushing water. Ruth shouted to people
to hold on to the kids. Unfortunately, in some areas, the
detour paralleled the river. We had to be careful because
entire sections of the road had fallen into the river, often
with the guardrails remaining. Worse still, someone would
always shout, and everyone would stop and watch when a
body or animal carcass floated past. At one point, we had
to cross an unstable bridge at risk of imminent failure from
the 'damming effect' from the accumulated debris jammed
up against it, including a house that had washed down the
mud-filled river.

I worked with Joe and Clark to scout up ahead for trouble
while Bill, Chris, and a few others brought up the rear, keeping
stragglers moving. Joe and Clark were the best archers, so
they took turns hunting before the approaching caravan made
too much noise and spooked everything. They'd already shot
two small deer, but there were eighty people to feed, and we'd
need to make jerky for midday meals tomorrow; not wishing
to stop and build fires to cook the midday meal, we were

always drying meat. They'd field-cleaned the two deer and loaded the meat into a wagon, working as fast as they could to stay ahead of the caravan. That wasn't difficult because we moved so slowly; we had to stop frequently so that the caravan wouldn't stretch out too long. Stragglers would be more vulnerable to attack. Our pace was also slowed as carts and wagons had to skirt around all the debris, the rusted-out cars, and the many blowdowns blocking the road. Within only a few kilometers, pushcarts and bicycles began falling apart. People started discarding possessions along the side of the road.

Since it was the first day, we planned to stop and camp early. I asked several people to collect firewood while we looked for a suitable spot. Once we found a stretch of straight road with no blowdowns that would obstruct our view, we camped right there on the road. I then helped people build campfires. Ruth and June went around and organized the cooking. Joe and Clark had shot and cleaned a third deer and several rabbits. It wasn't much, but it was enough. The unofficial travel committee met around one of the campfires.

"George, how far have we come today?" June asked.

"We only made ten kilometers; sorry, about six miles. Some of these people have never walked long distances before. But I think we'll pick up the pace tomorrow now that they're becoming more accustomed to it. And today we've weeded out the more unreliable carts and wagons."

"People ditching their stuff on the side of the road worried me at first," Joe said. "I thought highwaymen might use it to track us, but the road's already littered with all sorts of trash from the hordes escaping Philly."

"Do you have a watch set now, Joe?"

"Yeah, I've got three men patrolling the camp. We'll switch out in another two hours and then again four hours later."

"Ruth, did you hear of any major incidents?" June asked.

"I don't think I would describe any as major, but we had a few incidents. A cart fell into the river and was lost. There were several fights—just minor stuff. Donna and I helped people with their blisters. We need to caution everyone to conserve the clean water we brought with us. Some people were using it to wash up. We don't want to have to start boiling river water until we really have to."

I was glad she hadn't volunteered our water filters. They wouldn't be capable of filtering enough water for everyone, and, selfishly, I also hoped we'd need them for ourselves if later we continued on our trek.

"Okay, does anybody have any suggestions for improvements we should make tomorrow?"

Gloria raised her hand. "We need to ask people to walk a little farther into the woods when they answer 'the call of nature.' David urinated in front of a group of people that included children."

"But they should also let someone they're walking with know, so if it's while we're on the move, they'll wait to make sure they return to the caravan," Joe added.

"Alright, we'll spread the word," June said. "Anything else? If not, try to get a good night's rest; it's going to be an even longer day tomorrow."

Several families had brought tents. Ruth decided we shouldn't use our tent, but instead she put the orphans in it. We'd sleep under the stars.

"Hon, is this going to work? Are we going to get these people there safely?"

"I don't know, babe. We've got a long way to go."

"Yes, we do, but you're never going to make it if you don't learn to delegate better. You're running yourself ragged attempting to scout our route ahead with Joe while checking on the stragglers at the other end."

"I'll try to delegate, okay."

"You'd better. You know what a nag I can be." She kissed me, and soon we were both asleep.

* * *

I awoke early the next morning to find Ruth had already rounded up volunteers to take charge of restarting fires and boiling water for tea or cooking the rabbits that Joe and Clark had shot and cleaned the night before. After I'd had some tea, I went and found Joe.

"When are you and Clark going to sleep?"

"When we're dead; ha, ha. No. Clark got some sleep earlier and will take point this morning, so you'll need to tell him if there are any route changes. I'll grab some shuteye while you all get this bunch fed and rolling this morning."

"Any incidents during the night?"

"No, we've been lucky so far."

Our luck wouldn't hold much longer.

* * *

It was a slow process getting everyone up and going, but we did it. Then, two hours into our walk, it rained. Ruth and June smartly stopped the caravan so that everyone could fill every empty container with rainwater to replenish our drinking water supplies. It was a cold rain, so everyone was freezing.

Nevertheless, Ruth found the bright side. "At least everyone smells better. I just wish people had thought to bring soap."

Because we'd stopped to collect rainwater, we delayed stopping for the midday meal. It was just as well; we didn't have much jerky from the previous night's hunt. People complained, especially David, who seemed to relish inflaming people's anger.

Once we got underway again, the front of the caravan quickly caught up to Clark because he'd stopped when he came across a woman and her two boys traveling on their own. They'd been attacked two days earlier. Her husband had been killed, and they were robbed of all their possessions, including food and water. It took little for Clark to convince June to let the family join our caravan. Ruth gave them some food she had left over from our supplies. Ruth later told me the woman had confided in her that the attack they'd endured was far worse than she'd first described.

Later, we came to our first ghost town. Ruth and I weren't as disturbed as the others by what we found because we'd been out in the world and seen what it was like. The town had been razed to the ground by fire; worse, we had to walk around burnt corpses riddled with arrows lying in the street.

That night, people didn't complain as much after dinner. Even David was subdued. Joe and Clark had been lucky enough to encounter a herd of young deer and were able to shoot two, but that still wasn't enough to feed eighty-three people to satiation and to supply meat for jerky, so we'd all be going to sleep hungry.

When the travel committee met that night, it was with grim faces. The realization of how difficult this was going to be was settling in.

"George, how far did we make it today?" June asked.

"Today we made twelve miles. The problem is the stragglers. I'm surprised how far back the caravan can stretch with only eighty people. To prevent the rear from becoming separated completely and out of sight or earshot, we had to keep stopping. Add to that the rain break, and there you have it."

"But that's not a horrible pace, is it?" June asked.

"Well, at this rate, it'll take at least another four or five days to reach Lancaster County, if we don't run into any trouble. We should shoot for sixteen miles a day."

"I don't think we'll make that tomorrow," Ruth said. "Some of these people are in pain, either from blisters from all the walking in poor shoes, or chafing, but some also have poison ivy from going into the woods to urinate or defecate."

"Owchie," June said. "Okay, did Donna have anything for the poison ivy?"

"Not really. So, I collected some Jewelweed and made a lotion. It seemed to help."

"You're a lifesaver. Joe, are you and Clark going to be able to supply more food? We're already running out of what we

135

brought with us."

"We're doing the best we can. Right now, we're splitting our time between scouting for trouble and hunting. Maybe if we get more hunters up ahead of the caravan."

"I can give you a hand hunting tomorrow," I said.

"No, you won't!" Ruth said. "You're too busy running up and down the caravan trying to micromanage everyone."

There was the nagging she'd warned me about.

"I agree," June said. "We'll have to find other volunteers to help with the hunting. And we need someone to help George deal with the stragglers."

Great, Ruth had enlisted June to keep me in line.

* * *

The next day, we encountered a mudslide across the road. We could either backtrack and find another way forward or try to climb up and over it. We decided on the latter. Two men went up and bushwhacked a trail for us to use. They also took ropes and fashioned a pulley system to pull carts and wagons up and then lower them down on the other side. The steep and slippery terrain was tough for everyone, but nearly impossible for those with injuries from the tornado. Ruth had to help a woman named Janet, who could barely put weight on her knee. When Janet's knee gave out completely, she fell and almost took Ruth with her. I was behind them and was able to push both of them forward. Ruth landed hard and gave me a look as if to say, 'Why did you do that?' Later, I helped another woman who had a sudden case of acrophobia. She'd climbed almost to the top, but then she panicked and refused to go farther. People were having to step around her, putting themselves in danger of falling. She didn't appreciate my grabbing her arm and pulling her to the top. Everyone was exhausted after the steep ascent, but going back down was even worse because it was so slippery.

Later, while I was hurrying to catch up with Joe and Clark, I came across a fellow sitting on the side of the road. He was in his early thirties and had stringy hair plastered to his scalp either because it was wet or greasy; I couldn't tell which. He was dressed in rags, much like everyone else, but he wasn't wearing any shoes or socks.

"Hey, how you doing?" I asked.

"Not too good. You in the group with Clark?"

"Yeah, you met him earlier?"

"Yeah, he's a good jawn; gave me a piece of jerky and a sip of wooder."

"Where are you from?"

"I'm from Philly. We left a couple of months ago and have been looking for a place to live, but no one'll take us in. Coupla days ago, I twisted my ankle. My friends left me behind when I slowed them down too much."

"What's your name?"

"Mike Thompson. What's yours?"

"Mine's George Reynolds, but most people just call me Reynolds. Can I ask what happened to your shoes?"

"Oh, the people I was with took 'em. They figured I wouldna need them nomore."

"That's kind of harsh."

"Yeah, life sucks, and then you're dead."

"Did Clark tell you about our group?"

"Yeah, he said you're trying to move eighty people."

"It's actually eighty-three now."

"Well, good luck with that. I doubt any town'll let you in. There were only nineteen of us, and towns treated us like we had the plague."

"Did any of you have the plague?"

"No. None of us was even sick. They said if any of us were a doctor, nurse, or one of the tradesmen they needed, then they and only they could stay."

"Did any of your group have those credentials?"

"No."

"Where have you tried?"

"Every town from here to Harrisburg."

"Really, did you try any place near Lancaster?"

"Yeah—they said they'd been overrun with refugees. And it seems like everyone hates people from Philly."

"Did you tell any of this to Clark?"

"Yeah, and he didn't seem too pleased, if you ask me."

"No, I bet he wasn't. Listen, I'm going to run up ahead and see if I can catch him. Our little caravan should be coming up this road in a few minutes. Ask for June or Ruth. I'm sure they'll help, and I'd like you to tell them what you told me."

By late afternoon, it began to snow, followed by freezing rain and fog. Clark and I found an abandoned box store for us to camp. I ran back to the caravan to hurry them up. By the time I arrived back at the store with the rear of the caravan, six fires were burning in the garden center. The heat from the fires was welcomed, but I wished there'd been more more food to cook. The new hunters had increased our haul by only one additional deer. People wouldn't starve but would still be hungry after burning a lot of calories walking all day. That night, the travel committee had a lot to go over.

"Before we discuss today's revelations, let's find out how far we've come. George?"

"Dealing with the mudslide cost a lot of time. We walked only ten miles today."

"Well, it is what it is," June said.

Ugh, I hated that expression. It had become popular during the climate crisis to signal resignation and an unwillingness to act. If anyone dared to talk like that at the Center, they'd be met with disapproving stares. It should be 'it is what you make of it'.

"Ruth, any major incidents?"

Lots of fighting, which appears to be escalating. People are tired and are becoming frustrated. A couple of broken legs resulted from two people falling while climbing over the mudslide. We put them in carts and are taking turns pushing them. And we're drinking a lot of water, which is good, but we need to continue collecting rain or snow. I've got some people doing it tonight while we're here, and if it's still raining, we'll do it in the morning.

"Great, something else to slow us down," Joe said.

"Okay, what does everyone think about the information brought to us by Mike? By the way, we offered to let him travel with us if he's able to walk at all when we leave."

"I think we proceed, but be prepared to go to Plan B if they won't allow us to settle in Lancaster," I said.

"I agree," Chris added. "My cousin always said that while the Amish seemed standoffish, they were always willing to help one another and even outsiders."

"George, you said go to Plan B—do we have a Plan B?" June asked.

"Not that I know of, but we'd better come up with one before we need it."

"I think if they don't let us in for whatever reason, that we continue west away from the ocean and nor'easters."

"Does anyone have any other suggestions? Okay, well, keep thinking about it."

The next day, things became much worse.

* * *

We'd been underway for several hours when I heard screaming as I was headed back to the rear of the caravan to check on the stragglers. I rushed toward the sound and found a group of men I didn't recognize surrounding something on the ground. One of the men was holding another man by his arms. The man being held was someone I recognized, but had never heard his name. I yelled something, and the group turned toward me, and I could see a woman on the ground with a man standing over her, pulling his pants up. I yelled again and let loose an arrow. It struck one of the men, in his side. Suddenly, someone tackled me from behind. I went down hard with him on top of me. My bow and quiver went flying. We rolled around wrestling, but I pushed him off and got up. I drew my long knife. Surprise was written all over his face, then his nerve faltered, and he ran away. I felt like jumping up in triumph, but saw the men were moving toward me aggressively. Then Bill rushed up beside me and let loose an arrow, striking another of the men. They ran off.

"You okay?" he asked.

"Better now."

The man that was being held dropped to the ground, sobbing, and lifted the woman's head. She reached up and pulled him down to her. As I watched them, I could feel tears run down my face.

"I don't know where they came from," Bill said, visibly upset. "I was just here a few minutes ago."

Having heard the commotion, Chris arrived. "What happened?"

"Jim and Shirley were just attacked by some men," Bill said.

"Was anyone hurt?"

Wiping my eyes, I said, "I think they raped Jim's wife."

"We've got to go after 'em," Chris said.

"We need more men before we do that," I said. "You two stay here, and I'll go and send some men back. I'll also find Donna or Ruth and ask them to come back and see to the Shirely."

But I was thinking, *I can't track them down. I'm not that guy anymore.*

It didn't take long for the news to travel up the caravan. By the time I found Ruth, she'd already heard and was headed back to check on Shirley. Donna had been busy taking care of someone with a knife wound from a minor squabble that had gotten out of hand.

When Ruth saw me, she ran up and hugged me and asked, "Are you all right?"

141

"Yes, why?"

"I was worried about how seeing the attack on Shirley might have affected you, given your past."

"I'm okay. Go take care of her." I didn't want her to see how upset I was. She had enough to do without worrying about me.

"You sure? You look like you've been in a fight."

"It was nothing," I said.

"Okay. Then you're wanted at the head of the caravan. June's already on her way. Apparently, there is a town up ahead that won't let us pass."

When I reached the head of the caravan, after sending some men back to Chris and Bill, I could see a large group of people milling around in front of a large barricade across the road. It consisted of rusted-out cars, refrigerators, and other household appliances, and lots of wooden pallets. I walked up to June and Joe, who were whispering.

"What's going on?" I asked.

"They don't want us in their town," Joe replied.

"Did you tell them we're just passing through on our way to Lancaster?"

"Yeah, they won't allow us to pass through, and they say if we try to sneak through the woods, they'll set it on fire."

"Did they give any reasons?"

"They claim that the last time they allowed a group of people to pass through, the group trashed the town. Shitting all over the place, throwing rocks at people, all sorts of nasty things."

"George, how much time will we lose if we go around?" June asked.

"I don't know off the top of my head. I'll have to check the map, but what choice do we have? We can't rush them."

"He's right. If we try to rush through the gap in the barricade, they'd pick us off, and I don't think they're bluffing about setting the woods on fire."

"Okay, Joe, since you've been talking to them, go and tell them we're turning around. George and I'll get these people back a mile or so and make camp until we can decide on a course of action."

We made camp on the road again. Everyone had heard about what had happened to Jim and Shirley and about not being allowed to pass through the town. They were angry and scared. They were also hungry. Joe, our best hunter, had been busy arguing with the townspeople about letting us pass, so we had even less food that night.

"Okay, what should our next move be?" June asked, looking around at each member of the travel committee.

"We can backtrack and take U.S. 322 west and then U.S. 222 south to Lancaster, but it'll add another day or two to the trip," I said.

"Okay, that's not too bad," June said. "George and Ruth, I can't thank you enough for all you've done to help us, even though you just joined us. It's truly remarkable."

"Hear! Hear!" Gloria added.

Joe patted me on the shoulder.

"Okay, on to more sad news. I'm sure you've all heard what happened to Shirley. Well, apparently, the news upset Emma. Upon hearing about it, she became hysterical and later committed suicide."

"Oh, my God, no," Carol exclaimed. "What happened?"

"She'd been agitated after hearing about it, and then when we were on a rest stop, someone noticed she was missing,"

143

Ruth said. "We found her about a ten meters back in the woods. She'd slit her wrists. It was horrible."

"This is all my fault," Bill said. "If I'd been there, I might've scared the attackers off?"

"That's unlikely," I said. "They'd probably just have killed you before attacking Jim and Shirley. Were you able to track them down?"

"No, they got away."

"Perhaps we should add more sentries tonight?" June asked, looking at Joe.

"Already done," he replied.

"Okay, so we're all agreed then?" June said. "In the morning, we're heading back to the turnoff to U.S. 322. Correct?"

Ruth and I went over and spread our sleeping bags out in front of our tent, which was full of orphans. From the sounds coming from inside, at least one of them was crying themselves to sleep. Gloria was pacing back and forth in front of the tent. Either she was too keyed up to sleep, or she was attempting to calm the baby.

"Ruth, was it you who found her?" I asked.

"Yes. It was horrible, George. What if those men return?"

"We'll deal with them."

She began crying quietly. I reached over and wiped the tears from her face.

"Oh, babe, I'm sorry you had to go through that."

She took a deep breath. "Well, as Mike told me today, 'Life sucks, and then you're dead.'"

That worried me because it didn't sound like the Ruth I knew and loved.

* * *

Not surprisingly, that night I had the nightmare. It was always the same—I relived what had happened after I'd returned from my first trek. It always started with my finding April. She was my childhood sweetheart. No one had been surprised when we married at nineteen. Our lives were complete when our twin girls were born a few years later. April and I were inseparable. My trek was the first time we'd ever been apart. My dad was my trek partner, and I drove him nuts talking about how much I missed her and the girls. After he was killed and I had to complete the trek alone, all I could think about was getting home to them.

I'd found April lying in our dooryard, covered in blood. Her body was left in a horrifying position. It was obvious that death hadn't come quickly and that she had suffered terribly. She'd been killed by a raiding party of ravagers. I know I must've gone into the house to find the girls, but I almost never do that in my nightmare. Sometimes I see other things, but never the girls. After finding April in the yard, the next thing I know, I'm standing in front of the ravagers that I'd tracked down, shooting. I just keep shooting over and over until the gun's empty. Two of the ravagers are still alive, but I kill them with my long knife. The thing that scares me is the pleasure I have in the dream while reliving the act of killing them all.

I woke up and knew I wouldn't get back to sleep anytime soon, so I got up and went and sat in front of the nearest campfire. From the sounds I heard, other people were having their own nightmares. A few minutes later, Joe came and sat down beside me.

"Can't sleep?" Joe asked.

"Not tonight."

"What's on your mind?"

"The usual," I said. "All the horrible things I've done in my life and the people I've let down."

"Come on, we've all done things we're not proud of. I sometimes wake up and can't shake a bit of self-loathing too; usually after drinking too much cider. But I gotta tell you, I don't know what we would've done without you and Ruth."

"But does it make up for what I did in the past?" I asked.

* * *

Morning broke with torrential rain, so we were all soaking wet, cold, and very hungry. It took a lot of effort to find enough dry wood to start only a few fires. But we got them going. The hunters had been hampered by the rain, so all we had for breakfast was steaming birchbark tea. We'd already burned through all the supplies we'd brought with us and there wasn't enough meat last night to make jerky so we'd not be having anything for the midday meal either. At least we could fill our containers with rainwater.

Before the caravan got underway, four men came up the

road and approached the leading edge of the camp. They were all wearing faded, dirty army jackets and jeans. Three appeared as if their last haircuts had been done hastily with a knife, which was then used to scrape their faces. The stubble made their faces look dirty. The oldest-looking guy, who looked as if he were in his mid-thirties, had a full beard. They didn't appear to be armed. As they approached, they were intercepted by one of the men on watch and brought to June.

"So, you're in charge?" the older man with the full beard asked with a nasty grin.

"We have a council," June said. "What do you want?"

Joe, Clark, Ruth, and I took a position behind June to show our support.

The man nodded, acknowledging our arrival, and said, "They wouldn't let you pass, would they? We can get you through, but it'll cost you."

I couldn't be certain, but one of the men looked like one of the attackers from yesterday.

"How would you do that?" June asked.

"We know a way."

"Is it safe?"

"Is anything safe these days?"

"What would you want in return for taking us through?"

"From the looks of it, you ain't got no food. What about that beehive we seen you transporting?"

June shook her head and said, "No"

"Well, we also seen you got lots of little ones running around. Any of 'em orphans no one wants to feed? We're always looking for strong, healthy workers, 'specially girls. We'll take 'em off your hands and give 'em a good home."

"You mean slaves? Don't be ridiculous."

147

"Yeah, I didn't think you'd go for that. Okay, what valuables do you offer then?"

"I don't think we'll offer you anything. In fact, I think you should leave now."

He looked at all of us in turn. "You sure? I can see you got too many mouths to feed as is, and it's awfully dangerous out here."

"Mister, we're sure," Ruth said. "Leave!"

"Okay, okay, but we'll follow behind you a ways, just in case you change your minds."

The four men left the way they had come.

As soon as they'd left, David came rushing over and said, "I overheard what he said. He's right; we've too many mouths to feed. And we don't have the time to backtrack and detour around the town. You should've given him what he wanted."

June turned to him and said, "David, shut up."

"Who put you in charge?" David asked.

Bill moved towards him. David turned and left.

We got the caravan packed up and moving. We put all the orphans in the middle of the caravan and warned everyone, particularly those with children, to stay vigilant. Later, Mike told me his group had heard of slavers who would capture and enslave refugees from the city.

Two days went by, and although the scouts warned us that groups were in front and behind us, they hadn't attacked. Maybe they were waiting until we were weak from hunger. The hunters couldn't shoot enough game for so many people. Another problem was getting worse by the hour; we were running out of clean water.

* * *

You know those days when you wake up in a bad mood, but you aren't certain why. I was having one of those days. Everything was setting me off. Ruth actually told me to walk someplace else. So I raced ahead to find Clark or Joe and alert them we should be approaching the turnoff to U.S. 222. I hoped that turning and heading in the correct direction again might soothe my irritable disposition. I was about a kilometer ahead of the caravan, expecting to find Clark or Joe or one of the other scouts when I spotted the cart the hunters used to haul dressed carcasses in the center of the road. A body was lying next to it with an arrow sticking out of it; it wasn't moving. I couldn't see who it was. I got off the road and ran a short distance into the woods and crouched behind a large tree. All I could think of was, *where was everyone? Who's that out on the road?*

"Joe! Clark! Are you out there? It's George. What's going on?"

"George, stay down. It's an ambush."

"How many are they? And where are they?"

"There's at least five of them. They're on the south side of the road near the bent road sign."

"Hey, you men out there!" I yelled. "We've got lots of armed men coming up behind us! You can't win this!"

"All we want are the two deer in the cart!" a man with a rough, gravelly voice shouted.

"You can't have them. We've got eighty people to feed."

After a few minutes of silence, I spotted movement where Joe had said the highwaymen were hiding. Two men raced out toward the cart containing the deer. At the same instant, the others fired several arrows at a location where I assumed Joe was hiding. They didn't know exactly where I was hiding, so they were just sending arrows in my general vicinity. Suddenly, the two men, who were almost at the cart, both went down, hit by arrows. Joe must not have been alone. Another of the men ran out. I assumed he was running to aid the wounded, but instead, he ran to the cart and started pushing it.

On another day, I might have had more patience. I stood, took aim, and let loose an arrow; it missed. But they'd spotted me and shot me. The impact twisted me around, and I fell to the ground with an arrow in my shoulder. Fuck, it hurt.

"George, you alright?" Joe shouted.

"Yeah, just peachy!" I replied.

"That's too bad; I was taking a shine to Ruth. She's a looker."

"Thanks, Joe; knowing you'll be there for her gives me a lot of comfort."

Someone else then yelled, "What say we kill these fuckers?" It was Boyd, one of the new volunteers helping Clark and Joe hunt.

"We give up!" the man with a rough, gravelly voice yelled. "Let us take our wounded, and we'll leave."

"Joe, it's up to you!" I shouted.

"Okay, you men can take your wounded!" Joe shouted. "But if you go near that cart, you're dead."

It took about ten minutes for them to check on their men and help the one remaining individual who was still alive up and carry him off. It turned out that Joe had shot and killed the man that I'd missed. He or Boyd had also killed one of the two that had initially run out. The body that I had first seen on the road was Clark's. He was dead.

By the time the caravan caught up to us, Joe and I were sitting on the ground behind the cart with Boyd keeping watch in case the highwaymen came back. Joe was examining the arrow in my shoulder.

"Are you going to break it and push it through?" I asked, groaning with pain.

"Not unless you want to die a painful death. The arrowhead isn't very deep. The guy who shot it had no power, probably a crappy bow, or he hadn't been using it for long. I could push it deeper and through if you want, or I can just yank it out."

And with that, he suddenly, without warning, yanked it out. I screamed.

"Come on, buddy, butch up. People are watching."

When Ruth arrived, I thought she'd have made a bigger fuss, but no. Ruth was in nurse-mode, all business.

"Joe did a good job," she said. "I just need to put a couple of stitches in it. And I think I still have some yarrow leaves I can make a poultice out of."

We made camp early so we could bury Clark. While the two deer he'd died for were either roasting or drying, Boyd and another man from the caravan were able to shoot two turkeys. So again, no one would starve, but once again, no one would go to bed with a full belly either. Ruth used the extra time organizing volunteers to boil water to sterilize for drinking.

That night, when she and I were arranging our sleeping bags, she came up and hugged me and cried.

"I refuse to break down in front of everybody, but I was so

worried about you. What would I ever do without you?"

"Don't cry, babe. I'm not going anywhere. Besides, Joe's hot for you and said he'd be willing to step in if something happens to me."

"He did, did he?" She laughed, wiping the tears from her eyes, and gently slapped my chest, hurting my injured shoulder.

"Ouch."

"You're such a big baby. Remind me later to put some sulfa powder on it that we brought from home. We don't want it getting infected."

* * *

I think everyone was relieved the next day when we turned south and were headed in the right direction again. After a few kilometers, Boyd came running back and stopped the caravan.

When June arrived, she asked, "What's up, Boyd? Why've we stopped?"

"Joe sent me back to get you. We found something up ahead."

"What is it?"

"Three bodies hanging from a tree. They've been there a while. It's bad, but we don't know if we should cut them down."

June, Ruth, and I accompanied Boyd to see what they'd

found. Three bodies were hanging from a tree on the side of the road. They were just teenagers. They weren't wearing much clothing, so unfortunately, we could see their skin was blotched and had taken on a greenish color. The bodies were bloated and leaking fluids that were pooling on the ground below. Insects were everywhere. The odor was indescribable. My stomach churned with revulsion.

"Oh my God," June said as she gagged.

Ruth was also gagging and asked, "Why not just cut them down?"

It was obvious Joe had been crying while waiting for us. "Someone hung them there as a message. Whoever it was might not like it if we cut them down."

"I don't care if we piss somebody off," June said. "We can't march eighty people, including children, past this."

So she and Ruth returned to the caravan to send someone back with shovels. Meanwhile, Joe, Boyd, and I cut the bodies down, being careful to lower them as carefully as possible so they wouldn't hit the ground and burst open. I wasn't much help with my sore shoulder.

By the time the caravan reached us, the bodies were buried. Joe, Boyd, and I were in desperate need of a wash, so we stayed away from people. Fortunately, we soon came upon a small pond, and the caravan stopped to collect water for boiling later with the evening fires. After the containers were filled, everyone took the opportunity to wash up.

Shortly after we got back underway, Joe came running back.

"George, where's June?"

"I think she and Ruth are still back at the pond, dealing with something David instigated. Why, what's up?"

"We got another barricade up ahead."

"Damn, how far ahead?"

"A couple of miles."

Okay, I'll run back and get them to come forward as quickly as possible. We don't want a bunch of people congregating in front of the barricade.

When June, Ruth, and I reached the barricade, the caravan was right behind us. Boyd said he'd go back and stop them from interfering with our negotiations. We walked over and joined Joe, who was talking to someone from the town. The barricade was much like the previous one, except they'd somehow managed to move a semi-trailer across the road and flipped it on its side. They filled in the gaps with rusty old appliances and cars. We could see four men and a woman standing on scaffolding or something behind the semi-trailer with bows with nocked arrows pointed at us.

"Royce, these are the leaders of our little group. This is June, Ruth, and George. Guys, this is Royce. He's the 'Mayor' of this town."

Royce was wearing a suit. It was torn and filthy, but it was a brown suit with a matching brown tie. The tie was badly stained. The only person I'd ever seen wearing a suit, outside of magazine pictures, was Steven, back at the Center. Royce was my age. His hair was trimmed but greasy, and he was clean-shaven.

"Joe, I wouldn't characterize yours as a little group," Royce said.

"Mr. Mayor, is there a problem?" June asked. "We're headed for Lancaster County."

"That's your business, but you're not coming through our streets."

"Why not?" June asked.

"Because how do I know you'll actually keep going? We don't have the resources to accept any more refugees."

"I promise we won't give you any trouble," June said. "We will just walk through your town, and you'll never see us again."

"How do I know you're not scouting our resources and defenses so you can come back and raid us later? We don't let people steal from us. No, you must go around."

June pointed to the river that paralleled the road and said, "We can't cross that with our carts and wagons. And on the other side, there is a wood that looks almost impenetrable."

"Yes, we're careful about where we take trees for firewood, not to thin it out."

"Please, we've been on the road for a week and can't go much farther."

"Exactly my concern. How can you be sure some of your people won't just stop? They might try to take the town from our citizens."

Ruth moved forward. "Sir, can you answer a question of mine? A kilometer or so back on the road, we found the bodies of three boys hanging from a tree. Would you know anything about them?"

"Yes, that's where we caught up with them. They'd repeatedly stolen food from us?"

"You hanged kids for stealing food?" Ruth asked.

"Yes, we did."

Ruth's face turned red and she said, "You're fucking monsters."

Looking to each of us in turn, he asked, "What would you do if those animals repeatedly stole your food? And let me assure you, they were animals. They couldn't even speak like a human being."

I knew Ruth had been right to be upset, but any chance we'd had of him letting us through his town just vanished.

We looked at each other, shook our heads, and walked back to the others, who were milling around about twenty meters behind us.

David must have followed us up the caravan when I went back and got June and Ruth because he was standing at the front of the crowd and shouted, "What now?"

As she walked past him, June said, "They won't allow us to pass."

* * *

We camped about a kilometer down the road from the barricade. Since we camped early, the hunters had time to go out and hunt, but there was less game here so close to the town. They only managed to shoot one deer. Being hungry didn't stop people from complaining about having deer meat again. After dinner, the unofficial travel committee met.

"What are we going to do?" June asked. "I've gotta tell you, I'm at a loss."

"There is always Plan B," Joe said.

"I forgot, what's Plan B again?" June asked.

"We give up on the idea of Lancaster County and living with the Amish and instead go farther west and out of reach from the nor'easters coming in off the ocean. Besides, we don't even know if the Amish would take us in. Let's just stop in the next town that isn't occupied or at least that isn't blockaded. If it doesn't suit us, we can move again later."

No one spoke for several minutes. I raised my hand slightly to show I had something to add.

"Go ahead, George," June said.

"I agree with most of what Joe said, except I think you should be choosy in the town you settle in. I don't want you to fall into the trap of becoming nomadic. In our travels, we've come across towns occupied by squatters. They move from one place to another, usually after hunting all the game or polluting it with their waste and making it uninhabitable. Yeah, it might make sense to be able to pack up your belongings and move once you've used up the resources, or if you're attacked and, obviously, if a tornado destroyed your town. But that only makes sense if you haven't invested in that area. And I think you need to find a place you can invest in. If we ever hope to rebuild even a semblance of what we had before, we need permanent settlements heavily invested in farming."

Joe shook his head and said, "We tried that, and it didn't work."

"Well, you've got to try harder. But if you succeed, it will increase your food security and perhaps even result in a food surplus. This would free up some people to work on other things; to be doctors, engineers, or mechanics as well as farmers. My dad used to say, 'We need people to remember how to make lead pencils again,' but don't ask me why."

"George, you said we needed to be choosy in selecting the town," June said. "What should we be looking for?"

"Clearly, you should be looking for a place with a lower risk of extreme weather. Of course, these days there's no place without risk, but moving farther inland is a start. You don't want to be too close to mountains either, though. They can serve as a barrier to frontal systems moving in from the coast, they create a lifting effect that cools the air, causing the water vapor to condense, resulting in heavier rain or snowfall. You need to be near a river or lake for irrigation and drinking water. But you need to find an area that's not at a lower elevation than the surrounding area vulnerable to flooding. You need to find an area with fertile soil for farming. Like the town that just stopped us in our tracks, you'll want a town with natural defenses. But unlike this town, you don't want to be surrounded by a forest that might burn out of control. And while you'll want a town that is semi-isolated, you still want neighbors to build mutually beneficial relationships, like trade or possibly defense. We need to work together for the common good."

"Is that what you and Ruth are looking for to move your town?"

"Yes."

"I can't argue with his logic," Joe said. "But we also need apple orchards so we can make hard apple cider."

Everyone laughed.

"Anybody else?" June asked. "Okay, so George, where do we look for this ideal town?"

"I'd suggest turning around and heading northwest on U.S. 222."

Two days later, the decision on which town to settle in was made for us.

Chapter 9. New Town

We camped on Route 61, having already rejected two small towns that didn't meet our criteria, one of which was occupied but let us pass under guard. The travel committee was meeting around a campfire and listening to a disturbing report.

"Yes, despite our warnings, people have been drinking non-sterile water and, as a result, are getting sick," Donna said. "Based on the speed of progression and the symptoms, which include diarrhea, sometimes severe and bloody, abdominal cramps, fever, and nausea, we feel it's dysentery rather than cholera."

"Oh, no," Gloria said.

"Yeah, it's not good news," June said. "Ruth told me about this earlier today. She's taking care of a few of the sicker individuals now."

"Yeah, we're trying to keep them hydrated," Donna added. "Ruth's giving them tea made from blackberry leaves. But no way these people can travel tomorrow. The next day, maybe, but they're going to be weak and will not be able to go far."

June looked over at me and shrugged. "George, I think we need to be less choosy in our choice of a town and find one now. Perhaps you, Joe, and Boyd, if the three of you are healthy, can scout ahead tomorrow while we stay here and take care of our sick?"

"I'm good if Joe is," I said.

"We'll have to check with Boyd; he's patrolling the camp right now."

That night, when I went and found Ruth, she confessed she had given some of our antibiotics to four sick children. I told her that was okay.

* * *

The three of us left at first light, traveling fast. By midday, we'd passed several farms but no towns with enough houses. In the early afternoon, we entered what appeared to be a ghost town. It was on the Schuylkill River, so it would have a source of clean water, and the elevation and terrain look promising. There were plenty of houses and even small apartment buildings. It was surrounded by farmland. So much farmland, albeit fallow, meant that it was a low-risk wildfire area. But the town was in shambles. There was garbage strewn everywhere. There were animal bones and other debris piled in the street, along with partially burnt wood, suggesting bonfires. Furniture and other household items were pulled out of houses and left in the dooryards. Faded graffiti covered many buildings. Windows had been smashed with rocks. We also found dried feces in a few yards; they hadn't even bothered to dig pits. Clearly, squatters had occupied the town, but the question was, were they still here?

"Let's split up and search for anyone still living here," Joe suggested. "And keep an eye out for any signs of weather-related damage: watermarks or signs of mold, and any kind of roof damage, that sort of thing."

"Okay, from the map, it looks like most of the houses are oriented along the river and are west of this intersection. I'll go west until I hit the river and then work my way north. Joe, why don't you continue north on Route 61? Boyd, can you go east and check out the farms? If you find more than just a few people, don't confront them. Come back here, and we'll all talk to them together. Do you want to meet back here in two hours?"

They both nodded. "Okay, see you then."

Walking past a couple of gas stations at the intersection, I entered what surely must've been a lovely neighborhood in its day, now overgrown with vegetation. I went door to door and found no one alive. Over time, I became confident enough that I was alone to yell, 'Is there anyone here?' I found a few skeletal remains in the houses and a few fresher corpses, likely of squatters, but they were several months old, at least. The houses themselves were in relatively good shape. They had no musty smell and no obvious water damage except for a few with smashed windows and leaking roofs. There were no outhouses, so people probably hadn't lived here for long after the collapse and blackout. The road dead-ended just past what looked like a neighborhood tavern. Its front door was wide open, so I had to go in. It had a short but nice counter bar with stools. I sat down on one. The mirror behind the bar was broken. Empty bottles of liquor in front of the cash register had been smashed. Of course, I'd never been to a neighborhood bar. By the time I was old enough, they were all gone; in Phoenix, we gather in homes and drink home brew. But I could imagine how it might once have been filled with laughter and friends stopped in after a hard day at work. The people who had frequented this bar must've liked Coors, according to the wall hangings. I could almost smell the beer; I was famous for my home brew back in Phoenix. Just as I was getting up to leave, a black cat came out from behind the bar and sat down in front of me on the floor and stared at me.

"I know you're not Charley, but you look like him. I'm a dog guy, but I guess cats have their place in the world. Here, here's a piece of jerky. Don't tell anyone I gave it to you."

I walked down to the end of the road, where I found a fallow farm field rewilding. I jumped over a fence and walked farther toward the river. To the north, I saw more farm fields running alongside the river in various stages of forest succession. I then backtracked to the cross street and started walking north. The street was a mix of houses and a few businesses, all empty. It was lined with rusted-out cars. When I came to a couple of baseball fields almost completely taken over by vegetation, I turned east and circled back to the intersection where we'd planned to meet up. Boyd was already there waiting, and he had a smile on his face.

"This place is great. There's much more farmland; we won't have to farm on a golf course. The soil looks good, or at least better than the golf course, and it appears some of the fields may have remnants of crops that self-seeded. I think we could clear the brush and get them going again without too much difficulty."

"That's excellent, but did you see anyone?"

"Not a soul."

Just then, Joe walked up. "Glad to see you guys made it back in one piece."

Boyd was just as animated when he told Joe what he'd found.

"I also found farm fields," I said. "When they built the town, they appear to have left the farm fields along the river. Being so close to the river, they might flood occasionally, but it's going to make irrigation much easier. I found skeletal remains and mummified corpses in a few houses and on the street, but no one alive. There weren't many remains, and they didn't appear to have died in a large fight or skirmish. I also didn't find any evidence of significant flooding. No watermarks on buildings, and the rusted-out cars were still parked where they were left twenty-five years ago."

"That's great," Joe said. "I found a large elementary school and running track that still looks in good shape. We could use the school auditorium for town meetings. There's an abandoned distribution center a mile or so northwest of here with semi-trucks still parked in front of the loading docks, but it was already ransacked, and I doubt if there is anything worth anything still there. There were a few dried-out corpses outside, but as you said, they didn't appear to have been killed in any kind of large skirmish. You can see the old rusty water tower from here. I'm sure it's empty, but to be safe, we might need to take it down."

Looking at me, he asked, "So, what do you think?"

"I don't think you could hope to find anything better. The only thing that bothers me is why there aren't any people here. Why did the people who lived here before the collapse leave, and why did the squatters leave?"

"I don't know and don't care," Boyd said. "It's ours now."

"I agree," Joe added. "Hey, it's too late to walk back to the caravan tonight. Perhaps we should stay here tonight and see if the place is haunted. Maybe that's what scared everyone away."

Boyd shoved Joe and said, "You ass, why the fuck did you have to say that?"

Joe smiled at me and said, "There must be a reason they're called ghost towns."

I laughed, but I could see Boyd was serious. "Although that sounds inviting, I think we should try to get back to the caravan tonight, even if it takes most of the night. People will be worried if we don't return."

"You mean Ruth will be worried," Joe said.

"I think Carol might be a little worried, too," I said, smiling. "Ruth told me you've been spending a lot of time with Carol and that you're teaching Margaret how to hunt."

"I'm just helping out with the family after losing Phil."

"Right," I said, still smiling.

Boyd said he'd walk all night if necessary. I think he was spooked by what Joe had said. So, we began the long walk back.

* * *

We got back to the caravan just after one o'clock, but the travel committee was still awake and waiting for us. Ruth ran up and gave me a hug. Carol was still up too and went to Joe, but there was no public hug yet.

As soon as we sat down with a cup of tea, June asked, "What'd you find? I can tell from your expressions you found something."

"It's perfect", Boyd said. "It's got so many farms and plenty of houses for us to live in."

"I wouldn't say it's perfect," I said. "It's going to take a lot of work to clean the place up, but I think it's going to meet your needs. Most importantly, there's no one claiming it."

"The place is empty," Joe said. "Eerily empty."

"Let's not have any more of that," I said. "There'd been squatters, and they left it in a mess, but they aren't there now. There's no evidence of significant weather-related damage. No flooding, but there is a river."

"Sounds great," Bill said. "How far away is it?"

"We might be able to get there in a day," I replied. "We made it in about seven hours, but we were walking pretty fast. I don't think the caravan can match that pace. How is everything here? Everyone recovering?"

Donna shook her head and with a sullen expression said, "No, two people died from the dysentery. They were just too weak."

"Oh, that's a shame," I said.

"We were also attacked," June said. "They came in a few hours ago under the cover of darkness, and without rousing the sentries, killed a man and stole two carts."

Joe pounded his fist on his leg and said "Damn. Did you add more guards?"

"Yeah, that's where Chris is now. Patrolling with five others," June said.

"How are the rest of the people who were ill?" I asked. "Any of them sick enough they might die?"

"No, we don't think so, and the children are doing even better than the adults," Ruth added.

"Will people be ready to travel tomorrow?" I asked. "It'd be safer if we moved into the town and weren't camped out here in the open."

"No, I don't think so; we should give them another day to recover," Donna said.

* * *

It was late afternoon two days later when we walked into 'New Town' as people were now calling it. The caravan had not been attacked again. We'd made the trip in a single long day because people were so eager to see the town. The travel committee thought it would be best if we kept everyone together for the first few days and asked them all to camp in the parking lot of the elementary school. Joe, Boyd, and a few others had made it there earlier and were roasting two pigs and a deer they'd shot on their way. So for a change, there would be plenty of food.

Someone said he thought it was Thanksgiving Day, so everyone thought it was an auspicious day to have a feast.

Ruth and a few women even foraged and brought back greens. The large meal and gathering would also entice people to stay together and not go off on their own and try to claim houses or farms for themselves. We wanted the selection process to be organized, with the best farmers getting the farms. We also thought it best if people stayed together and occupied houses close to the town's center, at least initially. It was a very festive evening; people were singing and dancing. They were told there would be a meeting in the school auditorium at ten o'clock the following morning.

When Ruth and I were getting into our sleeping bags that night, she said, "George, doesn't it feel great to have been able to help these people?"

"Yes, but the burden of responsibility has been a little tiring."

"But we got them here, and isn't this a great place?"

"Yeah, but I'm a little worried about why such a great town is empty. I hope we haven't led them out of the frying pan and into the fire. The only reason I can think of for this great town to be empty is nasty neighbors."

"You worry too much."

* * *

Like many others, I slept late the next morning. When I awoke, I found Ruth had already gotten up and had gone off somewhere. Someone had restarted the fires and left water boiling. But there weren't many people up yet, or so I thought. While I was drinking my before-breakfast tea, I heard screaming, then saw someone running towards the camp. It was Carol's daughter, Margaret.

"Hurry! June's been bitten by a snake while swimming in the river."

I jumped up and, along with a few others, followed Margaret back to the river. On the way, Margaret explained that several people had gotten up early and decided to brave the cold weather and go wash up and swim in the river. I was sure that Ruth was among them, and Margaret confirmed it. When we arrived at the river, we found a circle of people around June lying on the riverbank.

When Ruth saw me, she jumped up from June and ran to me. She was still wet and, to my surprise, was only dressed in her underwear and bra.

"I'm glad to see you. We need you to identify a snake; no one's seen it before."

"Where is it? Did you kill it?"

"Yeah, it's over there."

She pointed to where Joe was kneeling over something, which turned out to be the dead snake. I rushed over.

"What do you got, Joe?" I asked. He was wearing shorts, but was also wet.

"I don't know. I've never seen a snake that looks like this. It was probably sunning itself since it's cold. I think June stepped on it."

"Shit, it looks like a water moccasin."

"We don't have water moccasins in Pennsylvania."

"You do now."

"Damn, and their bites can be deadly, right?"

"Yeah, they're venomous."

I rushed back over to Ruth and told her and Donna what the snake was.

"Should we cut the bite open and try to suck out the poison?" Donna asked.

As I moved to a position to lift June, I said, "No, that doesn't work, and it'd likely be too late now anyhow. Let's get June back to camp."

We carried her back to camp, and Donna and Ruth sat with her. Carol and Gloria put people to work preparing breakfast, mostly to get them out of the way. Many people had grown fond of June for all she'd done since the tornado, and so were milling around, looking worried. I went back to where Ruth and I had set up the tent to check on the orphans and to tell them what'd happened. After an hour, I went back to check on June, expecting to find the worst.

But when I found Ruth, I was surprised to find her smiling.

"She's feeling much better. The pain has reduced, and there's a lot less swelling around the bite than I'd have expected. Maybe you were wrong about the snake being a water moccasin."

"No, I'm positive it was a moccasin. Maybe it was a 'dry bite' where no venom is released."

"Either way, it's great news!"

The town meeting was delayed for two hours so June could have more time to recover. When everyone finally met, there were a lot of discussions, some very contentious. It started almost immediately as the travel committee, standing at the front of the room, began outlining our thinking.

Someone—I was sure it was David—yelled, "Who are you

to tell us anything? And why are you standing up front as if you're in charge?"

Several people agreed, yelling, "Yeah, who made you the leaders?"

"We should have an election!"

And the one I liked best: "Why are those two outsiders up there with you?"

When the topic of signing up for work crews was brought up, David complained, "That's implicit slavery."

When all was said and done, it was decided there would be a vote in two days for a town council of five people. Until then, people should explore the town and select a couple of houses they'd like to live in, but, for better defense, they should stick to the houses within a four-block area around the school. If more than one family selected a house, the council would decide who'd get it. Any person with a proven record of farming or gardening could make an argument for one of the farms, and it would be okay if they lived farther out of town. Frank and Charlene, who had successfully brought their queen bee to New Town, could have their pick of any house at the edge of town or select an empty farm. And lastly, lists would be posted for people to sign up for various work crews: to remove and bury any remains that were found, to dig wells, build outhouses, and begin repairing houses. The hunters who supplied the caravan agreed to continue to hunt and try to supply meat for everyone in town, at least for a while.

Ruth and I had no part to play, so we went for a walk.

"What do you think?" Ruth asked.

"I was surprised and a little disappointed at how quickly they forgot what the travel committee did for them and mutinied."

"Well, David didn't help."

"Yeah, one bad actor."

"Should we stick around and help them get settled?"

"While it would be fascinating to watch, I think our continued presence is upsetting a few people. And we've been delayed long enough; we should get going."

"But where should we head from here?"

"What do you mean? I thought you wanted to abort the trek and return to Phoenix?"

"I've changed my mind."

Trying to keep the excitement out of my voice, I said, "You have?"

"After helping these people the way we did, I can see how important the mission is."

"So, you're willing to continue on to Florida?" I asked.

"Yes. But we've got to hurry and get back to Dan as soon as we can. I know I'll never be his real mother, but I feel like he's my child, and I miss him so much."

Ruth began to cry.

I held her and whispered, "You are Dan's mother, the only mother he's ever known."

* * *

We stuck around for several more days to replenish our supplies including, besides food, first aid supplies like surgical

171

suture material and bandages. Ruth was careful to keep the kit well stocked.

In the end, June, Joe, Donna, Gloria, and Chris were elected to the town council. Bill almost won a seat, but people were likely worried he'd vote the way his wife voted, giving June too much power. David received only two votes. One was his own vote, but who else would have thought he belonged on the council? Oh well, soon David wouldn't be my concern.

Ruth spent much of her time finding families to adopt the orphans and helping set up and train a crew to forage in the nearby woods. They even started replanting some of the wild plants they'd need in the future for the beginnings of an agroforest. After convincing them to keep back any seeds from crops that had self-seeded for future planting rather than eating them, I took time out from digging pits for the communal outhouses to write up my notes.

* * *

Journal entry: 26 Nov, New Town, PA (formerly Shoemakersville) on PA 61

Helped lead 80+ people from the neighborhood outside of Norris-town, PA, destroyed by the tornado (see previous entries), to this abandoned town. On the way here, the caravan was attacked on the road several times. We also encountered towns that had been burned out, while others were barricaded, not allowing passage. Both are very troubling—when are they going to realize they must work with their neighbors??? We also found three feral children who were hanged by people from one of those towns for stealing food. I was horrified by the lynching, but was surprised Ferals could survive through the winter on their own this far north.

We found this town completely empty three days ago—it meets many criteria for long-term settlement. It does, however, have some drawbacks. Other than the river as a natural defense from the southwest, the terrain is not easily defended. I am also worried the town may be too close to the mountains, i.e., risk of orographic lift of frontal systems producing excessive rainfall or snows. Yet the town itself is not at the lowest elevation— the nearby river is in a broad lowland valley that appears to be capable of accommodating considerable runoff. Strongly urged the council not to dump waste in the river, but instead to recycle the waste for farming. Town had been used by squatters (e.g., as evidenced by condition of homes, recent burn piles, piles of excrement, game carcasses). Can't think of why they or the original inhabitants deserted this town; hopefully, they were not run off by neighboring townsfolk.

Meteorological data collected today and tabulated on the following page.

Note: a water moccasin was obs. 2 days ago, i.e., dry bit someone. Like other cold-blooded reptiles, these snakes are highly sensitive to temperature change but apparently have extended their range north due to a warmer climate; more poisonous snakes are likely on the way.

* * *

When it came time for us to leave, I was surprised by how many people turned out to say goodbye. The people closest to us—those on the travel committee—who knew about Dan, understood why we couldn't stay; we had to keep moving to get home to him.

Chapter 10. Just the Two of Us, Again

The first few days back on the road, Ruth went from being very talkative, reminiscing about someone or something dealing with the caravan, to being quiet and unresponsive. She also snapped at me several times. I knew she missed her friends and missed caring for the orphans. Being self-centered, I was simply relieved at no longer feeling responsible for so many people, but I had to admit I also missed the companionship of the friends we'd made. Attempting to lift her mood, I even offered to let her go first in a game of 'Would You Rather?'. But she wasn't interested.

Walking by ourselves, we had to relearn our pace and the scheduling of pee breaks and rest stops. I pushed us hard because I wanted to make up time. My plan was to take U.S. 222 back to U.S. 1. Traveling by ourselves without carts and wagons, I wasn't worried about being forced to detour around the town that had refused passage to the caravan.

It also took time for us to get back into our routine of

distributing tasks between the two of us. When we camped the first night, I tried to do everything myself, like when we first started the trek, which slowed things down and frustrated Ruth. But being on our own had advantages too. The second night after leaving, we had tension-relief sex, which was very nice. Afterwards, I returned to worrying about the fact that we no longer had the security of guards posted.

On the third night after leaving New Town, we were in the tent, which finally smelled of us rather than all the kids that had slept in it on the caravan, when Ruth said, "Hon, I've decided when we get back to Phoenix, I'm going to run for my mother's seat on the town council when she retires."

"Really, when did you decide that?"

"While on the caravan. I admired the way June handled herself, and I got a lot out of helping those people. I also thought I did a good job."

"I thought you were amazing at organizing people, especially since we were outsiders. I'd bet you'd be great on the town council, maybe even becoming the head of the council someday."

"But then I'd have to work with Steven, and you make him sound like such a pompous ass."

"He is, but you can handle him."

She gave me a strange look, "Yes, I think I probably can."

"What do you mean by that?"

Ruth just smiled.

The next few days were uneventful, and we did finally fall into our previous routine.

* * *

It took us four days to walk to the Conowingo Dam and Bridge over the Susquehanna River. On the way there, we found the bodies of a family slaughtered on the road. It was a man, a woman, and two young children. The man was stripped of his clothes. After that, I moved us off the road anytime I heard noises up ahead.

When we reached the bridge, we found that it was impassable. Entire sections were missing, probably because the floodgates hadn't been opened during the extreme high flows since the blackout. If that weren't bad enough, I could see that the steel towers that had supported the heavy transmission lines at the southern end of the dam had collapsed onto the bridge, leaving a mass of rusty steel we'd have to climb through.

"What's the plan, George? We might walk across those rocks, but that channel over there looks deep."

"Yes, it does. No, we'll have to find another way. We can go east toward 95 or west."

"Well, I hate backtracking over the same territory."

"Me too, so 95 it is."

It took us several more hours to walk to the I-95 bridge, but it was impassable too; large sections were missing. We found piles of discarded items at the bridgehead from the legions of refugees that had arrived here, like us, only to find the bridge out. I guess they were as disappointed as we were and, in frustration, lightened their load before going on.

"Why didn't they build bridges better back then?" Ruth complained.

"In this case, I don't think you can fault the bridge contractor or design engineers for what's happened over the past twenty-five years with no maintenance. The steel and the concrete would've expanded and contracted differently during the extreme temperature swings, which weren't likely modeled during the design. The steel components would have also rusted and deteriorated. All this, in combination with greater runoff volumes, made failure inevitable."

"Okay, where to now? And can we stop for the night? I bet you could catch some fish for dinner."

"Alright, let's make camp, and in the morning, we'll decide where to try next. I'll catch some fish and later use my scope to see if the U.S. 40 bridge is out too."

Fortunately, I'm a better fisherman than hunter, so dinner was a hearty meal of fish. Unfortunately, my view of the bridge was partially blocked by an island, but from what I could see, it didn't look good. Mangled, rusted steel from the trusses had collapsed at both ends of the bridge.

* * *

In the morning, we headed west toward the bridge on Route 372. I hoped that if it were also impassible, we could ford the river across the shallows there. I decided against the U.S. 40

bridge because I was reluctant to climb through rusted steel girders, and if we crossed, we'd have to turn and go back west anyway to avoid Baltimore and DC. It took us all day to get to the bridge, and when we arrived, we found a section missing. One of the support columns had toppled, probably from the bottom being scoured during a high-flow event. We'd have to climb down and ford the river over the rocks. But it was late, and I refused to get caught crossing the river in the dark, so we made camp.

The following morning, I surveilled the river from the vantage point of the bridge. It looked very different from the old satellite image I had of the area taken just before the blackout. The channel to the island was now much wider, but I found a spot that looked doable. It took time to climb down to the riverbank and walk to the spot I had chosen to cross. While we were doing that, the weather changed.

"George, I don't like this. It's too cold to go swimming, and it looks like it's going to snow. Maybe we should wait."

"I know, I don't like it either, but if we wait, the rocks will be covered in snow. We've got to do it now."

"Okay, George."

"I'm hoping the water won't be over our heads if we cross up by the dam close to the rocks. We'll have to hold our backpacks over our heads to keep them as dry as possible. It's shallower on the other side of the island. I think we'll just need to climb over rocks, but when we get there, I want you to keep your backpack unbuckled."

"Why?"

"That'll allow you to dump it quickly if you fall. I don't want it dragging you down."

"What about you?"

179

"We can't replace the contents of my bag, so we can't afford to lose it. I'll be okay."

Of course, I was the one who almost drowned. I'd misjudged the depth of the channel to the island. I was holding my backpack over my head, took a step, and suddenly was underwater. Fortunately, the backpack was slightly buoyant from the air inside, and Ruth was able to grab it and I got my feet under me. Because I don't know how to swim, Ruth had to swim her backpack to the island, come back for mine, and then return to help me. It was a humiliating experience being so helpless. Sadly, I lost the bag containing the food we'd stocked up on before leaving New Town.

Eventually, we made it all the way across the river with only a few bumps and bruises from falling several times on the slippery rocks. It'd started snowing while we were crossing. We were lucky the river wasn't flowing faster. Once on the other side, we kept going, even though we were sopping wet and freezing. We wanted to find a house because it was snowing harder. It took us only another twenty minutes of walking before we found a side street off Route 372 with several houses. The third one in was a yellow, three-story house with a fireplace and an intact roof. We quickly searched it, then I broke up some furniture and made a fire in the fireplace. We got out of our wet clothes and into our nightclothes. Since I'd lost most of our food during the river crossing, we ate some jerky Ruth still had and some hemlock tea for dinner. At least the tea warmed us up.

Once she stopped shivering and her teeth stopped chattering, Ruth asked, "Where are we headed, George?"

I grabbed the map that I'd taken out of my backpack to dry. "We're headed toward Wilmington, North Carolina, to take another sea level measurement, but it's going to take us well over a month to get there. My plan is to take U.S. 15 south to bypass Baltimore and Washington, DC, and then circle around Richmond."

"Sounds good, but I think you might add a day or two to your timetable. It's snowing pretty hard out there."

The snowfall was turning into a blizzard. We wouldn't be going anywhere soon. It continued to snow through the night. By the next day, there was over sixty centimeters of the white stuff on the ground. I was just glad we were in a house and not in the tent. This became even more fortuitous when the weather suddenly changed, and it started raining mid-morning. The rain melted the snow quickly, so there were torrents of meltwater flowing in all directions. We decided to take a zero day and burn the rest of the furniture. I'd go out and hunt later after the rain stopped. I had another cup of tea and wrote up some notes.

* * *

Journal entry: 2 Dec, Route 372 just south of the Susquehanna River

Frustrated by the amount of effort and time it took us to get across this one river, bridges on U.S. 1, I-95, U.S. 40, and on Route 372 were all impassable; several washed out. It must have been a huge deluge coming down the river to scour away the bed downstream from the piers or lifting the bridges to cause so many failures; that or the damming effect of debris on the bridges. This likely also weakened the supporting structures, causing their collapse. In the end, we had to ford the river and almost drowned doing so.

Continue to obs. signs of violence on the road: fresh corpses on the roadside; towns burned, occupants killed. Yet, also continue to obs. many small groups of migrants traveling south on the roads; the increased number of people moving around the country since my last trek may signal a greater sense of safety for traveling now (whether or not this is justified); this deserves further scrutiny in the weeks to come.

Heavy snowstorms followed by rain made traveling next to impossible. Must make up time, or we will be trapped by the weather later.

* * *

Over the next couple of weeks, I avoided communities along the route to make up time. This way I could also worry less about Ruth's safety. On three occasions, the towns were barricaded anyway. Ruth had finally learned her lesson and stopped trying to engage everyone we encountered on the road. The exception was when anyone traveled with children. When they did, we invariably gave them any food we had. I was able to shoot rabbits, squirrels, and turkeys with little difficulty, so we didn't go hungry. I also managed a couple of small deer, and so we dried some jerky. Ruth was very good at foraging mushrooms, dandelion roots, acorns, walnuts, and occasionally crabapples. When she came across them, she also collected edible insects. She favored cicadas that we roasted. But since we frequently gave away our food to families traveling with children, we never had a surplus, and so we were constantly looking for food.

We were frustrated by another bridge, this time over the Potomac. The steel trusses had collapsed onto the bridge in several places. Rather than spending days looking for a detour or risking drowning while fording the river, we climbed through the jungle gym of rusted steel. Although I knew that tetanus could be contracted just as easily from bacteria in soil entering a wound, I was glad we'd had all our shots in Phoenix before climbing through that rusted steel.

One afternoon, our spirits were lifted by the sight of a herd of wild horses running in a field.

"Oh, hon, aren't they beautiful?"

"Yes, they are," I replied.

"Hon, do you think we could get them to come over to us?"

"I don't think they're tame, babe. The only reason they didn't end up as a steak dinner is that a few of them were smart enough to be leery of humans."

"Well, I'm glad they were. We need more beauty in the world."

"Yes, we do. And we're going to need horses in the future, too, if we're ever to become an agrarian society; there'll be a lot of work to do."

One night sitting around the campfire, Ruth asked, "Hon, isn't part of the reason for going on this trek to assess the status of society out here?"

"Yeah."

"Then shouldn't you stop worrying about me and engage with the communities we're passing along the way?"

"Yes, I should. Okay, we'll stop at the next community that doesn't look dangerous, but we can't get delayed again."

Chapter 11. Evil in the Suburbs

We'd been seeing more and more desperate refugees on the road for the past two weeks. I wanted to avoid them and thought it'd be smart to hide in the suburbs again. So, we got off Route 288 to detour around the city of Richmond and headed east. As we walked past neighborhoods in various stages of neglect, I began to smell smoke. My first instinct was to turn around, but Ruth had reminded me that part of our job was to assess the status of society out here, so we walked toward the neighborhood where I could now see smoke coming from several houses. I checked the printed satellite image supplied by the Center, and the development we were headed toward had contained about sixty houses distributed on several cul-de-sacs. There was only one road in and out.

"Babe, you hang back here while I go in and look around."

"Okay, but it doesn't look dangerous."

Ruth was right. As I walked up the entrance road, I found no sentries posted. I detected another smell besides woodsmoke.

Something was being roasted over the fire. My mouth began to water. I immediately recalled the trap we'd witnessed weeks earlier. I did not want to be lured into an ambush by the aroma of food cooking. But I also noticed that every third or fourth house was being maintained. It was obvious which homes were occupied because the vegetation had been cut back and weather-related damage repaired by cannibalizing the adjacent houses. So one house would have all its windows intact, although different trim colors, and have patches of different colored shingles on its roof, and the next would be missing those items. I saw a man out in his yard with a sling blade cutting the brush back.

In what I hoped was a friendly voice, I shouted, "Hello friend, how are you this fine day?"

I could see that I'd startled him.

"I'm fine. What do you want?" he asked.

"I'm not here to cause any trouble, just looking for some information."

"You should go see Richard," he said with a worried look.

"Can you tell me where I can find him?"

"Keep walking down this road. It's the first left after the retention pond. His is the first house on the street, but he could be in any of the homes."

"Thank you."

I walked on.

I found the pond and the street. The houses all looked very similar to one another. Each was two stories with porticos or small porches. Unlike the other streets, all the houses on the street were being maintained, and there were no cars rusting in the driveways or on the street. I could see they'd built outhouses at either end of the street so the occupants in the middle houses would have the longest walk. I wondered if they drank the water from the retention pond or if they had a well; hopefully, a well. The first house on the block was the only one with a garage. It also had an enormous pile of firewood in the dooryard, along with a large wood smoker grill. It was the source of the amazing aroma I was smelling. If I wasn't mistaken, they were smoking venison. There were two picnic tables placed end to end and several chairs in the yard. I walked halfway up the drive. The garage door was up, and I could make out two deer hanging in the garage. Past the deer, I could see a very organized tool bench with various tools and impressive bows hanging on the wall. Whoever occupied this house prided themselves on being a hunter. I also spotted two bicycles leaning against the house and a large pull cart with fat, inflated tires. All looked to be in working order.

I had no desire to startle anyone by knocking on the door, so I shouted, "Hello, in the house!"

A woman came out of the house into the garage. She was in her late thirties, possibly even early forties. Her hair was chopped off very short, graying, and thinning. She was slim but not underweight. Her complexion was pale, maybe even a little yellow, probably from a lack of vitamins. She wore an apron on top of a faded housedress and had a wooden spoon in her hand. She looked very nervous upon seeing me.

She walked to the front of the garage but did not step outside. "Can I help you?" she asked.

"Hi, my name's George Reynolds. I was hoping to get some information."

"What kind of information?"

"My wife and I were walking past and couldn't help but smell the wonderful aroma."

Her expression immediately changed from nervousness to irritation.

"Don't get me wrong, we aren't looking for a handout. We're actually looking for a better place to live for our little community, and I just wanted information about this neighborhood. What kind of weather you're experiencing, if you're able to farm and, most importantly, if there are any other areas around here that aren't currently occupied that a few families could move into?"

She went back to being nervous. "You'll have to speak to my husband, Richard."

"Is he here now? Can I talk to him?"

"Another woman then came out of the house into the garage. She was in her late twenties, wearing a pink robe, and was very pregnant. She also looked pale and a bit yellow. "What do you want?"

The woman in the apron turned slightly and said, "I'm taking care of it, Nora."

"Then send him away."

"I'm sorry I didn't mean to disturb you," I said. "Perhaps I can talk to Richard?"

"He's not here!" Nora yelled in an angry tone. "Go away!"

"Come back later, if you like," the woman in the apron said, "but you really must talk to Richard."

Just then, I heard a laugh coming from behind me that could've only come from Ruth. She was walking up the road with an older man and a teenager. They walked up the drive. The man was my age, clean-shaven—not even stubble, had a horseshoe hairline, bald on top and hair on the sides, had striking blue eyes, and appeared very fit. He looked familiar to me somehow. Not that I'd met him before, but he looked like someone I'd seen before, maybe on TV when I was a kid, and there was still TV. He was wearing an oilskin jacket that, in the old world, would've been very expensive. It had a fleece lining, a leather top collar, multiple pockets, an adjustable drawstring waist, and snap-open back vents. The boy with him was in his mid-teens and wearing ripped jeans and a sweatshirt. Both were carrying expensive-looking bows; the boy also carried two turkeys.

"Hi George, this is Richard Havens. Richard, this is my husband, George Reynolds."

"Pleased to make your acquaintance, George," Richard said while shaking my hand and sizing me up. "I found your wife hiding in the woods just outside our little community. You really shouldn't leave her alone; someone might steal her away from you."

I didn't like his smile, and he held the handshake for too long.

"George, Richard has invited us to stay and share their Christmas dinner tonight. Did you know it was Christmas?"

I knew Christmas was days away, but didn't correct them.

"Why don't you both come up and have some refreshments while I get cleaned up?" Richard said. "Later, I'll show you around and answer your questions. Ruth tells me you're looking for some information. Evelyn, can you get them something to drink?"

Richard and the boy walked into the garage. Nora went over to the boy and whispered something, and then returned to the house.

Evelyn stepped out of the garage and, with a forced smile, asked, "Can I get you two some water?"

Giving her my best smile, I said, "No, thanks; we've got our own."

"Okay, well, why don't you have a seat while you wait for Richard?" she said, gesturing to the picnic tables. "I've got to get back to working on Christmas dinner."

She walked back into the garage, where the boy was pluck-ing the turkeys. Richard must have gone into the house. We were left on our own.

"So, what happened?" I asked in a low voice, attempting not to show my irritation.

"Nothing happened," Ruth replied. "Richard came walking up and noticed me standing off to the side of the road, and we started talking. He seems like a very nice man."

"I heard you laughing. What was so funny?"

"I don't know. He just said something about how I looked healthy."

"And that was funny?"

"You had to be there. He's offered to feed us and let us stay the night. We should be thankful, not mistrusting."

Just then, another woman and a young girl came out of one of the houses down the street and walked over. The woman was twenty or something, homely but sturdy-looking. She also looked nervous upon seeing us or, more specifically, upon seeing Ruth. The little girl looked about seven.

"Hello, my name's Leah, and this is my daughter Chris-tine."

"Hi, I'm George, and this is my wife, Ruth."

"Nice to meet you. Does Richard know you're out here?"

"Oh, yes. He's invited us to share dinner tonight," I said.

"Good, we don't get to meet new people very often." Leah sat down opposite us at the picnic table. "Christine, why don't you go help your brother?"

"I don't want to help Sam," Christine said in a whiny voice. "I want to stay here."

Giving us a sheepish smile, Leah said, "I don't care. Go. Now."

The girl walked into the garage and said something to the boy.

"The boy in the garage is named Sam, and he's your son?" Ruth asked quizzically.

"That's Sam, but he's Nora's boy."

"Oh good, I thought you looked too young to have a teenage boy."

"Have you lived here long?" I asked.

"About five years. We used to live a few blocks that way,"—she pointed to the north—"but Richard thought these houses were better, so we moved here."

Just then, Richard came out of the house wearing a crisp navy-blue tracksuit. He looked as if he might be out for a jog.

"I see you've met Leah. Good. Leah, I was hoping you might put Ruth and George up in your spare bedroom tonight."

She put on a forced smile and said, "No problem."

"Great, I knew there wouldn't be. I'm going to show Ruth and George around the neighborhood. Why don't you go in and help Evelyn with dinner?"

"Sure, that's where I was headed." Leah got up, as did Ruth and I.

"Follow me," Richard said. "You can just leave your backpacks here, if you'd like."

"We can carry them along," I said. "Maybe we can drop them off at Leah's as we walk."

I refused to leave my backpack unattended, at least not where Richard could get to it.

"Suit yourself. The first stop is the smoker—I need to check on the venison."

"I see you have two more deer aging in your garage. And you just brought home two more turkeys. You must be a skilled hunter."

"Actually, the boy shot the turkeys. I'm teaching him how to hunt. But yes, I supply most of the meat for this community."

"Do you mean this street or all the families in the neighborhood?"

As he opened the cooker, he said, "I hunt every day and share with all the families in the neighborhood, not just this street."

"Wow, they must be very appreciative," Ruth said.

As he closed the lid on the cooker, he muttered, "You'd think so, wouldn't you?" When he turned around, he had a tight smile that appeared forced. "Well, everything looks in order here. Let's take a walk, and I'll show you Leah's house, where you can drop off your backpacks."

He gave us a guided tour as we walked. "This is Nora's house, but she's living with Evelyn and me temporarily because she isn't handling the pregnancy as well as last time. Sam's living here on his own. And this is Leah's house."

Without pausing, he entered and went inside.

"Isn't Leah going to mind if we go traipsing through her house when she's not home?" Ruth asked.

"No, I'm sure she won't mind. She and Christine have bedrooms upstairs. The spare bedroom is down this hall. I'll leave you here to freshen up. There's an outhouse down the street and a cistern out back for water. As soon as you're ready, come back to the house. Dinner's not for a couple of hours, but there'll be snacks, and you can meet the rest of the family. I can answer your questions then."

"We can't thank you enough for your hospitality, can we, George?"

"No. Thank you, Richard," I said, as I shook his hand again. "And we'll see you in a little while."

After he'd left, I looked out the window to be sure he'd gone. "Something feels off."

"What do you mean?" Ruth asked.

"The deference everyone shows Richard doesn't feel right."

"I think you're imagining things. He's just filling the leadership role, just as Chad had. I think you're just jealous because he's so charismatic."

I turned away from the window. "You think he's charismatic? I think he's creepy."

"I think jealousy is ugly. I'm going to go find the cistern out back and get cleaned up for tonight's party."

"Alright, I'll go check out the privy. And by the way, it's not Christmas for another couple of days."

* * *

On my way to the outhouse, I met a man and a woman walking down the street. They were both in their late thirties. The man, who had a ponytail and a full beard, was dressed in jeans and a jeans jacket; faded and mended but clean. He was wearing

193

glasses with one lens cracked. The woman had brownish hair, cut very short, and was wearing a long wool coat. You might describe her as handsome but not pretty. They were both carrying covered dishes. As they approached, I could see they were both nervously scanning the area for more intruders.

"Hello. How are you two today?" I said in my friendliest voice.

"We're fine. Can we help you?"

"My name's George Reynolds. My wife and I are staying the night at Leah's. I was on my way to the outhouse."

The man gave me a quizzical look and asked, "Does Richard know you're staying with Leah?"

"Yes, he's invited us to share dinner at his place."

They both sighed and released the tension from their shoulders.

"Oh, okay," the man said as he offered me his hand. "We're Fred and Joyce. We live in the house at the end of the street."

"Well, I must say the homes are all very well maintained here."

"Thanks. Maintenance is our job," Fred said.

Joyce smiled and added, "We're the 'handyman' and 'handywoman.' We do all the carpentry, the plumbing; you name it."

"From all appearances, you do great work."

"You should've seen it when we moved in," Joyce said.

"How long ago was that?" I asked.

She looked at Fred and said, "It was about five years ago, wasn't it, when Richard moved us all here?"

He nodded and said, "Yeah, I think so."

"Oh, you all moved here together?" I asked.

"Yeah, Richard thought the layout of the houses was better,

and the pond."

"It was fortunate you found them all unoccupied," I said.

They glanced at each other nervously, and Fred said, "We've got to get these dishes over to Evelyn. We'll see you later at dinner."

I did my business in the outhouse and returned to find Ruth getting dressed in her cleanest and nicest clothes.

"Don't you look nice," I said.

"Thanks. It wouldn't hurt you to get cleaned up too."

"I was planning on washing up."

"You should put on some clean clothes too, at least a clean shirt."

"Or maybe a fancy tracksuit?" I muttered.

"What?"

"Nothing."

I went out back, found a bucket and a wash towel, and cleaned up. When I went back inside, I found Ruth in the spare room brushing Christine's hair. The girl had been sent to get us.

"Hello girls, are we having fun?" I asked.

"Christine here was just telling me she's going to have a little sister or brother soon. That her mommy's pregnant."

"Won't that be fun for you?" I said. "Is your mommy happy to be having a baby?"

"O'course. She says, it'll secur our future."

"Do you mean secure your future?" I asked.

"That's what I said," Christine said.

"Do you want a little brother or a little sister?"

"I want a little sister," Christine said.

"Are you looking forward to Christmas dinner tonight?" I asked.

"Yes, we're going to have my favorites."

"Like what?" I asked.

"Carrots," she said.

"You like carrots?"

"Yes, and beets."

"Whose garden do they come from?" I asked.

"Madelyn's garden."

"Who is Madelyn?" I asked.

"She's Julie's mom."

"Oh, we haven't met Julie yet," I said.

"Julie's my bestest friend," Christine said. "She lives in the next house. Her parents live in the nextest house. That's where they have the garden."

"So, Julie lives all alone?"

"Father stays there sometimes when he's not here," Christine said.

Ruth and I exchanged glances.

"Com'on, we hafta go," Christine said. "You don't wanna make Father wait."

"Okay, you go ahead. We'll be right behind you. I just have to put on a clean shirt."

"Okay."

When we were alone, I said, "I knew something was off."

"So what? He's a bigamist. Maybe the old rules shouldn't apply now. If he can take care of all these women and their children, who are we to judge?"

I put on a clean shirt and clean pants, and we walked over to dinner. On the way to Richard's house, we met Madelyn and her husband, Scott. I was surprised to see they were in their thirties. They must've had their daughter Julie, whom we still hadn't met, very early in life.

After introductions, I said, "We understand you garden and grew some of the food we'll be eating tonight."

"Yes, but Madelyn takes most of the credit," Scott replied. "I just do what I'm told."

"Don't we all?" I said. And we all laughed.

"So did you move here with Richard and Evelyn and the others?" I asked.

"Yes, we all moved at the same time. Richard made an excellent choice. The pond makes gardening so much easier. And Joyce comes up with ingenious ways to pump the water."

"And you supply what you grow while Richard goes off and hunts?" I asked.

"Yes, we all have our individual jobs. We have the garden, Joyce and Fred are fantastic at repairing and building things. Evelyn has knowledge of what plants are edible or medicinal. But Richard does much more than hunt. He also protects us."

"And your daughter, Julie, is married to Richard?" I asked, despite the stern look from Ruth.

"Yes, she was so lucky that he chose her. So were we. He's taken good care of us."

"Madelyn, what do you grow in your garden?" Ruth asked, obviously, to change the subject.

I stopped paying attention because I was trying to add it all up in my head; *Richard was married to Evelyn, Nora, Leah, and Julie.*

* * *

When we arrived at Richard's house, everyone was busy with preparations: setting the table or bringing food out. We were to eat outside on the picnic tables. It was a beautiful night, unusually warm for December. The men were all standing around the cooker while Richard was removing the venison. I went over to the men while Ruth went inside to help Evelyn. I'd already met everyone and so felt comfortable joining in the conversation about how good the venison smelled. At one point, a pretty young girl caught my attention as she was setting the table. She must have been fifteen or sixteen, had very long brown hair, and was dressed in a long cotton print dress. She was showing Christine how to set the table. When she looked our way, she had a troubled look on her face. At some point, the men moved off to take up various tasks or to just sit and watch the women work, and I was left alone with Richard. He moved closer to me, invading my personal space, and suddenly I was looking up at him. He was standing on a small rise in front of the cooker. It was as if he wanted to tower over me.

"So George, when did you take Ruth as your wife?"

"We were married six or seven years ago."

"She's very attractive."

"Yes, she is."

"Do you have any other wives?"

"No, my first wife was killed."

"I'm sorry to hear that. Any children?"

"Yes, a son. I had twin girls with my first wife, but they were killed at the same time as their mother."

"Well, Ruth is certainly young enough to supply you with more children."

"Yes, but we decided not to have any more"

"Really? She's healthy, isn't she?"

"Yes, she's fine. We're both healthy."

"Have you thought about taking more wives?"

"No, I think I'm satisfied with the one."

"I bet you are."

If this conversation went any further, I'd lose my temper and put both Ruth and me in jeopardy. I had to change the subject. "Richard, can you answer a few questions now?"

Just then, Ruth came up to tell us the other dishes were on the table. As we walked to the picnic table with Richard carrying a large platter of venison, I noticed a chair had been placed at the head of the table. Richard set the platter down in front of the chair and motioned for Ruth to sit next to him. The pretty young girl I'd seen earlier was seated opposite Ruth. She didn't look happy. There was no room next to Ruth, so I found a seat next to Sam at the other end of the second table. I couldn't understand why Ruth took the seat knowing that I was going to have to sit somewhere else. No matter how hard I strained, I could only hear snippets of what was being said at the head of the other table, but it sounded as if Richard and Ruth were discussing my hunting abilities. I also heard her laugh a few times. I was surprised to learn from talking to Sam that the pretty young girl was Julie, Richard's fourth wife.

Dinner was excellent. The venison was smoked perfectly. And the side dishes of carrots, beets, and potatoes were delicious. After dinner, Evelyn showed Ruth and me around their home. It was like a museum with very expensive-looking antiques. When we asked about them, she whispered that Richard was very good at scavenging. She pointed out the muzzleloaders and black powder rifles hanging on the wall. She explained that Richard could no longer find all the ingredients he needed to make gunpowder, but always preferred bow hunting, anyway. At one point, she removed a framed picture from a chest of drawers. It was of her two sons, Joss and Sterling, taken just before the blackout. They were two or three years old in the picture, so they would be almost thirty now. In a whispered voice, she told us how she'd lost them. Joss had been killed while hunting with his father five years earlier. A few months later, Sterling had run away. She made us promise not to say anything about either of them in front of Richard; he'd get very upset.

* * *

When we returned to the party, we found Richard holding court. I noticed Julie was absent and assumed she was inside washing dishes. Nora, whose face was apparently always scrunched up into a scowl, had taken her place next to her husband. Richard asked Scott and Madelyn to move to allow his guests to sit down next to him.

"So what'd you think of the house?" he asked.

"It's beautifully decorated," Ruth said. "You have some amazing things."

"Yes, very impressive, especially the antique muzzleloaders," I said.

"Do you shoot, George?" he asked.

"I used to, when we had ammunition."

"Ruth tells me you sometimes have trouble finding game for dinner. Why don't we go out hunting tomorrow, and I'll give you some pointers? I can also answer the questions you have about the area."

I glanced at Ruth, who avoided my look. "I'm not sure we have the time. We've been delayed recently and want to get back home as soon as possible."

"George, I think we have time for one extra day," Ruth said, without looking at me. "I'd like more time to visit with everyone before we leave."

"It's settled then," Richard said. "We'll leave at 6:10, an hour before daybreak. I'll bring the food. George, do you need an alarm clock to wake you up?"

"No, I have a pocket watch, thanks."

The rest of the evening was uneventful. Richard added extra logs to the cooker to supply light. Evelyn offered persimmons and assorted nuts for dessert. Eventually, we said our goodnights and walked with Leah and Christine back to their house.

* * *

When we were alone in our room, I turned to Ruth and whispered, "What the hell?"

"Hon, I never said you had trouble hunting. He asked, and

I told him what we were eating on the trail."

"Why didn't you back me up about leaving tomorrow?"

"Because you were right. Something is definitely off about this place."

"Well, that's something. What do you think is wrong?"

"I don't think Julie is happy with the marriage arrangements. I think her parents forced her to be with Richard, and I think it's been going on for years."

"Ick. That's gross, but not our problem."

"George, we can't just leave her to spend the rest of her life in his harem. There's no one in the community who's going to stand up against him."

"Oh, now it's a harem."

"George."

"What do you propose to do?"

"Well, I need time to get close to her and find out how she really feels about all this."

"Okay, I just hope I don't have a hunting accident tomorrow like Joss."

"What are you implying?"

"I wouldn't put it past Richard to pull a 'Vincent' and kill his own son for 'messing in his business.' Richard is obviously thinking of making you his next 'harem girl,' and I'm the only one standing in his way."

"George, don't be so dramatic. I can handle Richard."

She didn't see how dangerous Richard was. I hoped we weren't making a mistake staying another day. I couldn't sleep, so I wrote up my notes.

* * *

Journal entry: 22 December, Suburb off U.S. 60 west of North Chesterfield, VA.

Arrived here today to find 20 or so families living in this housing development. A single individual named Richard Havens is the recognized leader. People seem to welcome his leadership, but he seems more like a cult leader to me than a chief. From what I gather, he maintains a hold over these people by supplying food derived from his hunting abilities and protecting them against raiders. He has taken several wives (as tribute?). The people in the community are nevertheless well fed, maintain their houses, have a potable water well, and are properly disposing of waste; farming is limited, however, to small gardens. Richard may be violent, so we need to be cautious. I hope to learn more about the environmental conditions of the area tomorrow.

Walking south for the past two weeks, we've seen refugees traveling in various directions, not just south. Although this may be my own preconceptions, they may have realized they've reached the best climate zone, i.e., farther south would be too hot during the summer, farther north too cold during the winter.

* * *

I got up at the scheduled time, got dressed and grabbed my bow and quiver. As I was leaving, Ruth wished me a safe hunting trip. I met Richard in front of his house and was disappointed to learn Sam wouldn't be accompanying us. I'd wanted a witness.

As we walked out of the development, Richard said, "George, there's a large, wooded area about a mile from here. I've got a stand just above a pile of apples I set out last week. We should see a buck in no time."

I thought to myself, *that's how he's such a great hunter. He baits.*

"George, where are you and Ruth from?"

"We're from a ways up north. We're looking for a place to resettle our small community. Do you think there are any empty neighborhoods around here that we might settle? The weather here looks better than where we're from?"

"How long have you and Ruth been on the road?" he asked.

"A couple of months."

"That explains it, then," he said.

"Explains what?" I asked.

"There seems to be some friction between the two of you."

"Everything between us is fine," I said.

"Okay, if you say so," he replied. "She told me you two are visiting the Wilmington area next."

"Did she? I'm not sure where we're headed. It depends on what we find along the way. Maybe this area would suit us, and we could return home tomorrow."

"Oh, she sounded pretty confident you two were walking all the way to Florida."

It took a lot of effort for me not to reveal my emotions at that point.

"We were always headed south to get out of the freezing weather, and Florida seemed to be the obvious destination at first, but I doubt we'll have to go that far to find a place to move our community. Shouldn't we hurry and position ourselves in your stand before sunup?"

"Yes, we should." And we picked up our pace.

* * *

We sat in the stand for less than an hour before a buck with a ten-point rack showed up to feed on the rotting apples. Richard nudged me as if to suggest I should shoot it, but before I was set, he shot and killed the deer. As we were climbing down the ladder, Richard stepped on my hand. I was sure he did it on purpose. It was very painful, and I could have fallen and broken a leg or worse.

"Damn, that hurt," I said as I rubbed my fingers once we were on the ground.

"Sorry. I'm used to Sam practically jumping out of the stand to get to the kill."

I just shook my head and started walking over to the bait site, which was about thirty meters from the stand tree. When I was nearly there, I heard an arrow whiz by my head. I dropped to the ground.

"What the fuck, Richard?"

"There was another buck. You spooked him."

"I didn't see him."

"You aren't very observant then, are you, George?"

Getting up from the ground, I said, "Sorry, I spooked the damn deer but you could've killed me."

Laughter bubbled up from his throat. "If I wanted you dead, you'd be dead. You know, I saw your expression when I mentioned the apples. I don't have to depend on baiting. I'm the best hunter you'll ever meet. But you have no idea what a burden it is to keep these people fed and safe. They'd all be dead if it weren't for me."

"They seem very dependent on you."

"You would be too if you lived here. No offense, but you're not worthy of a woman like Ruth."

"What! What gives you the right to say something like that?"

"You can't even spot a deer when it's ten feet in front of you. What are you really doing out here traipsing around the countryside?"

"That's none of your business."

"We'll see about that. Now, let's gut this deer and get back."

I watched as he expertly field-dressed the deer. Even though he'd stepped on my hand, he asked me to carry out the buck, complaining of a sore shoulder. When we reached the road, we found Sam there waiting for us with the pull cart. Richard had been so confident he'd be successful he'd told Sam to meet us.

"Hello, Father, I'm here as you asked."

"That's good, Sam. Now help George here put the deer in the cart."

When we got back to the house, everyone came out and made a fuss about the buck. I looked for Ruth to give her a piece of my mind about what she'd shared with Richard. She was nowhere to be found. So I went back to Leah's house and cleaned up. As I was washing my blood-soaked clothes in the retention pond, Ruth came up and knelt beside me.

Before she could say a word, I exploded and practically screamed, "What were you thinking telling Richard where we were headed? What else did you tell him?"

"I didn't tell him exactly where we were headed, just the general direction and nothing else. And that was before."

"Before what?" I asked.

"Before I realized you were right. I'm sorry. I thought he was a nice, fatherly type."

"You and your daddy complex."

"What's that supposed to mean?"

We both needed to cool off so we could think clearly.

"Nothing, I'm sorry. And you're sure you said nothing about Phoenix?"

"Of course not."

"Okay, so what did you learn today?"

"He started molesting Julie, as his 'wife'"—she put air quotes around it with her fingers—"six years ago when she was only ten. She says he brings her to bed with him and Nora because Nora doesn't like sex anymore. Everyone is terrified of him. She thinks he killed Joss because he was upset about what Richard was doing to her. Joss was also in love with Leah. Christine may be Joss's child."

"Have you considered Julie might be making it all up because she's not first wife?"

"Leah confirmed she and Joss had a thing but wouldn't say any more. She's scared. And something else I found out today. These houses weren't empty when Richard moved them in.

Three families lived here right up until Richard and everyone moved in. No one knows why they gave the houses up."

"Okay, that's all very tragic, but what can we do about it?" I asked.

"We can get her out of here," she said.

"What?"

"You heard me, George. We take her with us when we leave."

"And you think Richard's going to just let us walk out of here with her."

"No, we'll need to escape under the cover of darkness tonight."

I just sighed and shook my head.

"What? I've got a plan."

I couldn't help but think, *what is she getting us into this time?*

Chapter 12. Putting Old Friends in Jeopardy

We escaped that night. Providence was on our side in that Richard wasn't scheduled to sleep at Julie's house that night. He made a habit of sleeping with his different wives on different nights—tonight he was home with Evelyn. Ruth and I packed up and left without waking Leah or Christine. We hoped that while our departure would be detected early when Leah and Christine missed us at breakfast, Julie's escape might not be detected until late morning. Julie was waiting for us outside. We cut across the backyards of the houses on the next street to avoid walking past Richard and Evelyn's house. The plan was to take U.S. 60 due east to Route 150 and then south on I-95.

By midmorning it began to snow, light at first, but then it became large, heavy, wet snow. As long as it continued to snow, our tracks would be filled in, but once it stopped, it would be easy to track us. So, we pushed on, hoping to get as far away as possible before it stopped snowing. Walking became difficult as the depth of the snow increased beyond thirty centimeters. We did not stop for lunch, but by midafternoon we could go no farther without snowshoes.

We found a deserted house just off the interstate that still had windows and a roof. Only wood and metal frames remained of the furniture, and debris covered the floor, but we cleared space and laid our sleeping bags out. Ruth and Julie were together in one bedroom. Not surprisingly, Julie was scared and didn't want to be alone, but was also mistrustful of men, so I was in another bedroom.

Julie had been tasked with bringing food from her house for the trip. She didn't have much as most meals were communal at Richard and Evelyn's, but she managed to bring some leftover venison jerky and a jar of honey. We didn't make a fire. It wasn't especially cold; only wet and snowy. After an unsatisfying dinner, Ruth and Julie went to sleep as they were exhausted from the escape. I'd take the first watch. Although I wasn't planning on waking Ruth for her watch, I couldn't stay awake any longer and so woke her about three o'clock. We agreed we wouldn't wake Julie. Ruth wanted to let Julie sleep as much as possible as she wasn't used to walking so far; I just didn't trust her.

The next morning, the snow was almost a meter deep, but the sky had cleared, and it was warming up fast. I didn't know how long it'd take for enough snow to melt to allow us to continue. Until it did, we were trapped. I was worried that if it had started snowing before he left to follow us, Richard might have taken snowshoes. If he did, he could be gaining on us now. Since there was nothing I could do except worry, I went back to sleep in the bedroom, leaving Ruth and Julie to talk.

I woke midmorning to raised voices. Julie and Ruth were in the living room of the deserted house staring outside. Julie was in a near state of panic.

"He's gonna catch us!" Julie said. "I know he is. I ain't going back!"

Ruth put her arm around Julie. "Don't worry, we won't let him take you."

"How can there be so much snow?" Julie asked.

"The warmer air can hold more moisture," I said as I entered the room. "Good morning."

"George, I think Julie's question was rhetorical."

"Is there anything to eat?" I asked.

Ruth got up and moved toward me. "Not unless you have something stashed away. Can I talk to you in the other room?"

We walked back into the room that I had just come out of.

"George, I don't think you appreciate how close she is to becoming hysterical. I've never seen such terror in a person's eyes before. We can't let him catch us and take her back."

"I understand that. How much of the snow has melted?" I asked.

"Some. Do you think we can walk through it yet?" Ruth asked.

"Let's pack up and give it a try."

We went back out to Julie and told her we were leaving and then packed up.

"Understand that as soon as we step outside, we're going to leave tracks, so let's try to walk in single file and step in the person's footprint in front of you. It should also make walking easier."

"Why don't we set a trap and ambush him?" Ruth asked.

"That's a great plan," Julie said. "Let's do that, then I'd be rid of him for good."

"First, we don't know if he's even following us," I said. "And more importantly, I don't think we're the kind of people who can kill in cold blood."

Ruth just shook her head. Julie slammed her fists down on her legs, but neither said anything. Walking through the snow was nearly impossible, especially for me since I was in the lead, but I took one step and then another. Fortunately, as we traveled south, less and less snow had fallen. In time, we walked out of the snow. We had no food, so we didn't stop for lunch but took a few breaks. When we came upon a power line corridor crossing I-95 through some woods, we got off the highway and found a house to camp in. We had to have food, so while Ruth built a fire, I went and shot four rabbits. Julie cleaned them. I was amazed to see that she, like Ruth, could do it without getting covered in gore. I took the time to write up my notes.

Journal entry: 24 December, Carson, VA off I-95

Addendum to 22 December entry. As suggested in my previous entry, I believe that Richard Havens was more of a cult leader than a chieftain. In talking to him, he gave the impression that people owed him everything and anything for feeding and protecting them. I also believe he had become infatuated with Ruth, which led him to make an attempt on my life. Accordingly, we left in the middle of the night last night. Ruth, concerned with the well-being of Richard's youngest wife, Julie (he claimed her as his fourth wife when she was only 10 years old), insisted we bring her along with us to Wilmington, NC. Ruth and I have agreed not to talk about our mission or Phoenix in front of the girl, and hope to leave her with the first community we stop at that has the resources and people to care for her.

Just after leaving, we encountered what must have been a near-record snowfall near Richmond; the snowpack for this single 12-14 hr storm is estimated to be over a meter. It was likely a result of an atmospheric river coming in from the Atlantic. The snowpack slowed our progress considerably, but thus far, there has been no sign of pursuit by Richard Havens.

On a personal note, it's Christmas eve and all I can think about is how alone and miserable Dan must be back home without his parents.

* * *

Although Julie tried to keep up, she slowed us down because she was unaccustomed to walking so far, day after day. I know she wanted to get as far away from Richard as she could, as fast as possible. With every mile, she talked more and more about things other than him. I couldn't be sure, but I suspected she was feeling more at ease because she assumed Richard wouldn't follow us this far. I, on the other hand, didn't think Richard would let her go so easily.

It took us almost two weeks, looking over our shoulders every step of the way, but when we finally reached Wilmington, we took U.S. 74 to Wrightsville Beach. I planned on staying at the motel next to the pier that my dad and I had stayed at when we visited ten years earlier. As we approached the bridge over the Intercoastal Waterway, we began seeing boats lying on their keels that had been tossed up onto the road.

"I know we're getting close," Ruth said. "Besides all the boats, I can smell the ocean and can hear the seagulls."

"I ain't never seen the ocean," Julie said.

"Then you're in for a real treat," Ruth replied. "It goes on as far as the eye can see."

Once we crossed the bridge and reached the fork in the road, we could see that the roads out to the beach were flooded.

"George, why's this area so flood-prone compared to Asbury Park?" Ruth asked.

"Differences in land elevation, slope, and topography."

"It doesn't seem too deep, maybe a foot or two," Julie said. "Can't we just walk through the water? I can't see the ocean from here."

"I won't stop you, but with all that debris scattered about, both above and below the water, it might be dangerous."

"That's not fair. We came all this way, and I can't even see it," Julie said.

"Maybe it's high tide, and later, when it's low tide, we can make it out to the beach," Ruth suggested.

To placate Julie, I said, "That's possible," even though I didn't think the tidal range was that large. I'd have to take my measurements at the foot of the Wrightsville Beach Bridge. But first, I needed Ruth to distract Julie and keep her busy somewhere else so she wouldn't ask a lot of questions about what I was doing or where I had gotten all the scientific instruments. So we walked back to the bridge. Ruth must've anticipated my needs.

"Hon, Julie, and I are going to scavenge in the stores we passed earlier. She needs to replace the clothes she couldn't bring with her."

"Okay, but stay away from the marina. That boat sitting up on the roof over there doesn't look very stable and could come crashing down at any time."

It took me only thirty minutes to collect and record the measurements and another ten to finish my notes.

* * *

Journal entry: 4 January, Wilmington, NC – West side of Wrightsville Beach Bridge over ICW

Arrived today to find portions of West Salisbury Street and Cause- way Drive *to Wrightsville Beach flooded. Took meteorological and water quality measurements at the foot of the bridge; data and distance to water's edge collected at 1500 hrs this date and tabulated on the previous page. Unable to reach survey monuments placed at Silver Gull Motel, so distance to water's edge measurement is from NE corner of Waterway Lodge to ICW. Seawater is only 0.6 m away from overtopping the western abutment of the bridge. Uncertain as to the tidal cycle stage— someone will need to check the models. Not surprisingly, storm damage is extensive, especially within the inundated sections of the island.*

I hope to find a community in Wilmington that will accept Julie Havens, who has been traveling with us (see previous entry).

* * *

Just as I was finishing my notes, Ruth and Julie came running up, out of breath.

"Someone's coming," Ruth exclaimed.

"Is it Richard?" I asked.

"No. It's three young men."

"What's the matter?" Julie asked. "Are they dangerous?"

I scanned up the street to see if anyone was approaching. "We treat all strangers with caution, particularly young men. Let's hide and watch to see what they do."

The three of us ran over to the deserted hotel as the marina looked too dangerous. We went up to the second floor to give us a better vantage point.

Three young men came running down the street from the direction of the city center, all carrying weapons. The one in the lead looked to be the oldest, at twenty or so. He was carrying a crossbow. The others carried a machete and an old rusty sword.

"We know you're here someplace!" the boy with the crossbow yelled. "We found the pile of clothes you dropped on the road."

I glared at Ruth and shook my head slightly. She shrugged.

"We would have seen you if you crossed the bridge, so unless you jumped in the water for a swim or learned to fly, you're hiding in one of these buildings! If you come out now, we won't hurt you."

I whispered, "You two stay here and stay down. I'll go out and talk to them." Handing my bow and quiver to Julie, I added, "Both of you be ready to shoot if they attack me."

Ruth began assembling her takedown bow as I walked, hunched over, to the door and went downstairs.

"How are you guys doing today?" I asked in a friendly voice as I exited the building.

"We're surviving. How 'bout you?" Crossbow Boy asked.

His two companions were smiling in a not-so-friendly manner.

"I'm good," I said. "You three gave me a start, so I dropped what I'd scavenged. You can never be too cautious."

"Where's your friend?" Crossbow Boy asked. "We saw two of you running."

"He's around?"

"So, those ladies' clothes were yours?" Crossbow boy asked.

"Yes. My wife's camped a couple of kilometers west of here. My buddy and I were scavenging new clothes for her. Is that a problem? You three don't need them, do you?"

"A couple of kilometers, huh?" Crossbow boy asked quizzically.

"I mean a couple of miles," I said.

"Your name wouldn't be Reynolds by chance, would it?" Crossbow boy asked.

I wasn't the only one with a stunned look on my face at that

217

moment. Crossbow Boy's friends were looking at him with questioning looks as well.

"It would," I replied. "Have we met before?"

"I'm Tom. You and your dad were here years back."

He lowered his crossbow and came over and hugged me. After getting over my initial shock, I hugged back.

"This is messed up," he said. "I knew it was you the second you walked out, but I wasn't sure until you said kilometers instead of miles."

His friends lowered their weapons and glanced at each other, with less menacing smiles, and shrugged.

"Whatcha doing here? And don't gimme that fish story 'bout looking for a place to move your people. You didn't fool me the first time you told it. Was that your dad with you?" Tom asked, looking around.

"No, he was killed while we were headed home after that last trip."

"Oh, I truly am sorry. I remember his telling all those great stories."

"What about your dad?" I asked. "It's Brian, right?"

"He's gone too."

"Oh damn, how'd it happen?"

"It was a dumb accident. Remember how we got that truck working? We didn't have any brake parts, so we played it safe and didn't drive too fast. But one day he was going too fast and hit a goddamn deer."

"Oh, that's too bad. But your mom is still good?"

"Yeah. You should come back and say hey, maybe hang out." Looking at his two friends, he added, "These two clowns are Pete and Tony, by the way. You prob'ly didn't meet them when you were here before."

"Good to meet you guys," I said, shaking hands with both of them. "I guess I should signal my wife and let her know it's safe to come down. She and a friend are hiding upstairs. It was them that you saw running."

I waved to Ruth.

"I'm looking forward to meeting her," Tom said. "I remember you pining away for her the last time you were here,"

I stiffened; that's the way my body always reacted when someone mentioned April or the girls.

"That was my first wife. She and my girls were killed in a raid. This is my second wife."

"Oh, I'm sad to hear that, man," Pete said. "My mom and sister were killed in a raid too. It's fucking hard."

Ruth and Julie came out of the building, and introductions were made.

When I finished, Ruth looked at me and said, "It took you long enough to bring us down. I would've come down after you two boys hugged, but didn't want to get yelled at for not following directions."

I smirked at her and said, "Tom has invited us back so that I can say hello to his mom, whom I met last time I was here."

"Sounds great," Ruth said.

I noticed Julie was standing slightly behind Ruth and not saying much. I also noticed all three boys looking her over. We walked back west and stopped to pick up the pile of clothes Ruth and Julie had scavenged and dumped in the road. On the way to his house, Tom filled me in on all the things that had happened recently in the town. Pete and Tony both chipped in as much as possible to get Julie's attention. We walked a few kilometers northwest on U.S. 74 and then took U.S. 17. In just

219

over an hour, we came to an old, historic red brick mansion with a wide portico supported by four tall white columns. It was mostly hidden behind overgrown vegetation, including several large trees. The yard and house were surrounded by a short red brick wall.

"You live here?" I asked when we stopped. "I don't remember you living in a mansion the last time we were here."

"Nah, we've only been here a couple of years. Mom and a few families live in the big house. I live in the carriage house out back. C'mon, I'll give you the tour."

"Tom, we gotta go," Tony said. "We've seen your place and need to hunt since we didn't catch fish, or we ain't eatin' tonight."

"Sorry 'bout getting sidetracked. I'll make it up to you guys next time."

"Nice meeting you all," Pete said. He looked at Julie and asked, "Think we could come see you later?"

Before Julie could respond, Ruth said, "That'd be nice."

As they left, we turned and went through some iron gates. Tom took us inside the house where we found a large hall with marbled columns and a staircase up to a second-floor balcony. The stairs were in rough shape, where the carpet had been ripped up. There were several holes in the ceiling, but the floor was clean of debris. Obviously, someone was living here. We entered one room with an enormous fireplace that had a fire going.

"There are actually nine fireplaces in the house," Tom said.

"That should be handy this time of the year," I said.

"You're welcome to help me chop firewood later."

"No, thanks."

There were three cats lounging in different areas of the

room.

"You've got cats," Ruth said.

"You're gonna have to get used to them," Tom said. "They're all over, and they'll come after you if you're not careful; they think they own the place."

"They're lovely," Ruth said. "Look, George, that one looks like Charley."

"Hon, there are a lot of black cats in the world."

"The cats keep the mice under control," Tom said, "but they piss in the courtyard and stink it up."

We then entered what Tom described as the dining room. It was large and wood-paneled, but there was no dining table. In fact, there was no furniture anywhere except for several plastic lawn chairs that'd been in front of the fireplace. There was also no artwork on the walls. Next, we entered a solarium. Many of the glass panels were missing and replaced with wood. Evidently, water had gotten in sometime during the past, based on the damaged floor and walls. Tom then took us out to a courtyard, where two couples were sitting in plastic chairs around a fire. The fire was burning in the bowl of a cement fountain with its centerpiece missing. Surrounded by a wall of vegetation, the courtyard felt very secluded. It also seemed the fire could keep the enclosed courtyard very warm, which was good because it was a chilly January day. Tom was right; I could smell ammonia from the cats out here in the courtyard.

"Hey, everyone, let me introduce you to some folks we met at the marina. Mom, you may remember George Reynolds. He and his dad, William, visited here many years ago."

She got up from her seat and came over to me. She was in her forties, with dark hair, and was wearing what appeared to be a clean cotton or linen blouse and pants.

"You'll have to bear with me. I broke my glasses a couple of weeks ago, and I'm blind as a bat without them." She took my hand, looked closely at my face, and said, "Of course, I do. It's so wonderful to see you again, George. And who are these people with you?"

"This is my wife, Ruth, and our friend Julie."

"So wonderful to meet you both," she said as she shook Ruth's hand. I'm Helen, and this is Andrew, and these two are Ken and Mary. All three were in their thirties, skinny but not emaciated, wearing clean but worn clothes. Like Helen, they all appeared to have dry, thinning hair, pale complexions, and dark circles under their eyes, suggesting vitamin deficiencies. *I thought to myself that maybe Ruth could suggest some plants they should be looking for when they forage.* Everyone was standing at this point.

"Why don't you take your backpacks off and have a seat? We can get acquainted. Can I get you some water or tea to drink?"

"No, we're fine," I replied.

"Well, I'd like some tea," Julie said.

"Julie, here, drink some of my water," I said, not wanting her to drink anything we couldn't be certain was bacteria-free. I handed her my water bottle and glanced at Ruth for help in controlling her.

"George, we're good; we boil our water," Tom said. "You sure you don't want any tea?"

I smiled at his ability to read my thoughts and said, "That'd be great, thanks." Both Ruth and Julie smiled and nodded enthusiastically as well.

"Julie, why don't you give Tom a hand with the tea?" Ruth

said.

"Okay." She and Tom went off somewhere to get the tea.

"She's a beautiful girl," Mary said. "Where did you meet her?"

"We met her west of Richmond," Ruth said. "It's a long and sad story."

"Aren't they all nowadays?" Helen replied.

We talked for about an hour. First, recounting what happened to Brian and my dad. We learned that Helen and Andrew had been together for three years and that besides Ken and Mary, there were two other couples: Gary and Brenda, and Mike and Judith, living in the house. Gary and Brenda were off hunting, and Mike and Judith were away visiting Judith's sister, who lived on a farm twenty miles away. We'd be staying in Mike and Judith's room while they were gone. We also learned there was an unofficial town council made up of people living in Wilmington. I put a pin in that, so I'd remember to ask about it again later. At some point during the afternoon, I looked over at Ruth, and she had the black cat in her lap and was petting it. We had tea, which led to dinner.

Fortunately for us, Gary and Brenda had a successful hunt and returned with several turkeys. They'd dropped off two turkeys already with a family down the street. Tom and the two boys were supposed to have brought fish home for dinner for several families living in the area, but we'd disrupted their trip. So instead of brining the turkeys overnight, we roasted them. Even without brining, the turkeys were moist and delicious. Conversations continued to focus on what was going on in Wilmington; I was good at deflecting questions about us. At some point, Julie asked about children.

Addressing the two younger couples, Julie asked, "Do you

223

have any children?"

"We tried for a few years, but after two miscarriages, we gave up," Brenda replied.

"Oh, I'm so sorry to hear that," Ruth said.

Ken then said, "We decided a long time ago that we couldn't bring kids into this world."

"Why?" Julie asked.

I was desperate to change the subject, but before I could say anything, Ken said, "Because it wouldn't be fair to bring them into this horrible mess."

Mary then added, "And we aren't the only ones to think that way. Mike and Judith share our feelings. Right now, they're at Judith's sister's place. They have to move her and her four kids into town because her husband abandoned them when their farm failed."

"Oh, that's too bad," I said.

"Well, I'm gonna have kids," Julie announced.

I couldn't help but think *that's because you've had it easy. That psycho took care of you all your life, so you'd bear his children*, but said nothing. The conversation continued, but I wasn't listening. I could see that Ruth was upset by the discussion. Before we'd married, I'd told Ruth that I didn't want any more children, not because of the conditions in the world but because of what happened to my twin girls. She'd said that being Dan's stepmom was enough, but I didn't believe her. Although I tried to stay out of the conversation about having kids, I foolishly opened my mouth.

"Well I think conditions are improving," I said. "More and more people are working together for the common good. We've met some really good people in our travels, and just look at what you folks are doing here for your neighbors."

From his facial expression, I could see that what I had said, had upset Andrew.

"Things aren't getting better; they're getting worse, and all this could have been avoided! We're living day-to-day here. A problem that would've been insignificant before could cause disaster for us. So don't you come in here and tell me things are improving."

He stormed off.

"George, you must excuse Andrew," Helen said. "His parents were professors here at the university, as were the parents of both Ken and Brenda. They all worked tirelessly to warn people about climate change and how we could take steps to avoid it or at least slow it down, so it'd be more manageable. But they were persecuted by the government."

"His father was put in jail for several years when he wrote a paper outlining the potential negative effects of geoengineering," Ken added.

"That's horrible," I said.

"You can appreciate how that affected a ten-year-old boy," Helen said. "And later, having to watch his father, consumed by despair as everything he'd warned about came to pass, commit suicide."

I thought about my granddad, who went through the same depression after he warned people, and they didn't listen.

Everyone remained quiet for a long time after that. Then we all said our goodnights and went to bed. I ended up sleeping on the floor of Tom's apartment while Julie and Ruth took the empty bedroom. Apparently, Julie was still worried about Richard. I wasn't happy about having to sleep on the floor when there was a bed available.

225

* * *

Breakfast the next morning was my favorite—scrambled eggs. I didn't ask what kind of eggs they were, but told myself they'd probably come from a bird. After breakfast, I volunteered to go for drinking water. I thought it was only fitting given how much of Helen's Yaupon tea I'd drunk.

"I'll show you where to get the water," Tom said.

"I don't think that's necessary. I saw a creek on the way here."

"We've been warned not to take water from Burnt Mill Creek," Tom said. "It's surrounded by several cemeteries and is thought to be contaminated with arsenic and formaldehyde from decomposed caskets. Instead, we go west to Cape Fear, but only during low tide. I'll go and show you the way."

"Can I tag along?" Julie asked.

"You bet," Tom said. "You can help tote the containers"

So we left the house and walked west toward the river. As we walked, Tom pointed out the few houses that were occupied. I noticed that neither he nor anyone else last night had used the terms 'squatting or squatters.'

When we reached the river, I was surprised to find it was so swollen, given its distance from the ocean. Most buildings lining the waterfront were now inundated. Having arrived from the north on I-40, we'd crossed a small branch of the river.

So I asked, "Tom, when we leave to head south, will we be able to cross the river on the U.S. 17 bridge?"

"The bridge is dry, but once you get across the island, the area to the west is flooded. I think your best bet is to go north, the way we're going now, and cross using the bridge on I-140. The road to the west is elevated. Then you can go south and pick up U.S. 17."

"Thanks!"

We walked along the flooded river north for a good kilometer before filling several containers, not from the main stem of the river but from a small creek draining a wetland.

"So, you only collect during ebb tide or slack low tide when the water is less affected by the tidal inflow, correct?" I asked.

"Exactly, so we could collect again tomorrow about this time or a little later, depending on how much we use today. We don't allow water to sit around for very long."

* * *

When we returned to the house, we found the women had gone out to forage in a woodland a couple of kilometers to the north. They avoided the cemeteries even when foraging for plants and small game because of the concern about possible contamination. Apparently, there'd been a lot of stillbirths and deformed babies born years earlier, and the locals believed it was due to the contamination of crops someone had tried to farm near the cemetery. I thought it could also have been because of poor nutrition, especially vitamin deficiency. Now they were attempting to farm in some former sports fields south of the house, but according to Tom, they weren't having much success. He said I'd have to talk to Andrew to learn more about the problems they were having.

We tasked Julie with boiling the water we'd collected while Tom and I went to the garage under his apartment to butcher a deer that had been aged for a week. We skinned it and cut the meat into various portions for storage and cooking, being careful to trim and save as much fat and sinew as possible. I then helped him build a fire to dry some of the venison for jerky. He was being extra careful in building the fire and hanging the jerky. I think he was showing off for Julie. He offered to give us some before we left. The women returned with baskets full of chickweed, dandelion roots, nettles, and oyster mushrooms. After we all shared a late lunch of leftover turkey and sliced venison backstrap, I helped Tom hand-cut some wood to replace missing panes of glass in the solarium while Julie took over tending the drying jerky. It was nice to see her pitch in to help. It was noticed by everyone, but especially by Tom. I was becoming hopeful that we'd found her a new home.

Later, I found Andrew.

"Listen, Andrew, I'm sorry if I appeared naïve or if I knew what you guys are going through," I said. "Trust me, I know how bad things are."

"No, George. I should be the one to apologize. I have a short temper."

"Helen shared a little of what your parents tried to do and what happened afterwards."

"It was hard on all of us," he said.

228

"Well, I can tell you that there are people out there, following in your parents' footsteps, attempting to make things better."

The discussion then turned to the difficulties they'd been having farming. Not surprisingly, they were mostly weather-related problems. I explained how agroforestry could be an improvement over conventional row cropping under the new climate. But then he surprised me when he speculated that some of their difficulties stemmed from a lack of insects to pollinate the crops.

As the afternoon waned, Pete and Tony showed up with a mess of fish. They'd returned to the marina and fished all day. I think they were desperate for a reason to come back and see Julie. They fried them all up while trying to keep Julie in conversation. We had another sumptuous meal.

After dinner, we were sitting around the fire in the courtyard when Tom surprised me when he asked, "George, can you explain how everything got all messed up?"

He must've read my surprised expression when he went on and said, "I've tried to repeat the stories your dad told when he was here, but I must not be explaining it right because Pete and Tony can't understand what happened."

"It's not really the best story to tell around an evening campfire," I said. I was also worried about how Andrew would take it, coming from me.

"I'd like to hear it, too," Andrew said. "After my father came back home, we stopped listening to the news."

"Well, don't say I didn't warn you," I said. "My dad was a kind of historian, collecting stories as we traveled. But I guess I should start where he always started—he'd try to explain that at first people refused to believe climate was changing

229

or, if they did, just seemed to accept the gradual change, but then it suddenly became so much worse."

"But George, what caused the climate to change?" Julie asked.

"Oh, sorry, I guess I should back up—that part is kind of important. Right, first you should understand that all animals, humans included, change their environment unintentionally just by living in it. Humans began unintentionally changing the climate over three hundred years ago when they burned coal to heat water to power steam engines, marking the beginning of the Industrial Revolution. Later, coal was replaced by other so-called fossil fuels. They're called fossil fuels because they resulted from wood or other organic material, which are any substances—chemicals—that include the elements of carbon and hydrogen, that fall to the ground and are slowly buried by accumulating sediment, and remain underground for millions of years. Unfortunately, when any organic material is burned, it changes into a simpler chemical called carbon dioxide, also known as CO_2, for carbon and two oxygens. You're doing this yourself right now as you digest the food we ate for dinner—you're not burning it, but more or less doing the same thing by oxidizing it, and then you exhale CO_2. Over the years, the CO_2 we emitted, from burning fossil fuels in particular, accumulated in the atmosphere—not a lot, but enough to change the climate. See, when sunlight comes in, it passes through CO_2 gas in the atmosphere and warms the planet. Much of that heat is given off or remitted by the earth back out toward space as another kind of light that we can't see. However, the CO_2 in the atmosphere can stop that type of light and reflect some of it back to the Earth, which warms the planet. A little is good, but too much trapped heat is bad.

"Okay, I think I get it," Tom said.

I saw Pete and Tony nodding; Julie still looked confused, but I went on.

"Alright, where was I? Oh yeah, so the climate was changing rapidly due to all the CO_2 in the atmosphere. Heat waves lasted longer; storms became much more intense. This killed thousands each year, but people seemed to accept it. Then the sea level rose suddenly, flooding coastal cities, forcing people to leave everything behind and move inland. Then lots of different things went wrong all at the same time. The heat and bad weather caused food crops to fail more often. There was still plenty of food, but people got scared and angry when they started seeing empty shelves in stores. So people bought up what little food was available, even if they didn't need it, which just made things worse. Then, the federal program that offered insurance to farmers was eliminated."

I saw I had confused them, so I added, "Insurance is like betting or gambling. If you're doing something that's risky, like farming or building a house near the ocean, you pay a small amount of money to somebody, usually a company, but sometimes the federal government. If whatever you're doing doesn't fail or isn't destroyed, they get to keep the money. But if it does fail, the company agrees to pay you for the loss or damage; so, in effect, they're gambling that it won't fail. When the government stopped offering insurance, the farmers stopped planting climate-sensitive crops, which led to more empty shelves. This ultimately led to food riots. Then the commercial insurance sector collapsed due to all the financial losses from weather-related damage. Without insurance, people couldn't get loans to buy homes, and those who did often couldn't rebuild after storms. The situation was made worse still when the federal government eliminated the agency that was supposed to go in and help people in different areas of the country rebuild after weather-related disasters. All these failures led first to the collapse of the economy and then the federal government."

"Wait, so the government didn't even try to prevent the climate from changing?" Pete asked.

"Andrew can probably answer that better than I can."

Andrew looked at me and then everyone else. "I'll give it a go. Despite all the warnings from scientists that CO_2 accumulating in the atmosphere could potentially warm the planet, little was done. Even after people noticed the climate was changing, we were slow to act. I don't have time to list all the excuses they came up with for continuing to burn fossil fuels, but from what my father told me, once they could no longer deny it was happening, they tried to geoengineer their way out of the problem. As George said earlier, all animals change their environment unintentionally, but sometimes they change it on purpose. For example, people have lit fires and burned grassland and woodlands for hundreds, if not thousands, of years for a wide range of purposes, including improving the land for hunting and agriculture. To try to reduce the warming of the planet, we sprayed chemicals into the atmosphere to reflect some of the incoming sunlight back into space before it could reach and heat the surface. Although it successfully reduced temperatures in regions where it was being used, mostly in the northern hemisphere, areas where it wasn't being implemented continued to heat up. Not surprisingly, people in those other regions became very bitter, particularly since people here in the U.S. thought we had a technical fix and so made no effort to reduce CO_2 emissions. Worse, the geoengineering had several unwanted side effects. Although the government claimed they were caught off guard by the side effects, my dad had warned them. Spraying the stuff in the northern atmosphere caused severe droughts in parts of Africa and India. It also reduced the natural chemical shield in the atmosphere that protects us against a part of the sunlight that can hurt us. And then when we finally stopped spraying the chemicals, temperatures soared back to where they would've been had we not done the spraying. I think all the money they spent on the failed geoengineering upset people and contributed to the collapse of the federal government."

"So, who actually launched the EM pulses that shut everything down?" Tony asked.

"I think I need to hand it back to George to answer that one."

"From everything my dad learned, he thought it was China, but he couldn't be certain. He thought they were emboldened to launch the Blackout War because most of the world's leaders were very concerned about securing the U.S. nuclear arsenal after the federal government collapsed. They were afraid that some rogue state governor engaged in a civil war with their neighboring state might start lobbing nuclear bombs. And because of all the anti-American sentiment across the world, China would likely have been confident there wouldn't be any retaliation. You must understand that while we focus on what happened here, there were lots of other climate wars going on at the time because of cross-border migrations and water disputes."

"You were right—that was the worst bedtime story I've

233

ever heard," Brenda said. "This fills in a lot of the details and will magnify the nightmares I already have."

"I know," Helen said. "After I heard George's dad tell it, my nightmares came back but were even more ghastly."

"But we can never forget how we got into this horrible mess," Andrew said.

"Yes, but at the same time, we also shouldn't dwell on the past," Ruth added. "We've got a lot of work to accomplish to make things better."

It was quiet for a long time after that. I was tired, so I said goodnight, and so did Ruth. Before parting ways, her to the upstairs bedroom and me to Tom's apartment, she came up to me and gave me a kiss and whispered, "You were in your element tonight, weren't you, explaining how it all happened?"

"Yeah, but I also learned a few things from Andrew that I didn't know."

"Really?"

"Yes, about the geoengineering. Babe, why does Julie have to stay with you again tonight?"

"It's not going to be for much longer. I think Julie will agree to remain here."

"That would be great. Okay, I love you."

"Love you too."

The other adults also went to bed to leave Julie and the three young men sitting around the fire. How much trouble could they get into?

* * *

The following day, I was finishing my breakfast tea when Ruth came running into the courtyard and asked, "Have you seen Julie?"

"Not this morning, but I've only been out here for a few minutes."

"Maybe she's with Tom," Ruth said.

"No, I just saw him go into the house to do some repairs."

"Well, I know she came to bed last night, but when I woke up this morning, she was gone."

"I'm sure she's around here somewhere."

We started searching. I searched the grounds, and Ruth searched the house.

As I was about to try the garage, Ruth shouted out a window to me, "George, Helen says Pete came by, and he and Julie went to get some fresh water!"

"Why would she go alone with Pete?" I yelled back.

"What's the matter?" Tom asked as he came into the courtyard. "Pete knows where to collect water?"

"Come on. We need to find them, now," I said.

Tom and I retraced our walk yesterday to see if we could find Julie and Pete, but before we got two blocks, Tom's neighbor came out of his house and called over to us.

"Tom, are you looking for a missing girl?"

"How'd you know?" Tom asked.

"She was here a little while ago with a man. He was dragging her by the arm."

"What'd the man look like?" I asked.

"He was fortyish, bald, and clean-shaven."

"Was Pete with 'em?" Tom asked.

"No."

"Do you know where they went?" I asked.

235

"Yes, the man made a big show of telling me—even waving to me in the house to get me to come outside. Then, I think he hurt the girl to make her scream. When I came out of the house, he told me to tell anyone that asked that they were going to the cemetery."

Tom and I exchanged glances.

"Thanks, Mr. Miller," Tom said.

"George, what's going on?" Tom asked as we ran back for weapons. "Who's the man and what did he do with Pete?"

"It's a long story, but the man who took her is likely her husband, Richard Havens. He forced Julie to be one of his four wives when she was only ten years old. We helped her escape. He's very dangerous."

"That fucking bastard better not have hurt Pete or Julie."

When we got to the house, we told everyone what we'd learned and explained again who the man likely was.

"But how did he find us?" Ruth asked.

I shrugged my shoulders and said, "He must have spotted us getting water yesterday and followed us back to the house."

"Why's he telling you where he's headed?" Andrew asked.

"He's baiting us," I said, "just like he baits animals when hunting."

"But why?" Ruth asked.

"I think he wants to kill me and take you back with Julie."

"He's not getting either of them!" Tom said.

"Tom's right. Even if we think it's a trap, we've got to try to rescue Julie," Ruth said.

"But which cemetery?" Andrew asked. "There are several around here."

"Considering where Mr. Miller lives, I think it's Oakdale Cemetery," Tom said. "Besides, it's the closest one and the first we'll reach."

Gary said he'd go and search for Pete. I convinced Andrew to stay behind in case Richard was using this as a diversion to get us out of the house. I could not convince Tom to stay behind. He and I rushed to his apartment and retrieved our bows and quivers. We met Ruth in the dooryard on our way out. She had her backpack but didn't have her bow. I knew that meant she intended to use her gun. I didn't argue with her.

* * *

The Oakdale Cemetery was at the end of a street immediately behind some homes. It was surrounded by wrought-iron fences and brick pillars. There were massive headstones and ornamental monuments, including obelisks and cement angels seated on benches in what must have been a park-like atmosphere back in the day, with old-growth trees and shrubs. Now it was an overgrown forest. I didn't know how we'd ever find them. But then we heard muffled screams. We ran through an iron archway and, after searching for a couple of minutes, spotted Julie tied to a tree in the center of twenty or so headstones encircled by more iron fence. There were only two narrow openings in the fence, so we'd have to enter through one or the other or hop over the fence to get to her. We hid behind headstones just outside the iron fence. I got out my monocular scope and tried to find Richard's concealed location. I knew he'd likely positioned himself in front of her rather than behind, so he'd just need to scan two hundred and seventy or so degrees around the circle, focusing on the openings in the fence.

"I know you're here, George!" Richard shouted. "What are you waiting for? Go help Julie"

"Richard, why don't you just go home to your other wives and children? Julie doesn't want to be your wife. She never did."

"Did you bring Ruth, George? I want her to see how helpless you'd be at protecting her. She'd be better off with me. I can protect and provide for her."

"Richard, you're the monster she needs protection from. Did you kill your son, Joss, because you were jealous of his relationship with Leah? Or was it because he was ashamed of you for molesting a ten-year-old girl? And did your other son run away from you, or did you kill him too?"

As I was saying this, I signaled to Ruth and Tom to circle around; he'd go clockwise, she'd go counterclockwise.

"Shut up!" Richard yelled. "They never appreciated everything I did for them."

"Did you murder the people who lived in the houses you now live in?"

"I wanted the houses, and they wouldn't give them up. George, why aren't you trying to save Julie? Here, I'll make the decision easier for you."

Just then, Julie screamed through the gag in her mouth as an arrow hit her left leg.

I yelled, "You fucking bastard."

As I yelled it, I saw Tom rush out and hop the fence, but

before he reached Julie, he was shot in the neck with an arrow. He staggered and fell. Julie continued to scream through her gag, not because of her own pain, but as she watched with horror as the blood pumped out of Tom's neck. Richard must have hit the jugular vein. I couldn't see Ruth, so I couldn't signal to her that I was moving off in a clockwise direction.

Then Richard shouted, "Who was that young man, George? I didn't mean to kill him. I thought it was you. I think I'm going to end this now."

When I heard that, I stood up to give him a target and yelled, "No!"

But he shot Julie in the heart. I sat down behind the gravestone and put my head in my hands. A second later, there was a gunshot.

"Did you hit him?" I shouted.

"I think so!"

"Where is he?"

"He's behind the obelisk at about nine o'clock from our original spot!"

"Stay where you are!"

I ran, still hunched over, to the next headstone and then the next until I could see behind the obelisk. There was a large amount of blood on the ground, but no Richard.

"You hit him, but didn't kill him! But I think he's gone."

We both got up and walked over to Tom and Julie. Ruth and I were both crying.

"George, we've got to track him down and kill him."

"Considering the amount of blood on the ground, he's badly wounded. He's no longer a threat to us."

"I don't care," Ruth said. "He's a monster. We've got to kill him!"

I slowly shook my head. "We've got to go tell Helen that her son is dead."

"Then we find him and kill him?" Ruth said.

I didn't answer. I hoped with time she'd get past her need for revenge. We walked back to the house we'd been sharing to tell a woman that her only son was dead and that it was our fault for bringing a monster into their lives. *I wondered whether Ruth felt any guilt for convincing Julie to leave Richard.*

Helen was stoic when we told her the news. Andrew, on the other hand, was furious that we hadn't warned them about Richard. I think he was worried about who would care for Helen in the future if he wasn't around. Gary had found Pete— dead. We helped them bury Tom, Julie, and Pete. We left the next day. Helen insisted we take food from their supplies with us.

While hiding it from Ruth, I couldn't help but look for signs of Richard as we were leaving. He'd now know we had guns with ammunition, and so, if he was following us, he would be more careful.

Chapter 13. The Lost Community

We didn't talk about it as we walked, but I knew Ruth was furious with me for refusing to track down and kill Richard; she was actually walking in front of me. Her anger towards me was at least allowing her to put aside, for the moment, her grief at the loss and the pain we'd caused those people. We were both emotional wrecks. We needed a place to rest and heal, so I thought we would visit the community that had given my dad such an emotional lift on our trek. I also thought they'd protect us if Richard was following us. We'd stay on the coast and take U.S. 17 to South Carolina.

When we stopped the first night after leaving Wilmington, she refused to eat, saying she wasn't hungry. She simply unrolled her sleeping bag and lay down. I set up the tent anyway, hoping she'd move her sleeping bag into it. I then built a fire and went out hunting for dinner. I shot two squirrels, skinned and cleaned them. When I got back to camp, she was sitting up but wouldn't look at me.

"Do you want to talk about it?" I asked.

"No."

"Well, will you at least eat something?"

"I told you, I'm not hungry."

"Okay, I'll save you some for breakfast."

"Do what you want." She got up, grabbed her sleeping bag, and went into the tent.

When I finished eating the charcoaled squirrel—I'd cooked them too low to the flame—I banked the fire and climbed into the tent. I found Ruth crying. I knelt and rubbed her shoulder. She rolled over to face me.

"George, she was only sixteen, and her whole life was shit."

"I know, but we tried to make it better for her, and she was happy in Wilmington with all the attention she was receiving from the boys. At least she had that."

I lay down next to her and held her while she cried herself to sleep.

The next morning, I woke up to find Ruth already up. She'd restarted the fire and was making tea as she scarfed down the dried squirrel I'd left for her.

When she saw me climb out of the tent, she said, "I love charcoal for breakfast. After you have tea, why don't you try to catch some fish, and I'll cook them?"

"Okay, boss," I said.

We smiled and gently kissed. Things were better after that, but I recognized the rage that was still simmering in her. *I knew that feeling all too well.* I doubted she understood why I couldn't help her get revenge on Richard.

* * *

Early on the fourth day after leaving Wilmington, we reached the little community that had given my dad such hope on our first trek—it was deserted.

We walked past abandoned auto parts stores, gas stations, and empty billboards on rusting poles. No one came out to meet us. Everything was covered in graffiti that was no longer readable. Individual stores were burned to the ground. Considering the size and amount of vegetation that had encroached into the town, whatever happened happened a long time ago.

"George, maybe they just abandoned the town, and later, squatters moved in and did this?"

We walked past the church where Dad and I had first met Debbie and the town council. It was burned to the ground, and the steeple was lying on its side. I walked up the steps in front of the church, where the front doors had been. That's when I saw them. There were charred bones everywhere. There must have been forty or fifty people in the church, probably sitting in the pews, when it was burned down around them.

"Goddammit to hell!" I screamed. "Who would do something like this?" I turned, plopped down on a step, and buried my face in my hands. "You were right, before. We should just give up and lock ourselves away in Phoenix. We've got everything we need. People don't deserve our help. Fuck 'em!"

Ruth rubbed my back. "What about all the good people

in New Town? What about Andrew and what his parents attempted to do? What about Russ, Jess, and Baby? Come on, let's get out of here."

* * *

I got up and wiped away the tears. We continued walking south on U.S. 17. I tried taking my mind off what we'd just seen by studying the forests and the marshes along the swollen Intercoastal Waterway, but they were all dying too, likely because of saltwater intrusion. Soon, they'd be ghost forests. I couldn't help but think, *I'm always so focused on the human tragedy that I rarely consider the devastation climate change is having on the ecosystems, other than what it does to our ability to farm.*

The landscape quickly changed from dead forests to a stretch of densely packed houses. It was getting cold, so we looked for a house to spend the night. We passed a hospital and then a small satellite campus of Coastal Carolina University and found a house with no occupants, live or otherwise, and settled in for the night. Ruth cleaned an area inside the house to roll out our sleeping bags while I built a fire on the patio beside a small pool that was now filled with mats of blue-green algae. Once I got the fire going, I walked over to what must've been a small park on the Intracoastal Waterway and fished using some grubs I'd dug up. I caught three large snook and was very pleased with myself. When I returned, I found Ruth preparing some greens left over from what we'd brought from Wilmington.

"Later, I'll make us tea from some Roman chamomile I found," she said. "I also found some lavender that I can boil and bring into the house. It'll smell nice while we're going to sleep."

I was no dummy—I knew she was attempting to use aromatherapy on me.

After dinner, we had the tea and then went inside to the smell of lavender. I guess it worked, for her at least. She slept through the coldest night we'd had since leaving Phoenix. I couldn't sleep because I was so cold and just lay there, shivering and going over things in my head—all the mistakes I'd made since leaving Phoenix. It kept me busy most of the night, but eventually I got up and went into another room and wrote up my notes using the small solar lamp we'd been issued before leaving on the trek.

* * *

Journal entry: 12 January, Hollywood, SC on U.S. 17

Addendum to 4 January entry. Immediately after recording the previous entry, we met Tom Davis—he was the son of Brian Davis, a man my father and I met on our first trek (see field books from that trek). It was great finding him alive and healthy. Ruth and I, along with Julie, the girl we helped escape, returned to his home and stayed with him, his mother, and other families for three days. Learned the people of Wilmington have taken an important positive step and have become more organized since our previous visit. They now have a town council and a farm. Typical weather-related issues have hampered their farming; however, their farm manager, who had been educated by his professor father, speculated on something new to me. He feels there is a mismatch in the timing of when the pollinating insects arrive and when the plants enter their reproductive stages. This idea should be further evaluated by our ecologists, if they haven't already considered this as a possible impact of sudden climate change.

Tragedy struck when Richard Havens showed up and abducted Julie; subsequently killing her, Tom, and another boy. We escaped; Havens was (mortally?) wounded but not killed.

Traveling south on U.S. 17, we stopped today in a community I previously visited on the first trek with my dad. As I reported on my return from that trek, my dad was very impressed with the level of cooperation and organization within this community back then. Today, we found the town empty and evidence of a massacre of 40-50 people inside a burned-out church. I am heartbroken by what I found. My dad would have been devastated if he had lived to learn of this.

Traveling south on U.S. 17, we are encountering more and more areas inundated with seawater in the low-lying coastal areas; these areas are susceptible due to elevation and grade. Near the coast, we noted a large tract of dead trees. However, mangroves are now moving in; the most obvious being the black mangrove (more resistant to cold as compared to the other two species of mangrove); it's surprising their range has extended this far north already. Likewise, because they are highly sensitive to cold, it is also surprising that snook (i.e., the gamefish) that I caught from dinner have also extended their range this far north.

* * *

The next day, I woke up early and, even though it was chilly outside, went back over and caught more fish. Although they weren't snook, which likely fled to deeper and warmer waters overnight, they were tasty redfish. While fishing, I wished I were on the other side of the Intercoastal so I didn't have to look back over my shoulder to watch the sunrise—in do so, I'd missed a couple of good fish taking my bait. When I got back to the house, Ruth had revived the fire on the patio. I went into the kitchen, took off my jacket so it wouldn't get covered in fish slime, and cleaned the fish on one of the counters.

As I handed the fillets to Ruth, she asked, "Did you get any sleep last night? I heard you get up."

"No. I thought writing my notes would bore me to sleep, but it didn't work."

"I'm sorry."

"It's not your fault."

"I know, but it was horrible, and I'm sad to see you in so much pain. I know those people had a special place in your heart."

"Yeah, meeting them was one of the few good things that happened on the trek with my dad. At least he died with the hope that things were improving. You know, Ruth, back right after the tornado, you said we had the emotional reserve to help those people. I think I'm running out of my emotional reserve."

"I know what you mean, hon."

She hugged me.

Later, as we passed Myrtle Beach, I realized that while it wasn't the worst mistake I'd made on this trek, taking U.S. 17 was a bad idea. The Waccamaw River and its floodplain were now inundated with seawater. We'd have to wade through water on some of the low-lying stretches of the road. And it was still cold. There was no way we could do this for long, so we detoured west on U.S. 501. But rather than continuing to I-95, we turned south again on U.S. 701 back to Alt U.S. 17. Although I'd never admit it to Ruth, my thinking was that if Richard was following us, he'd never think I'd be foolish enough to turn back towards the coast after encountering so much flooding.

As we approached Charleston, we encountered more swollen estuaries, flooded wetlands, and trees showing salt stress, but the upland vegetation also showed wilted or blackened leaves due to the cold, the drought, or both. All the waterbodies were too saline to drink. I was beginning to worry about how we'd replace our drinking water. As we walked, I tried to remember the attribution of a line from a poem or story that I couldn't get out of my head.

"Hon, can you remember the source of the phrase 'water, water everywhere, but not a drop to drink?'"

"Yeah, it's from a poem called 'The Rime of the Ancient

Mariner' by Samuel Coleridge."

"And that's why no one will play trivia games with you at home."

"Is that your way of telling me we should start conserving our drinking water?"

"It wouldn't be a bad idea."

Chapter 14. Wildfire

One day, we found ourselves walking across a low bridge over a shallow creek that fed an expansive marsh. As I stared down at the water in the creek, I felt myself begin to salivate. We'd run out of drinking water two days prior. I'd planned on taking the next road west, hoping to find freshwater, but it would be great to find water we could drink today. The trees along the bank of the creek were all dead. This could either mean a recent influx of saltwater or that they died from their roots being flooded, so I decided to check the conductivity of the water.

After crossing the bridge, we walked over to several run-down buildings along the creek that looked to be an old fish camp. When I tested the water, it was just as I thought—too salty to drink. I sat back on my heels and began beating myself up for getting us into this mess.

"George, maybe it's high tide, and it'll be fresher when it goes out?"

"It's possible, I guess."

"Do you want to catch some fish while we're waiting to see if the water recedes? We're out of jerky."

"Yeah, okay, but first I'm going to look around for anything that might have collected rainwater."

"I'll help, but we haven't seen any rain or snow for days."

We were in luck; we found a fifty-five-gallon drum sitting under the eaves of the main building of the fish camp. It still contained what I hoped was water collected as the rain, melted snow, or dew that dripped off the old, rusty metal roof.

"We're not going to drink that, are we?" Ruth asked. "You don't know what was in that drum."

"It's probably overflowed many times over the years, rinsing it out. We'll pour the water into a bucket or something so we can get a better look at it."

I found a five-gallon bucket in a shed, and we transferred about half of what was in the drum to it.

"It doesn't look too bad," I said.

"It smells."

"Let me get the water quality probe and test it to see if it's okay."

"But the probe only tests for certain things, right? It doesn't mean it's safe to drink."

"If none of the measured parameters indicate the water's bad, we'll filter it, and I'll give it the taste test."

"Can we boil it first?"

"With the filters we have, we don't need to boil it."

"It'd make me feel better."

The water had very low conductivity when I tested it, so that wasn't a concern. While Ruth filtered a few hundred milliliters, I made a fire so we could boil it. After the water

251

cooled, I sipped it, and it tasted fine. We both had our fill. Ruth filtered and boiled the rest of the drum's contents while I fished. We now had enough water for another day, possibly two if we rationed.

We made camp in the main building of the fish camp. We ate the catfish I'd caught from the creek. They tasted a little muddy but were okay since we could wash them down now with tea. Later, we climbed into our sleeping bags with our thirst quenched and fully satiated.

* * *

I woke up to the smell of smoke. It was heavy; the fire must be nearby. I scrambled out of my sleeping bag and went outside. The entire northern horizon was ablaze. I couldn't be sure, but it looked as if it was circling around to the west. We were in trouble.

I ran back inside.

"Ruth, get up. There's a fire."

"What?"

"Get up, babe! We've got to be prepared to leave."

We quickly packed up our things and went back outside. In that short amount of time, the fire had moved closer.

"Come on, let's get up to the road."

Once we'd done that, I saw my worst fear had been realized. The fire had circled around to the west and was now south of us. We were surrounded by the wildfire. *It suddenly occurred to me that Richard had set this fire to drive us toward him. It made sense; he knew we had guns and ammunition.*

"What are we going to do, George?"

"We're going to hunker down on the bridge. We'll be safe there."

We got down on the pavement next to the cement parapet on the side of the bridge. After twenty minutes, the roar of the fire intensified. We could hear the popping sounds of dead trees exploding. We could also see animals running and jumping into the water to escape the flames. Some were actually swimming downstream under the bridge. At one point, I thought I saw a bear running across the road to the south of us on fire. Maybe it was just a raccoon. Embers were swirling all around and would burn whenever they landed on us. I tried to cover Ruth with my body. The heat was becoming intense. It felt as if my skin was on fire. Hot blasts of wind whipped into Ruth's face. The smoke was getting thicker. We were choking for air, but it burned our throats as it went down, even breathing through the wet shirts I'd soaked with our precious drinking water. I could only imagine what it was doing to our lungs.

"Ruth, I'm going to take one of our sleeping bags and soak it in the creek to bring back to cover us."

"George, I can't take this anymore. Let's jump in the water?"

So we grabbed our backpacks and ran down to the edge of the water below the bridge. I wedged the backpacks and my bow and quiver under the bridge abutment. Ruth's takedown bow was disassembled and in her backpack. Then we lay down in the water on the side of the bank and covered our exposed heads and faces with cool mud. The bridge above us would offer protection from the swirling embers. At first, the water was freezing, and I was worried about hypothermia as most of our bodies were submerged under water, but then the water heated up. I wondered if we were going to be boiled alive. We had to fight the undertow of the ebbing water to keep from being pulled out into the creek and deeper water. At the rate it was ebbing, I was becoming worried that the tide might go out and leave us high and dry. Worse yet, we were still breathing smoke-filled, superheated air.

In the midst of a coughing fit, Ruth said, "I can't imagine a worse hell."

We stayed in the water for what seemed like hours. Finally, the surface fire burned itself out. But the grasses and the muck in the marsh were still smoldering. I climbed out onto the bank and managed to drag Ruth all the way out of the water. All around us, everything had burned, including the old fish camp. We were soaked, covered in mud, and there was no way to dry off, so I just tried to keep Ruth warm using my body heat. We slept or passed out; I don't know which.

I woke to the sound of Ruth in an uncontrolled, violent coughing fit. She wasn't fully conscious, and I couldn't wake her. I didn't know what to do. So I dragged her from under the bridge, picked her up, carried her up to the road, and ran.

Chapter 15. Finding Help

I tried to run while carrying Ruth in my arms, but had to stop frequently and walk because I was having trouble breathing. Ruth still wouldn't wake up, and her breathing was shallow and raspy. The smell of the smoldering fire was everywhere, but so was the rotten egg smell of the sulfidic mud we were both covered in. I couldn't stop thinking that Richard was out there, watching us; it was unnerving.

About seven kilometers, I came across a gated drive with brick columns on either side and a wooden plank fence. I could see that the vegetation had been cut back. Not only was this farm occupied, but they weren't afraid to advertise. More importantly, the gate was open. I walked in, past a large pond, and saw several buildings scattered around a farm about five hectares in size, much of it cleared. Dogs were barking somewhere. I then noticed a man driving a horse pulling a plow. I'd never seen a horse outside of Phoenix other than wild horses. Their numbers, along with other domestic animals, were greatly reduced after the blackout as people were eating anything they could catch. There were two other younger men watching the plowing from the edge of the field.

I screamed, "Help!" as loud as I could and fell to my knees.

All three men ran over to me, stopping a few meters away. Four dogs came out of nowhere and started jumping on Ruth and me, licking our faces. I think they were pit bulls. I'd seen many wild dogs on my previous trek, but hadn't seen friendly dogs outside of Phoenix. They were a welcome sight. The man who had been driving the horse was a bull of a man my age. He had a broad, flat face that betrayed an unreadable expression. His squint could signify hostility, curiosity, or just that he had sun in his eyes. The other two were younger; by the looks of it, his sons, but neither was as tall as thier father. All three were wearing Farmer John overalls.

"Get away, dogs!" the older man shouted. "Is she sick?" he asked.

"We were caught in the wildfire last night. I don't know what's wrong with her."

The man's face softened. "Jayden, go tell your Momma we've got guests, and one's hurt, but it's not the kind you can catch. Carter, give me a hand carrying her to the house. I think this man is done in."

They carried Ruth to the house, where a woman in her late thirties and a young girl were waiting for us at the door.

"Put her on the bed in the front bedroom," the woman said. As she rushed in behind us, she asked, "What happened?"

"We were caught in the wildfire last night. We took shelter in a nearby creek but breathed in a lot of smoke and very hot air."

"You boys get out; you too, stranger. Kayla, help me get her

256

out of these damp clothes."

She pushed us out of the room and closed the door.

The older man put his hand on my shoulder. "Come into the kitchen and sit. You look like you could use some water."

As I sat down, I said, "Thank you for helping us. And yes, I'd greatly appreciate some water."

Handing me a glass of water, he said, "When you showed up, all covered in ash and mud, I thought you were one of us."

I could see that he was smiling.

I coughed twice while drinking the water, spilling most of it. "Thank you for the water. My name is George Reynolds. My wife in there is Ruth."

Just then, we heard someone come out of the bedroom into the hall.

The girl I'd seen before came into the kitchen. She was fifteen and, lucky for her, looked like her mom, not her dad. She went to the kitchen sink, where there was a hand pump, and said, "Momma wants a bucket of water."

"That's my oldest daughter, Kayla," the man said. "I'm Caleb Freeman. These two are my sons, Carter and Jayden. The woman in there taking care of your wife is Jayla. We got a mess of other kids running around here somewhere."

Kayla went back into the bedroom with the pail of water.

"I can't tell you how much I appreciate this," I said.

"We saw the wildfire last night," Caleb said. "It scared us pretty bad."

Kayla again emerged from the bedroom and came back into the kitchen, grabbed a woven basket from the counter.

"How's she doing?" Caleb asked.

Kayla just shrugged. "I gotta go get stuff for Momma." Ticking them off on her hand: "She wants flowers from the

257

elder tree, roots from burdock, and bark from willow."

She turned to leave.

"Wait a minute!" I exclaimed, startling everyone.

Kayla turned back and looked at me and said, "But she needs 'em to care for your woman."

"I know, but I need to explain. It might be dangerous to help us. I think a man is following us. I think he set the wildfire last night."

"Who is he?" Caleb asked, now much more alert, as was everyone.

"We met him a couple of weeks ago up near Richmond. He was forcing a young girl to be one of his wives. We helped her escape. He tracked us to Wilmington, where he killed the girl and two young men who were helping us. He's an expert hunter and very dangerous."

"So, you believe he's out there?" Caleb asked.

"I can't be sure. He was wounded in the fight to rescue the girl. We haven't seen him since, but setting that fire would've been something he'd do. Listen, I have no right to ask you to help us. I don't want to get anyone else killed."

Caleb sat back in his chair and, after a moment, said, "Carter, go get your bow and go with your sister to collect what your Momma needs. Be careful. Jayden, round up your brothers and sisters and bring 'em back here; check the barns first."

"Thank you," I said, as I released the breath I was holding. When I inhaled, I coughed so hard I thought I was going to pass out.

When we were alone, Caleb asked, "You and your missus have been on the road a long time, haven't you?"

"Yes, and we still have a long way to go."

"Where you headed?"

Before I could answer, Jayla came out of the bedroom.

"How is she?" I asked.

"She's got burns in her mouth, throat, and nose, and soot in her sputum; she must've breathed the smoke down deep. I can't be sure, but I think she got fluid in her lungs. I can hear rumbling sounds when she breathes. She's also running a fever."

"But why won't she wake up?"

"I don't know. I think we just got to give her body time to repair itself."

"I want to thank you for taking care of her."

"It's the Christian thing to do. As soon as my daughter gets back, I'll make up some tonics that might help."

That made me remember the antibiotics we're given to bring on a trek. They were in my backpack.

"I've got some medicine in my backpack, but I had to leave it behind near the creek. I'll go get it and bring it here."

I started to get up.

Caleb put his hand out. "You ain't strong enough to go. I'll send the boys to fetch it when they get back."

"They wouldn't know where to look. I hid the backpacks under the bridge."

"Okay, you can go with them, but later," Caleb said. "You need to rest up first."

"Right now, you need to get yourself outside and wash up," Jayla said. "You and your woman are dirtying my house with all that mud you're wearing. Caleb'll bring you some of his clothes to put on. Then you can go in and visit with your woman before you rest."

Smiling, I said, "Yes, ma'am." I went outside but couldn't

259

find a hand pump, so I just walked over and into the pond and began washing my face and clothes. The dogs were barking at me as if they thought I was crazy for walking into the pond.

When I finished, I walked back up to the house to find Caleb holding some clothes out for me. I looked around to see that no one was watching and changed.

As I walked back into the bedroom, Jayla said, "I'll bring you in some broth."

I found Ruth lying in the bed, unconscious. They'd cleaned her up and dressed her in a cotton nightgown. She had burns on her scalp and face, and was making a raspy noise when she took a breath in. I sat on the edge of the bed, leaned over, and kissed her forehead. She was hot with fever. I held her hand and quietly cried.

"I'm here, babe."

She didn't respond. After a few minutes, I moved to a chair and promptly fell asleep sitting up. Sometime later, I woke up to find Jayla trying to get Ruth to swallow some liquid.

"It's elderflower tea for her lungs. I also made some balm from burdock root for her burns. You could use some too."

I reached over and touched Jayla's arm. "Thank you." I then broke down and started crying again.

"Your broth's in the kitchen."

I sat there trying to regain my composure. Looking around the room, really for the first time, I noticed all the books piled up everywhere and old pictures of white people, which surprised me.

I left Ruth with Jayla and went back into the kitchen and found Caleb surrounded by his 'mess of children.' I'd already met Carter, Jayden, and Kayla. Now I was introduced to his youngest daughter, Jasmine, and his two other sons, Levi and Keshawn, who were twelve and nine. It was nice to see that, like his other kids, they didn't have pockmark scars, but they all had horribly crooked teeth. I wondered how many times the clothes they were wearing had been handed down from one child to the next. Although obviously mended and worn, they were cleaner than I expected for people living on a working farm. I also met Grandma, who was seventy years old and white. She must have seen the surprise on my face.

"I used to live on a farm down the road, but they adopted me after my husband passed, some time ago."

"It's great meeting you. I assume it's your room that my wife is recuperating in. I'm sorry we're putting you out."

"It's no problem, I'll be bunking in with Jasmine."

"You must read a lot," I said.

"I can't get enough. We all take turns reading at night. It's a great way to teach the kids."

Kayla interrupted us, and said, "Mr. Reynolds, Momma wanted you to drink broth and willow-bark tea when you got up. I'll fetch 'em for you."

"Thank you, Kayla," I replied. "Caleb, when do you think we might go retrieve my stuff from the creek?" I asked.

"You, Carter, and Jayden can leave right after you've had your broth and tea. I'm staying here in case that man comes."

＊ ＊ ＊

The boys and I found the backpacks exactly where I'd left them under the bridge. Unfortunately, the tide had come in and somehow swept away our sleeping bags and the tent, but my bow and quiver were still lodged behind the packs. The boys offered to carry the backpacks back for me since they were soaking wet and very heavy. We saw no sign of Richard.

When we got back to the farm, I found Ruth awake, sitting up, supported by pillows, and drinking willow-bark tea. They'd cut her hair.

"Hi, babe, I'm so glad to see you're up. You gave me quite a scare."

"Well, imagine my scare, waking up alone here in a house full of strangers. I thought you were dead. But Jayla explained where you were, and she and the girls have been taking excellent care of me."

She coughed several times, pressing her fist to her chest.

"Well, I'm here now, and can take care of you."

"George, was it Richard? Did you see him?"

"No, we haven't seen any sign of him. I told Caleb, and everyone is being careful."

"Oh, George, I was so frightened."

"I know. But we're safe now. I'm sorry they had to cut your hair."

"It's okay. Jayla needed to put balm on the burns. It'll grow back."

After first checking with Jayla and receiving some linen, I made up a bed on the floor of Ruth's bedroom. Then I unpacked the instruments and guns from the backpacks and hid them in the bedding that Jayla had given me. I made sure the guns were empty before hiding them and hid the cartridges separately under Ruth's mattress to be on the safe side, since there were young children in the house. I then took one vial of amoxicillin we'd been given before we left Phoenix out to the kitchen to show Jayla how to mix it with Ruth's tea. Ruth would receive it three times a day. Jayla wasn't convinced it would be any better than the Elderflower tea, so she suggested Ruth continue taking that too. Later, I took our backpacks outside, washed them and the contents in the pond, and found a place to hang everything up to dry.

That night, we enjoyed roasted pork while Ruth stayed in bed and remained on a liquid diet. I asked for the fattest piece of pork. Over dinner, Caleb told me about the problems he'd been having with the farm. Before the blackout, his family had farmed peanuts predominantly, selling them to local stores and roadside vendors. Afterward, he switched to corn and sweet potatoes. He still wanted to farm peanuts because it was a family tradition, and he'd had success trading the harvest with surrounding farms, but couldn't get peanuts to grow in the extreme summer heat. He'd even tried testing different growing seasons. He also suffered losses from hail and was worried about saltwater intrusion into his well. I learned the pork we were eating was from one of many wild boars that were digging up his farm. The family ate a lot of pork.

* * *

We stayed for a week while Ruth recovered. I spent my time

trying to repay them for their hospitality by educating them on the benefits of agroforestry and helping them dig a deeper well to tap into a lower aquifer that might not be as easily contaminated with saltwater. I also enjoyed listening to the reading sessions at night with Grandma and playing football with the kids. After one particularly competitive game, I thought of Dan—*why don't we play football or any games anymore? We used to play catch, but each time it'd only last a few minutes before one of us would lose patience with the other. I've got to work on that when I get back. I wonder what he's up to right now.*

We saw no sign of Richard. Nonetheless, I couldn't overcome the feeling of dread that something horrible was about to happen. One day, as I was sitting with Ruth, she began to cry.

"George, can you ever forgive me for ignoring your warnings about Richard?"

"What are you talking about?"

She was sobbing. "I got Julie killed. If I hadn't offered to help her escape, she'd be miserable, but at least she'd still be alive."

"Babe, it wasn't your fault. And she knew what she was doing."

Ruth was then racked by another violent coughing fit, so I made her some tea and tried to calm her down. After a while, she fell back asleep. I took the opportunity to write up my notes.

* * *

Journal entry: 2 February, Farm Just South of Ashepoo, SC on U.S. 17

Two nights ago, we camped at a place called Joe's Fish Camp near a small bridge over the Ashepoo River. A wildfire swept through the area in the middle of the night. I am sure it was set by Richard Havens, although we never saw or heard him. He could have tracked us from Wilmington, and because he knew we had guns with ammunition, I believe he was attempting to drive us toward some ambush. We had to spend the night submerged in the river as the fire raged around us. Ruth suffered damage to her lungs from smoke inhalation. I found help here at the Freeman Farm; we will stay until Ruth recovers.

As reported from other areas, the intensity and rate of spread of the wildfire were amplified because of prolonged drought and strong winds compounded by high fuel load from excessive vegetation growth with higher CO_2 levels.

The Freeman family is a strong family unit of 9 individuals, including six children ranging in age from 9 to 18. They have been unbelievably generous in their hospitality, taking care of Ruth and me and, equally if not more importantly, guarding us in case Richard comes. The family's attempt at farming has suffered from excessive heat (preventing them from continuing to grow peanuts, which was a family tradition going back to before the Civil War), drought, and hailstorms. It was fortunate that the wildfire did not come in this direction. I plan on instructing them in agroforestry and especially ground cover as repayment for helping us. I also plan to offer some of our antibiotics to them, if they see value in accepting them.

The head of the family was not receptive when I suggested he consider moving his children from the family farm west to be farther from the coast. Not knowing the local elevation or topography, I do not know how many years they have until this area is underwater, but it will certainly be within the children's lifetime.

* * *

The day before we were to leave, I tried to convince Ruth to stay with the Freemans while I continued with the trek, but she wouldn't hear of it. She insisted she was fit to travel and wanted to see Miami. I knew it wasn't about seeing Miami; she wasn't going to let me go alone. She also refused to abort the trek and return to Phoenix.

The day we left, Caleb gave us two sleeping bags to replace the ones we'd lost. He said they didn't own a tent and so couldn't offer to replace it. I knew we'd have to scavenge one in a store somewhere before we reached Florida; we wouldn't be able to survive the mosquitoes without the screening. Caleb and Jayla forced more food and water on us than we could carry. He even offered to send Carter, Kayla, Jayden, and Jasmine out in different directions, disguised as Ruth and me, to draw Richard away if he were watching the farm. I wasn't sure if he was joking, but both Ruth and I firmly rejected the offer. We would never again put others in harm's way. Richard was our problem. Besides, I doubted whether Richard would've been fooled by the kids even if they were all bundled up in coats and scarves. Everyone cried, including me again. I didn't know what I'd have done if it weren't for these people helping me to save Ruth.

Chapter 16. Taking it Slow Avoiding the Militia

The first day after leaving the Freemans' farm, we walked along a narrow strip of road crossing the Combahee River and its vast wetland. It was rimmed with dead trees. Open water stretched for kilometers on either side of the road. The narrow embankment on which U.S. 17 was constructed was now less than a meter above the water. I really didn't want to be caught out here in the open, but Ruth was still weak and could only walk so fast.

"Babe, how are you doing?

"I'm fine, stop asking every five minutes. Ouch. Look at that, the little bugger drew blood."

"I know. Let's stop for a minute; I brought some mosquito mesh head nets for when we're down in Florida."

"Hurry up. I won't have any blood left. Why are they so thick?"

"I'm looking. Do you want me to stop and tell you the

scientific reason they're swarming?"

"You do, and I'll kick you. Just find the nets, hurry."

"Here they are; put this on!"

"What about my hands?"

"Put them in your pockets."

"Do you have any earplugs in there—the buzzing sound is driving me crazy."

"I know. Let's just keep our heads down and get across this marsh as fast as we can."

It took all day to cross the causeway, but we made it before dark. We had no tent and needed a house to take refuge from the insects. The first long driveway we passed was blocked by massive trees that had been cut down as a barricade. We kept walking for another hour and hadn't passed any more farms or houses, but spotted a small church set in a clearing of loblolly pine just off the highway. It was a simple white, wood-framed church with a steeple. It had lots of windows, but thankfully, they all looked intact. I was leery of entering the church after what we'd found in the last one, but when we went inside, we found lots of discarded items scattered about, but no human remains. It was clear that others had taken refuge here but had shown reverence by not ransacking it.

I was still worried about Ruth, so I made her sit and watch as I did everything. We still had plenty of dried food to eat, but I wanted to heat the medicinal teas that Jayla had provided. I also wanted to administer another round of amoxicillin, and it would dissolve better in hot tea. So I built a fire just outside of the church's side entrance, away from the highway. Not being religious, I was surprised that I had a tinge of reverence for the church and did not want to break up the church pews for firewood. So instead, I went and collected dried pine branches off the ground to build the fire. We sat on a pew as we ate, but I rolled the sleeping bags out on the floor, thinking one of us would surely roll off if we attempted to sleep on a pew. Actually, I'd debated sleeping outside. I had no desire to be trapped in the church like those other people, but, in the end, I put my fears aside—it was important for Ruth to get a good night's sleep, and it was still cold and buggy outside, and, without the tent, we would've been miserable.

The next morning, I got up and restarted the fire. We took our time with a breakfast of tea, cornbread, and jam that Jayla had provided. Eating carbs, as well as fat, is essential when consuming so much protein as we were. Our route that day would take us west so we could rejoin I-95, at least temporarily.

Near the I-95 on-ramp, we found a hotel with a retention pond, so we replenished our drinking water. From now on, keeping our water supplies filled would be one of our highest priorities.

* * *

Ruth's health slowly improved, and we increased our pace. There were also fewer distractions, at least in terms of exits off the interstate, to worry about. However, there were more refugees on the interstate. Many appeared even more haggard than the people we'd seen before. Interestingly, they were now, more often than not, walking north. Mostly, they ignored us, and we ignored them.

A few nights later, as we were passing Savannah, I pulled out the map and told Ruth that I was considering getting off I-95 again.

Pointing to the map, I said, "We're here. I think we should take 204 to 301 to avoid this stretch of 95. Once we're on 301, we can stay on it all the way down to Florida."

"But why the detour?"

"There's a former military base, Fort Stewart, located right here. It was the largest army garrison east of the Mississippi back before the collapse."

"So?"

"Long-haul trekkers are warned to stay away from former military bases, both federal and state-run, but most states took control of the federal facilities after the collapse. We've learned over the years that military personnel who didn't immediately desert and return home after the collapse often were drafted into State Guards or militias when they were from that area or didn't have a home to go to. And, depending on their leadership after the blackout, these militias often devolved into something no different from raiders taking what they wanted, even forcibly recruiting children."

"That's horrible."

"Yes, it is, and because of this and because they had ammunition stores to go with the armament, they're considered a long-term threat to any trekker. Because we knew the garrison was there, Dad and I were very careful when we came this way on our trek, particularly since there is a bottleneck here where 17 and 95 are both close to the coast, and there aren't many back roads. Fortunately, Dad spotted the roadblock on 95 and the sentry they'd positioned up in what used to be a cellphone tower, watching for people who turned around. Anyway, we were able to get off the road before they saw us. They even had functioning jeeps and trucks back then, probably running on biodiesel. Later, we learned from talking with people we encountered that this militia actually helped the locals, and the roadblock prevented raiders from traveling north or south. It wouldn't have mattered that they were honorable, though. If we'd been stopped and searched, we would've had a hard time explaining our guns and ammo and all the tech we were carrying. So the question is, do we take the detour that will add several days to our trip, or do we keep going and be extra careful in case the roadblock is still there?"

"If we take the detour, do you think it might also throw Richard off our trail, if he's still out there?"

"Maybe; it certainly wouldn't hurt."

"Then let's take the detour. I'll try to walk faster to make up the lost time."

"Okay, but don't overdo it and make yourself sick."

* * *

Although we saw fewer refugees once we got off I-95, they still worried me each time they approached. If I saw them first and there were a lot of them, I tried to move us off the road before they saw us. One morning, we were passing a family consisting of a man and woman, aged nineteen or twenty, and a little girl, probably five or six, who were headed north. The woman also had a baby in her arms. They were dressed in rags and looked emaciated, with loose, pale skin, hollow cheeks, and dark circles under their eyes. The smell was horrible. They seemed to stumble along and didn't look as if they could be a threat. As far as I could tell, they were carrying no weapons or belongings of any kind, except for the little girl, who was carrying a doll. The little girl waved at Ruth, so of course, Ruth had to wave back. I couldn't be sure, but I suspected Ruth had initiated the girl's wave with a look and smile. Ruth stopped and started up a conversation. I put on a smile to hide my frustration.

To the little girl, Ruth asked, "What's your name?"

"Millie."

"And what's your doll's name?"

"My baby's name is Debbie."

"I see your mommy has a baby too; what's its name?"

"Henry, but Dad calls him Hank."

Addressing the woman, Ruth said, "Hi, my name's Ruth, and this is my husband, George."

Addressing the man, I asked, "How are you folks doing today?"

Before he could answer, the woman said, "We're searching for clean water."

"Here, take some of mine," Ruth said as she handed the woman her water bottle.

All I could think was, how hard these people had it with a little girl and a baby to care for?

273

The woman took Ruth's water bottle and said, "Thank you so much." Before drinking from it herself, she gave it to the little girl, who took a drink and passed it back. The woman then dripped water onto the baby's lips. "My name is Ava, and this is John." After taking a drink, she handed the water bottle to John.

When he was done drinking, I shook his hand and asked, "Where are you all headed?"

"Maybe North Carolina," he replied. "Anyplace that's not so hot during the summer and where there's plenty of freshwater."

"Yeah, I can understand that," I said. "We ran out of water a week or so ago, but got lucky and found some after a day or two."

John tried to give the water bottle back to Ruth, but she refused it.

"Please keep it. Why don't we stop and all share a meal?" Ruth said. "I'm sure that George could shoot a few rabbits for us."

I could see hope flash across Ava's face as she turned to see her husband's response.

He looked uncomfortable with the question. "I don't know; we've got a long way to go today."

Knowing that Ruth wanted very much to feed this little girl and her family, I said, "John, why don't you make a fire, and I'll go hunt us up something to eat."

I wasn't sure if it was karma or what, but I shot three rabbits and two raccoons for our meal. The raccoons would be a better source of fat than the rabbits. Every morsel was eaten. During the meal, we learned they'd lived on his parents' farm, but the farm had failed due to the drought. They'd been walking for two months with a larger group, but fell out over where they should head next. John wanted to head north to escape the drought, while the others wanted to head toward the coast. He told me the drought had been going on for three years. They also informed us that the militia had disbanded a long time ago, and that Fort Stewart was now deserted; the rumor was that the water on the base was contaminated. We ended up giving them all of Ruth's water and the food she was carrying. I could tell from Ruth's expression that she wanted me to give them my water too; I ignored her but gave John my fishing setup and explained how to find grubs or other insects as bait and how to use a long stick to get the hook out farther away from the bank.

After we parted ways, I didn't even try to admonish Ruth for engaging with them on the road. But she felt obliged to tell me that my concerns about the militia and the possibility of a roadblock were unfounded and that I worried too much. She must have been feeling better; she was back to her old self.

* * *

The next day, as we passed through a small town that appeared to be deserted, I spotted a pharmacy that also advertised as a sporting goods store. Since we'd be traveling through a more rural area again without as many deserted

275

houses to choose from, I thought it'd be a good idea to replace the tent we'd lost in the Ashepoo River. The pharmacy had been ransacked, probably for drugs. All the guns and ammunition were gone of course, but there were still a few items on the floor of the sporting goods section. I sifted through the debris and found a two-man tent. It wasn't as good as the tent we'd lost so I'd keep a lookout for another store, but in the interim, it'd suffice. I then looked for hooks and fishing line to replace what I'd given John. Ruth had found a replacement water bottle and was busy looking for dry shampoo to brush through what was left of her hair. She didn't have any luck. On the way out, we heard yelling and saw four people running down the road toward us from the way we'd come. Not caring to learn what they wanted, we ran. To be honest, it was exhilarating. They gave up when we reached the edge of town. They were probably just upset we'd been scavenging in their town.

* * *

We passed several farms over the next few days that appeared recently abandoned. Someone had prevented reforestation of the fields and had planted. Unfortunately, the crops had all withered and died, probably due to a lack of rain.

One afternoon, we were attacked by a pack of wild dogs as we walked. But as luck would have it, rusting pickup trucks were a common feature in the driveways of rural Georgia, and we were able to jump up into the bed of one of them. I fired a few arrows, killing two of the dogs, which scared the rest of them off. Ruth even pulled her takedown bow out of her backpack and had it assembled just as they ran off. But the important thing was that she hadn't resorted to using the gun and, by the sound of its report, alert everyone within kilometers we had ammunition.

Not wanting to be caught out in the tent if the dogs were following us, that night we searched until we found a house to sleep in. Being forced to kill the two dogs had upset me because they looked like a mix of Black-mouth Cur and Pitbull and reminded me of our dog, Otis, that we'd left with Dan. I'd considered eating those two dogs for only a second before rejecting the idea. But it wasn't as easy to push the thought of Dan out of my head.

The house we found was a single-story, red-brick home with intact windows. I was able to open the windows only in the small back bedroom because aluminum oxide corrosion had built up on the casement of the other windows, and the cranks wouldn't turn. There were two large but shallow depressions in the earth behind the house that, during other times, would've been ponds. The house next door had a pool and a diving board. They were all bone-dry. I'd have to find a stream or deeper lake fed by groundwater tomorrow, or we'd be without drinking water again. Because it was getting late, I settled on rabbits for dinner. While two rabbits usually provided enough meat for Ruth and me, these two rabbits were very skinny.

The wild dogs did not trouble us that night. However, we had other visitors. Because I was worried the dogs would come after us, I slept little. An hour or so after we turned in, I heard a noise from outside. We were in the back bedroom, so I grabbed my long knife and, quietly, not to wake Ruth, moved into the front room. There was definitely something or someone in the carport. The house we were squatting in didn't have a garage but instead had an open but covered carport. I listened for a few minutes. Whatever it was, it was trying to be quiet, so it wasn't an animal. My patience was wearing thin, so I jerked open the door and screamed, "Who's out there?" In the moonlight, I could see three small shapes near the back wall. I then heard a loud whistle, and all three took off running. They were Ferals. They probably followed us and were looking to steal food or, more likely, water. Now I wouldn't get any sleep. But I found what remained of a kitchen chair and jammed it under the doorknob of the door to the carport. It wouldn't stop them from getting in, but they'd make a racket doing it. I did the same to the front door. When I re-entered the bedroom, I found Ruth still asleep. I thought to myself, *good, if she'd found out about the Ferals, she'd probably want to rescue them.*

In the morning, I woke to find Ruth had gotten up early and had killed a snake for our breakfast. She said it looked like a python. I knew they were all over Florida, but I didn't think they'd moved into Georgia already, but if there could be water moccasins in Pennsylvania, who knows? Ruth had already skinned it, so I couldn't be sure, but from its size and the rolled-up skin, it was possible. Regardless, there'd be a lot of meat for us to eat, and we'd likely have leftovers for jerky.

Ruth interrupted my trance as I was savoring the aroma of the roasting meat; at least it wasn't the gamey smell of roasting rabbit.

"George, there's something I've been meaning to ask you. I've been noticing that among the people we've met on the trek, there are young kids and teenagers as old as nineteen or twenty, like Ava and John, and a lot of people a couple of years older than me, but I haven't met many people around my age or slightly younger."

I noticed she was careful not to say there weren't many people as old as I was or older, but I simply said, "That's the missing cohort."

"The... what?" she asked.

"It's a term we've given to that missing age group. Trekkers have reported seeing the same thing wherever they go in North America. We think it's because of the vulnerability of infants and young children during the Time of the Great Dying. Infants born just before the blackout perished. And of course, for the first few years after the blackout, people weren't having babies either because they chose not to or weren't physically able to, due to poor health or nutrition. And if, somehow, they were capable of getting pregnant and carrying to term, the baby would be extremely vulnerable and would likely have died. So they're missing along with the very old, who are also extremely vulnerable."

"My God, that's awful."

"Even back in Phoenix, fewer people chose to have babies during those years because they were worried about how things would turn out. Of course, in Phoenix, we didn't see the early infant mortality, so a few people were born into that age group and survived. You didn't notice the small size of your class as compared to other classes in the consolidated school?"

279

"I just thought it was normal."

"To be honest, I'm surprised that Ava and John have been able to keep their baby alive for this long," I said.

"Me too. I feel so sorry for them and for little Millie and Henry. Maybe the two couples back in Wilmington were right about not bringing kids into this world."

I said nothing.

* * *

After breakfast, we got back on the road. While walking, I kept a lookout for any signs of water along the road, but all I could see was dry soil, dead grass, and wilting brown leaves on trees and shrubs. We ran out of water at our midday meal, which was leftover dried python. *I couldn't help but think about the water we'd given away to Ava and John.* We were fortunate that it wasn't hotter than it was, but we needed water. I worried about what it would be like walking back this way from Florida in summer rather than early February. We plodded on.

When we stopped for the night, we still hadn't found any water. Although both of us had parched mouths and weren't especially hungry, we forced ourselves to eat the rabbits that I shot for dinner. I noticed that game, even rabbits, were becoming scarce. Tomorrow, we'd have to stop walking south and instead put our energy into finding water.

* * *

The next day it took us over two hours walking down several side roads to find a lake with water. It was likely dredged for fill material to build the road, but fortunately for us, they'd dredged it so deep it was now hydrologically connected to the aquifer. The lake was covered with blue-green algae, but we were told our filters would remove phycotoxins. We boiled the water anyway to be on the safe side and to make Ruth happy. We put the tent up next to the lake and took the rest of the day off to wash ourselves and our clothes and to swim. It was a pleasant afternoon. I took the time to write up my notes before I fished for our dinner.

* * *

Journal entry: 16 February, near Glennville, GA, off U.S. 301

Walking south on U.S. 17 from Ashepoo, we had to cross the Combahee River. Its assoc. wetland is now twice the size it was in the satellite image I have with me that was taken 25 years ago. I confirmed the bald cypress trees on the periphery of the wetland were dead and had not simply lost their needles for winter. Over

35% of the wetland is now open water. Its conductivity was 3,500 μS/cm; I assume the trees and the submerged aquatic grasses were killed as a result of increased salinity or water depth.

Interviewed family met on Route 204, they reported: 1) their family farm had failed due to the drought in the southern portion of SC and the entire state of GA that has persisted for 3 years; 2) the militia that had occupied Fort Stewart has disbanded, and the base is now deserted. Accordingly, it won't be necessary to detour on the return trip or the next trek south.

The report of the failed farm was only one among many—we obs. 15-20 abandoned farms traveling south. This is, of course, particularly disheartening; if we're ever to recover, we need to build an agrarian society. We must begin supplying farmers with drought-resistant crops and the information on when it is safe to plant. I needed to get my model working and we need to publish our new Farmers' Almanac.

Drought conditions are moderate to exceptional; all vegetation showing signs of stress with some herbaceous plants dying. Although standing water is scarce, we found a lake today. Meteorological data measured at this location are tabulated on the previous page.

It is noteworthy that we were attacked by a pack of wild dogs the day before yesterday. Interestingly, they continue to be found here, where there are few wolves, but are no longer common farther north, where wolves are present; likely being killed or integrated into packs by the wolves. We were also visited by three Ferals the night before last—they nearly came into the house we were sleeping in; their brazen behavior was possibly due to desperation to find/steal water.

* * *

As the sun went down, it became increasingly apparent I'd made another mistake in setting up the tent next to the only water source within kilometers. The sounds of animals started slowly. The insects were first. Then the croaking of frogs and toads. The hooting of an owl was next. Other noises then joined in, perhaps just raccoons or opossums. But then I was sure I heard the high-pitched yips of a coyote. I debated going out and rekindling the fire. However, it was the loud rustling of the cattails and tussock sedges near the lake that worried me the most. I hadn't seen any alligators, but I was now imagining one approaching the tent. I kept telling myself it was just a deer or a boar coming to the waterhole for a drink. I would not get any sleep. Of course, Ruth was already sound asleep, missing the chorus completely.

I woke the next day to the sound of ducks out on the lake. I quickly crawled out of the tent and was able to shoot two before they all flushed. I told myself this was due to my hunting ability and not because animals were losing their fear of humans since there were so few of us left. As I stood there wishing I didn't have to wade out into deep water to collect my ducks, I thought how nice it would be to have a retriever do it for me, but even Otis wouldn't know how to fetch the ducks for me, at least not without ripping them apart first. I then gingerly walked out into the water scanning the nearby mud for tracks and retrieved our breakfast.

I put aside my aversion to plucking birds and just got it

283

done. The ducks tasted great and made it all worthwhile. After breakfast, we filled every container we could find with water. I even walked to a nearby house and found more containers.

As we continued walking south, the temperature rose, especially on clear days with the scorching sun beating down on us. Unfortunately, we were headed to the Sunshine State.

Chapter 17. Welcome to the Sunshine State

It took us another seven days of walking through drought-ridden Georgia before we reached Florida. Fortunately, it didn't appear as if the drought extended this far south. The few people we saw walking north behaved differently from other groups we'd encountered on the road. Rather than avoiding eye contact and refusing to engage, these people approached us and asked about conditions farther north. They were all desperate to learn when we'd run out of water. Because they couldn't understand why anyone would be headed south, they all assumed we'd turned around after not finding water. Apparently, others had been returning regularly after attempting to travel north, returning to tell stories of not being able to find water. When they asked if we were headed to the shelter, I told them I was always on the lookout for shelter. They then explained it was what people called the camp west of Jacksonville. It was a kind of way station for people migrating north. When pressed, they told us where it was located but warned us it was a nasty, disgusting place, and that they'd risked the drought only because they couldn't stand living there any longer.

Because I wanted to learn more about this camp, we stayed on U.S. 301 and headed west. We'd get on the beltway around Jacksonville, farther south. When we hit I-10, we turned east and encountered a man and a boy pushing a cart containing a field-dressed deer. The both carried bows and were dressed in camouflage, mesh bug jackets, and pants.

As we approached, I said. "That's a fine-looking deer, Mister."

"Thanks," replied the man. "We had a great day today," he patted the boy's shoulder—"didn't we, son?"

"Yup, we'll get a good price for this beast," the boy said.

"My name is George Reynolds, but most people just call me Reynolds. This is my wife, Ruth."

"Good to meet you. I'm David, and this is my son, Travis."

"Can I ask what your son meant when he said you're going to get a good price for the deer?"

"We bring our kills back for barter," he said.

"You wouldn't by chance be headed back to the Shelter, would you?" I asked.

"Where else?"

"Can we tag along?" I asked. "We're headed in that direction."

"Why not," he replied.

"Is game plentiful around here?" Ruth asked.

"No, it's been hunted out. That's why we gotta travel so far to hunt, and why this deer is worth so much. So you haven't been to the Shelter yet?"

"No," I said.

"Are you staying long?" Travis asked.

"We might stay a night or two," I said.

"That's what everyone says when they first arrive," David replied. "Then they hear all the horror stories, so they stick around for a while before headed north."

"We're headed south," Ruth said.

"South? Why you headed that way?" he asked.

"We're looking for a better place to live."

"Well, you ain't going to find it in the south. It's too hot, too humid, with too many bugs. Then there's the fucking storms, and if you go near the cities, you've got to hide from the machete-wielding gangs."

"It's that bad?" I asked.

"That's why we're outta here. I got a woman and another son back at the Shelter."

"How long have you been there?" Ruth asked.

"Seven months, but we're leaving any day now. Ain't that right, kid? Maybe with what we get for this deer, we can get the rest of what we need."

"What do you need to travel north?" I asked.

"Better shoes, and more water bottles," he replied.

Travis smiled with obvious pride as he patted the pushcart. "I found this baby for us the other day."

"What can you tell us about the Shelter?" I asked.

David stopped, shook his head and said, "You gotta see it and smell it to believe it. When you get there, you'll have to deal with a man named Leo. You'll find him in an office on the east side of the building. You can't miss him. He'll be the fat guy wearing a red armband."

I said nothing but noticed that Travis suddenly stifled a

287

laugh.

"All the enforcers wear red armbands. Steer clear of them if you can, but you gotta deal with Leo. He takes the first rent they charge to camp there, more if you want a space inside." Lifting his hand and wrist to show me. "He'll give you a short piece of ribbon to tie on your wrist: green if you rent space outside like we do or blue if inside."

"How much? What do you give him?" I asked.

"He'll demand first cut when I butcher this deer. I'll have to give him something else in three days, but again we live in a tent outside."

I stopped asking questions as I pondered what I could barter to stay at the shelter. After a few more kilometers, I knew we were getting close to the Shelter by the putrid smell of sewage and rotting garbage. Then I spotted some activity up ahead.

"They dump the camp's garbage over there," David said.

Garbage was spread out over an enormous field at least four or five hectares in size. There were two guys pushing wheeled carts full of garbage toward the field. Another guy was dumping his load. As soon as he pulled away, two men threw themselves on the pile and began fighting over the scraps. But what was most disturbing was the ten or so kids picking through the field of trash.

"On a bad day, the wind blows the stench toward the Shelter," David said. "Over there is the cesspool where they dump the piss and shit from the outhouses. They're constantly reminding us that's part of what's covered in the rent—hauling away the shit and garbage."

We walked for another kilometer or so, and then I spotted the Shelter. It was a massive warehouse or distribution center covering five or six hectares that must've had millions of square meters of floor space. There were sixty large bay doors on this side of the building; most were open, but large rolling steel doors were closed tight on a few. Semi-trucks were parked in front of them. Surrounding the building were hundreds of tents and makeshift shelters. There were many small fires burning.

"I can understand why you said we'd have to see it and smell it to understand," I said.

As we walked through the camp toward the building, I could see that most of the makeshift shelters would do little to protect the occupants against the weather. There were a surprising number of wooden pallets that people were sleeping on, probably hoping to lift the occupant away from the rats that must be rampant. I was surprised they hadn't been burned for warmth, but then I remembered this was Florida. A few people were living in rusted cars in the parking lot. I also spotted what I knew was a bus stop shelter that a family appeared to be living in. The metal framing was rusty, but it still had its plexiglass panels. A fire was burning in the rusty trash receptacle that was attached to the metal frame. There was also a family living in a trash roll-off turned on its side. Other trash roll-offs were being used for their intended purpose and filled with garbage. Yet, there was trash on the ground everywhere, but none of it appeared to be combustible; anything combustible was likely burned. I then noticed what must have been close to a hundred porta-potties lined up on the edge of the parking lot.

"This is where we stop. We gotta let my woman know we got back safe. Maybe I'll see you later. I've gotta give Leo his rent. Again, good to meet you two!"

"Thanks for letting us tag along. Good luck with your

bartering. I hope you get up north soon. Where are you headed anyway?"

"I heard North Carolina or Virginia is a nice place to live."

"They are nice," Ruth said.

"Have you been there recently?" Travis asked.

"Yes, a month or so ago," she replied.

Then David asked, "Maybe I could find you later and ask you some questions about your travels."

"Yeah, sure," I replied. "Well, thanks again."

As Ruth and I walked through the maze of tents and shelters toward the building, she asked, "George, what are we doing here? Let's just keep walking south."

"This is a great opportunity to interview people. Remember, you reminded me a few months ago, that's part of our mission."

"I can already tell you the status of society simply by looking at this place and by smelling it."

When we entered the building, we found a vast, cavernous space with high ceilings filled with a skeletal network of raised metal platforms and walkways. Men with red armbands were up on walkways monitoring the throngs of people below. Fishing line was strung everywhere. Sheets, blankets, and tarps were hung from the wires to offer some semblance of privacy for the people living in small spaces on the floor that were arranged in rows upon rows. We found the office that David had told us about, and inside was the heaviest man I'd seen outside of Phoenix sitting behind an old metal desk. But he wasn't fat, at least not fatter than I was. He just wasn't skin and bones like everybody else out here. I wondered if that was why Travis had laughed when his father had said Leo was fat? That little bastard thought I was fat too.

Leo was in his early thirties and had a neckbeard; it wasn't that he was shaving his cheeks and upper lip—he just couldn't grow facial hair anyplace but on his neck. The hair on top of his head hadn't been clipped in some time, and so contained many strays, which would be termed flyaways if his hair weren't so greasy. He was wearing a dirty gray jumpsuit with a red armband on his right arm. The front of the jumpsuit was covered in stains, clearly from spilled food. His office stank of body odor, which was saying a lot because the whole building stank of BO from a couple of thousand people that hadn't taken a bath or shower in a very long time, if ever.

"Are you Leo?" I asked as we entered the office.

As he looked up and smiled, a creepy smile at seeing Ruth, he said, "Yeah, whatdaya want?"

Without thinking, I took a deep breath to stop myself from punching the creepy bastard in the face, but had to choke back a gag because I tasted what I was smelling.

"We understand we need to talk to you if we want to stay for a night or two."

"Whatcha got to trade? Those backpacks look nice. What are those curved wooden things sticking out of your packs?"

"No, I was thinking of these." I dropped two ferro rods that I'd removed from my pocket on his desk. They hadn't been used much since they were backups to my backup. When he looked confused, I picked them up and struck them together, creating lots of sparks. "People always need to start fires."

He took them from me and struck them together and smiled at the sparks.

"This'll getcha a small space for one night inside, but I've gotta warn ya that rule-breakers are kicked out and forfeit all their belongings. Got it?"

291

"What are the rules?" Ruth asked.

"No stealing, no starting your own fires inside the building, no fighting or killing. We don't care what you do if it's voluntary, but rape will get you kicked out. And don't you ever pretend to be a Redband. That'll get you killed depending on who catches you."

"What are the Redbands?" Ruth asked.

He pointed to his red armband and said, "Redbands enforce the rules. Okay, take these blue ribbons—wear them on your wrists at all times or you'll get kicked out. Now go back outside the office, turn left, and find Larry—he's another Redband. Tell 'em I said you got an inside space for one night. If you want to stay longer than that you'll have to barter with him. And a word of caution, keep an eye on those backpacks. A lot of people are going to want 'em."

As I turned to follow Ruth out the door, he said loud enough to be sure she heard, "And the same goes for your woman."

* * *

We found Larry, and after navigating a complex labyrinth of stalls, he showed us to ours. It was only large enough to allow both Ruth and me to lie down. He also pointed out which fire pit we were assigned to cook any food we had. He told us we had to find our own food and water to drink and wash, and could only use the porta-potties on the east wall. While our little stall had sheet walls between us and the three spaces surrounding ours, it had no sheet for a door. I rummaged in my backpack and found the tarp I used to cover the tent when it rained and hung it up for a door.

Standing there in the middle of our stall, I couldn't resist and said, "Home sweet home."

Ruth just glowered at me and shook her head.

I then whispered, "Alright, I'm going to walk around and try to interview people. You stay here. Don't go out and don't use the porta-potties by yourself. When you need to go, I'll go with you and keep an eye on you to make sure you're safe."

"Are you kidding? I'm not using those toilets. I'll hold it until after we leave tomorrow. And we're definitely leaving tomorrow."

"You can't hold it until then."

"You watch me."

"Okay, I'll go see how bad they are and come back and report. But promise me you won't leave for any reason."

"Okay, I promise."

Taking my backpack with me, I walked over to the line of porta-potties. Before I even got there, I had to hold back a retch from the smell. Okay, maybe we'd just have to time it right and use them immediately after they were emptied. I walked around trying to strike up a conversation with anybody who looked promising. This was an exceptional opportunity to interview people and learn where they'd come from, the type of settlement they lived in, and about the weather they'd been experiencing. As is the case when meeting people on the road, most refused to make eye contact, particularly the women. Finally, a man sitting on a five-gallon bucket nodded, acknowledging me. He was in his early thirties, had dark skin, and looked to be of Hispanic origin. His cheeks were glistening with sweat.

"Hey, how's it going?"

"Same old—bored out of my mind," he said.

"You been living here long?" I asked.

"It's been a month since we got here."

"When are you planning on moving on?"

"As soon as we know the rains have come back up north."

"Why stay here?" I asked.

"We heard it was a safe haven, but when we got here, we found a shithole. But it's safer than being out on the road. You musta've heard 'bout the highwaymen on roads going north?"

"Yeah, we heard some rumors about them."

Just then, a woman came up and stood next to him. She was his age and also looked to be Hispanic.

"Manuel, why are you talking to this stranger? You're supposeta be getting water."

"I'm sorry if I delayed him," I said. "My wife and I just arrived, and I wanted to learn more about this place."

"Can't you see for yourself?" she asked. "Can't you use your nose? No one should live like this—there's no privacy, no proper food, no necessities that a person needs."

"Where did you live before you came here?"

"We lived in a place called Hialeah," the woman said.

"Why are you moving north?" I asked.

"Summer is so hot; it's awful. So are the bugs. We just couldn't live like that no more. Then a hurricane come and destroyed everything. It was time for a new beginning. Now, that's enough talk. Manuel, you go get the water before it gets dark."

She slapped him on the arm to get him moving. He got up off the bucket, picked it up by its handle, and turned to leave.

Before he got away, I asked, "Where do you get your water from?"

"You go two or three miles east of here to a canal to get water good enough to drink. Everyone goes there now. Just follow the line of people with buckets or cans."

I spoke to several other people who gave me the same reasons for migrating out of Florida. As I was sitting interviewing two men, a kid came up behind me and tried to steal my backpack. I grabbed it from him just before he got away. One of the two men yelled something and threw an empty can at the kid, but missed.

The other guy turned and said, "Hey, that was my water can. Now go fetch it back."

The man that threw the can made no effort to get up but said, "Those kids are nothin' but trouble. Always stealing and getting into trouble."

As I got up, I said, "I'll fetch your water can for you." I returned the can and went on my way.

Then I spotted an older Redband who, unlike the others, didn't have a permanent scowl on his face. He was leaning on a wooden crate that someone was sleeping in. I made eye contact and nodded. He nodded in return, so I walked over to him. He was my age, had very long hair, and was wearing a faded T-shirt, shorts, and flip-flops on his feet. I thought about telling him about the kid who tried to steal my backpack, but decided it was better not to make a scene, and instead, I would try to learn more about the shelter. When I approached, I got a whiff of something even more disgusting than the porta-potties.

"Can I ask you a question?"

"Why not? I ain't doing nothin' but standing here."

"Do you know how long this place has been in operation?"

"That's an odd question. Nobody's ever asked me that before."

"I just arrived, and I'm curious," I said.

"I dunno for certain. I've been here for five years, and it was already set up when I got here. It wasn't so packed back then."

"Why's it more crowded now?"

"It used to be a layover spot. Folks would stay a day or two before heading north. Now some stay put for weeks or longer hoping the rain returns up north. So it's been a bottleneck for the past couple of years."

"The conditions are pretty bad," I said.

"Things were better back then, but it's just too crowded now. And there's alotta bad people here, and it's not just them people on the floor. You should be careful talking to us Redbands."

I nodded. I could imagine the corruption and extortion that must go on here.

"But it's way worse in the summer," he said. "The open doors give us some breeze, and we have shade. But it's miserable outside in the scorching sun; we've got people dying outside every day from heatstroke during the summer."

"What do people do all day?"

"Folks mostly just sleep, unless they're looking for food or water. We prefer that, else they'd be fighting."

Just then, another Redband came up with a shovel in his hand. "It's dug."

"Good, I'm tired of standing here smelling him." Flip-flop Redband replied.

The second Redband leaned his shovel against the crate,

and they both reached in and grabbed the person sleeping, only he wasn't sleeping.

"What happened?" I asked.

"He died a coupla nights ago," the second Redband said. "I been out diggin' a grave for him."

I thought it was time I got back and checked on Ruth, so I said thanks and got the hell out of there. On the way back, I saw people cooking their dinner at the communal fire pits. The main entree on tonight's menu appeared to be rat. I also noticed lots of red plastic containers that were used for transporting and storing fuel. I knew it wasn't fuel they contained, so I assumed people were now using them to transport and store water.

When I finally found our little stall in the maze, Ruth was nowhere in sight. My initial anger was quickly replaced with panic. Then I heard her voice coming from down the row of stalls. I spotted several kids looking into one and guessed she was there. I walked down and looked over the heads of the kids in front of the stall. She was sitting on some blankets, stitching up a boy's arm. She looked up as the kids reacted to my standing behind them.

"Hi, hon."

"You promised me you wouldn't leave our area."

"Well, Levi walked past and was bleeding badly. I had to do something, didn't I?"

She went back to stitching his arm. The kids were sizing me up.

"Levi was one of the kids we saw scavenging at the dump today," she said. "That's where he cut his arm. Tina, over there with long brown hair, was scavenging with him. The fellow standing next to you is Chris."

Smirking at him, I said, "Yeah, Chris and I have already met."

"Well, next to Chris are Matt and Ellie," she continued. "The young lady who is obviously pregnant and standing behind me, watching my every move, is Carol. I think she has a knife in her hand."

Carol removed her hand from her pocket. They were all teenagers. Chris was the oldest, probably eighteen or nineteen. While the others had acne, he was the only one with pockmarks on his face. He also had other scars and was missing his thumb on his right hand; that was probably why he didn't have a good grasp on my backpack. Tina was the youngest, possibly thirteen, and was going to be drop-dead gorgeous, if she lived long enough to grow up. They were all dressed in filthy rags except for Matt and Carol. They were both wearing surprisingly newish clothes; at least they weren't ripped and torn. They also weren't as filthy as the others.

"Pleasure to meet you all," I said.

They didn't respond to my greeting and continued to size me up.

"Okay, now before I bandage this, I'm going to sprinkle some medicine on it to prevent it from getting infected, but you've got to keep it clean. Understand? No scavenging at the dump for a couple of days."

"We'll make sure he keeps it clean," Chris said. "What do we owe you for fixing him up?"

Shaking her head, Ruth said, "Nothing."

"Nobody here does nothin' for nothin'," Chris replied.

Ruth looked up and shrugged.

"I've got an idea," I said. "How about you all keep watch

on Ruth and our stuff, if I'm not around, to make sure no one steals anything or bothers her tonight or tomorrow?"

"We can handle that," Chris said with a smirk.

Ruth packed up her things, and I helped her up. We then returned to our little stall.

"That's an interesting group of ragamuffins," I whispered. "I assume they're all orphans?"

"Yeah."

"Well, at least it must have happened when they were old enough that they didn't turn feral. How do they pay rent for a space inside?"

"My impression is that the space belongs to Matt and Carol, and the rest of them aren't supposed to be inside. They were wearing strips of blue cloth on their wrists instead of ribbon, and they kept watching for any Redbands approaching."

"Well, how do Matt and Carol pay for the space?"

"I think they're prostituting themselves. Some of the others may do it as well or will do it soon. But I think Chris is out of the business now. He's probably too old. I don't know how long the little ones will continue to survive just scavenging on the dump. With the way Tina looks, she must get propositioned all the time."

"That's awful," I said.

"Yes, it is, and we should do something to help them."

"Like what? I'm sorry if I sound unsympathetic, but we can't take them all with us."

"I know, but we've got to do something. Let me think about it."

"Oh, goodie," I said, with the most sarcastic voice I could muster. "Do we have anything to eat? I really don't want to have to barter for a rat."

299

Just then, a voice from outside our stall said, "Ruth? You there?"

I pulled back our tarp door and found Carol standing there with a woman who was holding her arm at an awkward angle. The woman was grimacing and appeared to be in great pain.

"Ruth, this here is Barb. She burned her hand this morning and has been in agony all day. I told her you might be able to help."

"Let me see?"

I moved out of the way so the woman could enter our little space.

"How did you burn yourself?"

"I was cooking next to a woman who dropped a hot pan. I didn't think—I just reached for it to save the food before it fell into the fire."

"First, we need to clean the burn."

Ruth grabbed her water bottle from her pack and poured some water over the woman's hand. She then pulled a shirt from her pack and gingerly blotted the hand dry.

"Isn't there a healer around here you could've had look at this?"

Carol shook her head and said, "They demand too much for doctoring."

"Wait, I think I still have some balm we could put on it in my backpack." As Ruth rummaged in her pack, she said, "This balm was made for me to put on my face after I was burned. It's made from burdock root. It should help your hand."

Ruth spread some of the balm on the woman's hand.

"Oh, that feels better already," Barb said.

Handing her the jar of balm, Ruth said, "Okay, you keep this and apply some each day for the next couple of days. It needs to be covered, though."

Ruth reached down and picked up the shirt she used to dry the wound, ripped a strip of cloth off, and used it to wrap the wound. "Here, take this too; it's clean." She handed the woman the rest of the torn shirt. "Change the bandage tomorrow. You've got to keep it clean, or it'll get infected."

"How can I repay you?" the woman asked.

"Don't worry about it," Ruth said.

"Thank you so much."

Carol led the woman away.

Stepping back into our stall, I said, "You should open your own clinic."

"Somebody should."

"Now, can we think about dinner?"

"Ruth?"

We both turned to find Carol standing at the entrance of our stall again; I hadn't yet pulled the tarp door back to close the opening.

"I hear you guys talking about food when Barb and I get here. Take this as payment."

She handed me a large metal can containing some kind of soup, smiled, and said, "Don't worry, it ain't rat; it's rabbit stew."

"Where did you get it?" Ruth asked.

She patted her belly and said, "My baby's daddy provides for us, as long as I keep that secret from his wife and her brother. Thanks for doctoring us, Ruth."

Carol turned and left.

"Give me that," Ruth said as she reached for the can of stew.

"What are you going to do?"

"I am going to take it to our fire pit and boil it for a few minutes."

"Good idea."

I'd characterize the watery mixture as a soup more than a stew, but it was hot and didn't taste too bad. After dinner, both Ruth and I wrote up our notes. I had to leave the tarp door open for the the light from the fires to write by. We couldn't use the solar lamps here; they'd cause a stir.

* * *

Journal entry 25 February, 'The Shelter' West of Jacksonville, FL, just off I-10

Arrived today to find approximately 4000 refugees encamped in and around a large open warehouse called 'The Shelter' by the locals. Interviewed people staying here; all report they plan to migrate north once the drought lifts in GA and SC. Reasons given for migrating north include unbearable summer heat, repeated storm damage, insects, and gang violence. From the reports, it sounds as if the gangs are even more entrenched now than they were ten years ago.

This layover site has been in operation for at least five years. In the past, people remained for less than a week, but now live in the Shelter's squalid and unsanitary conditions for months. People running the camp exploit the refugees by charging/extorting rent and are called Redbands for the red armbands they wear...

* * *

Our writing was interrupted by someone blocking our light. When I glanced up, I saw the outline of a man standing at the entrance to our stall. I couldn't make out any details because the light was behind him.

"You the one providing medical treatment?" he asked in an angry voice.

"Why, do you need help?" Ruth asked.

"Oh, it was you."

"Why?" I asked in my own angry tone.

"Stop, or you'll be sorry." He turned and left.

"I wonder what that was all about?" Ruth asked.

"I bet we just met the local healer."

I got up and closed the tarp door, so we'd have at least the illusion of privacy, but realized I'd needed to visit the porta-potty.

"Are you going to need to relieve yourself before going to bed?"

"No."

"I'm envious of your large bladder."

The porta-potty that I used hadn't been emptied in a long while. Wishing I could take a shower after using it, I returned to our stall, closed the tarp door, and got into my sleeping bag. The concrete floor was going to be hell on my hip. I then heard the snoring coming from the next stall. It was actually comforting compared to all the crying, coughing, and arguing that was going on in other stalls around us. Great, another

303

night with little sleep.

* * *

I woke up in the middle of the night to the sound of torrential rain hitting the metal roof and a commotion outside our stall. When I looked out, I could see people scrambling to place containers under the streams of water raining down from the leaking roof. I placed one of our pans under a stream of water pouring down just outside our stall. I tried in vain to go back to sleep. When Ruth finally woke up, it was still raining. I took the pan of water I'd collected over to our assigned fire pit to boil for tea. Apparently, the fires were kept burning all the time, probably for the light they gave off. I was trying to decide what I could barter for food when I noticed kids with sticks running around chasing something by the big bay doors. I picked up the pot of boiling water, dropped the crushed tree bark we'd been using for tea into it, and walked over to see what the kids were playing. I discovered they weren't chasing a ball; they were chasing rats that were coming into the building. Someone was going to have a banquet of rats for breakfast. I looked out the bay opening and could see the sheets of rain coming down; water was pooling in the parking lot, flooding shelters and tents. The people outside were getting soaked, as were all their belongings. I hoped, for their sake, the rain would stop soon. It was weird living inside the vast building; you lost your awareness of what was going on outside. I went back to have my tea.

"When are we leaving?" Ruth asked as we were sitting there drinking our tea.

"As soon as it stops raining," I said. "Why?"

"You know why."

"No, why?" I asked.

"I'm going to have to use the porta-potty."

"Start taking deep breaths now. And don't forget to bring a rag or something. I can see the porta-potties from here. I'll watch out to make sure no one bothers you."

She got up and left, giving me a dirty look.

I couldn't help but think, *how this is my fault?*

Before Ruth returned, Tina brought us a roasted rat on a stick. I thanked her profusely. I then pulled the rat apart, removing various parts, trying to obscure what it was before Ruth returned and saw it.

On her return, Ruth announced, "That was the worst experience I've ever had to endure. Oh, where did that come from?"

"One of your ragamuffins brought it by."

"Great, I'm starving. But first, where's my water bottle? I've got to wash my hands."

* * *

The torrential rainfall was still coming down in the afternoon. The refugees outside began forcing their way through the barricade of Redbands standing at the open bay doors. There was a lot of pushing and shoving, but I didn't think the Redbands had the heart to keep them out. There was more than half a meter of water in the parking lot, and it was foul water, having flooded the dump and cesspool. Any objects that were buoyant, including a few rusty cars and several bodies, were now swirling around in the parking lot, driven by the wind. People attempting to get to the building, some carrying all their belongings, were being knocked down by the force of the rushing water. And it was still rising. A few centimeters more and it would be coming into the building.

People inside the building couldn't help themselves and stood beside the Redbands watching the disaster in the making. Fortunately, all seven of Ruth's ragamuffins were inside with us. I wasn't entirely sure why they were hanging out with us, but I guessed it was Ruth's motherly attitude toward them.

"We should get the hell out of here before it gets any higher," Chris said.

"Yeah, I don't know how to swim," Matt said.

Carol put her arm around his shoulders and said, "Matt, none of us do. Don't worry, it'll be okay."

"I wouldn't suggest leaving right now," I said. "Look, people are already having difficulty walking through the water. It doesn't take much water to knock a person off their feet if water is moving fast enough. And what if you're hit by one of those cars being blown around by the wind, or it pins you against something? Besides, it'll be dark in a few hours. We're fine here. If the building floods, we can climb up onto one of those platforms."

"George is right; we should all stay here at least until morning," Ruth said.

"When will the rain end?" Tina asked.

"It could last a couple of days if this storm stalls on top of us," I said. "You see, sometimes frontal systems can get blocked and stall—it's called an atmospheric block."

"Why doesn't the water just go into the ocean?" Levi asked.

"Flooding here takes longer to recede because the terrain is so flat," I said. "And the higher sea level doesn't help either when drainage outfalls are all submerged. But I expect the concrete and corrugated metal pipes used in the drainage system have all deteriorated over time, and any that haven't are now blocked with vegetation. So it could take a while."

"Well, I'm gonna go find something to eat while we wait," Chris announced. "Anybody with me?"

As they all moved to leave, Carol turned and said, "We'll be back, will you be here?"

"Yes, we'll be here," Ruth answered.

Carol smiled.

After they left, Ruth turned to me and said, "George, it was very smart to try to calm them down by boring them with scientific facts."

I smirked and nodded at her.

A few minutes later, the flip-flop-wearing Redband that I'd spoken to earlier came over. "Hey, dude, you should think about leaving ASAP."

"Why?" I asked.

"People are gonna start getting hungry. It ain't gonna be pretty."

"I was thinking of waiting until morning," I said.

307

"Don't wait any longer than that. Good luck."

"You too," I said.

And he walked off.

* * *

When the kids returned from looking for food, we suggested they grab their belongings so we could proactively climb up onto a raised platform. Ruth and I had already packed our stuff because I was unwilling to leave our backpacks lying around to get stolen. Once we got settled on our platform high off the ground, we sat there with our legs dangling off and watched all the activities below. Chris handed me a plastic bag.

"What's this?" I asked.

"Dinner."

I looked inside and found a lot of jerky.

"Where did you get it?"

"Don't ask?"

"Where?"

"Everyone here stockpiles food, thinking they're going to leave any day. I happen to know where some of it is stashed."

"That's stealing."

"It was gonna get ruined anyhow in the water, so it's better it gets ate."

I shook my head and pulled out a large piece of jerky and took a big bite; it tasted like venison. I then handed the bag to Ruth and said, "Don't ask."

I turned back to Chris and asked, "How'd you lose the thumb?"

"I messed up; I stole from the wrong guy."

"I'm surprised they didn't take the hand."

Smirking at me, he said, "I guess they had a kind heart."

After an hour, one of the ragamuffins shouted, "It's happenin'!" The water was flooding the building.

There was a moment of panic when people rushed around gathering their belongings. What most people failed to realize was that, besides swamping everybody's belongings, the water was going to extinguish all the fires that lit the place. It didn't take long for the entire warehouse to become flooded with a few centimeters of water. People weren't going to drown in a few centimeters, but it was pandemonium on the floor when the fires began blinking out, and the warehouse was plunged into darkness. Fortunately, a few of the Redbands had the foresight to stack tinder and kindling in strategic locations on the elevated metal raceways. Once they started lighting them, people calmed down appreciably. They also started climbing up. We had to fight off a few uninvited guests, but there were nine of us. Eventually, the kids started lying down on the platform to sleep. Ruth had me use paracord to tie the younger ones down so they wouldn't roll off. I wanted to do the same for her, but she refused. It wouldn't matter because I'd be there watching to make sure she didn't roll off and to make sure no one bothered us.

* * *

The rain stopped about three o'clock in the morning, but equally important, the winds died down as well. When the rain stopped pounding on the roof, the sudden quiet woke a few people up, but not Ruth or the ragamuffins. I woke them two hours later and told them it was time to leave. Carol and Matt upset everyone when they said they weren't coming with us. There was a lot of crying, but they said they had people there who'd take care of them. The rest of us climbed down to the floor, stepping on sleeping people as we went.

The water on the floor was only up to our calves, but we had to maneuver through a great deal of flotsam to get out. We made it over to the bay door opening to wait til sunrise. I wanted to be at the head of the line getting out.

As the sun rose, we could see the challenge ahead of us. Although the wind was no longer driving the floating debris outside, there was still a lot out there bobbing up and down. And there would be just as much or more debris under the water. I sat down on the edge of the loading dock and slowly pushed off. The water was above my waist, and it was cold. I caught my breath. After I got used to it, I turned, and began lifting Ruth and the kids off the loading dock. Being shorter, Ruth and the others had to hold their packs or sacks of belongings up to keep them out of the water. Fortunately, I was tall enough that I could wear my backpack, and only the bottom was in the water. I'd packed it so that it wouldn't matter. But most importantly, my hands would be free.

"Try to walk right behind me so that if I stumble over something or step in a hole, you'll know to avoid it. Chris, you bring up the rear and help anybody who gets into trouble."

We walked through the parking lot to the main road. Actually, it was more like a hip waddle than walking. I pushed flotsam out of the way, but when I encountered a large Styrofoam board, I pulled it over so we could float out at least a few of the sacks the kids had. I banged my leg on submerged objects only about a hundred times, but never stepped into a hole deep enough to go completely underwater. Tina fell once and went under, but Chris was there and lifted her up. When we got to the main road, it was elevated, and so the water was only thigh-deep. Wading became much easier. We sloshed east toward I-295. We'd made it through the worst of it, I hoped.

* * *

It took several hours, but it was a tremendous relief for all when we finally stepped out of the floodwaters onto the I-295 on-ramp, though there was also sadness. We'd have to part ways. The kids would go left and head north, whereas Ruth and I would go right and head south.

Ruth hugged each of the kids, smiling through her tears. When she got to Chris, she said, "I want to give you a present." She pulled her backpack off and removed the three pieces of her takedown bow. She attached the limbs to the riser. "You'll need to hunt for food. Have you ever shot a bow?"

"No," he replied.

"Ruth, we should've talked about this," I said while clenching my jaw.

While avoiding looking at me, she said, "Why? I know what you would've said. Chris, you'll still be able to shoot even with your hand the way it is."

Using the bowstringer, she strung the bow.

"Here, pull the bowstring. It should be easier for you than for me."

With a broad smile, Chris took the bow from her and dry-fired it.

"George, give him three of our arrows."

I was still clenching my jaw. I removed three arrows from my quiver and handed them to him. Ruth showed him how to nock an arrow. He lifted the bow and began lining up a shot.

"Wait a minute, you're doing it all wrong," I said. "First, you need to take a deep breath, then draw the string back to the same spot on your face or jaw every time. This'll improve your shooting consistency. Let some air out and then aim, but don't focus on the end of the arrow; focus on your target. And don't forget the follow-through. When you can find an object that won't dull the tip or snap the arrow's shaft, you'll need to practice, a lot."

"Thanks," Chris said.

"Be certain to retrieve the arrows when you hunt," Ruth added. "It's going to be very difficult to scavenge replacements because they're so valuable, but always keep an eye out for more in sporting goods stores and wherever you find yourself. And while you're doing that, look for better boots for Tina."

"Okay, come on, Ruth, they have to leave and so do we," I said as I put my arm around her waist.

I knew she was worried about them; so was I, but the bottom line was—they'd either live or die. We walked up our ramp, and they walked up theirs. They waved, but before she waved back, I turned and walked away from Ruth. I was furious.

Ruth followed me and a few minutes later, asked, "Are we going to talk about it?"

I kept walking and didn't turn around. "Why bother? You know what I'm going to say, right?"

"We couldn't let them go off without a way to hunt for themselves," she said. "I told you I'd think of a way to help them, and that was a way that wouldn't affect your timetable."

"How could you give up your bow?"

"We've got your bow and the guns. Besides, you hardly let me hunt anyway. I bet if these cars were running, you wouldn't let me drive either."

I just kept walking. Then I turned and said, "For the record, in the range checkout before we left Phoenix, you were more accurate with your .22LR than I was with my 9mm, but you've got a floating anchor point when shooting your bow and have less power. That's why I do most of the hunting."

* * *

I'd intended to get back onto U.S. 17 south, thinking it was west of I-95 and, thus, farther away from the coast. I didn't want to find ourselves surrounded by seawater with no drinkable water again. But U.S. 17 was flooded, so we cross

313

the Henry H. Buckman Bridge and continued to I-95, which, because of its elevated base, wasn't. The number of broken grocery carts, wheelbarrows, and little wagons abandoned alongside the road was impressive.

After an hour or so of walking, we passed a side road that wasn't flooded and decided to camp at a Courtyard hotel. It was in front of a hospital. That might have been why the side street had been elevated. We hung our wet clothes on the metal frames of the pool furniture out back to dry; the plastic straps had deteriorated in the sun and had fallen off. The pool was filled with green water and covered with algae. I broke some chairs in the lobby and left it to Ruth to build the fire. I still wasn't talking to her. I walked back toward I-95 to a swollen retention pond and caught several bass using little bits of jerky that I had. I took my time fishing because I didn't want to go back right away. When I finally returned, it was apparent that Ruth wasn't talking to me now. She always gets angry at me when I'm mad at her, even when it's clear she did something wrong. After eating the fish, which mercifully didn't taste like rat, I busied myself writing up my notes. Since we were alone, I could use my solar lamp for light.

* * *

Journal entry 27 February, south of Jacksonville, FL, off I-95 east of Julington Durbin Creek Nature Preserve.

Addendum to 25 Feb entry: While I cannot be certain until I review the historical weather in this area, we likely weathered a 1000-year storm while staying at the Shelter. The intensity of the rainfall was unprecedented in my experience; however, I could not take measurements without having to answer a great deal of questions. The deluge lasted for over 25 hours with little change in its intensity. Local inland flooding was dramatic, resulting in over a 1.5 m of standing water in some areas. Attributing this extreme weather event to climate change versus other natural processes will be tricky without further data from the field. I have no plans of taking sea level measurements here; I will to do that once we reach Miami.

* * *

To avoid any conversation with Ruth, I went to sleep early and slept like a rock. The next morning, I woke up refreshed. I got up and went fishing. While I was sitting there waiting for my third bass to bite, I heard bird activity in some Brazilian peppertrees on the back of the retention pond. I went over to investigate and found eggs in several nests. I tried to candle one using the sun, but the light was too diffuse, and I couldn't see any shadows. So I had to sacrifice one to determine it's developmental stage; I didn't want to sacrifice several eggs only to learn their development was too advanced to eat when I got back to the hotel. They were recently laid and were

315

perfect for scrambling.

After a breakfast of fried fish and scrambled eggs, we began our long trek down to Florida. The argument and the not talking to each other were over, at least until the next time Ruth unilaterally decided to put our mission and our lives at risk. Now I could begin worrying about the gangs that I heard about at the Shelter.

Chapter 18. South Beach

It took us almost two weeks to reach south Florida. As we walked south on I-95, refugees streamed past us heading north.

"George, have you noticed that people are staring at us? Do you think it's because we're the only ones headed south?"

"I don't know."

"Well, is it always this hot in Florida this time of year?"

"Yes, it is." I was sweating beneath the noonday sun, and it kept getting into my eyes, blinding me. And a mosquito buzzed near my ear. "Just imagine how much hotter it's going to be walking north in another couple of weeks."

All I could think of was, *we've got to pick up the pace.*

A few hours later, as we walked past West Palm Beach, Ruth asked, "George, have you noticed there haven't been as many fires in the suburbs down here?"

I sighed and said, "Yes, I've noticed it."

"Why the tone?"

I'd heard it immediately after I'd said it. "You're right, I'm sorry. I'm just in a mood and was thinking about something."

"What?"

"Our slow progress."

"I'm sorry! I'm walking as fast as I can!"

Even though that was part of the problem, I said, "No, that's not it. It's just that it's already getting hot, and I'm worried about the trip back. But to answer your question, the reason there weren't as many fires down here is that they didn't depend so much on natural gas for heating as up north, and, so after the blackout, fewer gas leaks. There were also fewer homes built entirely out of wood down here, at least in the PUDs."

"What's a PUD?"

"A planned unit development."

As we passed Pompano Beach, we spotted flooded streets in a neighborhood to the east. I didn't know if it was simply inland flooding or high tide. I should've walked over and checked but I was in a hurry. Regardless, I hadn't seen that kind of flooding on my last trip.

That night as we slept under an overpass west of Fort Lauderdale, I was woken up by the sounds of distant gunfire. I couldn't believe there was still ammunition available out here. I got up quietly and walked over to get a better look at the city, and saw several fires burning off in the distance. My stress level shot through the roof.

The next morning, I needed to find out if the gunfire was a one-off or a common occurrence, so I tried to engage with people who had also camped under the overpass. The first few people that I could tell were awake ignored me. Then I saw a man my age and a boy about twenty. The man looked healthy, at least he had no obvious deformities; he was balding but had a beard. The boy also looked healthy. Both were wearing orange and green basketball shorts and white cotton tank tops that were filthy. The older man's tank top was plastered to his body, and beads of sweat broke and ran down his face. They were stuffing their belongings into garbage bags.

"Excuse me. Buddy, can I ask you a question?"

Without even looking up, he said, "We got no food. We got no clean water."

"No, I just wanted to ask if you heard the gunfire last night?"

The man shook his head. "I ain't heard nothin'."

"He never hears nothin'," the boy said. "I heard gunshots, yeah."

"Is that a common occurrence down here? The gunfire, I mean?"

"It ain't uncommon," the boy replied.

"Thanks. I'm George Reynolds, by the way. My wife is over there still sleeping."

I knelt down on one knee, hoping to prolong the interview and get more information.

"I'm Luke, and he's my old man. He's named Grady."

"Do you live near here?" I asked.

Looking at his father, Luke said, "We used to live out west in Sunrise, but the old man is making me leave."

The old man stopped what he was doing and looked up. "The house was moldy from being flooded all the time, and the mosquitoes made life miserable. I hated it."

"Is that why you're leaving?" I asked.

"Nope, the real reason were leaving is I need to get that boy away from the gang," Grady said, looking pointedly at Luke.

"Right, old man." Luke turned to me and said, "I only agreed to leave because the heat ain't good for him. Mom died from the heat last summer."

"I'm sorry to hear about your mom, but you were in a gang?"

"Yeah, but it weren't no big deal."

"I was surprised by the gunfire last night," I said. "How do they still have ammunition? It's all been used up in most other places."

"Lot of people here had guns back in the day," Grady interjected.

"I betcha we'd find guns and bullets going through just a few of the houses on that street right over there," Luke said as he pointed off to the east.

"Yeah, I hadn't thought about how many people lived down here that had guns. Luke, what was it like being in the gang?"

"I said it weren't no big deal. We hung out and kept the neighborhood safe."

"Who'd you protect it from?"

"Other gangs trying to steal our stuff. We helped people too."

"How'd you help people?"

"For one thing, we get food and bring it back for 'em. They wouldn't still be alive if it weren't for us."

"You gotta be kidding? You kids don't know how bad it was right after," Grady said.

Luke shook his head and frowned. "Yes, we do old man. I can remember the smell and seeing all the bodies being burned."

"You couldn't. Your memories must be from hearing the stories," Grady said.

"Luke, where did you get the food to bring back to the people in the neighborhood?" I asked.

"Mostly from other neighborhoods. But some of us hunt gators and birds."

"Did anyone ever talk about attempting to farm?"

"No. I think it was too flooded to farm."

"Well, thanks for talking to me. Good luck with your trip north."

"Ain't you going north too?" Grady asked.

"No, we're headed south."

He leaned back and shook his head with his mouth agape. "What the fuck you doing that for?"

"We need to find something, and then we're turning around and heading north."

"You one of the looters that showed up after the blackout?" Grady asked.

"No, we're just looking for information."

"Well, you crazy. I wouldn't go south, not for anything. You think the gangs are bad here, wait till you get down to Miami."

"We'll be careful," I said as I got up. "Again, good travels to you both."

I walked back to where Ruth was still sleeping.

* * *

321

Later that day, Ruth and I saw more flooding in the neighborhoods surrounding Fort Lauderdale airport that definitely wasn't there ten years earlier. Much of the airport was also flooded to a depth of twenty or thirty centimeters, given how much of the landing gear of the planes was submerged. We walked in silence for a long while, but then, out of the blue, Ruth asked, "George, can we visit South Beach?"

"What!"

"There's that attitude again."

"Why do you want to visit South Beach?"

"I've read a lot about it and want to see it."

"Why haven't you mentioned this before?"

"I doubted we'd make it down this far."

"Thanks for the vote of confidence. That's not where Dad and I collected data from on the last trip."

"You had to shift sites in Wilmington, so does it really matter if it's just a few kilometers?"

She had me.

I signed and said, "I guess not."

As we walked through North Miami, we saw only a few people moving on the side streets. I got us off I-95 to find a place to sleep. I wanted to time it so we could get in and out of downtown Miami the same day, and thought camping overnight in an industrial area might be safer than going into a suburb. We found a plumbing supply store off U.S. 41 that had two bay doors for loading trucks, but no windows, so fewer points of entry to monitor. It was perfect. Although it was faded, it also had a cool mural of a lion taking a bubble bath in a tub on one of the outside walls. Not wanting to have a fire, we ate leftovers for dinner: fish I'd caught in a canal and fried for lunch, and warm water from our water bottles.

It was quiet during the night. I was feeling hopeful.

The next day, as we got closer to downtown Miami, Ruth asked about all the destruction we were passing.

"Did it look this bad the last time you were here?"

"Yeah, mostly. Hurricane Walter came through in 34, it was a Cat-5. It was the first direct hit for the City of Miami in over a hundred years. Of course, when the earlier one hit, the city wasn't so built up, but the damage was still catastrophic. Another direct hit was bound to happen eventually. A lot of the damage from Hurricane Walter hadn't been rebuilt when the insurance sector folded. Actually, the losses from that storm and from the sudden sea level rise that devastated Miami Beach likely hastened the failure of the insurance sector."

* * *

Rather than taking the Rickenbacker Causeway out to Virginia Key as I did with my dad last time, we took I-395 toward MacArthur Causeway and South Beach. We were both surprised by the flooding when we reached Biscayne Boulevard.

"Wow, look at all the flooded streets," Ruth said. "It's worse than Wilmington. Was it this bad the last time you were here?"

"I don't know; we didn't come this way, remember."

"Are you going to give me grief about that all day?"

"Maybe. But it's interesting that the flooding is mostly

to the north of 395. It's not as bad to the south. It must be differences in ground elevation. But look at those skyscrapers, that architecture's cool. What do you think that globe-shaped structure is in front of that building?"

"It was a planetarium where they projected images of space on the ceiling. The building next to it was a science museum."

"How do you know that?"

"I did my homework before we left. We've got lots of travel books in the library back in Phoenix, probably for you long-haul trekkers."

"Don't forget you're a long-haul trekker now too."

"Oh, yeah."

"Let's get out on the causeway. I'm hoping to catch sight of Virginia Key to see if there's been much change since the last visit."

We walked out to the highest span of the bridge.

"Wow, look at that cruise ship grounded on the island," Ruth said.

"It's surreal, isn't it—to see it like that?"

"I wonder what a cruise ship was doing here at the time of the blackout. Why wouldn't it have left after sea level flooded the islands and the coast?"

"No idea? That cruise ship terminal over there couldn't have still been in operation then."

"Maybe the cruise was sold as a tour of the country's new 'flooded city.'"

"I wouldn't be surprised. But I am surprised by all the smaller boats here too. I would've thought they would've at least been sailed or trailered away after sea level rose. We're going to have fun walking through all that debris on the causeway."

"Where's Star Island?"

"Farther east," I said pointing east. "That's Watson Island in front of us."

"Come on, I want to see Star Island—where all the rich people lived."

"I think you had to be rich to live on any of these islands. But give me a minute...I want to check to see if I can get a look at Virginia Key from up here. No, damn it."

It took us almost an hour to reach Star Island; there was so much debris on the causeway. Ruth was disappointed she couldn't go out on the island. Like the others, it had been swallowed by the bay. I noticed that the mangroves on the periphery of the island were much taller than the trees growing in the center. The houses were just shells of what they'd once been.

We continued on to the second section of the causeway that connected Watson Island to South Beach. When we reached its highest span, we saw that the streets on the beach were flooded. Most of the buildings remained, albeit severely damaged and flooded, but there must have been almost half a meter of water on the streets.

"I'm sorry, babe. Come on, let's go back to the foot of the bridge and take the measurements there."

"No, look over there in the distance beyond that collapsed high-rise. Palm trees with green fronds. There must be dry land. We can wade through the water to get to it."

"Babe, you know how dangerous it would be to do that?"

"Yeah, like we haven't done it before—like back in Jacksonville?"

"We didn't have a choice then."

"I don't care—I'm going."

325

She walked down the bridge toward the flooded street. I had no choice but to follow. The water was thigh to waist deep, depending on where you stepped and, of course, the length of your legs. I had an easier time than Ruth. Fortunately, this water was gin-clear, so we could see submerged objects to avoid. We walked through the flooded water to Ocean Drive and found the southernmost tip of the island dry. Rubble from the collapsed high-rise was spread far and wide in various directions. It was interesting that one of what must have been twin buildings had collapsed, but the other had remained standing. Vegetation, including coconut palms, many filled with yellow coconuts, had overtaken the property. Looking up Ocean Drive, we could see sections of the road were flooded, but farther north, it looked dry.

"Come on, we can walk on the beach," Ruth said as she started walking. "You've got to love that salt air. Hurry, I want to take a swim."

It was a gorgeous day; breathtakingly clear turquoise waters reflected the blue skies. As we trudged through the brilliant white soft sand, I checked my pocket watch. "Ruth, we need to stop and take the measurements so we can get out of Miami before it gets dark."

"No, just a little farther."

We walked past several blocks of flooded and damaged buildings along Ocean Drive. The side streets were also inundated, but as we walked north, the water flooding the streets became shallower.

"This is terrific!" Ruth shouted as she ran through an opening in the seagrapes that lined the seaward side of Ocean Drive.

"What's terrific?" I asked when I caught up with her. I then looked back over my shoulder at the opening in the seagrapes and wondered *who was keeping that gap open*?

She pointed to the street sign and said, "This is where the Art Deco district began. It's still here and isn't flooded. And that over there"—she pointed to a large, strange-looking building—"is where we're spending the night."

"No, no, no, no, I don't want to stay overnight in the city. It's too dangerous."

"We're not. We're staying out here on the island, in the 'Versace Mansion.'"

I knew I'd lost the argument before it'd even begun. "Why's it called that?"

"For the guy who owned it. I mean, he owned it up until he was shot right over there on those marble steps. Then it was sold, and they reverted to calling it by its original name, Villa Casa Casuarina, for some silly tree. It was built back in the 1930s out of coralline limestone blocks. That's why it's in such good shape compared to the other buildings."

As we walked across the sand-covered street, I asked, "Why was it called the Art Deco district?"

"For its unique architecture and the bright colors and pastels they used, and the chrome."

"Well, the buildings are all faded now, and all the chrome is corroded and pitted."

She gave me a look and said, "Don't be an ass and spoil it for me. Notice all the marble. Darn it, there was rumored to be a statue of a kneeling Aphrodite here at the entrance when Versace bought the mansion. I couldn't find out what happened to it, searching the World Wide Web archive we have. I was hoping we find it still here."

As she walked through the massive archway into the mansion where a door should've been, she said, "I wonder when the front door was lost. I hope the inside isn't destroyed. Come on, I'll give you a tour."

The inside courtyard was empty except for the piles of sand covering the floor. There was a frame for ceiling panels, but they were missing, so there was nothing to prevent rain from getting in. The wooden banisters on the upper floors still looked to be in relatively good shape, though. When she brushed the sand on the floor aside with her boot, she found a tiled floor underneath.

"Hon, look, the tile still looks good."

She then rushed out back. I followed. It was another courtyard with a large pool area. The pool was half-filled with sand and other debris, including some large urns that had been overturned. But we could still make out the tile mosaic on the wall, so Ruth was beaming. I wasn't that impressed, so I went back inside and searched the place to make sure it was empty. I walked up a bunch of small staircases to what looked like an observatory. There was nothing in the small domed room, but the view was amazing. I found a large room on the third floor, which was high enough to allow us to see the beach over the seagrapes. It was also empty of furniture. I made a space in the debris on the floor from the ceiling falling in and unpacked my instruments. I'd had to give in to staying the night here, but, if I had anything to say about it, we'd be leaving first thing in the morning. I went back down to the beach and began collecting and recording data, leaving Ruth to explore the mansion.

* * *

Journal entry: 17 March, South Miami Beach, Fla, at 'Villa Casa Casuarina'

On the trip south, we camped west of Fort Lauderdale and heard small arms gunfire in the distance, also obs. many small fires. Until now, I'd been confident we'd be able to fight our way out of any situation because we'd be the only ones with guns and ammunition, but now, we didn't have any advantage. Interviewed a father and son leaving the area who complained of summer heat, insects, and inland flooding. The boy was a member of a gang. He described fighting over territories, but also helping people—providing food. Good sign?? He also reported that it was too flooded in their neighborhood out west, called 'Sunrise,' to farm.

We arrived here this morning by way of I-95, I-395, and the MacArthur Causeway. We have obs. small groups of people moving throughout the city, but have not made contact as yet.

Obs. extensive flooding of Biscayne Blvd north of I-395; yet only about 0.5 km of Blvd south down to the arena flooded with 0.25 m from the bay (someone needs to check tidal stage - observations made at about 1230 this date). However, Blvd was littered with large debris, including boats. Bicentennial Park was not inundated but also littered with boats and other debris likely from storm surges. The number of boats here at the time of the blackout was surprising, given migrations had begun a decade earlier after the sudden rise in SL. Out on the causeway, approximately 30% of Watson Island's periphery was underwater (again, someone will need to check tidal status). Lots of debris, e.g., boats, dead trees, cars, and a grounded cruise ship on Watson Island. One can only speculate why a cruise ship was here at the time of the blackout. Most of Star, Palm and Hibiscus Islands flooded by >0.25 m of bay water; homes all flooded and have extensive damage with missing roofs and many walls collapsed. Height of mangroves in the interior of islands suggests relatively recent inundation. Lots of debris, e.g., cars, furniture, is also on the causeway and washed into the bay. All of western and much of the southern portion of Miami Beach is underwater up to 1 m deep in some places. I can't be sure, because we visited Rickenbacker Causeway and Virginia Key on a previous trek, but SL appears much higher. We waded through thigh-deep water on 5th St. to reach Ocean Drive, which was flooded in some areas. Land on the southern tip of the island is still exposed, along with about a 100 m-wide foredune running N-S along the beach face. We walked on the foredune @ 0.8 km north to 11th St., where the sand ridge was wider—exposed land extended from the beach back to Collins Ave. We will stay overnight at the Villa Casa Casuarina Hotel—a famous building Ruth had found in her research before the trek. From water marks inside the building, it has flooded up to the top floor and possibly higher in the past. Building is completely empty. No furniture remains, likely removed just after the initial increase in SL.

Results of meteorological and water quality data collected off the beach are tabulated on the previous page; also took measurements of distance to the edge-of- water from the front of the building at 1630; also tabulated on the previous page. Surprised that in March, water temperature of the surf was 29°C (i.e., few degrees shy of bathtub warm) while the air temperature *was a couple of degrees warmer at 31°C.*

* * *

On the way back in, I handed Ruth my field book so she could copy the data table into her book. After returning the instruments to our room, I quickly rolled out our sleeping bags. Unfortunately, these bags, given to us by the Freemans to replace the ones lost in the Ashepoo River, weren't designed to be zipped together. I then grabbed my fishing setup and went in search of bait. I found termites infesting the building next door. I tossed a few boards crawling with termites out into the surf along with a line with several bare hooks. This setup allowed me to catch small forage fish attracted to the termites as they sank through the water. I then used them as bait on larger hooks to catch our dinner. While I fished, Ruth swam. She looked gorgeous.

After I pulled in my third or fourth fish and was busy removing the hook, she swam over and shouted, "You know, you could use a good wash."

She wanted me to come out and swim with her, but she knew I didn't know how to swim. I looked down at the number of fish I'd caught and decided they were enough. So, I dropped the line and ran into the ocean, fully clothed. I sat down in the surf and began washing myself.

"I meant take your clothes off first," she said as she

331

splashed me.

"Why, they needed to be washed too."

I'd considered making a huge bonfire on the beach but didn't want to draw any unwanted guests, so I settled for a small fire just seaward of the seagrapes. I collected firewood and built a fire, but left the cooking to Ruth. I had a small project to do.

I went back into the mansion and out to the pool area and found a stark blue tile that was not too small. Most of the tiles in the mosaics were tiny, but I found one of the larger ones. It took me a while using my long knife to pry the tile off the wall without it breaking, but I did it.

After dinner, we sat around the fire, staring out at the ocean. With the sea breeze, it wasn't oppressively hot.

"Babe, do you realize that tomorrow we'll be headed home? I can't wait to get going. I'm so looking forward to this trip being done and to being home with Dan again."

"I can't wait either."

"Babe, what are you going to do first, after hugging Dan?"

"I'm going to take a long, hot bubble bath, with a glass of wine."

"What are you going to do?"

"I'm going have a tall frosty glass of beer and watch you take a long, hot bubble bath."

That got me a kiss and a smile.

"I've got something for you," I said.

"What is it?"

"Just a little memento of your visit to South Beach and the Versace mansion."

I handed her the tile that was wrapped in one of my T-shirts.

"What, your dirty laundry?"

"No, it's what's wrapped inside."

As she unwrapped it, I said, "It's a tile from the pool area."

A smile spread across her face, and she reached over and gave me a hug and then a kiss. "It's such a thoughtful gift. Thank you."

She gave me another hug. "Are you going to carry it all the way back to Phoenix for me too?"

"Yes, I'll carry it back for you."

She gave me a still longer kiss. *I liked where this was headed.*

"Maybe we should go inside?" she asked with a smile. "It's getting chilly."

It wasn't really getting chilly.

Using my most playful voice, I said, "Why not right here?"

She leaned toward me and whispered, "Sand!"

We both laughed, remembering the last time. We got up, joined hands, and walked back up to the mansion.

As we crossed Ocean Drive, we heard a man's voice say, "Good evening."

I almost jumped out of my skin. Then I got angry at myself for being so careless; two people were walking towards us on the street and I had only my knife on me. Enough light remained for me to see that it was a man and a young girl, so a wave of relief washed over me. I couldn't make out much detail, but could immediately tell the girl was walking with a limp.

"Sorry, didn't mean to startle you, but I couldn't think of any other way to get your attention. My name's Paul, and this is my daughter, Abby."

As they approached, Paul reached out his hand. I shook it and said, "You gave me quite a fright there. I'm George Reynolds, and this is my wife, Ruth."

333

"Hello," Ruth said.

"We saw you fishing earlier. When we saw your fire while taking our evening walk, we thought it'd be safe to stop and say hello," Paul said.

"Dad makes me exercise every day," Abby added.

"Do you live around here?" Ruth asked, looking pointedly at Abby.

"The Towers over on the next street," Abby said. "Where are you from? We know you don't live around here."

"We're from a ways up north," I replied.

"And you thought you'd take a vacation in Miami Beach?" Paul asked, with a puzzled expression.

"It's a long story," I said, nodding my head.

"Well, I'd be interested in hearing it, but maybe another time. I want to get Abby back inside."

"Why don't you come back in the morning for breakfast?" Ruth asked.

I wanted to scream, No!

"Okay," Paul replied. "How about I bring my fishing gear and help catch us breakfast?"

"Sounds good," I said, trying to hide my frustration at not being able to leave first thing.

"See you then," he said as he and Abby turned and walked off.

Ruth and I walked over to the mansion and up the short staircases to the room we were staying in, but the mood had been broken. This was evidenced by all the rhetorical questions Ruth kept asking about Abby. I was also still mad we would not be leaving at first light and a bit unnerved by getting caught out in the open without my bow or my gun. I tried to view it as a chance to interview someone living in

Miami.

* * *

We woke as the sun streamed through the opening where the doors to the balcony should've been. I was surprised there weren't more mosquitoes, but we had a strong sea breeze. We got up and went out onto the balcony. We had to be careful since the guardrail was rusty and wobbly. The sun rising over the flat ocean was an amazing sight. Seagulls were screaming. The salt air was wonderful. We went down and had tea on the beach. I'd stopped asking what she was making the tea from.

Paul and Abby found us sitting near the fire, drinking our tea. In daylight, Paul appeared to be in his late thirties, had sun-bleached brown hair, a clipped beard, and a very dark suntan. He was dressed in a T-shirt and shorts. He looked to be healthy except that he was rail thin and, like most people his age, was missing several teeth; the remaining teeth looked severely decayed. Abby looked to be eight or nine years old, but could be suffering from stunted growth. She had very thin hair that was sun-bleached like her dad's and cut very short. She also had exceptionally large brown eyes and was wearing a dress that revealed her misaligned right leg, which was the cause of her limp.

As promised, Paul brought along two surfcasting fishing rods. This would make getting the bait farther out into deeper

335

water much easier, as would the weights he had rigged on the poles. He showed me how to find and dig up what he called sand fleas to use as bait. They were in fact some type of crustacean. As we fished, I learned a lot about Paul and Abby.

"So how long have you lived out here on the island?" I asked.

"Only a few months. We've moved around a lot the past few years. My wife and I were kids living in the Keys when it all went to hell, but I guess we were fortunate. Many people had already evacuated from the Keys when the water came up. Afterward, our two families pooled our resources and survived down there for years in relative safety. But the water continued to rise, so we had to move north. Abby and I have been slowly moving north since my wife died."

"As Ruth and I passed Fort Lauderdale a couple of days ago, we heard gunfire, so I was surprised I heard nothing last night and didn't see any fires."

"No, it must have been one of their nights off, I guess. But don't be fooled into thinking it's safe to go into the city."

"No, I was actually hoping to leave right after breakfast."

"Where you headed?"

"North."

"Really? I've been planning to take Abby farther north, but I keep putting it off until she's stronger. But we've got to get out of here before the hurricane season."

"Are the storms bad?"

"Oh yeah. You know, maybe Abby and I could walk along with you for a ways. No, that won't work. I'd need to pack and get her ready."

"If you don't mind my asking, how did she hurt her leg?"

"She broke her leg three years ago, and it didn't heal

properly. She's had it pretty rough. As a baby, she was really sick. We thought she wouldn't make it for a while. You may have noticed she's small for her age. I'm worried she ain't getting any bigger."

"How old is she?"

"Twelve."

That surprised me.

"She took the loss of her mom a few years ago really hard."

"How'd she die?"

"Some damn flu that was going around."

"That's horrible," I said.

"Yeah, but Abby's a brave little girl and never complains. I just don't know what would become of her if something were to happen to me."

"I agonize over that too—about what would happen to Ruth."

We were both quiet for a long time before I said, "Well, I think we have more fish than we can eat. Let's go fry 'em up."

We walked the fish back up to the fire that Ruth had going. I could immediately see that Ruth and Abby had hit it off. Laughing and talking while tending the fire and washing seagrapes to go with the fish. I was surprised the fruit was ripe this time of year, but I guess now summer started earlier down here.

While eating, I asked Paul how it was to live in a high-rise without electricity or sewer.

"We live in an apartment on the first floor over in the Towers. But before we moved to the island and before Abby broke her leg, we lived on the third floor of a high-rise on the east side of 95. It had missing windows, terraces without guardrails, and crumbling walls, but it was home. You gotta understand that living above street level in a high-rise, even one that's not structurally sound, is safer than living on the streets or in the suburbs. It's funny, the opulent apartments with their breathtaking views, originally meant for the rich and powerful, now belong to squatters."

He hadn't really answered my question, but I let it go.

"Can I ask where you find freshwater out here to drink? We're running low."

"Oh, I can show you where rainwater collects in several places later."

"That'd be great. What do you eat besides fish?"

"We do eat alotta fish. I have several other rods back in our condo, but when we tire of fish, I trap and snare iguanas and other small animals."

"Dad spends hours rigging his snares," Abby added.

Then the discussion turned to our leaving and returning north.

"Please don't go," Abby cried, grabbing Ruth's arm. "We just became friends."

"I know," Ruth said as she put her hand over Abby's hand. "I'd like to get to know you better too. But we've got to get home. We've got a little boy younger than you waiting for us."

"Too bad you have to go today," Paul said. "George and I were talking about Abby and me traveling with you a ways."

"You're leaving and going north?" Ruth asked.

"Yeah, we've been planning it for some time, haven't we, pumpkin?"

"Yes. Daddy doesn't think the weather here is good for me."

"Why can't you leave with us?" Ruth asked.

"I'd need time to pack and get ready."

"How much time?" she asked.

I didn't like where this was headed.

"I'd need at least a day to pack."

"I'm sure we could wait a day, couldn't we, George?"

I sighed heavily and said, "I guess we could wait another day."

Paul clapped his hands together. "That's great! But would you consider staying just a bit longer. Before heading north, I thought it would be a good idea to dry and salt alotta fish to bring along on the trip to eat. It'd mean staying for an extra day to dry the fish. But I've already stockpiled the salt and have the wire racks we'd need."

I knew I was already screwed, having agreed to stay for one day.

"Okay, bringing dried fish along to eat sounds like a good idea," I said. "Hunting along 95 down here isn't very productive."

"Why don't you spend today fishing while I'm packing, and later, I'll come back with the salt and racks, and we'll get started drying."

* * *

Later that day, while fishing and waiting for Paul to return, I became concerned about a storm brewing on the eastern horizon. After what we'd gone through, I kept watching to see if it was going to spawn a waterspout or tornado, turn out to be a 1000-year rain event, or maybe even a hurricane. I was seriously debating whether I should grab Ruth and get off the island before it hit when Paul came walking down the beach with his fishing rod in hand.

"How's it going, George?" he asked. "Catching anything?"

"I'm worried about that storm over there."

"Oh, that's probably nothing; we get storms every couple of days. It won't rain for long. It might even fizzle out before it gets to us."

"You sure?"

"Well, I can't be a hundred percent sure. You know that's one of the many things I miss from before—weather forecasts that would tell you if a big storm was approaching. Now we can never be sure what to expect. That's one of the reasons I want to get Abby away from here before the real storms get here."

* * *

It took us two days to dry the fish to the desired moisture content. While Paul and I fished, salted and dried the fish, Abby showed Ruth around the Art Deco Historic District. The two of them were having a ball. It was a shame everything had been moved out of the shops, but I guess I should be happy the nightclubs were closed, or they might be out partying.

On the afternoon of the second day, I took a break from fishing and walked back to the mansion to see what Ruth was up to. I knew she was around because she'd left the sleeping bags hanging over the balcony railing. She called it air washing. I just hoped she was being careful because the railings were loose. I wondered if any guests of Versace, or staying in the posh hotel later, had hung their bathing suits out there to dry. When I came into our room, I found Ruth brushing Abby's hair with her favorite silver hairbrush, which she carried all the way from Phoenix. I'd assumed she'd discarded the heavy brush when she had to cut her hair, but apparently not. They were giggling about something.

Wrinkling her nose, Ruth said, "You smell fishy. Be sure to jump in the water and wash before dinner."

"Well, hello to you, too," I replied. "Nice to be greeted with such affection."

"Hello, George," Abby said. "I'm happy to see you."

"Hello, Abby, I'm happy to see you too. Are you gals having fun?"

"Yes, much."

"I'm glad to hear it. Ruth, I just wanted to let you know we've caught all the fish we need and should be ready to leave in the morning."

That night, Paul and I discussed our route out of the city. He suggested we walk north along the beach and take Broad Causeway to 123rd Street to avoid much of the city. He said we'd have to wade through some water on the causeway, but that it'd be a lot safer than going back through downtown. I just wanted to get out of Miami as fast as possible, so I agreed.

After they left to return to their apartment, having promised to return at dawn, I added an addendum to my journal entry.

* * *

Journal entry: 19 March, South Miami Beach, Fla at 'Villa Casa Casuarina'

Addendum to 17 March entry: We stayed two extra days to salt and dry fish for the trip back. Last night, for the first time while in Miami, I heard lots of small arms gunfire and obs. fires. We plan to leave first thing in the morning. We will travel north with two individuals, a man and his 12-year-old daughter. Although I haven't shared this with Ruth, I am worried the girl's disability (improperly healed broken leg) will slow us down.

Chapter 19. Homeward Bound

It took all day for us to walk the twelve kilometers north to 96th Street. We tried walking on the beach when sections of Collins Avenue were flooded, but Abby, with her bum leg, had trouble walking in the sand, so instead we just waded through the calf-deep water on the road. When we got there, we saw that 96th Street was also flooded, so we'd have to do the same going west. We could tell Abby was worn out, and so we camped for the night before attempting that. Paul wanted to find a condo so she could sleep inside. I refused, imagining the condo collapsing while we slept.

While Paul searched for a condo, Abby stayed with us. Ruth and I set up the tent in a clear spot within the sea oats. She and Abby then searched for firewood while I got dinner for us. I thought we might as well save the dried fish for later, so I borrowed one of Paul's two-piece rods and fished. I caught several fish using the sand fleas as bait again. We all turned in early, knowing that tomorrow would be another strenuous day getting off the island.

In the morning, we had a cold breakfast of dried fish so that we could get an early start. Once we got out of the water and onto the elevated span of the causeway, we took a long break to rest and to look around; we could see that NE 123rd Street was also flooded all the way west to Biscayne Boulevard. But we got going again and made it to I-95 before stopping for the night. Abby had been a real trooper. After getting out of our wet clothes and eating a cold meal, we slept under the overpass. Thankfully, we were alone.

The next day, we started with another cold breakfast and got underway, happy not to be wading through water. As soon as we climbed up and got onto I-95, we were joined by other people walking north. At least they weren't staring at Ruth and me as if we were crazy because now we were going with the flow.

As we walked, with Paul and me in front and Ruth and Abby behind, Paul said, "You know, there was a common saying or a truism voiced down here when I was a kid, one sure-fire way to stop the snowbirds from coming south was to turn off the air conditioning and stop spraying for mosquitoes. It turned out to be accurate."

"Dad, you say that all the time."

We all laughed.

"But it's true," he said. "Florida has become unlivable."

A couple of hours later, we came across the bodies of a man and a woman on the side of the road. They hadn't been there long. They both had been stripped naked.

We made it only to Pembroke Pines before Paul wanted to stop. We'd just passed a flooded suburb on the east side of the interstate that had converted to marsh. The west side was also flooded up ahead, but we found a four-story Best Western hotel just off the interstate that was on dry land. I was okay with sleeping on the first floor. Leaving Paul to get Abby settled and Ruth to make a fire, I went out to hunt us up something other than fish. I found a sports field overgrown with vegetation just to the north of the hotel that must have been associated with a nearby high school or park. There were plenty of rabbits. Not knowing Abby's disposition toward eating rabbits, I skinned and cleaned them before returning. I was surprised at how much I was looking forward to rabbit after eating all that fish. That night, sitting around the fire swatting mosquitoes, Abby asked about Dan.

"You said the other night that you had to get home to a little boy younger than me. What's his name?"

"Dan," Ruth replied. "He's nine years old and is living with my parents while we're away."

"Why didn't you bring him along on the trip?"

"George and I knew we'd be gone for a long time and that the trip would be too dangerous for him to come with us."

"How long have you been away?"

"It's been almost a year now."

"Wow, that's a long time to be away. He must miss you terribly."

"We miss him terribly every day, I know that," she replied.

We sat there for a while talking about nothing and then turned in.

* * *

The next morning, Paul and Abby were gone. We checked their room, and it was empty.

"Where could they've gone?" Ruth asked.

"They must have left early this morning."

"Why?" she asked.

"Maybe they figured they were slowing us down."

Ruth was crying. "I didn't get to say goodbye. Maybe we can catch up to them."

Knowing Paul had asked me just yesterday why we weren't taking the turnpike north, I said nothing to give her false hope. The first thing I'd done when we couldn't find them was to check the stores of dried fish. I then felt like shit when I found he had left half of it for us. Ruth was quiet for the rest of the day. I knew she'd grown very fond of Abby. I held her hand as we walked.

* * *

Without Abby slowing us down, our pace quickened considerably. We were averaging twenty to thirty kilometers a day. We made it to Vero Beach before I began worrying about having to walk through the drought up north. I hadn't realized it until one evening sitting around the campfire, but Ruth had her own worries. That's the problem with hiking—you've got too much time to live inside your own head.

"Do you think there's any chance Richard's waiting for us?"

"No, I'm sure he thought he killed us in the fire, so he went home to his cult. I'm sure of it. And we're not going anywhere near them."

"What do you mean?"

"The most important thing now is to get home safely as fast as possible to make our report, so we're going straight home. No more stopping to take measurements or engaging with people. To avoid people, we're going to get back on the AT and take it home. It's more up and down, but fewer refugees and barricaded towns. The higher altitude will be cooler too."

"Oh, that'd be wonderful. It seems to be getting very hot, doesn't it? And it's not cooling down at night."

"Yeah, I noticed that too. I'm hoping it's just that we've had several clear days and the sun has been beating down on us. It's also been heating the road. We may need to move farther away from it at night to get away from the heat it's radiating."

"Will we have time to stop at New Town or to visit Russ and Jess to check on them?"

"Maybe, but it depends on what we encounter on the way. There is some risk taking the AT. If we're delayed, we could get caught in winter storms. And it would be colder and the snows deeper at the higher elevations."

"Where do we get back on the AT?"

"In Georgia."

She smiled and said, "That's a weight off my mind."

* * *

One day, walking through north Florida, I realized I was unconsciously 'cameling up,' which is a term trekkers use for refilling their water supplies before they actually need to. It's not a bad practice, but it adds to the weight you must carry. I think I was doing it because I was constantly feeling thirsty. I was bathed in sweat all the time and was becoming dehydrated from all the sweat I was generating, even at night. So was Ruth. I'd also begun noticing signs of stress in the vegetation and the animals; animals were no longer moving during the day. It was then that I understood it wasn't just the sun beating down on us over several consecutive days of clear skies; we'd walked under a heat dome. I felt as if I was burning up, so I decided we'd stop at the rest area that was coming up and I'd break out the instruments to see how bad it was.

* * *

Journal entry: 13 April, St. Johns County Rest Area on I-95, south of Jacksonville, Fla

I believe we've been under a heat dome for several days. Meteorological data measured at this location are tabulated on the previous page. Air temperature is 38°C, but the heat index is 53°C, well above normal body temp. Although we're covered in sweat all the time, it's not evaporating fast enough to cool our body temp because of the high humidity. So there is an increasing risk of heatstroke. We've stopped walking today and will try to cool down. We will resume our trek tonight after the sun sets. I am surprised at how dry it is here following the rain and the flooding that occurred here on the trek down just a month and a half ago. The drought appears to have extended down into Fla now.

Wilting and browning of vegetation is noticeable; if memory serves, plants stop photosynthesizing somewhere above 40°C or 45°C—not sure which.

* * *

Fortunately, the rest area had a stormwater retention pond that still contained a few centimeters of water—it wasn't exactly boiling, but I wouldn't intentionally run a bath that hot. So while keeping a lookout for alligators in the mud, we sloshed water all over ourselves. We then found a clump of trees away from the asphalt that offered some shade. We both slept for several hours. When I woke up, I walked out into the mud and fished the deepest part of the pond. Ruth came and harvested several arrowhead plants growing around the bank for the starch and moisture in their tubers. I braved the heat and built a fire when I returned with the fish.

Once the sun set, we got back on the road. It was treacherous maneuvering through all the debris on the road with only a quarter moon lighting our way. It wasn't the rusty cars abandoned after the blackout; it was the trash discarded by the legions of refugees that had streamed north, and their shoes.

Around midnight, clouds obscured the quarter moon, making it almost pitch black. Then, the booming sound of thunder filled the air and lightning streaked across the sky. It was very intimidating, but we began to hope for rain. None came. Lightning then struck the ground next to us on the road, terrifying us. Then another. Somehow, it made the darkness even darker. One minute it'd be pitch black, then everything would light up when the lightning struck. During those times, we'd look around, expecting to see something or someone sneaking up on us; it was very eerie. Slowly, the dry storm waned.

We walked all night and late into the morning. We realized that navigating in near pitch-black conditions would not work, so we changed our plan to wake before dawn and walk during the early morning hours. This worked well, but the drought that had extended down into Florida was even worse in Georgia. Finding game to hunt was next to impossible. We resorted to eating bugs and worms and the occasional snake. I told Ruth to carry her gun and be ready to shoot if we saw an animal. Concealing the fact that we had ammunition for our guns had been eclipsed by our need for food.

When she mocked me by widening her eyes and allowing her jaw to drop open, I said, "We've entered the territory of last resorts."

I could feel the air getting drier, so I again pulled out the instruments and took measurements.

* * *

Journal entry: 23 April, Circle K Truck Stop off I-95 just north of East River, GA

Addendum to 13 April entry: averaging only 6 km per day, walking only during morning hours. Dry storm last night with much lightning, but the raindrops must have evaporated before reaching the ground. We are now finding it difficult to sleep during the day—it's just too damn hot even in the shade. Meteorological data measured this location tabulated above. Air temperature is up to 40°C, but the heat index has decreased to 44.1°C, only because it's less humid. While sweat is now evaporating (leaving dried salt all over us), we ran out of drinking water early yesterday, so we have no water to replace sweat and to quench our constant thirst. Drought in GA continues and is worse than in north Fla. The only standing water I can find has elevated conductivity and thus is not potable. I am worried about Ruth. With blood being diverted to the skin, our organs are probably beginning to shut down. This can't go on much longer.

* * *

When we woke up, we immediately realized the temperature overnight had dropped below the dew point because there was condensation on the grass. We both quickly changed into our cleanest socks and began shuffling our feet through the grass to collect the dew. Sucking the moisture out of the socks produced little water, but it wet our mouths and cracked lips. I noticed Ruth had blisters on her face from the sunburn. *I then realized I had matching blisters.*

About two hours into our morning walk, I felt ill.

"Ruth, I gotta stop and rest a while. I feel sick."

"That's understandable. That little taste of water we had this morning isn't going to help much, and we haven't had any proper food for days. George, you're looking flushed. And why aren't you sweating? Do you have any of that brackish water left? I can at least pour it over your head."

"What water?" I asked.

"What did you do with the water? You didn't drink it, did you?"

"I don't know."

"George, tell me how you're feeling."

"I've got a headache, and I'm dizzy."

"George, your head is lolling to one side. George, George..."

Chapter 20. Running into an Old Enemy

Someone's in the room with me—I can hear them arguing. I've got to sit up. I scream and try to lift my arms. I realize I'm having a night terror. I don't want to hit Ruth with my flailing arms; I've done that before. Why isn't Ruth waking me up? I think I'm crying but there's no tears. Suddenly, someone is pouring water into my mouth. I instinctively gulp it down, but a lot of it spills down my face onto my neck and shoulders. It's cool. I wake up enough to register that I'm lying in bed, but I'm tied up. I try to think coherently, but I'm so tired.

* * *

I woke with a start. I couldn't roll over because I was tied to a bed. I looked around and saw that I was in a darkened bedroom alone. *Where's Ruth?*

After a few minutes I start screaming. "Is anybody there? Anybody, I'm awake in here! Ruth! Ruth!"

A woman came in with a bowl in her hand. "Shut up, you'll wake him."

"Where's my wife?"

"Shut up." She sat down and spooned something out of the bowl. "Drink this; it's broth."

"Where's my wife?"

"She's safe for now."

"Let me see her."

"I ain't got no say-so 'bout that. Swallow."

She spooned the foul-smelling broth into my mouth. It was burning hot and tasted awful. It spilled down my chin.

"You know you got me into a mess a trouble," she said, as she kept spooning the horrible-tasting stuff into my mouth. "I figured he expected me to fix you up; but how was I supposta know he wanted you dead."

"Who? Where's Ruth?"

She spooned a few more mouthfuls of the stuff, got up, and as she was leaving, said, "Yell out when you gotta piss. I'll send my son in to help you; I don't want you messing that bed."

I tried to wiggle my arms free from the rough ropes. It was of no use. I felt so weak and tired, as if someone had drugged me. All I smelled now was my body odor. I stank, but I also kept tasting the horrible stuff she'd fed me. I lay there feeling sorry for myself. I was so pathetic.

354

* * *

I was jerked awake in the middle of my recurring nightmare. But I remembered that instead of finding April dead sprawled on the ground in the nightmare, it was Ruth. I felt utter despair. I'm such a worthless failure, I can't protect anyone.

Someone kicked the bed. "Hey, you awake? You need to pee?"

"Where am I? Where's my wife?"

"She's okay for now; she's locked in my room."

There was enough light in the room for me to see a surprisingly large, black kid in his early teens sitting in a chair tilted back on the rear two legs.

"Why is she locked in a room, and why am I tied up? What's going on?"

"Father wants it that way. Answer me—do you need to piss yet?"

"No. Let me see my wife. Ruth! Ruth!"

"She can't hear you; she's on the other side of the house."

The woman whom I'd seen earlier came in. She was probably in her thirties, but her skin was so tanned and leathery from working in the sun, it was hard to tell. She could've been a decade older or younger.

"Camden, make him be quiet! Do he need to piss?"

"No, not yet."

"Then we've got to get more water into him."

The boy picked up a glass of water, tipped it to my mouth, and poured. I gulped instinctively, but most of it spilled onto

355

my neck and chest, wetting my back and the bed sheet. The woman left, closing the door.

Coughing up water, I said. "Who're you and who was that?"

"My name is Camden, and that was my mom."

"How'd I get here?"

"Your woman found Dawson. Said you were in a bad way and asked for help. He went with her and brought you back, cos we were told to watch for you."

"Watch for us? What do you mean?"

"Father told us you'd be coming. He had me watching 303 and Dawson 95."

"Who's your father?"

"What do you mean? He's Father."

"Who's Dawson?"

"He's a goddamn redneck. He came with Father."

This kid wasn't making any sense.

Just then, the door opened, and I was horror-struck by what I saw. It was Richard.

"Camden, you can leave now."

"Yes, Father," the boy said as he got up to leave.

My head was spinning; maybe I was having another night-mare.

"How are you feeling, George? You're lucky I wasn't here when Dawson brought you back. I would've let you die, but Gloria thought she was pleasing me, so I won't punish her."

"Where's Ruth?"

"She's in another part of the house. She's fine."

"What do you want with us?"

He sat down in the chair that Camden had just vacated. "I want lots of things. But most of all, I want to pay you back for shooting me and stealing one of my wives."

356

"What are you talking about? I didn't steal Julie from you. I helped her escape!"

"Oh, and you didn't want her for yourself? I know you fucked her. You spoiled her for me."

"I didn't sleep with Julie."

"Now I need a replacement because you made me kill her. Ruth's old, but she can still give me babies. My onus is to father as many babies as possible. You know, Ruth still looks good even with the scars. But they'll fade, and her lovely hair will grow back."

"You're a crazy, sick fuck."

"I told you that you weren't worthy of her. You can't even protect her."

"I'm going to kill you."

"No, George, I'm going to kill you. But first, I want to know where you got all the electronics in your backpack? What does it all do?"

"None of your fucking business."

"Well, I'm going to find out."

He got up and left.

He's right, I thought. *I did a lousy job protecting her. I couldn't save my dad; I couldn't save April and the twins, and now I won't be able to save Ruth.*

* * *

I was having difficulty keeping track of time; I'd fall asleep and then wake up and remember where I was. At some point, a skinny little white kid, maybe fifteen years old, came into the room. He was filthy and dressed in rags. He was carrying a bucket.

"You ain't dead yet? I figured you'd be dead by now for sure."

"Are you Dawson?"

"Yep, I'm the one who found you. Made Father happy. Too bad about your woman; she's pretty."

"What's too bad? She's still alive, isn't she?"

"Yeah, she's alive, but Gloria hates her and treats her like shit."

"Can you get a message to her for me?"

"Are you kidding? I ain't doing anything against Father. He's teaching me how to hunt. He's teaching that stupid bastard, Camden, too, but I'm his favorite. I saved him."

"How did you save him?"

"You shot him. He would've died if I hadn't come along. I thought he was dead and was taking his bow and arrows, but he waked up and grabbed my arm. I almost shit my pants."

"You were in Wilmington, North Carolina?"

"No, I don't think so. I found him on 95."

"Where on 95?"

"I dunno. I got no maps. Pretty sure I hadn't made it all the way to North Carolina yet."

"How long ago?"

"I ain't here to answer your questions.

"Come on, how long ago?"

"Long time ago."

"Weeks, months—what?"

"I dunno. Lots of days"

"You said you thought he was dead when you found him. Was the gunshot wound still bleeding?"

"No, but it weren't healed yet. It was all red and was seeping a thick pus that smelled real bad. He said it was 'infectated.'

"And you brought him straight here?"

"Yep, he wanted to walk south to catch you. I wanted to keep going north, but he said he'd give me his bow and teach me how to shoot it if I were to help him. So I did and brought him this far south. I dunno why he wants us to call him Father, but who cares as long as I get that bow."

I wasn't listening; I was thinking how stupid I was. He couldn't have started that wildfire. He was chasing us on I-95.

"Enough 'bout that. I was sent in here to help you pee. Gloria is all upset about you pissing in her bed. I ain't going to hold your thing, so I'm going to untie you and let you do it yourself in this bucket. If you try to escape, I'll beat you to death. Father won't care."

I had to pee finally. When I tried to stand up on my own, I almost collapsed. I would have if Dawson hadn't caught me. After I was done, I fell back into the bed, and he retied me.

* * *

I woke up later to find Gloria in the room pulling the sheet off me.

"What are you doing? I didn't mess the bed."

"It stinks in here. Move so I can change the sheets."

"Untie me."

"No. If you don't move, I'll strip the bed and leave you with no sheets."

"No, you won't because then I'll sweat directly on your precious mattress. Ouch, okay, let me lift my butt. You know he has other wives and children back in Richmond."

"He said you killed his wife."

"He killed her, and that was only one of his wives; he's got three others and three or four kids. I'm not sure how many because two of his wives were pregnant when we left. Can you give him more kids? If not, he's not going to take you with him when he leaves."

"Shut up!"

She left the room. Damn, she left before she put the bottom sheet on the bed, and the buttons on the mattress hurt my backside.

* * *

Sometime later, Richard came into the room, dragging Ruth. She broke free from his grasp and ran to me and knelt beside the bed. She buried her face in the crook of my neck and hugged me.

360

"George, I thought you were dead!"

Richard yanked her up and tied her to the chair.

"One of you is going to tell me how to work that electronic stuff, or I'm going to gut George."

"You're going to kill us both anyway!" Ruth yelled back at him.

"I'm not going to kill you. I'm taking you back. You're going to love living in Julie's house. And I'll take care of you better than he did."

"I'll kill you in your sleep," she replied.

He laughed. Then he left, closing the door behind him.

"George, I'm so sorry."

"What for?"

"For getting us into this mess. I was near panic when you passed out, and I couldn't cool you down. I thought you were going to die. So I went to get help and found Dawson. He seemed okay at first, but when we got here, Gloria locked me in a bedroom. I was practically hysterical worrying about you, and then Richard showed up. He thinks you wanted Julie for a wife. He also thinks you were the one who shot him. Its all my fault. I told him we were traveling to Wilmington and then down to Florida. He knew we would be coming back this way. He had Dawson watching 95 and Camden watching 303. They've been watching for months."

"I know. It's okay, and it's better that he thinks I shot him. But none of this is your fault. I should have listened to you and ambushed him at the start or tracked him down and killed him after he murdered Julie and the boys."

"What's our next move, George?"

"I want you to show him how to charge the instruments with the solar panel and then show him what they do. They're of no use to him anyhow."

"But how are we going to get out of here, George?"

I started crying. "Babe, we both may not make it out of this."

She was crying. "George, I'm working on Gloria; telling her about his families back in Richmond."

"She's not going to do anything against him," I said. "Listen, I want you to stop fighting and go with him. Later, you can kill him in his sleep. Then make your way back to Phoenix. You'll need the maps in my backpack and journal. If you can take the journals back, too, great, but you've got to make it back for Dan."

"No," Ruth said, sobbing.

"Ruth, you've got to face facts. I can't win against him and the two boys."

"No," she said, struggling to get out of the ropes.

With tears streaming down my face, I whispered hoarsely, "You said I didn't love you as much as April. But that's not true. I do love you. It's different, but I love you very deeply, and I no longer feel guilty for loving you; it's not a betrayal to April. I wish we could spend the rest of our lives together, but it looks like that might not happen. Just promise me you'll do everything you can to survive."

Suddenly, Richard came back into the room. "So what's it going to be?"

Ruth snarled, "I'll show you how they work."

"Smart choice," Richard said as he went around to the back of the chair, untied her, and dragged her from the room.

They left me wondering if I'd ever see her again.

* * *

A short time later, Richard stormed into the room carrying my portable weather station.

"What the hell is this?" he asked, shaking it in my face.

"Ruth must have told you. It measures air temperature, pressure, humidity, and a few other weather-related parameters."

"What good is that? What the hell are you two doing with this stuff?" He threw the instrument on the floor and stomped on it, smashing it into pieces. He left the room, slamming the door as he left.

* * *

A few hours later, Gloria came into the room with another bowl of noxious-smelling broth.

"I don't want any!"

She sat down. As she ignored me and began spooning the hot broth into my mouth, she said, "I'm gonna get you and that woman outta here tonight."

I couldn't believe my ears.

"I'll bring her here after everyone goes to sleep. I'll try to get your backpacks, but your electronics are all smashed up. I'll try to get your guns too, but you've gotta promise you won't try to kill Richard. If there's a fight, Camden might get hurt, and I can't have that. Will you promise?"

"I promise," I said. "Why are you helping us?"

"I heard him talking; say he's taking that woman back home with him. He was supposeta stay here and care for me and Camden. You got no idea what I've had to do to keep us alive."

"No, I don't. But thank you for saving me and helping us get away."

"Okay, scream out if you need to pee or the other thing. Dontcha mess that bed."

She left.

I had a newfound sense of hope, but at the same time, I began listing everything that could go wrong.

* * *

I was going crazy waiting. The sun had gone down hours ago, and there was no sign of Gloria. I knew I shouldn't have gotten my hopes up. He probably enlisted Gloria in some kind of mind game. Then I heard the door open. Ruth snuck into the room and ran over to me and started untying my arms. When they were free, I grabbed her and hugged her.

"Where's Gloria?" I whispered.

"She said to wait, that she'll bring the backpacks."

"Okay, we'll give her five minutes, and then we're leaving. Do you know where we are?"

"We're in a suburb west of Brunswick, Georgia."

"Do you know which direction any of the major roads are?"

"No."

"Well, do you know which way is west?"

"Yes, it's that way," and she pointed and noticed my frown. "The front of the house is oriented to the south."

"Okay, now I've got a bearing. We'll take anything going west, but keep an eye out for U.S. 341. Richard'll think we headed north."

"Why can't we kill him in his sleep?"

"That would wake the boys, and we'd have to fight our way out. I promised Gloria I wouldn't hurt Camden."

The door quietly opened, and Gloria slipped in and closed the door behind her. She had our backpacks. I grabbed mine, opened it, and found my gun. I made sure it was loaded and chambered a round.

"You promised," she said, sounding alarmed.

"I'll keep my promise unless I can't. Where's my bow and quiver of arrows?"

"I couldn't find them."

"Okay, at least I've got my gun," I said, holding the gun up.

I could now fight my way out if need be. We were almost free. I couldn't help but smile. Ruth was crying with a smile of her own. I then thought of my journal. I looked, and it wasn't in my backpack.

"Ruth, check to see if your gun and journal are in your backpack."

"Yeah, they're both here."

"Well, leastwise we have your journal, if we can't recover

365

mine." I turned to Gloria and asked, "Do you know where mine is? It looks like hers?"

"After finding that electronic stuff in your backpack, Richard started reading it to find out how it all worked. Last time I saw him with it, he was in the living room."

"We've got to try to get it back."

I got up and took two wobbly steps, leaning on the bed's footboard.

"Can you walk?" Ruth asked.

"Yeah, I just need to get my legs under me."

The three of us snuck into the living room and found the journal. Another wave of relief washed over me. Trekkers are careful not to give any clues as to Phoenix's location in their journals in case they're read by the wrong person, but I was relieved to have mine back. I could only imagine what Richard thought as he read my entries.

"Okay, what's the best way out of here?" I whispered.

We were at the bottom of the driveway when we heard Richard scream. Ruth and I looked at each other and ran.

Chapter 21. The Final Showdown

We were moving as fast as I could but I couldn't run far; I hadn't fully recovered from the heatstroke. Ruth was carrying both backpacks, but I carried my 9mm in my hand. I would not let that monster get his hands on Ruth again.

After several wrong turns, we'd found our way onto U.S. 341. I planned to take it west to U.S. 441. We had nothing to eat or drink, but didn't care; we were both alive. We couldn't stop smiling at each other. I didn't want a recurrence of getting dehydrated and having heatstroke, so we looked for water as we ran. Fortunately, the drought seemed to lessen as we traveled west. The vegetation didn't look as wilted and brown here.

We found a pond just off the road. It even had a short wooden pier out to a gazebo-looking thing over the water. I was surprised the dock and gazebo were still intact. We were filtering water when the first arrow struck. If I hadn't been leaning over to fill a container, I'd have taken the arrow in my neck. Ruth and I dropped to the ground and lay flat, but there wasn't any cover. I scanned the trees frantically, trying to pinpoint the source of the arrow. I couldn't believe Richard had found us. From the angle the arrow had traveled and the way it was sticking out of the bank, I had a general idea where to shoot. I grabbed and pulled my backpack over and fumbled for my gun in the mesh pocket I'd tucked it in while filtering water. Thankfully, I hadn't put it inside the main compartment with the leather straps, or I'd never've gotten it out.

I whispered to Ruth, "When I fire, run to that tree."

I let off two rounds. Ruth and I bolted like rabbits and dove behind the trunk of the tree. It wouldn't give us much cover, but it was better than nothing. In the frantic dash to the tree, Ruth had somehow had the presence of mind to bring her backpack. She shoved it in front of her next to the tree to serve as cover.

Richard then shouted, "You didn't think I was going to let you escape, did you, George?"

An arrow embedded itself in the trunk of the tree next to my head.

"George, I thought it strange you'd take the Appalachian Trail north, but I figured you'd be taking this way to Springer Mountain. Was it just because you were so terrified of me? Have you ever been on the AT? You know, my dad took me hunting on the trail in Virginia when I was a kid."

Shit. While I'd been careful about obscuring Phoenix's location, I had a hand-drawn map of how to get to the AT in my journal and a foldable map of the complete trail in my backpack. He must have surmised our route based on reading my journal.

"Didn't you two appreciate Gloria's hospitality? It was naughty of her to help you escape. Camden was a bit put off by what I did to her last night."

I immediately thought was Dawson—he was likely out there too. I scanned the area for any movement but couldn't see any sign of either of them.

"George, I've got to tell you that I found your journal amusing. You worry too much about people. All that stuff about your father being devastated by what you found in South Carolina was pathetic."

"Ruth, do you see where he is?"

"No," she replied. "What are we going do?"

"You know, George I couldn't help but laugh when I read you thought I started the wildfire. I wouldn't have resorted to that, and besides, I don't want to kill Ruth."

I whispered to Ruth, "We're going to stay calm. We've got the advantage. We've got the guns, remember."

"You're right, we've got the guns." She took a deep breath and said, more to herself than me, "We've just got to stay concealed."

"Yeah, but Dawson may be out here too, so keep an eye out."

Just then, a searing jolt of pain shot up my left leg. There was an arrow sticking out of my thigh.

"I hit him! I hit him, Father!"

"That's good, but follow the plan!" Richard yelled.

Little bastard. That hurts. And that's my arrow. Goddamn bastard's shooting me with my own arrows.

I let off two more rounds in the general direction I thought Dawson had shot me from.

"Let me see it," Ruth said as she tried to roll me over to look

369

at it. "Good, it didn't pass through to the femoral artery; it must have hit the bone. But its still bleeding badly; let me put a tourniquet on it."

"Aren't you gonna pull it out?" I asked.

"Not now. Later."

"Why not? It hurts."

"That might increase the bleeding, and besides, I don't know what kind of tip it has. I may have to cut it out."

"It's my arrow. It's a bullet point. You can pull it out."

"Later!"

As she tightened the tourniquet, she yelled out, "Hey Richard, George didn't shoot you, I did!"

"What are you doing?" I asked, grimacing in pain as she tightened the tourniquet more.

"Screwing with him," she said. "He can't even conceive you and I are equal partners in this or that I was the one who shot him."

"You little bitch!" Richard yelled. "You almost killed me!"

"I wish I had!"

An arrow hit her backpack.

Another arrow then embedded into the ground near my leg. I'd been busy straining to see what Richard was up to, but now I focused on scooting my lower body over to the right. When I looked up again, I spotted Richard. He'd exposed himself by looking at something to the left of his position. That must be where Dawson was hiding. I shot at Richard but missed.

He shot two more arrows in rapid succession.

Then, from behind us, Dawson said, "Don't move."

Fuck. How had he circled around us without me seeing him? I didn't move.

"Drop the gun. I got 'em, Father!"

I knew if I dropped the gun, Ruth and I'd be dead or worse, for her. All I could hope for was that when I twisted around to shoot, and he was busy shooting me, Ruth could shoot him. Of course, I didn't have time to tell her my plan.

It all seemed to happen in slow motion. I rolled, twisted, and pulled my arm around to shoot. An arrow passed dangerously close to my chest and into the ground. I completed my twist and roll move and saw the kid. And then froze. *All I could see were the faces of the raiders I'd killed so long ago, who weren't men but kids no older than Dawson.*

He was already nocking a second arrow when Ruth shouted, "Shoot him!"

I just couldn't make myself pull the trigger.

She shot him. She then shot Richard twice as he was running around the side of the pond.

I sat there stunned for a couple of minutes and then, using the tree for support, got to my feet. Ruth had gone over to Richard, kicked him with her boot, and then knelt beside him to check his pulse. I hobbled over to the kid.

"Richard's dead!" she shouted.

"Dawson is still alive for now, but unconscious," I replied.

I checked him for a knife and found my long knife wedged under his belt. I then picked up my bow and quiver.

Ruth ran over, grabbing her bag as she went and knelt beside Dawson. She pulled out her first-aid kit and started working on the kid. I walked over and dropped my bow and quiver on the ground, and sat down in the shade of the tree. I then buried my face in my hands. I was so angry with myself; I'd almost gotten us both killed.

* * *

Despite Ruth's efforts, Dawson died.

A sob of anguish broke from her throat. "I wasn't trying to kill him." She sat back on her heels and cried.

I got up, hobbled over, and plopped down beside her. As I rubbed her back, I said, "I know. I should've been the one to have shot him. I froze. I'm sorry."

"It wasn't your fault either," she said. "You didn't turn him into a killer."

"Yeah, but if I'd tracked Richard down after you wounded him like you wanted, none of this would've happened."

She was quiet. *So she thinks this whole thing is my fault,* I thought.

After a couple of minutes of continued silence, she said, "You don't know that; he might have been able to kill us before we got him, and then we would never've seen Miami." She smiled and squeezed my hand. "Let me take that arrow out of your leg."

She wanted to make me feel better, but I knew her too well. She was trying too hard. Something was bothering her. When she yanked it out, agonizing pain coursed through my leg. I screamed, but this time, she didn't call me a big baby. I wished she had. When she was done putting a couple of stitches in it, she got up and buried Dawson. I hobbled over and finished collecting and filtering our drinking water.

We left Richard where he lay to feed the wildlife. I took my bow and quiver, picking up my arrows and taking Richard's, but left his bow on top of Dawson's grave. I found a sturdy stick to use as a cane, and we were off.

* * *

We walked in silence for several hours. Actually, she walked, and I hobbled along, leaning heavily on my cane because my thigh was killing me. We desperately needed to get away from that pond, but we were also exhausted from walking all night, making our escape. Because we'd left our tent and sleeping bags at Gloria's, we need to find a house to spend the night. We spotted a nice cabin-style house off the road. It had a green metal roof, two dormers, and a double garage. It also had a pool in the backyard, but it had unfortunately suffered a crack in the past, so it only held a couple of shallow pools of stale rainwater.

We went through the motions of searching the house mechanically, as if in a daze. I found the remains of two people in the back bedroom, but didn't tell Ruth; I didn't feel like searching for a different house to sleep in. She found that an animal had nested in the bed of the master bedroom sometime in the distant past. I had a moment of dread thinking she'd want to go back and check the rooms I'd already checked, but I simply removed the mattress and threw it onto the floor.

Because of my bad leg, Ruth smashed some furniture for firewood and dumped it on the patio near the empty pool.

"Babe, I don't think that's going to be enough."

"Well then, you go out and find some more. I'm going hunting. And I'm using my gun. After all the recent gunfire, I don't think making a little more noise matters."

I didn't argue with her. I hobbled out to the woods behind the house and looked for branches on the ground I could use for kindling. It took a long time to collect it and then figure out a way to carry it back to the house. I had to give up my cane and carry the wood with both arms. It was painful, but I wasn't going to cry. While I was doing all that, I heard the report of her .22LR.

When I got back to the house, I found Ruth already there, sitting staring at the pile of firewood; she hadn't built the fire. There was also a turkey carcass on the patio next to it. She hadn't plucked or cleaned it.

"Ruth, did you have a problem with the fire?" I asked.

"You and your damn upside-down fire."

She got up and rushed inside. I built the fire, plucked the bird, not caring if mites crawled into my ears, and started it roasting. I went inside and found her curled up on the box spring in the master bedroom. I sat on the edge of the bed.

"Ruth, are you going to be okay?"

"I'm sorry, I'm just exhausted."

"That's understandable. Maybe you'll feel better if you have something to eat."

"I'm not hungry, but I'll get up and sit with you."

She hadn't foraged for greens, so I just picked at the roasted turkey. It was the first solid food I'd had in some time, so it tasted great. After sitting there a while, Ruth also began picking at the turkey. We weren't 'not talking', we just had nothing to say to each other, at least not yet.

Suddenly, Ruth announced, "Hon, when we get back, I think you should go and talk with Ralph Jameson."

I smiled at her. "I was thinking the same thing about you. You were forced to do something today that no one should have to do."

"Okay, maybe we both need to see a counselor, but your problems have been festering for a long time,"she said.

I couldn't argue with that. Nonetheless, I got defensive anyway.

"I'm sorry I refused to exact vengeance for you! I'm sorry I froze when faced with the idea of killing a kid!"

My outburst must have stunned her because she just sat there and stared at me, saying nothing for several minutes.

"Hon, there's nothing to be sorry about. And nothing to feel guilty about. No one should have to do those things."

That's why she was so good at nursing suicidal long-haul trekkers, I thought.

"But you must be willing to protect yourself when faced with life-or-death situations."

I knew she was right; I had some things I still needed to work out.

We were both silent for a long time, then she got up and came over to me, sat down, and put her arms around me. We both cried quietly for a while, sitting there hugging each other.

Then she squeezed me and said, "Right, I think we should put everything aside for now and instead focus on the fact that we're both alive and we're going home!"

"That's a wonderful idea. Can we go to sleep now? I can't keep my eyes open."

She kissed me and said, "First, we've got to find some blankets since we don't have sleeping bags."

In a cedar chest, we found blankets that hadn't turned to dust and lay down on the box spring. A couple of hours later, I woke to the sound of her sobbing. I rolled onto my side, nestled in behind, and put my arm around her. I held her like that until her steady breathing told me she'd fallen asleep.

* * *

The next morning, we woke up and, without saying a word, made love. I didn't know if it was stress-relief sex or happy-to-be-alive sex, but it was good sex. Ruth did all the work since I had a bad leg. The firm box spring was, surprisingly, an excellent platform. Afterwards, we lay holding each other. She then got up and went out back to restart the fire. I followed her out.

As I picked up my bow and quiver, I said, "Babe, I'm going to go find us some breakfast."

"No, you're not. I'll go. I want you off that leg as much as possible."

I heard two reports from her gun while boiling water for tea. She came back with a couple of rabbits. She skinned them, cleaned them, and cooked them. More importantly, she wore a weary smile as she did. I thought, *we're going to get through this.*

* * *

We stayed at the house for two days for my leg to heal. It took us sixteen days to walk to the Amicalola Falls Lodge near Springer Mountain and the southern start of the Appalachian Trail; I limped most of the way. I was fortunate we still had sulfa powder and that the initial infection that set in wasn't a resistant strain of bacteria. On the walk there, the chemistry between Ruth and me had returned to almost normal, but there was an underlying tension that we pretended wasn't there. It took us a long time to find a sporting goods store to replace the items we'd lost. It seemed as if there were no towns on this road, only farms returning to forested lands. But in Jesup, we found most of what we needed in Sheffield's Sports Shop. Besides the tent and sleeping bags, Ruth replaced her winter coat. I was pleased to find the deerskin coat my mom had made still rolled up at the bottom of my backpack. I'd be needing that in the months to come.

Once we arrived at the lodge and determined it was empty, we found two mattresses still in reasonably good shape. All the box springs had disintegrated into wood and metal, so we doubled up the mattresses for a bed. I was sure they were going to be too soft, but this might be the last time we'd sleep in a bed for six months. We selected a room with a balcony and an excellent south-facing view. The two Adirondack chairs on the balcony were still sturdy enough for us to sit comfortably and enjoy the vista. I finally took the time to write up my notes; I'd been hesitant to do so. I had to do it by firelight because we'd lost our solar lamps when we escaped from Gloria's.

* * *

Journal entry: 19–21 May?? Amicalola Falls State Park, GA

Uncertain as to the exact date because I lost my pocket watch while being held captive and may have lost a few days while suffering heatstroke (Ruth believes I was delirious for three days, but even she is uncertain about the passage of time while being held). But we arrived here today.

A lot has transpired since my last entry over a month ago. I suffered heatstroke and was incapacitated as we traveled through the heat dome and drought in GA. Ruth and I were then captured by Richard Havens just outside Brunswick, GA (he somehow had found willing assistance from a lone teenager after being shot, and then by a family who took him in). We managed to escape with help; however, within a few kilometers, Havens and his teenage assistant caught up with us, and we had no choice but to kill them. Havens destroyed all my instruments, so no further measurements will be taken on this trek. We also lost several items in our escape besides my pocket watch, including solar lamps, monocular telescope, backup ferro rods, tent, sleeping bags, and some cooking supplies; but, importantly, we were able to retain our guns, maps, and, of course, our journals.

To avoid people and the risk of getting further waylaid, I plan to take the Appalachian Trail home, leapfrogging around some of the highest sections.

Conditions here in northwestern GA have much improved— while hot, temperatures are no longer dangerous, and radiative cooling at night drops the temperature; the drought is also not as severe here. By starting northbound now, we should have good weather during the early hike; however, if we are delayed, we may encounter early snow by the time we get close to Phoenix, especially at higher elevations.

* * *

We spent three days and nights at the lodge. I wanted to stock up on jerky and other supplies before we got on the AT, so I spent my days hunting and drying venison and pork. I'd been lucky to shoot a sow. She'd completely ignored me when I came upon her, and so I made a clean shot just above her armpit, avoiding the thick shield of cartilage on her shoulders. Ruth spent her days foraging for any edible plants, including more chickweed, dandelions, garlic mustard, plantains, elderberries, pawpaw, and even found some persimmons. At night we made love. The sex was wonderful, but there was still an unspoken tension between us. I was conflicted as to whether it was her resentment of me for putting her into a situation where she had to kill two

people or if it was my nagging guilt at failing to protect her.
It was probably a little of both.

Chapter 22. NOBO on the AT

Hiking the Appalachian Trail was now an established family tradition. Granddad had done it as a kid. My dad and I had taken it on our return trek, and both appreciated reconnecting with nature and the solitude of the trail, up until he became sick, and we were ambushed coming back from a medicine run off-trail. Ruth and I had only one minor misstep during our short southbound hike, and I was now hoping we wouldn't have any problems on our northbound hike.

The morning we left, we took the east ridge trail from Springer Mountain's parking lot to avoid the 600 steps and the steep initial climb on the approach trail near the lodge. After walking the flatland of Florida for weeks, walking up steep inclines would be challenging at first. But by skipping the approach trail, the first few kilometers would be downhill. One of the first things we did was to find sturdy walking sticks.

"The view is breathtaking from up here, isn't it?" Ruth said.

"Yes, it's beautiful."

"I bet you can see the entire Appalachian Mountain chain from here."

"Wait until you stand on Preacher's Rock," I said.

"It's nice to be back in the forest again, isn't it George? I'd almost forgotten what it smells like. I think the heat down south burns off all the wonderful smells."

I wasn't too worried about the shelters constructed of stone, but I wanted to get a sense of how the wooden shelters had held up this far south, and so we took a side trail to check on the Hawk Mountain shelter. The footbridge was out, but fording the narrow stream was no big deal.

As we walked up to the shelter, Ruth said, "I'm just amazed its in such good shape. It's in better shape than some houses we've stayed in."

"It's in the simplicity of its design and the fact its tucked within these trees."

"Are we staying here tonight?"

"Babe, we've only gone a little over ten kilometers; we can do better than that even on the first day, can't we?"

"Okay, but I'm ready for a break soon."

"We can take a break at Preacher's Rock."

Ruth wasn't disappointed when we reached the rock out-cropping.

While we were eating jerky and enjoying the view, she said, "Hon, we've got to bring Dan with us when we do this trek again. This is amazing."

I tried to hide my shock at hearing this and said, "Are we making this trek again?"

"Of course we are. Consider all the things we've learned. Besides, you only live once."

I couldn't believe my ears. I had to restrain myself from asking, 'What have you done with my wife?' Instead, I said, "Do you think he'd want to come with us?"

"I think he'll jump at it. He's always asking about the world outside of Phoenix."

That wasn't the kid I remembered. Whatever had changed her mood, I hoped it would last.

We finished our food and got back on the trail, which now would be a steeper incline.

"George, can you explain again why we're climbing up this damn mountain?"

"To avoid the crazies, remember."

"I know, I know."

"Don't worry, our calves will stretch out in no time. I'll bet you'll be used to climbing again after we get through the first fifty kilometers to Neel Gap. You didn't have any difficulty hiking the Green Mountains in Vermont, did you?"

"That feels like a lifetime ago. I was younger then."

"Well, I was planning on leapfrogging sections with the highest peaks, like in the Great Smoky Mountains and the White Mountains."

"Good thinking."

"Talking about the Green Mountains, do you remember Russ and I shot that bear? We need to be mindful of them here too; Georgia's got its own bears."

"Don't worry, I've still got my bear bell." And she rang it.

Not passing any more shelters that day, we set up the tent after I checked the area for bear scat. We'd brought lots of food, which I hung in a bear bag, but we had a fire for making tea and to deter wildlife.

The next day, I shot a raccoon for breakfast. Since we would

383

hike away from the area after breakfast, I wasn't too worried about the offal from gutting it, but, nonetheless, dragged it a hundred meters or so from the trail. When I got back to camp, I found Ruth stacking rocks to create a cairn to mark our location.

"If we pass a town, we should get some paint and repaint the blazes for our next trek."

It sounded like a lot of work to me, but I would not argue with her when she was in such a good mood. Besides, she'd probably bring it up again when we reached Neel Gap, but I doubted the outfitter store there had sold paint before the collapse and blackout, so there'd be none to scavenge.

The blazes saved us that very day. We'd followed a trail across a prairie, and when it entered a mature forest, we couldn't find a blaze. We hadn't seen any rock cairns either. So, we backtracked and realized we'd missed a turn and were following a game trail. Later, Ruth witnessed for herself wildlife using the AT when we watched a deer parade down slope from us. A more alarming sight was the mountain lion we watched as it tracked the deer. We decided then and there that we'd find a shelter to stay in that night.

A couple of nights later, a bear came into camp. If we'd been in the tent rather than a shelter with a solid wall behind us, I don't know what the outcome would've been. I considered kicking embers from the fire at it, but didn't want to piss it off, so instead, I jumped up with my sleeping bag in hand, waving it and making as much noise as possible. Ruth sat there ringing her silly bear bell. Whatever we did worked; it ran away.

Two days later, we spotted something black lying on the trail ahead of us. We crept closer.

"I think it's a bear," I said. "It may be asleep." I started clapping. "Hey, you bear, time to wake up and leave." No response.

Ruth hit her stupid bell. No response.

I walked up to it and saw it wouldn't be a threat. "It's dead," I shouted.

As she came up behind me, Ruth asked, "Do you think it's the same one that came into the camp the other night? Oh, shit. What could've done that?"

The bear had been half-eaten.

"No idea, and I don't want to find out; but it's fresh."

I looked around, clapped my hands and shouted, "Hey, whatever you are, we don't want any."

"Let's get out of here?" Ruth said.

"No, wait. Take my 9mm." I got it out of my backpack and handed it to her.

"What's this for?" she asked.

"You're going to keep watch as I harvest some meat and as much fat from the bear as I can," I said.

"First, yuck. And second, why can't I just use my gun?"

"I want you to have more stopping power."

"Okay."

We never found out what had killed and partially eaten the bear. But we were hypervigilant for the next few days.

It didn't take long before it all became routine. We'd walk, stop and have lunch, and then walk some more until we found a shelter. I'd build a campfire while Ruth foraged for greens and water. I'd shown her how to use her walking stick to point in the direction back to the camp if she stopped and got distracted by foraging at a particular site or filtering water. Once I got the fire going, I'd hunt, being careful not to leave

385

any offal from butchering the kill close to our camp or the trail. After dinner, we'd sit around the fire and talk about nothing really, or just stare up at the stars, or watch the fireflies. In the morning, we'd wake up at dawn, have tea and some breakfast, and do it all again.

Occasionally, we'd see smoke and would be tempted to check out who was living on the side trail or still in one of the small towns near the trail, but I had no desire to be waylaid again. We did, however, go off-trail to leapfrog around some of the higher peaks in the Smoky Mountains, like Clingmans Dome. We also had to go off-trail to look for water several times. On one of those occasions, we even picked up some white paint in the nearby town and repainted some blazes, but Ruth quickly saw how much work it would be.

I made sure we were back on the trail before reaching the Grayson Highlands. I wanted to surprise Ruth. So one day, we were hiking and playing 'Would You Rather' when we came upon them.

"Babe, would you rather get eaten by a mountain lion or a bear?"

"Hahaha, I think a bear; a cat would play with you for a while before killing you. My turn. Would you rather die from heatstroke or freezing to death?"

"That's easy—freezing to death. I've tried both, and heatstroke is worse. The last time I almost died from freezing to death, I just went to sleep."

"When was that?"

"Don't ask. In fact, let's not talk about freezing to death again on this trip."

"Well, there's plenty to look at up here. The open grass-lands allow for magnificent views. Where are we anyway?"

"Mount Rogers in Virginia."

"Why aren't trees growing up here? We aren't above the tree line, are we?"

"No, we're not above the tree line. This area was cleared for farming a long time ago."

"Why hasn't it returned to forested lands like almost every other farm in North America?"

"They intentionally introduced an exotic species to maintain the grassland or, as it was called here, 'grassy bald.'"

"What exotic species?"

"You obviously haven't seen them yet. There's a herd of them over there."

Ruth squealed and said, "They're ponies."

"Yes, and they might not run off if we approach."

"Can we pet them?"

"In the past, hikers weren't supposed to, but what the hell?"

We stayed and played with the ponies all afternoon, but I was disinclined to camp out in the open, so we found our way back onto the trail and located what was left of Thomas Knob Shelter.

It took us just short of three months to reach the halfway point in Pennsylvania's Michaux State Forest. So we were making good time. I'd considered stopping at the nearby Appalachian Trail Museum, but I preferred the one in Monson. That night, we celebrated with a grand feast of fire-roasted turkey, mushrooms, and walnuts; like we hadn't had that every night for the past two weeks.

"Babe, your roasted turkey is especially delicious tonight."

"Are you being sarcastic?" she asked.

"No, it's good but can you imagine the party they're going to throw for us when we get back?"

387

There's a party after any long-haul trekker returns and gets out of quarantine.

"I'm sure it'll be nice, hon. I can't imagine how difficult it is to throw those parties for the entire village."

"Well, you might be the one doing it if you become the leader of the Village Council."

"We'll see," she said.

"I really hope we get back in time for Christmas so we can be there for Dan."

"Oh hon, that would be wonderful."

"I was thinking we could give him a recurve bow this Christmas."

"Isn't he a little young for that?"

"No, I don't think so. I want to start taking him camping and teach him how to hunt."

"They sound like excellent father-son bonding activities, but you're also thinking of the next trek, aren't you?"

"I want him to take his rightful place at the Center, and being a long-haul trekker will ensure that."

"Who do you think he'll intern with?"

"I don't know."

"Well, he's interested in history, like your dad. Maybe he'll join the social science group."

"That'd be nice."

I got up, cleaned up the dinner mess, and then wrote up my notes before turning in.

* * *

Journal entry: 3rd week of August, Toms Run Shelter on the AT in PA

Again, uncertain of the exact date, but it's been over eleven months since we left Phoenix and are now at the mid-point of the AT returning home; having leapfrogged several of the more rugged sections. We plan to leave the trail in Vermont.

Evidence of recent wildfires at lower elevations. Southern portion of the AT still under drought this past summer. Trees and native plants are stressed with signs of disease and often heavily infested: hemlock woolly adelgid, ash borer beetles. As a result, many widowmakers to watch out for. Many water sources have dried; we've had to go off-trail to find water several times; however, we did find microclimates in north-facing valleys where water was available and veg less stressed.

Nonetheless, wildlife and game still plentiful (e.g., deer, raccoons, but also coyotes, bobcats & bear and we observed at least 1 mountain lion—confident it wasn't a bobcat due to its tail length and size; heard wolves, but they have stayed away); the AT is still very much an active wildlife corridor. Unfortunately, rattlesnakes are also plentiful amongst the rocks in PA. While we observed a few moose (population still being affected by winter ticks) and several elk, I didn't hunt either (too wasteful). Bear interactions have been increasing, possibly as they get ready to hibernate, i.e., hyperphagia; we hope they still hibernate under this climate, so we can have fewer interactions.

Precipitation also appears to be increasing as we move north; HOPEFULLY it will stay as rain; I am always worried we won't get home before snow makes the trail impassable.

* * *

The next morning, I woke up to the sound of Ruth vomiting outside. I became very concerned, but she said it was nothing, maybe a bad mushroom in our dinner last night. I wasn't so sure because I felt fine and we'd eaten the same food. She lay back down while I got the fire restarted and made tea for us both. The tea seemed to quiet her stomach. I ate leftover turkey we'd saved in the bear bag. She said she wasn't hungry. I felt relieved when she kept lunch and dinner down.

The next day, I woke to find she'd already restarted the fire and was off foraging. I didn't like her going off without telling me. Who knows what could happen? So when she returned, I asked her to be sure to wake me next time before she went off.

"Do you want me to wake you if I need to go pee?" she snapped.

She then busied herself making tea using whatever she'd foraged.

"Babe, can I have some of your tea?"

"Make your own."

Thankfully, her mood improved as the day went on.

A couple of days later, I woke as she was climbing out of the tent. I found myself in a quandary: should I give her some privacy, which is almost nonexistent on the trail, or should I find out what was going on? I chose the latter and strained to listen while I crawled over and peered out the tent flap. While I couldn't see her, I heard her vomiting. She came back into camp flushed, wiping her face. She was trying to hide her illness from me. My mind was racing; I was in a near state of panic.

As I climbed out of the tent, I said, "Ruth, what the hell is going on?"

"Oh, you startled me!"

"You're sick aren't you?"

"It's nothing," she said.

"It's not nothing," I said. "It's just like what happened to my dad. I told you he got sick on the trail as we were headed back. He couldn't keep anything down. I can't lose you, Ruth. I can't."

"It's nothing."

"Stop saying that."

"She sat down on a log and began to cry."

I ran over and sat next to her and put my arm around her.

"What's the matter?"

"You're going to hate me."

"I could never hate you. Just tell me."

"I'm pregnant. I know you said you didn't want any more kids. I musta messed up when we lost track of the date but my periods have been irregular since we started the trek, so my ovulation cycle might have been off."

"Are you sure?"

"I'm definitely pregnant. And George, I'm not sorry. I know I said that being Dan's stepmom was enough, and I love him like he was my own, but I've come to realize I want a baby. Our baby. Do you hate me?"

"No, of course not. I think I like the idea."

"But you said..."

"I know, but I've changed my mind. I want to have a baby

with you."

"Why didn't you tell me? I've been so scared the past few weeks that you wouldn't want it."

"I only realized it just now."

"Oh, George, I love you."

"I love you too. Wow, a baby!"

"I thought I was going to be lucky and not have morning sickness. I've already passed the peak time for it, but I've got it now."

"How far along are you? Should we get off the trail and find a place for you to have the baby?"

"No, George. I'm just over three months. We both instinctively looked down at her stomach, which still looked flat. The baby shouldn't come until well after we get back. And I've already picked out a name. I want to name her Abby. Would that be okay, George?"

"What if it's a boy?"

"It's a girl, I'm positive."

"Wow, wait till we tell Dan he's going to be a big brother."

"Hon, do you think he'll be upset—you know how he feels about the twins?"

"I think he's going to love the idea."

* * *

Her morning sickness ended a few days later, maybe because she was less anxious and no longer hiding it from me. Time flew by, but our progress slowed appreciably, likely because of my doting on her. It was almost as bad as the start of the trek, where I tried doing everything but did nothing very well. Hunting took longer now; I needed to find game with fat. Couldn't have rabbit poisoning now. Ruth also had to spend more time foraging for the plants she needed now that she was pregnant. A few weeks later, she had to borrow my pants to wear when hers became too tight. I was smart enough to have kept my comments to myself. I thought we should go scavenging for clothes off-trail, but she said it was fine and that we should get home as fast as possible. We also gave up any idea of stopping and checking on New Town or on Russ and Jess. Of course, I kept them in my back pocket in case Ruth showed any signs of early labor.

The temperature started dipping into the teens at night. Ruth said she preferred it, but I was becoming more and more concerned about the dropping temperatures. Then one day, my fears were realized. Out of the blue, it snowed, which wasn't great, but we could handle a light snowfall. As we descended a mountain trail, the snowflakes were replaced by rain, but as soon as it hit the cold ground, it froze almost instantly, making it much too slippery to continue hiking. I set up the tent as fast as possible. The rain was freezing on the tent too. Worse, if ice started accumulating on tree branches, they could snap and break off. This was bad. I wasn't sure what to do: stay here or run for a shelter. I hated indecisiveness, especially when I was the one displaying it. I grabbed both backpacks and made Ruth use my walking stick as well as hers, and, slowly, carefully, we walked back to a shelter we'd passed a kilometer or so back. It was up a positive grade which I thought would be better than walking downhill.

393

We left the tent where it was; we could pick it up later. It took an hour, but it was still a nerve-wracking hike. Thankfully, there was plenty of light to find our footing.

There was no way I'd find dry wood to start a fire, so we both just climbed into her sleeping bag with my sleeping bag on top as a second layer. We were uncomfortably cold but wouldn't freeze. We stayed in that shelter until the next afternoon, when all the ice finally melted, making it safe to hike again. A week later, we were hit by a near blizzard.

Chapter 23. Home Again

By my reckoning, it was the first week of December when we caught sight of Phoenix. We almost started running, but Ruth was in no shape to run and the snow was deep. She could no longer button my pants; her belly was so large. The only thing holding them up was the suspenders I'd let her borrow. Because it was so cold, she had three shirts and her heavy jacket on, so it was no surprise the home guard, who lived in the house at this entry point, didn't comment about her pregnancy; we also were keeping our distance until after quarantine.

"George. Ruth. You're back safe. Welcome home! But you two look like you've been to hell and back."

I turned and looked at Ruth and laughed.

"I hadn't realized until just now, but you finally look as if you've hiked across the country."

She flipped me off with a smile.

I turned and said, "Hi Nick. It's wonderful to be home.

What's the date?"

"It's December 2nd."

"That's fantastic! Can you let our families know we're home safe so they can come visit us at the house?"

"It'll be my pleasure, George. Can't wait till the party. Two other teams arrived yesterday. You'll see them at the house."

We walked down the road, which was plowed of snow for a change, towards the quarantine house that all long-haul trekkers had to stay in for the first three weeks back. It was a large white house with many rooms. It was an extensive property with a white picket fence. Back in the day, it was a frat house as part of the college. There were a dozen or so rocking chairs on the porch, but there was also a line of Adirondack chairs in the dooryard facing the house for family and friends to sit when they came to visit.

When we arrived at the house, before walking up the steps, I turned and hugged Ruth.

"George, are you crying?"

"We're home safe."

"I love you, George."

"I love you too, babe. I can't wait to see Dan!"

We dropped our backpacks onto the porch and knocked on the front door before entering.

"Hey, is everyone decent?" I said as I opened it and went inside.

A young man I'd only met a few times came in from the large living room and said, "Ruth, what are you doing here?"

"Hi Eric, we've just returned from our trek."

"You went on a trek? I hadn't heard. We must've left before the news came out. Ben and I just got back yesterday."

"Eric, this is my husband, George."

As he extended his hand, he said, "Oh yeah. Hey Reynolds. We've met a couple of times at parties and Center meetings."

"George, did you know that Eric and I were in the same class together?"

"Me too," a man said as he came into the room and hugged Ruth. "Whoa, Ruth, what are you hiding under your coat?"

"Ben, you've got a lot of nerve asking a woman that." She laughed, as did Ben. "I'm pregnant."

"Holy crap. That's amazing," Ben said, as he hugged her again. "Congratulations, George. I bet no trekker has ever come back pregnant before."

He shook my hand. Ben was one of Ruth's best friends from school, so he'd come to dinner many times.

"Well, considering she's the first woman to return from a trek, I wouldn't be surprised if that's the case," I said.

We learned that Raymond and Terry, two more of Ruth's school friends, were upstairs sleeping in. I was feeling ancient, and it wasn't from the trek.

"It'll be great having a woman in the house," Eric said as he took our coats and hung them up.

"Just don't expect me to do all the cooking," Ruth said. "Listen, it's great seeing you guys and catching up, but I've been looking forward to using a toilet again for a long time. Can someone direct me?"

"It's down the hall to the right," Eric replied.

Ruth waddled down the hall.

"Oh yeah. George, you must've stayed here after your first trek," Ben said. "It's our first time. It's going to be weird having people bring us food and beer."

I hadn't stayed in the quarantine house after my first trek; I'd gone directly into the hospital because I was in a catatonic state after killing the raiders that had murdered my family, but I didn't correct him.

Suddenly, from the end of the hall, Ruth shouted, "George, come here!"

Ben and Eric were as startled as I was, and the three of us ran to her. "What's the matter?"

"Look at that?"

There was a black cat in the hall, standing in front of Ruth.

"Oh, it's just the cat," Ben said. "We found him sitting on the porch when we arrived yesterday. He sits looking at the front door, but won't leave when we open it for him."

Eric then added, "We asked Toby, the guy assigned to run errands for us while we're stuck in here, and he says no one knows where he came from."

"Does he have a name?"

"No, we haven't decided whether we'd keep him or give him to Toby to find it a home," Ben replied. "We're leaning toward putting him outside for Toby, but no one can get close enough to catch him."

Ruth went over, picked it up, and started petting him. "Well, I want to keep him, and we're naming him Charley."

Realizing that I had no say in the matter, I asked, "Are there any leftovers in the fridge?"

"Yeah, I'm sure there's something in there if Raymond or Terry didn't eat it all. They were up late last night, partying."

As I walked toward the kitchen, I asked, "And what about beer?"

"No, sorry, man, we drank it all but have already asked Toby to bring us some more."

"Damn." But I was mollified when I found spaghetti leftovers in the fridge. "Pasta! You're lucky," I said, as I opened the container and stuck two fingers into the spaghetti.

"Aren't you going to warm it up or get cleaned up first?" Eric asked.

"There's no point in getting cleaned up until someone brings us clean clothes," I said as I scooped up the cold spaghetti and shoveled it into my mouth.

"I bet my standing beer order gets here before yours."

Just then, a knock came at the front door.

"I bet that's it now." Carrying the container of spaghetti with me, I walked to the front door and peeked out the window to make sure it was clear before I opened it. There was a small pitcher of beer sitting on the table beside one of the rocking chairs. I stepped out and waved to John, who was standing in the dooryard. He was my best friend and drinking buddy.

"Hey, pal, welcome home! How's Ruth?"

"She's great, John. More than great, actually. How's Libby and the kids?"

"They're fine. They'll be here shortly. She'll bring some more of my homebrew for you. I wanted to drop off a pitcher before I ran to your house to get some clean clothes for you."

"How's Dan and everyone else?" I asked.

"Everyone is fine, George. Any preferences on what clothes to bring?"

"Not for me, but can you stop at your place and ask Libby to bring some of her old maternity clothes for Ruth?"

"What! Ruth's pregnant? That's great, George! Congratulations! Wait until I tell Libby. She'll be thrilled for the two of you."

"But John, don't tell anyone else, please. Ruth wants to tell her parents, and we both want to be the ones to tell Dan."

"I understand. But this is great news!!" He pumped his fist

into the air and ran off.

I took a swig of beer directly from the pitcher and walked back inside.

"I should've known," Ruth said as I entered. "We're not home ten minutes, and you're swigging beer already."

"It's a present from John."

"Could you please at least wash your face before my parents get here?"

I'd never really gotten along with her parents. They knew about my past and thought I was unstable. They also thought I was robbing the cradle when Ruth and I got married. But they loved Dan and I was sure they'd be overjoyed at seeing Ruth home safe. I wasn't sure what they were going to think about my fathering their grandchild, though.

"Do you want to start airing out our backpacks?" Ruth asked.

"Can't that wait?"

"Till when—the next time we go on a trek?"

I spilled beer down my shirt. "That works for me."

"Now you need to go find a not-too-dirty shirt in your backpack to put on before they get here. Come on, stop being an animal."

I knew that even though I had only two sips of beer, I was acting like a drunken fool, but the incredible relief of returning Ruth home safe was intoxicating. And I was excited to see Dan. I'd missed him so much, but at least we got home in time for Christmas.

I heard snickering coming from Ben and Eric, who were standing in the hall behind Ruth.

"Okay, let me put this in the kitchen and clean up. You go grab me a shirt to put on."

"What, you want me to smell your shirts to find one that isn't too stinky? You know my sense of smell is heightened right now."

"Your parents will not be able to smell me from outside the quarantine zone. Just find one that isn't covered in blood or has stains on it."

"I told you to wash some clothes when we crossed that last river."

"Okay, you take this, and I'll find a shirt." I handed her the container of spaghetti and pitcher of beer. "And don't let them drink any of my beer."

I turned and checked outside again to make sure it was clear; then, went out and grabbed both backpacks and brought them inside.

"Ben, which rooms are free?"

"We're all on the second floor. You can have the entire third floor to yourselves unless someone else comes in."

"Great."

I went upstairs and got cleaned up. When I came back downstairs, I found Ruth outside in a rocking chair.

"Hey, I wanted to return this," I said, as I gave her the tile from the Versace mansion that I'd carried all the way back from Miami. "Look, I managed to get it here in one piece."

"Come here, you."

I bent over, and she kissed me.

Just then, someone said, "Hey, none of that. There are kids present."

John, Libby, and their two boys were standing by the Adirondack chairs.

"We've got a few things for you," John said. "I can bring them up if you go inside, or I can leave them here on the chair?"

"I brought some of my old things for you to wear, Ruth," Libby added. "I'm so thrilled for you." Even from this distance, we could see Libby shaking with delight.

"I guess the cat's out of the bag, then?" Ruth said.

"Oh Ruth, we haven't told a soul."

"Babe, I thought you might like to put on women's clothes that fit for a change, so I told John."

"Okay, that was very considerate."

Ruth and I were both scanning over the heads of John's family in anticipation of seeing Dan and her parents.

"I wonder what's keeping them?" Ruth asked.

Then we heard barking. A minute later, Otis came running into the yard and up the porch steps to us. I bent down and got a face full of dog tongue.

Still seated, Ruth petted him, but we both restrained him from jumping up on her.

"Oh, Ruth, I've been so worried!" Ruth's mom, Evelyn, shouted as she and Tom Prescott came into the yard. "Thank God you're back."

"Welcome back, baby girl," Tom added. "We've missed you."

"I'm sorry it took so long for us to get here, but we had an issue," Evelyn said.

"Where's Dan?" I asked. He's alright, isn't he?"

"Well, that was the issue," Evelyn replied. "He refused to come with us."

"What? Why not?"

"I'm sorry, George, but Dan said he didn't want to see you," Tom said.

I felt my knees buckle and thought I'd collapse, but I

managed to stay upright. I thought, *God damn that kid,* and started to cry.

"John, I want you to go get him. Tell him I want him here now. I don't care if you have to drag him here."

"Calm down, George," Ruth said. "You can't do that."

I hate it when she tells me to calm down; it just makes me angrier.

"George, Ruth's right," John added. "I'm sure he just needs time. I'll go by and talk to him tomorrow. I'm sure he'll want to see you then."

"Hon, let John talk to him after Dan's had some time to think. It was probably just the surprise and excitement of our arrival. Maybe he just wants to come by himself, so he doesn't break down in front of everyone?"

"Maybe you're right." *But I knew deep down my relationship with my son had been strained for a long time and now might be broken completely.*

"George, help me up," Ruth whispered.

"Mother, Father, I've got a little surprise for you." Ruth opened her jacket, turned sideways, and put her hand on her extended belly. "I'm pregnant."

"Oh, my goodness. That's wonderful news. My baby is going to have a baby." Evelyn began walking forward as if she were going to break quarantine.

"Evelyn, you can't come up here!" I said. "Tom, stop her!"

My outburst startled both Evelyn and Tom. Still being angry with Dan, my voice was probably a bit too harsh.

Tom gently took her arm. "He's right, Evelyn. You shouldn't break the quarantine."

I muttered to Ruth, "How bad would that have been to be stuck in quarantine with your mom for three weeks?"

Ruth turned and gave me a stern look.

Still looking at me, Ruth said over her shoulder, "Don't worry, Mom, you can come stay with us and help with the baby after it's born."

My first thought was *maybe ten years is too long to wait to go on another trek,* but then I thought about the baby, and Ruth, who was now grinning at me, and I *knew I needed to be here for my family, especially to build a bridge back to my son.*

* * *

Journal entry: 3 December, Phoenix

We arrived home yesterday, so this will be the final entry by George Reynolds in book 1 of my journal of the Florida trek (for the record, my wife, Ruth Reynolds, who traveled with me, filled two books). We will submit these journals and my report to the Center in three weeks, once quarantine is over. Having had time on the return trip to reread this journal and to read my wife's journal, I realized we came away from this trip with completely different perspectives. I often focused on the extremes of weather and social decay. She, on the other hand, focused mostly on the resiliency she obs. in people; she was surprised more people had not surrendered to despair after living through such tragedy. I concede that only a special kind of person survived the time of the Great Dying, but I did not have the heart to point out to her that a great many people surrendered to despair—they are just no longer here to be counted. Putting aside for the moment the social disintegration, I remain very concerned about climate instability as more and more critical thresholds are exceeded. For my model to have any forecasting capability, the climate must achieve a new steady state. Yet, we must confront the realities and find ways to limit the damage while we wait for this to happen.

Chapter 24. Epilogue

Journal entry: 3 December, Phoenix

This will be the last entry in my journal for our trek to Florida (2nd vol.). After arriving yesterday, my husband, George Reynolds, whom I accompanied on this trek, asked me to write my final thoughts—so here goes.

It was a heavy responsibility to be the first female long-haul trekker. We had many close calls and witnessed horrifying sights on our trek. I was unprepared for what we encountered. No one who has lived their entire life in Phoenix can truly be prepared for what awaits outside. I fear that my innocence put us in needless danger.

Despite that, I believe I played a crucial role in this trek, in no small part simply because I am a woman. My presence reduced the appearance of threat. A team of male strangers signals danger; a man and a woman look like a family. I don't know if George noticed, but many of the people we encountered looked to me before answering his questions. When I smiled and nodded, they visibly let their guard down. Thus, I strongly believe that women should be encouraged to go on long-haul treks, but I am not sure that married couples should go together, especially if they are leaving children behind (on a personal note, I feel this adventure brought George and me closer, but I worry that our son, my stepson, Dan, viewed our long absence as abandonment. While I would gladly accompany George on another trek, I know we can never leave Dan alone again or allow our new baby to go through that).

Additionally, as a nurse, stepmom, and mother-to-be, I had—and continue to have—a different perspective. I need to believe in the possibility of healing and the strength that comes from hope. I feel there is room for optimism, perhaps stubborn optimism, that we are going to come out of this, maybe even stronger than before.

Nevertheless, I worry about the people we met on our trek. So many have lost their humanity: Vincent, Richard Havens, the town that hangs feral children. But I feel that in the long run it will work out. I will always remember the quiet strength of Abby and her loving father, and the simple kindness of Russ and Jess, who had so little but shared so much. I was inspired by the people in New Town and Wilmington, by the Freeman family that adopted a grandmother, and by the band of kids in Jacksonville. They all have a desire for community, and ultimately, that is what will save us.

Many of the scientists working at the Center, especially my husband, focus on the negatives, but that is due to the urgency of their work and their overwhelming desire to improve the lives of people around them. They do not take time to consider how far they've come but focus on what remains to be done. Still, to ensure continued successes, we must keep hope alive through fellowship and joy of purpose. I feel that optimism is more than just an attitude—it's a strategy to accomplish our mission to rebuild a livable world for future generations.

The End